The Day of the Lie

William Brodrick

W F HOWES LTD

This large print edition published in 2012 by
W F Howes Ltd
Unit 4, Rearsby Business Park, Gaddesby Lane,
Rearsby, Leicester LE7 4YH

1 3 5 7 9 10 8 6 4 2

First published in Great Britain in 2012
by Little, Brown

A CIP catalogue record for this book is available
from the British Library

ISBN 978 1 40749 962 8

Typeset by Palimpsest Book Production Limited,
Falkirk, Stirlingshire
Printed and bound in Great Britain
by MPG Books Ltd, Bodmin, Cornwall

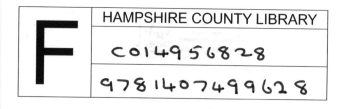

For Gerard J. Hughes
Head of the Department of Philosophy
Heythrop College,
University of London 1974–1988
Master of Campion Hall,
University of Oxford, 1988–2006

A great teacher

After the Day of the Lie gather in select circles
Shaking with laughter when our real deeds are
  mentioned.

Czesław Miłosz, 'Child of Europe'

PROLOGUE

An autumn sun lit the beads of dew upon the pink tiles of Larkwood Priory, the seventeenth-century manor that had once belonged to a king's trumpeter. For services rendered – belting out pomp for the Reformation – he'd been given a Benedictine monastery in Suffolk which he'd briskly demolished to the benefit of the local building trade, holding back enough stone and timber to erect a residence of more secular appeal. All that remained of the former abbey was a line of soaring, broken arches, the white limestone speckled with lichen and charged with the memory of cowled voices that had sung while the world lay sleeping.

With a troubled *humph*, Father Anselm Duffy, jazzman, beekeeper and brooder upon life's conundrums, put the phone down and turned away from the calefactory window that faced the glistening, tangled rooftops.

'You want a *lawyer*?' he complained, entering the cloister, still hearing his friend's anxious tone.

After the trumpeter had blown himself out – and following a noisy inheritance dispute that triggered three hundred years of real estate trade – a group of monks had returned to the quiet valley divided by a fast-flowing stream. Penniless and footsore, they'd taken a boat from Calais after the First World War, a motley band of men from different shattered nations with eyes on a wider horizon. By then the manor had crumbled from a prized asset to a maintenance headache that could only be resolved by donation to a cause deemed worthy. The monks – Gilbertines this time – had solemnly accepted the title deeds only to mislay them within a week. Far from the concerns of ownership, their minds had wandered elsewhere, slowly restoring the tiles, the thatch and the chant, helped by passers-by and well-wishers: anyone with a mind for the value of reflective living. In time, a deep music had pervaded the surrounding countryside, its pulse reaching as far as the holding cells of the Old Bailey where Anselm, then a restless barrister, made a living explaining the difference between justice and mercy.

'So you don't want a *monk*,' he mumbled, with a frown.

He opened the door that led to the reception area and paused to glower at Sylvester, Larkwood's timeless Watchman. White-haired and ascetically thin, his bones almost pushing through his soft flesh, the old man had never fathomed the relationship between a telephone and the noise it makes to announce an incoming call. In fairness there was a large console, flashing lights and three internal lines, each with their own receiver, but Sylvester would have been baffled by anything more complex than two tins linked by string. And even then . . .

'Sorry, Anselm,' said the Watchman, scratching the soft down on his cranium. 'The thing is, you don't get any *warning* . . . do you see what I mean? It just rings.'

'Sylvester,' replied Anselm, wondering how to break the news gently, 'the ring *is* the warning.'

'Don't talk nonsense.' Sylvester shook a loose fist at the countless thousands who rang without writing first. 'It's folk today. They never use pen and ink. What's wrong with paper? Stamps? Envelopes? Copperplate and decent grammar?'

'Things aren't what they once were,' sighed Anselm.

'They're not.'

'Much that was good has passed away.'

'Too true.'

'These are the dark times.'

Sylvester prodded the phone as if to check it was still alive. 'Anyway, no harm done. You got the call.'

'I did. Your triumph, at least, remains.'

Having bowed with that special ceremony reserved for Larkwood's most frustrating yet best loved elder, Anselm stepped outdoors remembering the pithy conversation with John Fielding, the old friend whose urgent call had initially been routed to various extensions in the

3

monastery where Anselm was least likely to be found.

'I need a lawyer,' he quoted, heading towards the woodshed.

The phrase was laden with the past. It rang from nineteen eighty-two when Anselm had still been at the Bar and when John, booted out of Warsaw by the Communist Junta, had come back to London with a swollen jaw talking about a violent arrest in a graveyard. The real, abiding injury, however, had been out of sight. The look in John's eye told something of the pathology but Anselm had never been able to properly construe the symptoms. Like Sylvester, he'd needed something simple to hang on to, and John had become . . . complicated; he wouldn't explain. Part of him had been secretly dying; and localised death – the inner kind – had ultimately left its imprint. Dragging open the large door that hung on one valiant hinge, Anselm paused to inhale the warming aroma of dry wood shavings mingled with the zest of fresh cut timber.

I'd better explain in person, John had continued. *You know I don't like the phone.*

There'd been no further elaboration. John had simply asked if he could come to Larkwood that evening. *I'll make a fire*, Anselm had replied, knowing from that pointed reference to the law that John intended to go back to the cold part of his life: to his secret meetings with dissident thinkers and his brush with State violence. But

4

Anselm was also apprehensive. John's voice had been tense, his breath catching on the line.

'Why now?' murmured Anselm, running his thumb across the dull edge of an axe. 'What has happened to bring back that unforgotten year?'

Lengths of wood, old and new, were stacked in different piles at opposing ends of the room. Anselm went for something green, something that was still holding sap.

PART I

THE FRIEND OF THE SHOEMAKER

CHAPTER 1

'Oh no,' snapped Róża. 'It's him again.'
The lawyer had written formally to
Madam Róża Mojeska. He'd telephoned,
late and early. He'd left brisk messages on the
answer machine. He'd written more letters. He'd
trailed Róża around Warsaw in that battered blue
2CV, pleading his case through an open window.
Undeterred by the constant refusals, he'd turned
up cold and knocked on Róża's door. He'd pushed
lightly against the frame, with Róża shoving back
from the other side. He'd flicked a business card
through the closing gap. And now he was having
another go – late on a Sunday afternoon.

'Blast him.'

Róża had only looked out of the kitchen window
by chance. She'd just thrown back a Bison Grass
snifter – on her doctor's orders – and was about
to rinse the glass when she glimpsed that car
parked on the main road, three floors down. Which
meant the lawyer must be on his way up.

'There's no stopping him,' muttered Róża.

*He's brought a sleeping bag; he won't leave until I
give in.*

9

Without grabbing a coat or knowing where she was going, Róża slammed the door behind her and ran down the corridor towards the fire escape that led to a courtyard of bins and slumped refuse sacks. She might be 80, but Róża could move. Every day she walked through the city going nowhere in particular. The exercise kept her strong. It burned up the energy of untold memories. They were burning now as she nipped across the yard and entered the dark passage that linked her block of flats to a neighbouring complex. She hurried close to the wall, her gaze fixed on the autumn light framed by stained concrete. A plan was forming . . . she'd head into town and hang around the Palace of Culture and Science. A gift from the Soviets, she liked to imagine its demolition. Stepping into the warmth and light, Róża paused. There were children in the quadrangle. Two girls turned the rope while a third skipped, her white dress bright and clean, flying like bunting in the wind. A boy in a track-suit, bored and brooding, sat on a step offering advice and insults.

'Do they know your story?' came the voice.

Róża turned wearily to her side. Leaning on the wall, legs crossed, hands in his tatty jean pockets, was the lawyer. He'd kept his good shoes on – Róża always noticed shoes and clothing; it had come with life in an orphanage, that never-forgotten world of shapeless hand-me-downs and patched elbows – and they still hadn't been polished.

10

'They need to hear what you have to say.'

'Will you ever leave me alone?' asked Róża, quietly.

'I doubt it.' The lawyer didn't smile but his mouth made the shape in sympathy. 'All the others have passed away. You're the last, Róża. You're the only one who knows what happened in that prison. You're the only one who can bring justice to that most unjust time.'

Róża closed her eyes. She listened to the whip of the rope as it struck the ground. She frowned as the girls counted triumphantly against the boy's jaded mockery. A small part of her surrendered.

Sebastian Voight, thirty-something, unshaved, and endowed with a charm as exasperating as it was unconscious, worked for the Institute of National Remembrance, a body formed, inter alia, to preserve the memory of patriotic resistance against tyranny and – coming to Mr Voight's neck of the woods – to prosecute crimes committed by officials of the former Communist state. There was no statute of limitation: the guilty could not escape judgement; all that was required were witnesses; then the law could take its course.

Róża didn't know why Sebastian rehearsed all the technical stuff. She'd already read it in the letters, heard it from a car window and listened to the endless messages. Perhaps spelling out the government's intentions was meant to insinuate an obligation to co-operate. Róża watched the slim, young man, vexed by his natural confidence, drawn to his easy, unrushed manner, almost amused by his ill-concealed watchfulness: he'd finally got Róża sitting down, and he was wondering if the old fish had enough strength to wriggle off the hook.

They'd come back to Róża's small flat. Tea had been made. Cherries had been washed and piled in a bowl. They sat facing each other across the dining table, Róża like a patient, somewhat stiff, Sebastian like a doctor on a house call, hands knitted, and arms resting on the table. His white shirt hadn't been ironed below the collar; the blue linen jacket was loose and creased. He spoke with a low, reassuring tone.

'Six months ago we came into possession of some lost documents. They were compiled by the secret police back in the eighties, ours and the East Germans'. It's a joint archive covering joint operations against certain high profile dissidents. One of the files deals with the Shoemaker.'

Sebastian waited a moment to see if Róża would react. Everyone had heard of the Shoemaker. He was one of the giants of dissident thought, an intellectual of the velvet revolution, a writer who'd helped craft the ideas and tactics that would bring down authoritarian communism. While his collected essays were required reading in every university, they'd remained in demand where they'd first appeared, on the street. Unlike other philosopher kings of East-Central Europe, however, the Shoemaker had never been crowned with political office. His identity remained unknown. Sebastian's expectant pause dried out. Róża wasn't going to take the bait and reveal his name; instead, she reached for a cherry.

'The Shoemaker was the voice behind *Freedom and Independence*,' resumed Sebastian, as if Róża didn't know already. 'The paper published his essays every two weeks, beginning in nineteen thirty-eight. For no apparent reason, he fell silent after twelve years . . . in nineteen fifty-one, during the Stalinist Terror.'

Róża nodded, feeling her throat go dry.

'Most people think he'd said all he had to say but then, out of the blue, he spoke again . . . thirty-one years later, just after martial law had been declared. *Freedom and Independence* suddenly appeared on the streets as if there'd been no hush. This time he dried up after eight months.'

'That's right,' said Róża, finding her voice, thinking the best line of defence would be a passive contribution. She ate the cherry to do what normal people do when they're not worried.

'Again, the view of historians and critics is that there was nothing else to be said – he'd been a writer with a sense of economy . . . no wasted words, no repetition. Why go on? He'd sent out his ideas and he was content to wait for the harvest.'

'Exactly,' said Róża.

'No one seriously considered that he might have been betrayed. Twice. In fifty-one and eighty-two.'

'No.' Her throat was drying again.

Sebastian paused for a while, waiting for the received version of history to fall apart without any help from him. He sipped his tea, as if leaving Róża's arms to weaken; waiting for her to drop what she was carrying.

'The Shoemaker didn't operate alone,' he said, casually. 'The entire operation depended on a group around him called the Friends. No one knows how they were structured or how they'd organised the printing and distribution of the paper. In fact no one knows how many of them were involved and who they might have been. Like the Shoemaker, they appeared with the paper and they vanished with the paper. Which brings me back to the archive found in Dresden . . . and a file on the Shoemaker.'

Róża nodded, her resistance beginning to flag, the very sound of the words seeming to press down upon her.

'The file contains documents compiled during an operation to catch him in nineteen eighty-two after the breaking of his long silence.'

'Yes.' Again, the act of speaking gave Róża something to lean on, something to hide behind.

'The operation was run by Otto Brack.'

'Yes.'

'It was called *Polana*.'

Róża, already reeling, frowned at the name; she felt a kind of tug on the line, but the hook was snagged deep in the past. Something stirred but slipped away.

14

'It failed,' said Sebastian.

'It did.'

'He only caught you . . . the only known Friend. The papers call you "the pre-eminent Friend". You were betrayed.'

Róża waited, her gaze falling on to Sebastian's lips. He'd fished out the slice of lemon and was eating the fruit, wincing at the bitter taste. After placing the rind on the saucer, he said, 'But you see Róża, I'm not here to talk about what happened in eighty-two. What interests me is fifty-one. The really dark year that no one knows about, except you and Otto Brack.'

Róża froze. She hadn't expected this. The letters, calls and messages had all been vaguely about justice, forgotten wrongs and the strength of the law. Cleaning up the past. She imagined he'd come across some slip of paper that mentioned her name; that he'd wanted her to fill in the gaps . . . but not this. He'd found his way into the cellar of Mokotów prison.

'Róża, we have a vast archive at the IPN,' said Sebastian, like a man laying his cards upon the table. 'It's the paperwork of the old secret police machinery. But it was cleaned up. Officials like Brack took the opportunity to get rid of incriminating material before going home from the office for the last time. They went away with smiles on their faces. But these lost documents, now found, change all that. Or to be precise, they change everything in relation to you. The file opened on

15

the Shoemaker in nineteen eighty-two has an enclosure: the file opened on you in nineteen fifty-one. In it are the transcripts of your interrogations carried out in Mokotów, when they asked you about the Shoemaker. I've read them, Róża. I've read between the lines. I know that off the page the gravest offences took place.'

Róża didn't dare to lift her cup of tea for fear her hand might shake. All at once she felt terribly old, too old for this. And Sebastian didn't understand that no lawyer could penetrate that lost time; no one could cross the divide constructed by Otto Brack. Sebastian was leaning forward, unaware of the abyss yawning in front of him.

'Róża, there's hardly anyone left who survived the Terror,' he said, quietly. 'You're the only one alive who knows what happened in fifty-one. Strenk is dead. Only you know what crimes took place when the questions were over . . . you and Otto Brack. He was there, too, at the beginning of his career. He's still alive.'

Their eyes met. Oddly, it gave Róża a kind of support; she held on to the gaze as if she might fall over.

'Do you know what Otto Brack did after the fall of Communism?'

Róża shook her head. She'd often wondered, not wanting to know; yet wanting to know, with the terrible heat of an old, quiet fire.

'He took early retirement and began stamp collecting.' He nodded at Róża's vacant face,

16

crediting a surprise that she hadn't shown. 'Yes, that's what he does to while away the hours. He collects little pictures of days gone by, the good old communist days. That's what he was doing when I asked him to comment upon your interrogation papers. He was going over his stamp collection.' Sebastian came an inch or two closer. 'He regrets nothing, Róża. He remains convinced of the cause and the merit of the cost. It's as if he'd done nothing wrong . . .'

Sebastian's eyes dropped remorselessly upon Róża's left hand. They both stared at the two wedding rings on her third finger, the one public avowal of what had happened in Mokotów when Róża was barely 22.

'Róża, help me bring him to court.'

'Why?' The whispered question was patently disingenuous born of a desperate longing to not know the answer.

'For murder and torture. Your torture. And the killing of two men . . . one of whom was Pavel, your husband.'

The sun had slipped away. A pink light warmed the apartment, illuminating a shabby brown sofa, a landscape painting hung askew, a half empty bookcase, an oval dining table and three matching chairs: the detritus of a life crushed by the secret police. Róża looked calmly upon her new inquisitor. She'd been in this type of situation before. After the exhaustion that comes with dodging questions,

17

there's a strange second wind, an energy born of knowing you've won, at least for the time being. Róża knew when it was time to make a controlled confession, and it was now. It was time to give the other side a little bit of what they wanted so as to keep back an awful lot more.

CHAPTER 2

Róża fetched out the bottle of Bison Grass. With two small glasses cupped in her other hand, she resumed her place at the oval table. A feeble light trapped by a thick orange shade just about reached them from the standard lamp in the corner. It picked out strands of Sebastian's roughly parted black hair. There was a pallor round his eyes and Róża concluded he didn't eat many vegetables. She filled each glass.

'How old are you, Sebastian?'

'Thirty-six.'

'You were fifteen when the Wall came down.'

'Yes.'

Róża sniffed at the coincidence. 'My age when Stalin replaced Hitler.'

This was an apt meeting point. At fifteen Róża had seen the birth of totalitarian communism while Sebastian, at the same age, had seen its death: the corpse seemed to lie between them, stretched out on the table.

'I didn't join the resistance immediately,' said Róża, her mouth and tongue warmed. 'But one

19

day I was given a secret. I was brought as close as you could get to the Shoemaker. And, like it or not, that made me a Friend . . . shortly afterwards, a Friend in prison.'

'Róża, who was the Shoemaker?' asked Sebastian, tentatively. 'That era has been and gone. They lost, we won. The fight's over, isn't it?'

'No, not mine.'

'Even though it's—'

The question died on Sebastian's lips. He was looking over Róża's shoulder as if Otto Brack had stepped from behind the curtain.

He'd seen the bullet.

Róża kept it standing upright on a shelf beneath a wall mirror. Most people didn't spot it; and if they did few dared or wanted to venture a question. But that little brass jacket with the lead on top, once seen, grew large and filled the room. It changed those who saw it: changed how they saw Róża. And Sebastian's eyes, finding again the old woman in the white blouse with a silver brooch clipped at the collar, were no longer so sure of themselves. He'd just learned something new about surviving the Terror.

'They came for me in November nineteen fifty-one and took me to Mokotów prison,' continued Róża, as if the air between them had been cleared. 'I remember the night even now, the biting cold, and the snow crunching underfoot. They'd already lifted my husband and others whom I'd never met or even heard of . . . people who'd never been told the secret. Maybe that's why Otto Brack thought of me. He was a young man, then. An angry, unquiet man. He'd just joined the secret police.'

Sebastian nodded. Impatiently, to clear his line of vision, he flicked back his fringe.

'He asked your question,' said Róża. 'He wanted to know about the Shoemaker and *Freedom and Independence*. He, too, said the fight was over, though it had only just begun. And I didn't give him any answers either.'

Róża took the smallest sip, letting the heat suffuse her lips and attack her throat. She couldn't continue with the chronology of her confession. To do so would only bring back the dim grey cell, the sound of thundering water in the cellar. To do so would only bring back the sound of the pistol.

'They let me out in nineteen fifty-three,' she said, airily, vaulting the years. 'All I had left was a secret. I came out burdened by knowledge of the one thing that Otto Brack had wanted to know. Only I could bring him close to the Shoemaker.'

The muffled sound of a television came from the flat below, a smudge of noise made of high voices and laughter. Observing Sebastian, Róża sensed his disappointment: he was still in Mokotów; he wanted a statement about the torture and the killings. He was trying to find a way into the cellar.

'I was helped by good friends,' continued Róża, drawing him on. 'Ordinary, decent people whose

21

names will never be immortalised by the IPN. People I would defend with my life. But I did nothing for the struggle, not for thirty years. And then, one morning, I went back to the Shoemaker.'

'Why?'

'The time was right.'

'And the Shoemaker . . . he'd been waiting?'

'No. Grieving.'

Sebastian nodded, outmanoeuvred. 'And this brings us to nineteen eighty-two?'

'Yes.'

'The year when *Freedom and Independence* reappeared on the streets?'

'Yes. Eight months later Otto Brack came to arrest me again. Oddly enough, it was a freezing cold November. Once more I was taken to Mokotów.'

Only there was no cage; no endless interrogations during that eternal twilight that emerges when you've no idea whether it's night or day. This time it was a single session like a brief visit to an undertaker. Unknown to Róża, the coffin had been sized beforehand. Brack was simply waiting with the lid in his hands, a hammer on the table, the nails in his teeth.

'I've read the papers, Róża,' Sebastian said with a note of warning. He'd picked up the crisp edge to Róża's voice. He'd seen her face stiffen. 'I've reviewed the operational file from eighty-two. It was cleansed. Brack got there first. All that's left are a few vague clues, marks on the wall . . . Brack looked after his informers. He made sure they were safe, that no one could trace them. You'll have to accept that—'

'I'm not bothered about the file,' said Róża, suddenly brittle. 'If you're really interested in what happened off the page, listen to me. If you want to understand how crimes can be protected by silence then give me your undivided attention.'

The orange light fell upon Sebastian's slightly parted lips.

'I'm going to tell you my only other secret,' continued Róża. 'You've been chasing me for weeks and now I'll tell you why I run away. This is my confession. It explains why I've done nothing about the murder of my own husband.'

For a brief moment, Róża lost her thread. She reached for her glass to get rid of the bitterness in her throat. Recalling that last interrogation in 1982, Róża began hesitantly, trying to erase the memory of Otto Brack's ashen face.

'When I entered the room, I thought I'd won. He'd wanted so much more, and all he'd got was me. Again. He'd got nothing the first time and he was going to get nothing now. I was so much bigger than the prison system, so much taller than its walls. He couldn't contain my spirit. Or so I thought.' Róża paused, smiling at her foolishness. 'I hadn't realised that on this occasion he didn't intend to ask any questions.'

'What do you mean?'

'*Polana* wasn't simply about catching the

Shoemaker and suppressing *Freedom and Independence*. He wanted to find *me*, to tell me that if I ever sought justice in the future, it could only be bought at a heavy price . . . a price I wouldn't pay. He'd found a means of silencing me for ever.'

'About the murder of your husband?'

'Yes.'

'And the other man?'

'Yes.'

'How?'

'He turned the tables. *He* gave information to *me*.'

'Information?'

'Yes. He told me the name of the informer. He told me their secrets. He told me things they didn't even know about themselves. He gave me the awful power that comes with knowledge.'

Sebastian stared back, expectant but uncomprehending.

'It was a special kind of blackmail,' explained Róża, patiently. 'He was warning me that if I ever accused him of murder, he'd not only expose the informer, he'd release all the details of their undisclosed past, as a means to shatter their future.'

Sebastian waited for a long time, holding Róża's gaze, wondering if there was any more to come; and then he realised she'd finished speaking, that she'd explained herself in full.

'He threatened to burn your enemy,' he asked,

eyes closed and brow furrowed, 'and that threat silenced you?'

'Yes.'

'How? Help me. Why not let 'em fry?'

'Because they might never recover from the shame, from the public destruction. They could very well end their own life.'

'Don't get me wrong, but so what?'

'In part, it would be my fault and I'd share the responsibility. I would be no different to Brack. I might as well have pulled the trigger myself . . . and that's why Brack put the gun in my hand. He knew I'd never take aim and fire.'

Sebastian blinked rapidly, one hand scratching the back of another.

'No, no, no, Róża, you've got it wrong, so wrong,' he laughed without humour. 'That's not how the world works, not now, not then. If a shamed collaborator opts for suicide that's *their* choice . . . that's *their* way of dealing with responsibility. Everyone at some point has to face up to what they've done. They can't run off or hide behind your . . . what is it? Decency? That's the one thing they threw away . . . you of all people can't give it back to them.' He seemed to come closer but he hadn't moved. He was still now, almost predatory. 'Róża, you're talking about an *informer*. They got a handful of silver. They've had their . . .'

Sebastian's voice trailed off.

Róża had stood up and walked to the mirror.

She picked up the bullet and returned to the table, placing it between them as if it were a tiny storm lamp, something from a doll's house. She sat down, looking at it as if she, too, was perplexed by its meaning.

'When I was first in Mokotów, Brack used one of these.' She turned it slightly, as if to adjust the flame. 'The next time round, I discovered he was no ordinary executioner. He'd learned how to silence someone without violence, without committing a crime. He did something I never could have imagined: he used me against myself. I won't vindicate Pavel at the cost of another life, Sebastian, even that of an informer. When people are stripped down in public, when every sordid detail of their past becomes cheap gossip at the bus stop, they can lose the will to live. That's not the kind of free speech we fought for. I won't use words to bring about another death . . . not when words were all we had to keep ourselves alive.'

Róża insisted on walking Sebastian to the street below. It was a mild night with a soft breeze carrying the hum of distant engines and downtown activity. Sebastian loitered, hanging back, making Róża walk more slowly. His hands were in his pockets in that relaxed way of his that was somehow smart. He was thinking hard, trying to find a way to end the meeting on the right note. His car keys jingled and he struggled with the lock in the driver's door.

'I won't trouble you any more, Róża,' he said, yanking at the handle. 'But I've got one last request. Come to the IPN. Let me show you something else that lies beyond your imagination.'

CHAPTER 3

For a long while Róża considered the two trees. They stood by the entrance to the Institute of National Remembrance. One was upright but the other seemed it might lose balance and fall over, its trunk curved as though it had grown in a gale. The lower branches were stretched out like arms ready for the fall. They were just the right height for a boy wanting to climb and get a better view of any commotion.

'Welcome, Róża,' said Sebastian, holding open the door. 'This is the place where we try and clean up the past.'

She shrank from the towering block. The Shoemaker had once said that history was our sacred curse; that we were forever torn between the duty to remember and the joy of picking daisies.

'Are you okay?' queried Sebastian.

'Yes . . . just something I read in the paper.'

Alongside the windows were canisters hiding external lights. Róża had seen them illuminated after dark during one of her walks. Reminded now of the building's purpose Róża wondered why she'd got into that taxi. She'd made another mistake: first, she'd said too much; now she'd come too far.

'We've got lots of papers here,' quipped Sebastian, leading Róża inside. 'You can read them, too.'

His suit was charcoal grey, verging on black. His white shirt had that factory gleam, persuading Róża that it had been torn from its cellophane wrapper earlier that morning. The maroon tie was slightly loose at the neck.

'The lifts are out of order, I'm afraid,' he explained, passing a couple of vexed technicians. 'So we'll have to use the stairs.'

On the other side of a door marked 'Private' they were met by a man whose job description did not permit a smile. An officer of the Internal Security Agency – Special Forces – said Sebastian in a low voice. He followed them down three floors, along a corridor and to a locked grey door. Róża felt unsteady, her stomach churning at an old memory. The cage had been three floors down, too; there'd been guards who didn't smile; and the cellar door had been grey. The paint had been peeling and the ground was damp. Brack had fumbled for his keys, breathing recrimination.

'Most people aren't allowed to see what I'm going to show you,' said Sebastian. 'Special clearance is needed. I had to fight to get yours.'

He pushed a card into a narrow slit and the electronic lock flashed green.

'Come on in. This is part of what Brack and his friends left behind.'

The room comprised nothing but shelving: row after row of long metal units jam-packed with buff folders, box files and bound reports. Between each block was a narrow walkway providing cramped access to the documentation. A musty smell tainted the air. Róża felt vaguely ill. She'd said too much, she'd come too far and now she'd gone too deep. She hadn't expected this.

'Lined up, there's about one hundred miles of material,' said Sebastian, leaning on the wall, legs crossed. 'Over ninety thousand informers from all walks of life. Here is some of what they said, noted down by the secret police. As I explained before, a lot of the really damaging stuff has been destroyed, though we reckon a duplicate archive exists in Moscow.'

Sebastian walked down an alleyway, drawing Róża along by a tilt of the head. She lingered, looking right and left, feeling the weight of information leaning towards her, the spines of the files like the backs of their authors turned in shame. All at once she wanted to get out of this terribly silent place. The intimidation of the handlers had been left behind like the harsh smell of cheap aftershave. When Sebastian opened a door on to an office, Róża entered with a sigh of relief, but then instantly recoiled as from a slap to the face.

The room was brightly lit. There were two comfortable chairs on either side of a table. In the middle of the table was a microphone wired to a recording machine. Beside the machine were two folders, one a dull orange, the other a pale green. Both were secured by a black lace tied in a bow. There was a jug of water and an upturned glass. A coat stand watched like a sentry. Sebastian appeared before Róża's frozen gaze.

'Róża, I'm not going to make you stay here. You don't have to say anything. You're a free woman. You can turn around and I'll call another taxi. But I want you to understand what you're doing.'

Róża smiled thinly at the offer of advice.

'Out there, behind you, is *their* story,' said Sebastian. 'They've had their say. The secret police and their informers have put their slant on every event since you were fifteen – and not just the politics but what your neighbours had for breakfast.'

It was far more complex than that, objected Róża, not bothering to say so. It had been so much more *involved*. Yes, some had taken the silver for a better standard of living . . . but there'd been others: parents, desperate to obtain medical treatment; one time adulterers, blackmailed to save a marriage; careerists who'd bought promotion with cheap gossip known to everyone but the cat; the stupid, who'd thought they could play the game better than the ones who'd made up the rules; and that special class – the almost innocent, the trusting kind who didn't even know they were being used. They'd all been informers. They'd all betrayed someone. But there was no true equivalence, not really. The many faces of choice and coercion kept them well apart.

31

All they shared was exile, deserved and undeserved. Róża looked at Sebastian's mouth as it moved, not hearing the words, wondering why his generation couldn't differentiate between the varying shades of wickedness and co-operation; why they smudged together malice, blabbing and whimpering; why they found it so easy to apportion blame.

'—but the files are with us for ever, and we have to make sense of them, here in a building that's meant to house your memories,' he continued, searchingly, trying to win Róża back. He'd sensed her drift away. He'd felt a remote coolness in her appraisal of him. 'If you ever decide to speak, everything you say would count as a memorial to the kids playing with the rope. Otherwise, this is what they're left with. The lies, the obsessions, the compromise. *Their* story.'

Róża turned around. Ahead was the narrow passage, walled by fading covers. At the far end the grey door seemed wedged between distant protruding binders. For those who'd grown while the shelves were being filled, the place was frightening. There was a terrible implied intimacy between lives lived ordinarily and these secret memoranda; these notes on what others had heard while you poured the tea or washed the cherries.

'On the table are two files,' said Sebastian. He'd moved to the door and taken its handle, ready to show Róża the way out. 'The orange holds your interrogations from nineteen fifty-one. The green is the Shoemaker file and what's left of Operation

Polana in nineteen eighty-two. If you leave now, that's what you're turning your back on. When I return the folders to the shelf, there'll be no other version of your life and times; the beginning and end of your resistance. Brack gets the first and last word. It doesn't have to be that way.'

Róża appraised the orange file. It was thick, the cover faded and bulging. With the sudden jolt of an electric charge she recalled a little man with a tatty briefcase, a spectacled pen-pusher who'd come to Mokotów shortly before she was released.

'Can I be alone for a moment?' she asked, suddenly hoarse. 'I need to gather my wits.'

'Sure.'

As soon as the door closed, Róża quickly untied the bow on the orange file and lifted the cover, her eyes scanning one side of the stacked grey paper. They came to a halt towards the bottom, when she spotted a pale blue line, a single sheet. With a quick tug, her memory shuddering with emotion, she tore it free from the binder. Without even a glance at the columns and boxes she crumpled the paper and thrust it deep into her pocket. Hastily closing the file, she made a new, tight bow, and then opened the door.

'I've thought about it, and I'd like to leave immediately, thank you very much.'

Sebastian's mouth opened in stunned disappointment. He stammered some sympathy but finally said, blocking her way, 'You only gave it a minute, Róża, whereas that lot –' he nodded past

33

her towards the table ' – was built up over years. Don't you want to take a little more time? Just give the proposal the consideration it—'

'What do you want me from me?' Uncontrolled feeling spilled from some inner guttering. He was watching her expectantly, not realising how deep despair can run. 'You bring me here . . . you push my face into my past; you ask me to clean it up? You ask me to explain to children I don't know why I failed, why I leave Brack's account on the table, why Brack won and I lost . . . lost everything I loved and cared for? You bring me here and offer me a glass of water and a chance to redeem myself? You expect me to sit down and smooth out the creases in my life?' She paused, unable to express the extent of her subjection. 'You have no idea – and I mean *no idea whatsoever* – of Brack's power, back then; of its *reach*. You don't understand. You haven't the faintest—'

'Róża,' Sebastian's whisper stifled her indignation. 'We have something in common. I've got a story too, you know. Not as bad as yours, I accept, but it's a story. It marked me and others. It's why I became a lawyer.'

Róża blinked and noticed that her hands were clenched; her teeth were tight against each other. Relaxing her bite, she made a low moan, wanting to get away from untold stories, other people's and her own. Not telling them saved a lot of harm; kept life manageable. She swallowed hard, knowing it wasn't true.

'We're not that far apart,' said Sebastian, opening wide the door. 'Which is why I have the courage to bring you here and the cheek to ask you to have the last word.'

'What on?' snapped Róża. She wasn't beaten but she felt a reluctant attachment to Sebastian, to his starched shirt, the wrinkled suit and his scuffed expensive shoes. She was drawn to his relentless, tousled energy. 'There's nothing I can say.'

'Yes, there is,' insisted Sebastian. 'We keep a voice archive. Recordings of interviews with those who fought the fight. I just want you to relate everything that Otto Brack didn't contaminate. Afterwards, you'll get a transcript and you can change anything you like.'

Róża felt herself surrendering again. 'But there's nothing . . . nothing at all.'

'Are you so sure?' asked Sebastian, coming back into the room and, by default, edging Róża towards the table. He was smiling hope and fascination. 'You had a childhood. You survived the Occupation; you were there when Warsaw was razed to the ground. You saw the Nazis leave and the Communists arrive. Tell us what you saw and heard. Don't you understand, Róża, there's so much to say? And no mention of the Shoemaker, Mokotów prison and Otto Brack's hold on your life . . . his reach from then to now. I'm also looking towards a kind of desert, Róża. A part of your life that escaped his touch . . . the thirty years you spent between leaving Mokotów and coming

35

back. Three decades of experience that wasn't chewed up and spat into a file. Tell us what happened out of his sight. What were you doing? Why did you go back to the Shoemaker? How did you put *Freedom and Independence* on to the street? Give us a taste of the time untouched by Otto Brack. If you want, I'll open some Bison Grass.'

Sebastian slipped his hands into his pockets. The appeal was over. He was waiting for Róża to reconsider her decision.

'Sebastian,' said Róza, not wanting to disappoint him, 'you have to understand . . .'

Her voice trailed off. She couldn't help noticing the two perpendicular creases to the front of his shirt. She was right: he'd put it straight on, probably leaving a few pins in the shoulder or cuff. Had he bought it for her or was shopping a desperate measure to avoid the ironing board? Either way, Róża was moved. If he'd been her grandson, she'd have told him what she could about her life, within the limits that remained available; she would not have allowed the shadow of Otto Brack to fall so heavily between them. She'd have told of small glories and some vanquished pain. Róża took off her coat and hooked it on the nearby stand.

'You have to understand,' she repeated. 'I only drink on Sundays.'

CHAPTER 4

Aventilator purred in the corner. House plants rose from mulch in plastic pots. There were various pictures on the walls – grainy shots from the forties and fifties, images of party leaders proclaiming change from a balcony, and then colour photographs of mass demonstrations, portraits of jubilant unionists: the whole a symbolic litany of the last sixty years. The snaps and clips took the place of the windows. It was as though Róża had an elevated view on to history. Wherever she looked she saw landmarks from her own passage to this basement deep beneath the city.

'Speak as and when you like,' said Sebastian, standing behind the facing chair. 'The machine's running.'

Where do I begin? thought Róża.

One of the pictures on the wall showed Warsaw in ruins: gable walls teetering over bent and twisted iron, smoke rising from open pits. But Róża recalled the elements that no image could capture: the terrible grunt of a building just before it collapsed; the moaning from heaps of rubble; the smell of burning flesh. Explosions thundered in her memory, shaking the ground and her teeth. Dead horses on the pavement had been stripped of their meat. Five years later she'd joined an Uprising with Otto. He'd been angry then, too. And unquiet; remote with his grievances. She'd finally held his hand and he'd wept: they were child soldiers facing annihilation. But they'd escaped through the sewers, each taking a different tunnel, each finding, eventually, a sudden peace and the Communists. No, Róża couldn't speak of her childhood or the war. They'd been incinerated. And Brack was there, as a friend. Oddly, she thought it something worth keeping. He'd been Otto back then.

But neither could she speak of Pavel and the brief time they'd spent together rebuilding their shattered city. Anything she might say led inexorably to the Shoemaker: for while her war had ended, Pavel had begun another. She hadn't known at first, but then he'd told her a secret, the keeping of which had eventually brought her to Mokotów.

All that remained was what Sebastian had called a desert: the thirty years that joined two shattering periods of imprisonment. And, in truth, it had indeed been a wilderness – a period of wandering and dryness in exile, striking rocks for water and begging for bread. But the barren ground had flowered, suddenly and unexpectedly. Even Róża had been stunned. She'd gone back to the

Shoemaker immediately. Yes, Sebastian was right: Otto Brack hadn't followed her into the wasteland on the other side of prison. It was hers alone . . .

Sebastian hadn't followed her either. The blue sheet of paper had been the one clue to the meaning of her exile – and that was now in her pocket, its significance having escaped Sebastian's attention. Throughout his pleading, he'd shown no inkling of the true scope of Róża's journey.

'In May nineteen fifty-three a guard opened the cell door,' she said, knowing she was in control. 'He called my name. I followed him out of the building with another guard walking behind. The sun was full and the sky that deep blue you find on old plates and teapots. It was a glorious moment . . . a moment of exhilaration and joy. I thought, "At last they're going to shoot me." My heart raced with anticipation and a sort of bubbling gratitude but he led me across the yard towards the gate that fronted Rakowiecka Street. The next thing I knew the thing swung open and there was Otto Brack, standing on the pavement – he'd come to say goodbye. The guard behind shoved me out . . . but I didn't want to leave. I'd forgotten how to live and I didn't know what to do out there, on an ordinary street. For years I'd been in a cell with a tiny window so high that I had to strain my neck to see the clouds. I turned round and banged on the gate, I kicked it and screamed but they wouldn't let me back in. Brack just watched me and, when I finished beating on the gate, he watched me wander to a junction a few hundred yards up the road. That's when I thought of a friend . . . I can't use names, you appreciate that, don't you?'

Nearly five hours later Róża's testament drew to its close. Her story was ending where it had begun, in Mokotów prison.

She'd described her meandering journey but now she rehearsed that last encounter with Otto Brack following her second arrest: when he'd told her the price of any future justice.

'Róża . . . are you all right?'

She could still see Brack's death mask face.

'Do you want a glass of water?' Sebastian's hand was reaching for the jug.

'Yes.'

Brack was in a posh grey suit and a business man's camel-coloured overcoat. The cut was too big, like the trousers, their hems slumped on his brown leather shoes. When they'd last met he'd been writhing in a drab uniform. His head had been shaved.

'Róża, drink this.' Sebastian was at her side, holding out the glass.

'Thank you.'

She sipped the water, waiting for Brack's presence to fade. He was sauntering towards the prison door, confident they'd never meet again.

'I'm sorry, Róża. I should have known . . . I did know.'

'Forget it. You may have lured me here but I chose to speak.'

The ventilator purred in the corner; the plants seemed to watch from their pots. After a while Sebastian coughed and laid a hand on each of the two files. 'Do you want to read them?'

Róża didn't even look at the covers.

'No thanks,' she said, putting on her coat, 'I was there.'

They walked down the alley of files, closely followed by the man from the Internal Security Agency. The lift had been fixed so they rose to ground level, John discreetly checking his pockets for his electronic card, the Special Forces officer standing at ease. When the doors opened, Róża walked straight towards a chrome waste bin situated at the main entrance, into which she ponderously divested her coat pockets of two bus tickets, some sweet wrappers, a ball of crumpled blue paper and a used tissue. Sebastian watched patiently, touched by the strange rituals of the old.

Outside on the pavement they huddled awkwardly as if wondering where to go next. It was evening now and an autumn chill made them both shiver.

'My grandmother was arrested during the Terror,' said Sebastian, blowing mist at the cold. He seemed to be confiding to the passing cars on Towarowa Avenue. 'She never spoke about it. All she'd say was that the cell was damp. I tried to find out more but she wouldn't be drawn. So I turned to my parents – and even they knew nothing. We all knew nothing – and yet whatever happened remained part of the family structure, like a locked room in the house. I grew up trying the handle, never putting a direct question. Now I make a living picking the locks to rooms a lot of people would rather leave closed.'

This time it was Róża's turn to talk at the passing cars. She watched them chase one another's lights, feeling cut loose from the rush of ordinary life.

'What about your grandfather?'

'The Terror tracked him down.'

'He's dead?'

'Yes.'

Róża felt close to the young man, wanting to better understand him. At the same time she felt a kind of heat coming from his memory. She said, anxiously, 'Why are you interested in Otto Brack?'

His eyes followed the roar of a motorbike and he smiled, as if he'd just hitched a ride to make a getaway. 'I'll tell you on the day he's convicted.'

But Róża gently shook her head, knowing there would be no trial, suddenly and acutely sad that she wouldn't meet Sebastian again; that there'd been no more letters, messages, or trailing; no final ambush. A siren wailed far off as if to say the raids were over. But Sebastian hadn't finished.

'Róża . . . find a way, if you can.'

'A way?'

'Yes. Find a way out of your silence.'

'There is none.'

'Think again.' He looked at her with an expression of intimidating seriousness, no longer just a lawyer but something of a renegade, a young man who would never accept that his investigation was over. 'Do the one thing Brack would never expect.'

'And what's that?'

'Speak to the informer.'

Róża visibly recoiled but Sebastian wouldn't listen to any more objections. 'You might as well, because one day someone else will do just that . . . a journalist, a scholar, another lawyer, someone with an interest in the Shoemaker. The file might be half empty, but now these papers have come to light, someone cleverer than me will start poring over the holes. If they ever find your informer, they won't be chary, like you. There won't even be a warning. Their name will appear on the front page of every newspaper. Capitalised. Why not beat them to it, while Brack's still alive? Do it *your* way, with decency. Lower case.'

'What others do is their affair,' replied Róża, fidgeting.

'And what you do is yours,' he barked, aggression getting the better of him. 'You know their name already. You're half way there. Speak to them. If Brack thinks you'd never confront them, then speak without confrontation. If you're scared they'll end their life, give them another reason for living. Do anything, Róża, only do something beyond his imagination. Use Brack against himself. Make up with his informer. Become friends once more.'

43

Bewildered by the challenge, Róża wavered; she felt her knees slacken. Sebastian was walking to the kerb, one arm waving in the air. A taxi swung out of the stream. She found herself seated by an open window with Sebastian stooped on the pavement, his face pale with cold, his lips blue.

'Find your way back here, Róża,' he urged without a trace of parting in his voice. 'Don't leave us with his story.'

CHAPTER 5

As the taxi pulled away, Róża muttered, 'Powązki.'

'Whereabouts?'

'The cemetery.'

The driver nodded and took her to the one place that haunted Róża more than the prison. She hadn't passed through its gates since the evening of her arrest in 1982.

Róża faltered down a darkening lane.

On either side carved figures with bent heads grieved eternally. A few candles flickered behind coloured glass. Vases with flowers stood propped by inscriptions. Róża's hand slipped into her pocket and reached for the ball of crumpled blue paper . . . but then she remembered: she'd got rid of it, just like the guards got rid of Pavel's body.

Her husband had no grave. Róża didn't know what had happened to his corpse. Rumour had it that some of those who'd been shot in Mokotów were thrown into the back of a truck and taken to building sites or the main rubbish dump in Słuzewiec; others were tipped into empty cement sacks and buried without markers in an open field. In her waking dreams, Róża had stormed into a Ministerial office or she'd knocked timidly at the door of some underling. She'd screamed and begged and whimpered and pleaded. Where is he? Where have you put him? All to the air; no one listening, save her conscience.

Róża turned right.

Another man had been shot, too. Róża didn't even know his name. She'd just seen him being dragged along the floor of the cellar, his two bare feet, angled in, broken or limp. Who was he? Who mourned him? What had happened to his body? Did he lie with Pavel in the foundations of an office block?

Awful questions. Questions that trailed you with a low whine.

Róża turned left.

Time was not a healer. Year after year Róża's attention would fasten on to the back of someone's head – the curls at the nape of the neck – and she'd wonder, insanely, if it might be Pavel, expecting some magic to have occurred, even though she'd seen his broken face and heard the kick of the gun. Then, as if waking, she'd grasp that he was dead, and off she'd go to that imagined door in the Ministry, full of hell or timidity. It was an endless cycle, rolling across the sand.

Don't leave us with his story.

Sebastian had brought the law close to Róża and she hadn't seen it coming. Yes, he'd said he was a lawyer, and he'd pleaded with her about forgotten crimes, but to have him in her flat, to deflect his questions and divert his hopes, had gradually made the law come to life. It was there, dressed in a blue linen jacket with silver buttons. He'd made her feel afresh the pain of justice denied. Year on year Róża had read of men convicted of monstrous crimes against women and children. She'd seen photographs of judges and barristers in their robes, knowing that they would never sit to consider the case against Otto Brack. And now here was a lawyer who wanted to put Brack in a courtroom.

Don't leave us with his story.

Róża turned right again and came, finally, to a large granite monument. It was the grave of Bolesław Prus, the writer. This was where she'd been arrested. The light was fading, so she couldn't quite make out the girl, carved in relief, reaching up to the inscription. But she knew the figure well enough: the thin legs, the pretty dress and the smart shoes. She'd always loved the little buckles by the ankles. Though she was the grey of stone, Róża had seen different colours, materials and textures, changing them every time she came.

You owe it to the children you might have had.

What a devastating phrase.

Speak to the informer.

How could she?

You might as well, because one day someone else will do just that . . . someone cleverer than me.

Sebastian's throwaway remark had nearly

47

knocked Róża off her feet. He was right. The informer's days of quiet obscurity were coming to an end. It was only a matter of time. Others would come to pore over the archives. And that changed everything for Róża. Why wait until the informer was shattered by exposure? She could get there beforehand and . . .

Give them another reason for living.

Róża clung to herself, feeling cold and lonely. All around stray lights flickered like scared moths trapped in a jar. A breeze unsettled the trees. Throughout, Sebastian's voice repeated that final beguiling command. After a while Róża ceased to follow the words. She held her breath. She was staring at a troubled ghost. He was there, clothed in shadows before her eyes, offering to help while pleading his innocence.

Róża could barely sleep. An overwhelming sense of urgency came crashing into the night hours, sweeping aside the decades of submission, the patient acceptance of defeat. With each passing minute her imagination grew bolder, her resolve all the more firm. By the time dawn light filtered through the worn bedroom curtains she'd devised a simple plan to bring Otto Brack to court. Ironically, it involved handing over all the names she'd refused to disclose when in Mokotów. But that time had come. They were all safe, now. The epoch of fear and secrets was almost over.

For three days she paced round Warsaw, waiting

for the transcript of her narrative to arrive from the IPN. When the post came, on the fourth day, she set to work. First, she carefully checked that the text presented a balanced picture of her life between 1951 and 1982. Second, with a red pen, she inserted all the names she'd left out while making the recording. Third, with a black pen, she deleted convoluted expressions, repetitions and digressions. The result was a crafted manuscript that suited her newfound purpose – something the Shoemaker would have been proud of. Every word had its place. They presented a kind of landscape ordered by signposts, only the most important indicator was missing, its absence serving to point without pointing, identifying the informer without a trace of condemnation. When she'd finished she went straight to the IPN and gave it to Sebastian.

'I've changed my testimony,' she said quickly, standing in the entrance hall. 'Could you type it up, please?'

'Sure.'

'Now, while I'm waiting.'

'Consider it done.'

Róża stepped outside to pace some more, refusing the offer of coffee, tea or Bison Grass. After what seemed an age, Sebastian returned with a clean copy in a brown envelope.

'Changed your mind, as well?' he quipped, seriously.

'Yes.'

'What are you going to do?'

A phrase of the Shoemaker's came to mind. 'Raise the dead and shatter the illusions of many.'

'Okay, sounds reasonably apocalyptic. That's fine. And in the meantime, what do you expect from me?'

'Nothing.'

'Not fine. Tell me what you're up to.'

She shook her head with approbation. 'You'd never have survived the fifties. You ask far too many questions.'

With that judgement, she left him bewildered by the leaning tree. On returning home she rang her old friend Magda Samovitz in England, a woman who'd survived the Nazi holocaust only to be hounded out of Warsaw by a Communist pogrom in 1969. Magda had bought a ticket to a new life. For years she'd been sending Róża postcards of Trafalgar Square which bore one simple message: 'Come and feed the pigeons'. That time, too, had finally arrived.

By the evening of the next day Róża had bought her flight and packed her bags. There was no need for a phrase book. She'd been learning English since 1989. It had been a hobby, of sorts. Twenty-four hours later Róża was in the upstairs box bedroom of Magda's Georgian house in Stockwell, south London, lamenting the absence of a phrase book that would have helped an elderly dissident cope with a different kind of Underground. Once again she couldn't sleep. Her mind whirred like the air vent back in Warsaw.

Sebastian had been right about something else. He'd seen something obvious to which Róża had been blind; blind because, as a matter of principle, she'd excluded the possibility from the outset. The last thing that Brack expected was that Róża would arrange to meet the informer. That she'd sit down at their table. That the betrayer and the betrayed would somehow find the courage to talk together, deeply, of all that lay hidden. That Róża would open up the possibility – for the informer – of another, more authentic existence, a public and private identity based on the truth. This was the landscape that lay beyond Brack's imagination: that his informer would stomach disclosure of the past and face the dread of an uncharted future. And that defined Róża's task: to persuade the informer that even now, after all these years, the pain of a life in the open was preferable to a numbed existence in the dark.

There was, however, one remaining catch. A relatively large one, too.

There could be no forced entry. The door had to be left unlocked from the inside. Róża would have it no other way. She needed an invitation to enter and sit down, her host knowing full well that the unexpected guest intended to talk about their mutual relationship with Otto Brack. It was a great gamble with great risks . . . but if this, Róża's stratagem, worked, Brack would be left defenceless. Once the informer accepted exposure, Róża would be free to accuse her husband's killer.

Róża switched off her bedroom light, her thoughts and prayers resting with a man she'd first met in 1982. He'd found her through the distribution chain of *Freedom and Independence*. She'd thought of him looking at the monument to Prus – they'd met there countless times. He'd been a romantic. An outsider. An Englishman of ancient courtesies. He'd been kicked out of the country for getting too close to the fire. His name was John Fielding, a British journalist who'd longed to find the Shoemaker.

PART II

LIVES LIVED IN SECRET

CHAPTER 6

Anselm cut the engine dead. The wipers swung home with a soft thud. Outside autumn rain fell quietly in the darkness, the drizzle lit a strange yellow by the distant street lamps. A mist had drifted east off the river Cam smudging the clean-lined portico of Cambridge station. It was the same back at Larkwood: an afternoon of intense sunshine had brought a fog off the Lark to hide the fields and smooth the tangled roofs and walls of the monastery. An apple wood fire blazed in the calefactory and Anselm was keen to get back to the hearth and warm his hands.

'I need a *lawyer*,' quoted Anselm, pensively tapping the steering wheel.

Those had been John's exact words. Not, it seemed, a *monk*.

'I'd better explain in person. You know I don't like the phone.'

'When do you want to come?'

'Tonight.'

Anselm had put down the receiver and shuffled off to the woodshed. There, musing and recollected, he'd split some green logs and sized them for a decent fire.

John Fielding was Anselm's oldest friend. They'd been to the same boarding school where, following a walk around the cricket square, they'd become allies in mutual understanding, a hallowed state that was later sealed over a bottle of purloined altar wine. While at university – John at Exeter, Anselm at Durham – they'd skilfully negotiated the transition from boyhood to manhood, that time of awkward flowering when, in making momentous decisions, many who were once close find themselves subtly apart. John, a linguist, had chosen journalism. Anselm, drawn by the thrilling mix of courtesy, high theatre and linguistic violence, had opted for the Bar. Both noted, with satisfaction, that the distance between Fleet Street and Gray's Inn was negligible.

While Anselm had forged a career defending the washed and unwashed alike, John had secured a position as foreign correspondent, serving first in East Berlin with Reuters and then landing a prized BBC posting to Warsaw in early 1982. He'd arrived just after the Communist Junta put its troops on the streets in their doomed fight against Solidarity. He'd covered the scrap meticulously until, much to the surprise of his employer, he'd been shown the door. More accurately, he'd been tossed on to a plane bound for Heathrow. Following which he'd told Anselm that he needed a lawyer.

56

Only there'd been a short interlude; a brief time when John was something of a reluctant hero in the pubs scattered around Gray's Inn and the watering holes favoured by writing hacks at the bottom end of Chancery Lane. John had clout. He'd been a friend of Lech. And everyone wanted to know what had happened out there in the cold. John parried questions from all quarters, only disclosing – with reluctance – the barest of details. He'd gone to a graveyard for a clandestine meeting with an underground activist (a remark that pulled a few laughs) but no sooner had he arrived at the chosen spot when agents of the security service appeared, arresting both John and his contact. Three days later his accreditation had been withdrawn. No amount of coaxing or flattery from the audience would persuade John to add anything further, either about the activist, or the candidates for betrayal – the person close to home who'd sold him down the river. The troubled disinclination to elaborate simply buffed up John's unwanted glamour and increased the aura of mystery surrounding his narrative.

Alone with Anselm, however, he'd been a fraction more informative, not so much about the events that had led to his arrest as to the nature of his work, its risks and obligations. But Anselm had sensed a link between the two, as if John were examining the chain of causation that had led to his expulsion.

Investigative journalism (he'd said, without

preamble, while they were playing chess) involves talking to anyone with insight and authority, regardless of their standing or the provenance of their information. It's about the search for truth, and sometimes you had to put your hand into the sewer. One of his sources had been a disaffected official with access to the darker corners of the government's mind. He'd phoned John cold. He'd called himself 'The Dentist'.

'As in teeth and fillings?'

'Is there another kind?'

'I suppose not.' Anselm was distracted, considering a dramatic sacrifice late in the game. His queen for a pawn. Something unheard of in the annals of their many confrontations. 'What about him?'

'Well, he was just a voice at the end of the line, feeding me inside stories . . . he remained hidden . . . until, one day, I met him.'

'Really? He dropped his guard?' All sacrifice involves a gamble, thought Anselm coldly. He made his move.

'Yes,' replied John, his voice light with surprise. 'He came to see me just before I left Warsaw.'

Anselm looked up.

'You know –' John hesitated, his brown eyes alight with subdued anxiety – 'I think I might have reached too far.'

'What do you mean?'

'Into the sewer.'

'Why?'

'He was a hood. The stories had been jam. Something sweet to get me on side.'

'To do what?'

'I don't know . . . and it doesn't matter any more. Because they kicked me out.'

Even as he spoke, John withdrew into himself. He looked at the board in confusion and, three moves later, trapped Anselm's king with vicious intellectual satisfaction, the brutality – Anselm was sure – having nothing to do with the game, and everything to do with the lingering memory of that 'Dentist'.

Anselm wondered if there was some connection between this shady individual and John's arrest in the graveyard, an intuition that acquired sudden weight when Anselm raised the matter, delicately, and John brushed it away with the same gesture one might use to slam a door. The conversation, he seemed to say, was over.

The subject appeared to have died a friendless death until, one morning, it gave John a sudden kick, demonstrating that it was very much alive – for others if not for him. A short article appeared on the third page of a national broadsheet intimating a more involved explanation for the sudden ejection of John Fielding from Warsaw. Its substance, fleeced of insinuation, lay beneath the headlines of two major tabloids.

'They're saying I was moonlighting for MI6,' seethed John. 'That I'd been using journalistic cover to gather intelligence.'

And so much more: that he was a key player on the ground with access to dissidents in hiding and liberals in the government. A spy.

'How do you hide a "dead drop" in a graveyard?' asked Anselm, not displaying the supreme tact advertised by his clerk.

'Don't you realise what this means for me?' barked John. 'For my career?'

They were sitting in the upstairs bar of the Bricklayers' Arms in Gresse Street, near Soho, lodged deep in soft armchairs near a low-lit corner. Perhaps it was the clinking and raised voices – the sense of festival away from the office – that had nudged Anselm's sensibilities off course. He apologised profusely, but John wasn't listening.

'Don't you see?' His deep brown eyes were anguished. 'If I leave the accusation unchallenged, I'm finished. No media outlet will employ me. It means I'm tainted. I can't be trusted.'

'What do you mean by unchallenged?' Anselm was shaking his head in disbelief. 'You're not squaring up for a fight, are you?'

'Not personally. It's your round,' said John, pointing at his empty glass.

John wouldn't listen – either that night, the following day, or during the tense weeks after the writ of libel had been served. He'd resolved to sue the most powerful news corporations in the United Kingdom. No warning or cautionary tale from Anselm would deter him. He remortgaged his flat in Hampstead to pay his solicitors' costs.

He duly begged Anselm to handle the trial, despite compelling evidence that his old friend's speciality was bread and butter crime, cut from the rough end of the loaf at that, and served with margarine. In the end, worn down, Anselm agreed, insisting on a CD of Johnny Hodges in lieu of payment.

Then relations between the two friends became strained. John wouldn't give any detailed instructions about his arrest in 1982. No information was forthcoming beyond what he'd revealed to his recently disbanded fan club.

'I'm protecting a contact,' he said, blinking like a mule.

'Which one?'

'The person I went to meet in the graveyard.'

'Tell me about him or her.'

'I can't. I made a promise.'

'To whom?' Anselm was twirling a pencil, conscious that it wasn't going to be used.

'The contact.'

'Promising?'

'To do and say nothing.'

'About what?'

'I'm not falling for that one.'

'John, I need an account. I need an explanation stronger than theirs.'

'Forget it. Put them to proof.'

Anselm bit the pencil, watching John sat cross-legged in the chair facing his desk. He was a worried man – one knee bobbing, a moist hand constantly smoothing back his combed sandy hair

– but he wouldn't help himself. He was the worst kind of client.

'What about the Dentist?'

'He was a legitimate source.'

'This is like pulling teeth,' sighed Anselm. He leaned back and pulled a little harder. 'He was – I use your words – a hood.'

'But our dealings were purely journalistic. He was channelling information into the western media. I was just the conduit. Like I said, he gave me jam. It never got to the point where he asked for anything from me.'

Anselm came from another angle.

'Did you keep any private papers when you were in Warsaw?'

'Like?'

'A diary, taped or written.'

'Yes.'

'Which kind.'

'Written.'

'Did it contain material germane to the matter in hand?'

'Decidedly.'

'Can I see it?'

'No.'

'Why?'

'I burned it.'

'You didn't. Tell me it's a joke. Okay, it's not a joke. Tell me why?'

'Pique. I'd hoped to use it later for a book. Cold War memoirs.'

'Why pique?'

'Because a handful of British newspapers accused me of spying and the substance of my experiences – rich, varied and well worth recounting – would, if printed, be interpreted from that perspective.'

'You shouldn't tell me you destroyed evidence.'

'You should be careful what you ask.'

'I'll have to tell the other side.'

'Go right ahead. Tell them I burned it after they burned my career.'

Anselm chewed his pencil. The mule with the bobbing leg wasn't going to budge.

'Character witnesses,' he said, hopefully. 'Do you know anyone who was close to the ground in Warsaw who can vouch for your professional integrity?'

'No.'

Anselm was getting nowhere. He decided to bring the conference to an end.

'Forget the cemetery and your burned journal and the friends you might have had. While in Warsaw, or anywhere else for that matter, did you have any form of contact – be that written, oral, signs, numbers, sounds – with any individual or organisation or their representatives which was inconsistent with your status as a foreign corres-pondent or any other capacity that you might have held or assumed, given the limitations conferred by your visa?'

'None whatsoever.'

Anselm dropped his pencil and closed his empty pad. 'It's a fight, then.'

The defendants had pleaded justification, implying that hard evidence would be forthcoming, presumably from credible persons with knowledge about John and the work of the intelligence community. However nothing was disclosed. Like John, they claimed to be protecting their source. Which, while admirable, was not a recognised defence to libel. They'd thought the little man wouldn't stand his ground. Negotiations began at the court door.

What should have been one of those rare experiences of uncomplicated joy for Anselm – knowing he'd won before he'd opened his mouth – turned out to be a remarkably unpleasant tutorial in humiliation. He was pitted against the most renowned performers from London's specialised libel chambers who viewed him, not altogether unfairly, as a mole on their lawn. Every offer of settlement refused by Anselm was met with soaring contempt.

'Now you're being greedy,' said one, with a slow, patrician sneer.

'I'd thought your client was being better advised,' mused another, a short man who seemed to look down while looking up.

They eventually caved in. And John won a retraction, a public apology, and what is always called, enticingly, 'undisclosed substantial damages'. That outcome ought to have been the signal for celebration: he'd recovered his reputation with compound interest. But within two weeks neither meant anything to him. He'd lost far more than his standing or its abstract value. Tragedies are like that. They redefine what is important.

Anselm tapped his fingers on the steering wheel. The train from London rumbled out of the darkness, its brakes screeching, the carriages shuddering. The tannoy crackled and a low Suffolk voice announced the arrival from London and a few pending departures. Anselm got out of his car, opened his umbrella and shambled pensively towards the station entrance.

The first tragedy to strike John took place the day following his victory. He'd not been alone in quitting Warsaw. A dissident and colourful intellectual had taken the same plane to London. Celina Something-or-other had irked the censors for years through her ambiguous documentary films but she'd finally had enough of the intimidation and restrictions placed upon her work. She'd chosen exile. John had adored her, from the tangled dyed hair, past the plastic belt, and down to the green canvas shoes. Anselm had imagined that before long they'd marry and that tiny feet with garish, painted nails would patter round Hampstead – a happy vision that was only blurred by his inclination to anticipate all manner of crises best expressed in German.

Though unfounded, his *ängstlichkeit* turned prophetic. John's association with Celina came to an abrupt conclusion on the very day that the

65

agreed apologies were printed in the various newspapers. John never spoke of the matter save to say, in clinical terms, that things hadn't worked out.

'It's over.'

'Why?'

'Why not?'

The accident occurred within a month of that conversation, though John refused at any point afterwards to call it a tragedy. He'd been screaming up the A1 when he went off the road after skidding in slurry. It turned out the farmer was on his way back to clean up the mess, but John had got there first, blown through a fence and hit a couple of trees. After a few weeks in intensive care, surgeons in Leeds and London achieved quite astonishing results in facial reconstruction.

'You wouldn't know the difference,' Anselm said, polishing his glasses on the lining of his jacket.

'I'd banked on improvement,' observed John, his voice flat and dry.

A year or so later Anselm left the Bar to join the community at Larkwood. The sound of monastic bells had been ringing in his memory ever since he'd stumbled on the Suffolk retreat in his youth. He'd been stung by simple words on a leaflet . . . something about tasting a peace this world cannot give. Like water dripping on a stone, some moisture in the phrase had finally got through to his heart. Surreptitiously, he'd gone back to the quiet valley. He'd mooched around the enclosure, knowing, even before he knew why, that this remote place was home. When John had said he was off to Warsaw, Anselm had lured him up the bell tower, intending to reveal the strange longing that had seized hold of him: but they'd ended up talking cross purposes. Looking down upon the fiery green of the cloister Garth, they'd spoken of love and reasons – that the twain would never meet – and John had thought Anselm meant an ample Jazz singer who reigned over a basement club near Finsbury Park. When, following the accident, Anselm finally disclosed his intention to leave the Bar, John had been hurt and stunned.

'You're not serious?'

'I am.'

'A monk? Sandals? Sackcloth?'

'Yes.'

'Covert flagellation?'

'No, communal.'

'You kept that to yourself.'

'Sort of.'

'Bloody hell. Why didn't you tell me when we were up the bell tower?'

And yet, in a curious way, Anselm's departure proved decisive for John's long-term rehabilitation: a deeper healing beyond the visible injuries. Unsure of where his future might lie now that his career as a journalist was over, he came to Larkwood. For months he shared the simple rhythm of Anselm's life, the experience communicating with depth what his friend could never have expressed in words. He returned to Hampstead understanding not only Anselm but his own future, bent on academia with a resolution only comparable to his first day at Reuters.

Over the following years John frequently made the trek to Larkwood. He told Anselm everything, from the contents of his dissertation to the underground politics that shaped the common room rebellions. They chewed over the past, as old friends do. But 1982 remained the year they never spoke about. Which, of course, made it for ever present. Because that was the time John had been in Warsaw. Whatever had happened over there he'd come home to lose everything that had once mattered. And a little bit more.

Passengers appeared in the mist. They moved quickly and purposefully, shoulders hunched, hands buried in pockets. John was the last to leave the station. He stepped outside, tapping his stick in a wide arc before his feet. Anselm had cut it down shortly after John had moved into the guest-house. The bottom half had been painted white in deference to city life and the conventions that announce disability.

'I need more than a lawyer,' he said, knowing that Anselm was out there, reaching for his arm. 'I need you to be my eyes and hands.'

CHAPTER 7

The fire hissed and spat. Anselm had chopped young wood, not old. The apple timbers hadn't had enough time to dry out so the resin boiled and ran. Heat efficiency was reduced, but you got that unusual smell, the warming aroma of smoky cider, hot pies and an imagined cinnamon. Anselm threw on a couple more logs and shambled to a small oak cupboard built into the wall of the calefactory. Situated as it was within the monastery, the room was not accessible to any of the guests. But Larkwood always made exceptions. To quote the Prior, it's what the rules were for. And Anselm wanted complete privacy and the surrounding silence that promoted absolute candour.

'Whisky?'

'Yep.'

'Water?'

'Nope.'

A couple of burgundy armchairs, the leather shabby and worn, faced the stone hearth, their feather cushions plumped and yielding. Between each stood a small round table with a faded military insignia dated 1916. They'd been picked up way back for a few quid by Father William at a Salvation Army secondhand furniture store in Manchester. Like all Larkwood's cobbled furnishings, they carried the secret histories of many unknown lives. They linked the community to the world they served. Anselm handed John his drink and then sank into his chair.

'You asked about the person I met in the graveyard?' said John, as if they were still in Anselm's chambers at Gray's Inn.

'Yes.'

'I need to wind back first, to December of nineteen eighty-one, just after midnight. That's when it all began.'

John sat hunched forward, nursing his glass with both hands. Reflected flames danced on his dark glasses. He angled his head slightly, attuned, as always, to the breathing of anyone nearby.

'Tanks rolled on to the streets and within days ten thousand people had been thrown into detention camps. The army were in charge. Helped, of course, by the secret police . . . the *Służba Bezpieczeństwa*, the SB, the *ubeks* . . . to use their more polite names. This was martial law. People called it *stan wojenny*: a state of war.'

Most of the Solidarity leadership had been captured. The free trade union that had pressed for reform and change – wielding industrial chaos to speed up things – had been decapitated. Remaining activists had gone underground and

70

settled into a long war. For their part, a war of words. They didn't take up the gun, they took up the typewriter. Illegal publications burst out from hidden places. By the time John arrived there were hundreds in Warsaw alone. In March 1982 one of them caught his attention: *Wolność i Niezależność* . . . *Freedom and Independence*. Running along the bottom of the page in tiny letters was this mysterious declaration:

PRINTED BY THE SHOEMAKER FOR THE FRIENDS OF THE SHOEMAKER

'The Shoemaker?' echoed Anselm.

'His selected essays are available in translation. You'll find a lengthy appraisal of his work (with citations) in my doctoral dissertation, a copy of which – furnished with a warm dedication – was presented to you in the manner of a gift.'

'I still recall the lucid opening and the magisterial conclusions. Remind me about the cobbler.'

'Every child in Warsaw knows the story. A dragon ravages the kingdom. All the knights are slain. Eventually a poor shoemaker turns up with a scheme to blow it to pieces, a sheepskin filled with sulphur . . . think takeaway kebab stuffed with Czech Semtex. The dragon has a night on the town, fancies a quick bite after closing time, and bang. Peace returns to the land.'

The meaning was stark ('and concludes Chapter Two') – the Shoemaker was back to save the kingdom, this time with another kind of foreign explosive: words and ideas. John's interest in the publication, however, wasn't only limited to an enticing byline. A few probing questions revealed that the Shoemaker's paper had first appeared before the Second World War. It had continued in print right through the transition to Communist rule, abruptly disappearing off the streets in 1951 during the Stalinist Terror. For those old enough to remember – 'Ring any bells? Chapter Three?' – the reappearance of *Freedom and Independence* in 1982 was a wake-up call. The title was heavy with the meaning of struggle. It situated martial law squarely alongside the Occupation and the subsequent burden of totalitarian rule.

'In retrospect, it was extraordinary,' said John. 'The response of ordinary people to the tanks and guns was spontaneously democratic. They set up "the other circuit", *drugi obieg*. They devised their own secret institutions, run by and for themselves. *Freedom and Independence* was a perfect example . . . it was produced by friends. Someone printed it, obviously, but the operation didn't end there. A whole distribution network was set up, right under the noses of the army and the *ubeks*. Teams of volunteers, *kolporters*, people who believed in the Shoemaker's ideas, spread the paper all over the city. They called themselves the Friends and, to this day, nobody has the faintest idea who any of the key players might have been. I first came across a copy in a café near my apartment. The owner had a pedal bin that functioned as a kind of secret magazine rack. Those in the know would turn up, buy a coffee and wait for the nod to go and fish out their morning paper.'

A nod given in John's presence, telling him that he was trusted. A nod that told him the owner had some link to the Friends of the Shoemaker. John saw his opportunity to get to the voice behind the paper: he left a message asking for an interview.

'Instead I met Róża Mojeska,' said John. 'The most remarkable woman I have ever met in my life. And she doesn't even feature as a footnote.'

She had two wedding rings on one finger, he said, running ahead of himself. He'd never had the courage to ask why. It had been a priest's idea, that's all she'd said, seeing John's gaze. But it was the single most potent 'message' that accompanied every movement of her hand, every gesture and action. She was not alone; she was two people. She was part of an alliance. Anyway, returning to that request for a meeting, a week after leaving his message with the owner, he'd been stirring his coffee when a huge bearded guy in a checked jacket loomed over the table and told him to wear his overcoat like a cloak and wait at the grave of Bolesław Prus in the Powązki cemetery, a writer famed for his love of children.

'Where you were arrested six months later?' asked Anselm.

'Yes.'

'What happened in between?'

John had become a friend of Róża, as much personally as professionally. He'd been her link to the western media and she'd been his entry to the underground, but something else had grown: the sort of confidence and affection you can't choose or nurture; it's already there, waiting to catch light. But there'd been no meeting with the Shoemaker.

'I asked every time I saw her and she always said no, which frustrated me no end because whoever did the writing wasn't only a Václav Havel, he was a pimpernel known by his shoe rather than his glove. The paper just turned up out of nowhere. Every page kept alive the dream of an independent culture and society. There was poetry in the simplest lines.'

And Róża was the only link to this central figure of resistance: no one else knew who he was or where he was hiding. Then on the morning of the first of November, while walking to work, John felt a big hand grab his elbow. Turning to his side, he saw the towering figure who'd loomed over the café table. 'The Shoemaker wants to meet you. Tonight. Six p.m. At the grave of Prus.' Then he crossed the road and was gone, leaving John stunned in the middle of the pavement.

'It was All Souls' Day.' John was still leaning towards the fire. He sipped his whisky. 'The place was alight with thousands of candles. People were gathered everywhere, but Róża was nowhere to be seen. And then I saw her walking over to one of them . . . a hard-looking bastard with a dead man's face.'

★   ★   ★

74

John leaned on the huge stone lintel and looked down, unseeing, towards the complaining fire. His jacket was a neat fit, a slate grey herringbone, on top of a black roll neck sweater. He was tall and slim, the black trousers well pressed and shoes highly polished.

'I was arrested, too,' he said, stroking his jaw. 'For some reason, taking photographs of the secret police in action was considered bad taste. I got a good kicking and then they threw me on to the street.'

But not before learning that Róża had been taken to Mokotów prison.

'I found her home address through a contact in the jail. I had to tell her it wasn't me, that I'd been careful, that no one had followed me, but she wasn't listening, she wasn't *present*. That's when I realised she'd told others, and they'd been waiting like me, the Shoemaker among them . . . but she'd seen one of the *ubeks*. She'd handed herself in. It had been a spontaneous, desperate signal to whoever was watching to make a run for it. So she'd won. They got no one else and they had nothing on her . . . and yet she was a broken woman. She was completely shattered.'

Straightening up, he tapped his jacket pockets. 'May I?'

'Yes.'

He'd always smoked Sobranie Black Russians, ever since his student days when he'd first got hooked. Like the Zeha East German trainers he'd

75

picked up in Carnaby Street, they'd given him a sort of nonconformist allure. He still had the sheen as he fumbled for the crumpled packet, bent his head and struck a match.

'I told her I'd find out who it was,' stressed John, gesticulating with a sweeping arm towards Anselm. 'I said I had connections, friends on both side of the fence, that it was my job to investigate, that I'd walk through fire . . . and she just cut me dead. She stared ahead, face stricken, and told me to do and say *nothing* . . . to forget what had happened in the cemetery, to forget the Shoemaker and the Friends – to forget her.' He pushed smoke out of the side of his mouth, shaking his head in a kind of sickened wonder. 'I don't know what they did to her in prison, or what they'd said, but make no mistake. She'd lost. This was a defeated woman.'

'Shortly afterwards you were thrown out,' recalled Anselm.

'Yep.' John blew hard and took another deep drag.

'You kept your promise.'

'Yep.'

'Which was why you couldn't tell me anything during the libel proceedings.'

John nodded.

'What's changed John?' Anselm removed his glasses, and held them up to the light of the fire. Cleaning them on his scapular, he said, 'You've kept that promise for twenty-eight years. Why break it now? I'd have thought . . .' He paused, suddenly understanding.

John counted the steps back to his seat and carefully lowered himself into the armchair. Taking his drink, he nursed it again and said, 'Róża knocked on my door last night. She wants my help after all.'

Anselm listened with the helpless compassion that he often felt in the confessional. He identified with other people's lives and dilemmas; he railed against the random sequence of events whose ordering caused as much grief as any want of goodness. John evidently blamed himself for Róża's collapse. He was the one who'd badgered her for that interview. And someone had used the circumstances to engineer her spiritual obliteration.

'She rang first,' explained John. 'There was no "How are you?" or "Long time no see". She just said she was in London and went straight to the point. "John, I wear two wedding rings. You've seen them. The second belonged to my husband. He was shot in nineteen fifty-one. Pavel, and another man . . . they were killed like beaten dogs. I was there, in the cellar of Mokotów. After my release, I could do nothing for him, for both of them, except wear the rings. I feel them every day; I've never forgotten the sight and the sound of that gun, or the face of the man who pulled the trigger." She was whispering hard and I told her to slow down but she sort of pushed past me, her English breaking up as she ploughed on.'

Róża had switched to her mother tongue, speaking with deadly emphasis.

'She said, "You, too, have seen his face. It belongs to Otto Brack. He arrested me at the grave of Prus in nineteen eighty-two. Do you remember?" I said I did, and then her voice dropped even lower. "When we got to Mokotów, he warned me that if I ever chose justice for Pavel consequences would follow, that he'd expose the informer he'd used to catch me . . . he'd spill their past all over the floor. Then he let me go. Do you understand what he did? He gave me power over their future, a power that could end their life or save it." Her voice cracked again and seemed to vanish down a hole and I just waited and waited . . . and all I could hear was her breath dragging at the other end of the line. Then she said, cold and quiet, "That power . . . I'm going to use it."'

John gave the remaining exchanges without commentary. Anselm seemed to pause in a Hampstead corridor, listening hard.

'Why now, Róża?'

'Because sooner or later someone else will name the informer.'

'Really?'

'Yes. There are files in Warsaw. Lawyers are reading them.'

John paused to light another Sobranie, struggling with the matches.

78

'If they're named later, Brack might be dead. I have to act now.'

'Absolutely.'

'But the informer must know that I don't seek to condemn them. That's not my objective, it's not what I want.'

'That's . . . generous, Róża.'

'If they face the past, then I can, too. This is the only way to catch Otto Brack.'

'Yes, I see that now.'

He leaned forward, feeling for an ashtray.

'You once offered to walk through fire, John, do you remember?'

'I do.'

'Well, I've written something that'll help you get to the other side.'

'You better bring it round. We need to look each other in the eye.'

Sitting back, it was as though John had put the phone down in London and returned to Larkwood's calefactory, short of breath and vaguely agitated.

'She obviously wanted me to find the informer, to reassure them and appeal to their conscience, prior to some sort of meeting . . . but she couldn't see me of course, she didn't know that I'm as blind as a bat, that all I could do was stumble in the dark.'

'Did she come round?'

'Yep.'

'And?'

'I made roast beef and Yorkshire pudding.'

'Any reference to that fire?'

'No. We just talked about the old days. No mention of Otto Brack. Just a passing shot at the Shoemaker.'

'What about whatever it was she'd written?'

'Kept it to herself. Seems Braille didn't get a look in.'

'What then?'

'She left.'

'Just like that? No proposal to meet at the Tate or the Festival Hall?'

'She was too upset. Couldn't see her, of course, but she held me by the arms once more and I knew she was leaving me as I'd left her the last time, a devastated woman. She realised I couldn't help her, that Brack had won again.'

He'd finished his whisky with an intake of breath and seemed to be waiting and listening, as he'd waited and listened to Róża on the phone. The resulting space in the conversation seemed to have Anselm's shape, so he filled it.

'John, what is it you want me to do? You said you needed a lawyer, someone to be your eyes and hands.'

The wood had ceased to spit or hiss. Embers glowed, turning black and red. Outside the rain had stopped and a wind had begun to loosen the trees.

'I want you to do what I can't do,' said John, resigned and tentative. 'I want you to walk through fire. I want you to find out who betrayed Róża Mojeska in nineteen eighty-two. And once you've found them, I want you to coax them out of the dark. Failing that, bring them kicking and screaming into the light. Rough or smooth, give them a helping hand.'

CHAPTER 8

Anselm went to his cell and threw open the window, wondering how he was going to tell John that life's changes intervene. If John was blind, Anselm was lame. He was a monk, now, not a lawyer. He couldn't go where he pleased, even for the sake of lost justice. The trees began to lift and sway in the darkness, restless and strong, fighting back. Looking towards the lights in the guesthouse, warm and comforting, like banked fires on a headland, he thought of other trees, and other storms, of first disclosures and the binding, unforgettable confessions of childhood.

Anselm first met John at the school gates, shortly after his eleventh birthday. His father had just driven off and tears were rising in a great wave of sadness, their force jamming in his throat. He was about to sob when he heard a twig crack among the rhododendrons that fenced off the woods which flanked the school entrance. Peering into the darkness Anselm saw a stained face, a stiff white shirt, and ruffled sandy hair.

'What are you doing in there?' asked Anselm.

'I'm not entirely sure, to be honest,' said the boy, emerging with a trombone case in his hand. On his back was a leather satchel. He whistled nonchalantly and looked around, as if he often made irrational excursions into nearby woodland, instrument oiled for action just in case he came across a brass band. He, too, had been crying. Anselm understood at once. His parents had gone, and, unable to let anything else go, the boy had wandered about the school grounds clinging on to his music and his books as if they were someone's hands, finally hiding in the trees when the weight of isolation grew too heavy, when the indignity of tears erupted into this grown up world of boys who didn't cry, least of all for love of one's family.

'Are you new?' asked the boy.

'Yep.'

'Good.'

There was nothing else to be said for the moment. They'd each found their Man Friday. They were going to survive. They shook hands and swapped names.

Neither of them, in the true sense, had been abandoned, though from Anselm's perspective there'd been an element of shipwreck. Two years earlier his mother, Zélie, had died of cancer, leaving her husband, Gilbert, bereft in his soul and all fingers and thumbs in the home. A chancery lawyer not gifted in the management of emotions, least of all those of other people, he'd been unable to handle the grief of his five children.

They'd all started swearing in French with shocking ingenuity. There was no obvious link, but boarding school for the three oldest eventually surfaced like a message in a bottle, bobbing up and down on the waves of unchartered feeling.

For Anselm the passage of bereavement had been smoothed by treachery. Gilbert, clumsily, had instructed his children not to reveal that an operation to save their mother's life had failed. 'Let the end come like an unexpected guest,' he'd said, like General Custer sighting the Indians. But within days of Zélie's return home, Anselm broke rank. Handing her a cup of tea, he said, 'You're going to die.' From that moment she was free – free to say goodbye. Free to look upon her family with the clarity of vision that comes from knowing the last grains of sand were falling fast through the egg timer. In public they kept up the pretence that she would survive while, as between themselves, there grew an excruciating pain, a liberating simplicity coming, on occasion, mysteriously close to joy. They'd grieved while she was still alive – a gift lost on the others who'd taken refuge in the numbness of make-believe. In the two years that followed Zélie's death, all that Gilbert had noticed, as he pondered what to do and how best to manage his own incipient breakdown, was that Anselm had sworn the least.

'So that's why he sent you here,' said John, with a sigh.

They were walking around the cricket square. In fact, they'd walked around it three times, ultimately missing one of the most savage displays of fast bowling attack the school had ever known. All John had done was to try and open up the territory between them by asking, off-hand, 'Why did you come to Roper's Hall?' and Anselm had delivered what John later called a long and sparklingly honest confession. He'd evidently been scared off, since (Anselm surmised) most disclosures work on a *quid quo pro* basis and John hadn't wanted to say anything beyond the commonplace. After all, there was a match on.

'What about you?' asked Anselm, vaguely hearing another cheer from the field.

'Eh?'

'Why Roper's Hall?'

'The price.'

'Sorry?'

'No story such as yours,' explained John, ruefully looking over Anselm's shoulder. 'My father just went for the cheapest prison he could find.'

Of course, Anselm hadn't sought any treaty by mutual revelation. He'd simply answered the question, but in so doing he deepened the contract of friendship between them. Regardless of John's personal reticence, or being irked at missing seven wickets in two overs, their alliance shifted level. They became blood brothers, even though Anselm was the only one who'd opened up his skin. They looked out for each other. They ambled round the school corridors, hands in pockets, planning dark mischief against the dorm prefects on the top floor.

John's quip had nonetheless intrigued Anselm, and did so for years. What John didn't seem to realise was that holding back anything important from a friend always communicates something profound. It wasn't that term 'prison' or the jibe at the cost. Rather it was the silence within the words. As life at Larkwood confirmed, silence has a shape and content, but even back then as a twelve year old Anselm sensed in John's rejoinder something momentous and defining, another manner of ship-wreck. Anselm didn't find out what it was, or why John had come to Roper's Hall, until they were about to leave it, some six years later.

Final exams were approaching and, all classes being finished, John invited Anselm to his parents' home in Cornwall, a large, white house that faced the sea at Bude Bay. There, protected from the wind and soothed by Atlantic sunsets, they might revise by day and revel by night. The idea was to occupy the building without the benefit of adult interference, an objective happily guaranteed by John's father's diplomatic career. Without drop-ping any particular clangers, George Fielding had singularly failed to attract any major promotions, finding himself exiled to a basement office in the outskirts of Washington dedicated to trade and foreign licence agreements. 'Not that happy a man,' John had said. 'He never found his way out of first gear, so now he's just waiting to retire . . . prior to which the house is empty and available for our undisturbed occupation.'

Except that things didn't work out that way. John's American mother, Melanie, insisted on coming over to 'cook, clean, and entertain'. It was the latter that took Anselm's orderly – one might say restrained – life by storm.

'Okay, boys, you've been working too hard,' she said on the first night before they'd even opened their books. 'Time to play.'

'Mother, no,' said John, closing his eyes.

'C'mon, you old bore,' she replied, winking at Anselm. 'Follow me.'

She swept down a corridor, opened a door that led to a basement, and vanished down the stairs. Anselm tracked her descent, John groaning to God from behind. Entering a low, windowless room Anselm saw a pool table, centrally placed beneath a frame of harsh lights. Mel – as she insisted on being called – placed a cigarette into a long, black holder, flicked open a silver lighter and settled a hard stare upon the two friends. 'Forget exams, degrees, and the ladder to high office. All that matters, for sure. But there's something else you need to learn. Misery. Sometimes called Alabama Eight-ball.' After lighting up, she took a slow, deep draught and blew a stream of smoke towards the cue-rack. 'Let's go to school.'

Moments later Mrs Fielding – Anselm couldn't quite make it down the Mel route – crouched over the green felt, tossed back a fringe of brown hair and smacked the ball, her dazzling teeth biting the cigarette holder.

'By the way,' she said, reaching for the blue chalk, 'I play to win.'

In effect a tournament began which threatened to take over the object of coming to Cornwall. Each evening they played Misery, cracking open bottles of Budweiser, the day's revision dramatically pushed into the background. Anselm would have enjoyed himself without equivocation – and not just because Mel played to lose, handing the victor's mantle to Anselm – if he hadn't noticed that John was three steps removed from the fun, that his smile was half forced, that he was – to use his mother's term – an old bore. With the same puzzled eye Anselm also noted, very gradually, that Mrs Fielding's capering wasn't so simple or spontaneous: that it had a target; that her verbal tricks were dealt towards John; that she was trying, desperately and unsuccessfully, to please him, to win him over. She was too much an extrovert to show her disappointment but, as Anselm's French grandmother used to say, the skin speaks, too. And at the corners of Melanie Fielding's eyes were fine lines of suffering, deepened by a ready laugh that they might be hidden. Anselm let the matter pass.

It was John who raised it, two weeks later when they were back at school, drinking the remnants from a bottle of altar wine lifted from the school's sacristy.

'I just love her,' said Anselm, pouring an inch into two mugs stained with coffee. They'd locked

88

the door to their shared room facing the second floor showers.

'Who?'

'Your mother.' Anselm shook his head at the memory of her face, the twang in her soft voice. 'She's clever, rude, funny, and irrepressible. She's good company. She's—'

'Not my mother,' inserted John.

He walked over to the sink and poured the wine down the drain.

'Too sweet,' he said.

Anselm waited for John to elaborate but, for a moment, he said nothing. He washed his mug, scouring the coffee stains with his toothbrush. When he'd turned off the tap and dried his hands on the curtain he came back and sat on the edge of his bed, looking at Anselm from some distant place, far from school and the recollection of Misery in Cornwall.

'I'm not like you, Anselm,' he said, almost regretfully. 'I can't just open up and tell you what's inside. I wasn't made that way. And, you know, sometimes, there are things you can't talk about. They have to be left where you find them. Six years ago I found my birth certificate. That's how I learned my mother's name. You see, Anselm, the difference between me and you is this: I was the one that was lied to. I'm like your mother, only nobody sat down and told me the truth, not until I asked; and when I did . . . I preferred the lie.'

John would have left it there, but he saw the

question in Anselm's face: his wanting to share the load.

'She betrayed my father,' he said, frowning, loathing the harsh atmosphere roused by the charge. 'And I don't appear to have featured on the balance sheet . . . at a time when I couldn't eat unless she held out the spoon.' Shuffling back on to the bed to lean against the wall, he looked at Anselm with undisguised envy, as if to say parental death has its compensations. 'I came to Roper's Hall not because my father thought it was cheap, but because I didn't want to stay at home. I needed to break out of the make-believe. Find myself. You wouldn't understand that.'

Gazing out over Larkwood's restive trees Anselm mused how these differing experiences of family trauma had shaped them both. Speaking for himself, the loss of his mother had opened a wound on to life itself – that the rich grass, soft to touch, rich to smell, withers too soon, an insight that had prompted a quest and helped illuminate the narrow path to monastic life. Rooted very much in this world, Anselm strived to see every-thing as a mirror on to the other side of the fence, where the pasture was a contrasting green, and unfading.

As to John, the effect of the loss of his mother was a far more complex matter to gauge, not least because her great going had been voluntary. She'd turned away from her son and husband, presumably for someone else and a new life weighed and checked as having far more appeal. But Anselm, remembering these ancient, nearly forgotten disclosures, now received a glimmer of understanding. In retrospect – and Anselm had never quite noticed this before – John had always been on the move, in search of something out of reach. Throughout his school days, as soon as he was able, he'd run after the big ideas – from Zeno to Marx, never quite finding satisfaction at the end of the book. He'd wrestled with theories of right and wrong, wanting a rational basis for why one should be moral at all, searching – Anselm thought – for some intellectual mechanism that might excuse if not explain his mother's conduct. At university, he'd chased the reticent, colder girls, sometimes breaching their fragile defences, never staying with any of them for long. They'd thought him heartless. And his first job had been in East Berlin. The next in Warsaw. He'd learned languages increasingly far from his own. If the accident hadn't happened, he'd probably have ended up in Shanghai. In every way he'd been on a quest, like Anselm, only he'd never arrived at a moment of stillness – a recollected, clear-sighted understanding of where he'd come from and where he was going. Seen like that, Anselm recognised another facet of John's character. The man who searches is looking for something; and until it's found, he's waiting. That was John . . . a man who'd been left waiting ever since his mother turned away.

Anselm shut the window, muffling the clamour of the trees and the great sighs of the wind. He was troubled by his unremitting failure to recognise the pikestaffs in his life. All these years he'd thought 1982 was the one subject they'd never spoken about, forgetting that this other, older crisis remained, for the greater part, unexplored. They were blood brothers, but John had kept two secrets beneath his skin, not one. The first had now been ventilated. Strange, really (thought Anselm, climbing into bed) that tonight he should think of the oldest. He'd forgotten all about it.

CHAPTER 9

Anselm dreamed vividly, receiving the special enlightenment that comes from the paradox of watching oneself in action. It was as though his psyche – exasperated once more with its host's predilection to skate past the obvious – hit back, hurling into the sleeping mind something simple but significant about John's motivation in coming to Larkwood. Something else he'd forgotten. Faithful to the facts, the drama unfolded like a black and white newsreel from a forgotten war.

Anselm had been a monk for about eighteen months and hadn't heard from John at all. For his part, Anselm had sent tape recordings in place of letters, describing the rough and tumble of life around a cloister. He'd told funny stories about the older duffers. He'd passed on some of the wisecracks from the Prior. But nothing came in return. With the passage of time Anselm had grown anxious because he couldn't expunge his last memory of John: unshaven, the buttons out of order on his shirt, the coloured socks that didn't match. And so, with the Prior's permission, Anselm had taken an early train from Cambridge and turned up unannounced at John's flat.

'I thought we might have breakfast,' said Anselm, as the door opened.

'Have they kicked you out?'

'Not yet.'

'Are you wearing sandals?'

'Yes.'

'O God.'

Anselm followed John down the dark corridor, weaving between unopened mail and slumped rubbish sacks loose at the neck, horrified at what he'd just seen: the bloodless face behind dark glasses; the creased, slept-in clothing; the saffron stains on the open shirt. Cautiously, he entered the kitchen, smelling a nauseating blend of cigarettes, stale beer and spices. The work surface and sink overflowed with filthy crockery, half empty aluminium take-away trays, empty bottles and crushed cans. On a table, by a tape recorder, lay a saucer heaped with ash and stubs. One of Anselm's cassettes was in the deck. The others, salvaged from the corridor but still in their envelopes, were piled to one side.

'I take it you've made a significant effort to continue your engagement with the local community?' queried Anselm.

'I feed my neighbour's cat.'

'You've sought help from professionals trained to help a talented young man come to terms with restricted vision?'

'Don't be shy. The word's "blind".'

'You take frequent and regular exercise?'

'Without fail. I go upstairs . . . and then I come down again.'

John was opening cupboards, patting his hands inside, trying to find a jar of instant coffee.

'You're relatively happy, grappling with the exciting question of what comes next in your life?'

'I'm raring to go.'

'I assume you have a suitcase?'

John turned around, letting his arms drop.

'A suitcase,' repeated Anselm. 'Let me pack it. You're expected at Larkwood. I realise you'll be leaving behind a vast, carefully constructed support network, but you'll find another community, different help, lots of exercise and as much time as you need to grapple. Sandals, too, if you want.'

'And a whip?'

'No. And leave yours behind. The point of coming is to learn to do without.'

John was not the first person overwhelmed by depression to stay at Larkwood. Many tortured men and women had taken a room in the guesthouse while learning to grope through various kinds of darkness. John was allocated a room on the ground floor. In lieu of a white stick, Anselm cut down a sapling with twists and turns produced by a struggle with a winding creeper. John was given a job picking apples, alternating with bottle washing and waxing floors. He was given a structure. Early rising, quiet, work, more quiet, more work, recreation (sometimes raucous), a Great Silence, early to bed. Between times: mysteriously bad meals.

'This is good, Anselm,' he said after three weeks. 'I'm beginning to find my way.'

It was a warm, grateful but cryptic comment. Anselm had anticipated that John would eventually start shaving, pick fruit and – when the moment was ripe – open up about the terror of finding himself blind, haunted by the memory of colour. However, only a portion of those expectations came to pass. He did shave. He went one step further: despite strong warnings to the contrary, he asked Larkwood's unskilled barber for a haircut. He wandered through the orchard, arms reaching up into the lower branches feeling for apples that were ready to fall, removing them with that gentle twist required by Brother Aiden. But he didn't open up. At least not to Anselm. In the evenings, in that quiet hour before Compline, Anselm often saw John walking with *the Prior*, the man whose pungent remarks had made it on to the cassette left in the tape deck. Heads bowed, they ambled along the Bluebell Walk; they sat on the railway sleeper overlooking Our Lady's Lake; they paused in the woods, suddenly alert, as though wondering if someone had tailed them. Moving once more, the Prior listened intently, his arm hooked into John's, nudging or pulling as the turns of the lane required.

'You're back to your old self, John,' remarked

Anselm six months later as they rinsed bottles in the scullery. 'And I'm glad, real glad.'

'I'm not quite there,' he replied, plunging his hands into the hot water. 'But I'm learning . . . slowly learning . . . to bide my time and wait.'

Wait for what? Anselm wanted to know but he couldn't ask. There was something confessional about John's talks with the Prior which, by their nature, excluded repetition, even to a close friend. Anselm understood this, but it didn't erase the jealousy: his wanting to be an important – if not decisive – part of John's recovery. The sense of exclusion was all the more difficult to manage because John became increasingly relaxed with Anselm. He joked again, as they'd done at school. He sought him out to talk about everything but the past: he confided to Anselm not the path travelled, but his plans for the future.

'I can still contribute,' he said cautiously, almost lapsing into the Prior's strange Glasgow-Suffolk dialect. 'I can write. I can teach. I can see certain things without my eyes . . . things I might not have seen unless I'd been forced to look in a different way. Do you know what I mean?'

'Yes.' Anselm did. It applied to his life of faith.

John left Larkwood after seven months. By his own account he wasn't ready to handle life alone in Hampstead but the time was right – like one of those apples that need a little twist to leave the tree. Anselm drove him home, a restored but still broken man – that contradictory state of the injured who

97

have come to accept their injury and the limitations it brings.

'Thanks for the tapes, Anselm,' said John after they'd tidied up the kitchen.

'No problem.'

'Thanks for coming to get me.'

'Sure.'

'Thanks for bringing me back. I can take care of myself, now.'

A pause fell between them. Anselm's failure to reply contained the unspoken hurt: that he'd planned his own wisecracks and counsel only to find himself employed as the chauffeur.

'Anselm?'

'Yes?'

'If ever I needed help – real help . . . with something far more difficult than what to do when you can't see the end of your nose . . . I'd only come to you.'

At those words Anselm woke up as if someone had snapped a thumb and forefinger.

He showered and threw on his habit, glancing afresh at the milestones to John's professional rehabilitation. After leaving Larkwood he'd found a place at St Anthony's College, Oxford, and completed a PhD, a *meisterwerk* on the contribution of dissident thinking to political theory in East-Central Europe. Honoured with a copy, Anselm had confined himself to the first and last pages, thus missing those abundant references to the Shoemaker. Fortunately, more discriminating readers had considered its merits and John had been offered a tiny room in Birkbeck College, London. There, speaking from a cloud, Sobranies to hand, he'd entranced successive generations with tales of the movers and shakers behind a peaceful revolution; of how he'd once rubbed shoulders with greatness.

But the dream had left another imprint on Anselm's mind: the recollection of something altogether personal. The bell for Lauds came like a herald: John's request for help had been planned long ago, even as he'd stumbled through the woods at Larkwood.

CHAPTER 10

The jubilant opening antiphon did not command Anselm's undivided attention. He kept thinking of Melanie Fielding propped up in a facing stall, pool cue in one hand and a bottle of Bud in the other. Beside her stood another phantom, this one empty handed: John's real mother, the woman he'd never named. They seemed to watch Anselm with different kinds of appeal, wanting by turns to be understood and forgiven. They were at his shoulder when, after Lauds, he tugged at the Prior's scapular. Standing in the cloister, he spoke in a hushed voice from one cowled shadow to another, the shamble of feet around them growing still. Given the hour and the place he restricted himself to the sparest details.

'John Fielding has asked for my help,' whispered Anselm.

Nod.

'He wants me to walk through fire.'

A reasonable-request nod.

'If I make it to the other side a killer from the Stalinist Terror will be brought to justice.'

An as-you'd-expect nod.

'Will you tell him it's just not possible? Monastery walls, and all that?'

The Prior nudged his glasses and the two round discs glinted suddenly in the darkness. His reply was barely audible. 'This afternoon, two-thirty.'

The meeting was convened in the parlour, a bright and draughty room opposite the reception desk where Sylvester endured his long face-off with the telephone. Anselm strongly suspected that the Watchman had quit the front line trench and had scouted silently to the door where he could listen to John's explanation.

The Prior listened, too, but in that intimidating way for which he was renowned. He didn't move, sitting on the edge of his seat, his dark eyes alive with an intense concentration that threatened to consume whoever was speaking. His cheap wire glasses, round and slightly out of shape, seemed to have been damaged by the force behind them.

'Where is Róża now?' he said, the accent more Glasgow than Suffolk.

'I don't know,' said John. 'She'd gone before I could ask where she was going.'

The Prior made a humph. 'She waited fifty-nine years,' he calculated, drawing out the words. 'And then, when she finally decided to use the power given to her by this man Brack, she turned to you. Not one of the many Friends who'd served the cause of the Shoemaker, but you, a man she'd only known for a matter of months . . . it's as though

101

she could trust no other. It's as though you were part of her lost opportunity.'

The Prior humphed again, and Anselm winced, waiting for his spiritual father to express pained regret: that the monastic enclosure represented an environment of inner freedom born of stability and that Anselm, without duress, had chosen to live within it; that he was no longer free to be anyone's eyes and hands. Instead the Prior sat back and said, 'What can be done?'

Like Róża said, explained John, there are files.

During the eighties, the Warsaw SB and Stasi personnel from East Germany formed a unit to tackle underground printing in the city. They kept a joint archive in German. No one knew of its existence until six months ago when a plumber found two crates in the basement of a condemned office block in Dresden. The contents were now lodged with the *Instytut Pamięci Nardowej* in Warsaw, the Institute of National Remembrance, commonly known as the IPN. After Róża's disappearance John had lunged for the phone, wondering if she'd been there and hoping to track down a contact number. He'd failed on both scores for reasons of confidentiality but mention of the Shoemaker and his own arrest elicited a reference to the newly found documents. As a victim of the former communist regime and someone directly linked to the fortunes of *Freedom and Independence*, he was entitled to inspect them.

'The operation that led to my arrest was called *Polana*,' he explained. 'Obviously, the target was Róża, not me. The point, however, is that the file generated by the operation was stored in one of those crates. As I say, all the paperwork is in German.'

The last observation came with an angling of the head towards Anselm, neatly making reference to his passable competence at the language. As an adolescent Anselm had been enthralled by all those dark words for dread and anxiety, along with heavyweight mindbenders like *vergangenheitsbewältigung*: the assumption of one's past. He'd relished that one, even before he'd had a past to assume. With the same hunger he'd scoured a dictionary for like terms in a fearless endeavour to acquire intellectual depth. He'd drop them carelessly into ordinary discourse as if to say English had unfortunate conceptual limitations. It was only much later, after the war criminal Eduard Schwermann had claimed sanctuary at Larkwood, that Anselm returned to the language with the sober application that comes with middle age. He'd been taught by the community's gardener, Brother Eckhart, a former bookseller with unsubstantiated connections to the Austrian aristocracy. His tuition had been unconventional, grounding Anselm's vocabulary in horticultural matters, thirteenth century mystical theology and the requirements of polite table conversation.

'The file ought to contain everything compiled

by this unit to catch Róża,' said John, fidgeting with a button on the cuff of his jacket. 'And that would include the name of the informer.'

'Whom Róża has, in effect, protected from Otto Brack,' mumbled the Prior, recapitulating.

'Yes,' said John.

'Because if she accuses Brack he, in turn, will accuse his own informer.'

'Exactly.'

'Who would then be exposed for what they were and are.'

'Which Róża, until now, has refused to contemplate.'

'For fear they'd take desperate measures to avoid the shame.'

This was Róża's dilemma, neatly summarised. For a long while, the two monks and their guest meditated on Otto Brack's scheme to avoid justice, their heavy silence almost certainly shared by Sylvester who, ear to the door, was straining to catch the Prior's considered response. Finally, Larkwood's reluctant superior made a kind of speech. If Anselm hadn't sought the conference that morning he'd have thought the Prior had prepared his words the night before. He spoke deliberately with measured phrasing:

'Such is the ingenious plan of Otto Brack. But Róża's is all the braver, all the more daring and all the more laden with risk. Her aim is nothing less than to turn Brack's world-view upside down. She's placing all her hopes in the hands of the one person who has everything to lose. Brack, it seems, has no faith in the human condition, in *humanity*. He has never contemplated that his informer might be prepared, if asked, to face their past. Róża, on the other hand, holds firm to a belief that I sometimes fear is waning . . . that a longing for truth lingers in every man. This, I suspect, is why she dares – at last – to seek their co-operation. She thinks they'll agree to a manner of dying. For their own sake if not for hers.' The Prior adjusted his glasses and a trace of Glasgow pragmatism entered his voice. 'As with any great endeavour the risk of failure far exceeds the chances of success. Someone has to reach out and tip the balance. Someone with the right kind of experience.'

'My sentiments precisely,' endorsed John.

'Anything else?'

'No.'

'We're all agreed then.'

Anselm frowned, not quite following the drift of accord that had left him behind. Puzzled, he watched the Prior worm a hand into his chest habit pocket and take out a diary and the chewed stub of a pencil. Flicking the pages, he said, 'Anselm, I take it you've persuaded more than one criminal to enter a guilty plea?'

'Indeed I have.'

It was an art. They had to come out of the discussion believing abject surrender was a smart move. He coughed modestly.

'Well, you better go to Warsaw and read that file.

The sooner you find this informer and get to work the better. It seems Róża needs your kind of help.'

Anselm's mouth dropped open. What had happened to 'monastery walls'? It was the Prior's phrase, used to emphasise the importance of the enclosure, and not just when restless monks fancied a jaunt up the road for some ostensibly worthwhile purpose. The remark enshrined the withdrawn nature of Larkwood's communal life, its witness of recollection and stability to people forever on the move. And yet here he was, trading dates and times with John, resolving incidental details.

'I'll meet all the expenses,' insisted John. 'There's a reasonable hotel right by the IPN.'

'We'll contribute.'

'No, really.'

'Three days?'

'A week, he might as well visit the place.'

'Call it ten. We'll pay the difference.'

'I think not.'

At the close of the meeting, the two negotiators shook hands and, with a curiously solemn nod to Anselm, the Prior disappeared through the arched door that led to the cloister. It was as though his companions had just finished one of their old walks, when John had been overrun by despair and Anselm had kept watch from a distance. His presence had finally been acknowledged.

Quite apart from the 'monastic walls' aspect, the Prior's decision had been unprecedentedly swift.

Ordinarily, he didn't sleep on a proposal; he hibernated with it, emerging after some private winter of reflection. But now, without the slightest equivocation, he'd agreed to Anselm acting on John's behalf. Leaving his old friend in the parlour, Anselm hurried over to Sylvester who was back behind his desk, eyeing the telephone as if it were a child that might talk back.

'Were you listening?' whispered Anselm, leaning down.

'How dare you.' Sylvester lurched for his walking stick as if it were a Lee Enfield with fixed bayonet.

'Why did he let me go without a fight?' pursued Anselm, fearlessly.

'Can't you guess? Or are you just plain stupid?'

'There are two schools of thought on that one. But seriously, why?'

'Exodus Twenty-two.'

'Yer wot?'

'Defend the widow and the orphan.'

Anselm gave a knowing sigh, but before he could pull away Sylvester gestured him closer, nodding towards John. 'I've seen him before.'

'You have.'

'Thought so.'

'Countless times.'

'Really? Well, I forgot to ask . . . was he ever in the scouts?'

'No.'

'Ah, that's a pity.' The Watchman tried to fathom a boyhood without a knife, a ball of string and nights under canvas. 'It would have made all the difference.'

'Steady on, he was still the outdoor type,' objected Anselm defensively. 'Took his trombone into the bush, damn it. Marched through nettles.'

'Good heavens.' The old man frowned, reluctantly won over. 'All right, you can tell him.'

'Tell him what?'

'That as a lad I met Baden Powell. At Olympia. Shook his hand, I did. Do you know, it was during the Second Matabele War that he first . . .'

After lunch Anselm drove John to Cambridge. They waited on the platform, John tapping an erratic rhythm on his toecaps. Anselm wanted to snatch the half-white stick and break it over his knee. A sort of chasm had been growing between them since they'd left the parlour. It had been filled by practical chat and Baden Powell and, finally, that tat-tat-tatting. But both of them knew that something of importance had been left unsaid. As the train approached, Anselm took a deep breath and stepped back nearly three decades.

'Do you remember I asked for a character witness? Someone who could speak to your professional integrity?'

'Yes.'

In the car, Anselm had suffered a sudden and terrible premonition that John still loved her; that part of his desire to fulfil Róża's appeal was a crazy attempt to somehow win her back. He didn't dare say it, and he couldn't say it now. But he sensed he was close to the reason for their separation.

'Did you ask Celina?'

'Yes.'

'And?'

'She refused.'

'Do you know why?'

John's stick made a sort of full stop and the carriages crashed along the rails. 'I never asked. She'd gone before I could pop the question.'

CHAPTER 11

It was not, perhaps, the most prudent decision. Having decided to brush up his German, Anselm had turned not to the likes of *Der Spiegel* or any number of crackling long-wave radio programmes, but to the ruminations of Ludwig Wittgenstein. Drawn by the remark, 'I don't know why we're here but I'm pretty sure that it isn't to enjoy ourselves' he'd made a cursory examination of selected oeuvres (expecting more laughs) only to find the insight unambiguously confirmed. It was therefore with mild relief that he abandoned a knotty paragraph in *Philosophische Untersuchungen* to answer the library telephone. It was from the Prior. Ten minutes later they were on the Bluebell Walk, heading towards Our Lady's Lake. The summons had been far from unexpected. Since John's departure two days earlier, Larkwood's guardian had been observing Anselm across the nave with a paternal, subdued disquiet.

'I want you to be vigilant, Anselm,' began the Prior, watching where he was putting his feet. Branches had fallen during the recent bout of high winds. His solemn manner evoked the conference, erasing the interlude. 'I don't wish to offend you, but regardless of your many years in the criminal courts, you have no experience of the place to which you're now going and the dangers it holds. It's not the Old Bailey, with hefty policemen at the door. Nor is it a prison cell where you're protected by that strange respect which even the most violent men hold for representatives of the law, including those who propose to demonstrate their guilt. You'll be entering the world of Otto Brack, this frightening man who learned how to bring about evil by exploiting someone who is good, laying – in part – the evil at their door. I have never come across that before. You must take special precautions.'

Anselm was unnerved by the Prior's declamatory tone. It was reserved for funerals. He was surprised, too, by the warning. The plan was to fly to Warsaw, open a file, have a quick read, eat some pickled cucumber, drink himself senseless, and then come home. The chances of mishap were remote. He said so.

'I hope you're right,' replied the Prior. 'Perhaps you can walk into Brack's world and walk out again unscathed, but I have my doubts. Twisted people lead twisted lives and the roads they build around them are never straight and true. You might find yourself on some back street wondering where to turn next.'

The evening sun filtered through the copper leaves overhead. Water glinted at the end of the

111

winding track. Listening to the fall of each other's feet, they stepped out from under the trees on to a pebble beach that skirted the edge of the lake. To one side lay a blackened railway sleeper, sunk deep into the bank by Sylvester when he was a young man who couldn't stop talking. He'd been banished here by his novice master to work alone and learn the infinite vocabulary of silence. It was here, too, that Father Herbert Moore, one of the founding fathers, had broken the rule against speaking to suggest a name for the derelict buildings under restoration, for this hidden school dedicated to sane living. He'd uttered one word: 'Larkwood'.

'You mentioned precautions,' said Anselm, hitching his habit to sit by the Prior. He picked up a handful of stones and threw one towards the reflections of yellow and crimson cloud. John had sat here thirty years back when the Prior didn't need glasses. Anselm had wondered what the Prior had been saying.

'First, your task isn't simply to find a name. Anyone can read a word upon the page. You need to look far deeper. You can't arrange to meet this informer until you know why they betrayed Róża. They, like Brack, occupy a world very different to yours, but you must enter it, seeking to understand its logic, its values, its Gods and idols . . . its empty spaces that long for meaning. All you will have are the papers in the file. Peel back the words. Look inside.'

Anselm nodded and threw another pebble along the same trajectory as the first. The water creased and the colours ran from the splash of light and dark.

'Remember they have lived unchallenged for over thirty years,' continued the Prior. 'They'll have restructured their past to make it manageable, perhaps even attractive and virtuous. We all do. We all write these narratives so that we have something good to read when we wake up at night, troubled and unsure. You need to find a better story. That's the only way to bring them back on to Róża's side of tragedy and injustice.'

Anselm nodded again and lobbed another stone.

'Secondly, bring this place with you. Bring all it represents and means. Though you leave the enclosure keep faith with the rhythms of our day. This is your best precaution on entering Brack's world. I don't know why, but it changes what you do, how you see things and what you say. It's what separates you from many a better detective.'

The Prior had finished. He picked up a dried twig and cast it high in the air. It landed almost without a sound, floating on the water's surface, barely visible against the reflected evening sky. Beyond, on a plinth in the middle of the lake, the statue of a woman looked down in calm resignation, isolated but resplendent.

'Be careful, Anselm,' he said, quietly. 'Don't let Brack know that you're coming.'

★　　★　　★

A week later, after Lauds, Anselm knelt down in the nave to receive Larkwood's traditional blessing for the travelling monk. Surrounded by hunched figures who almost certainly weren't listening, the Prior commended his son to the dispensations of Providence, adding a few suggestions for compliance with best practice: to guide his steps, thoughts, and deeds, and procure a safe return. In the afternoon Anselm met John for lunch at the airport. They sat in a bar, Anselm stirring a preposterously large carton of strong coffee, John – forbidden by law to smoke – nervously chewing a match, his hand squeezing a pack of crumpled Black Russians. As if in tandem with the Prior, he, too, had come with warnings and a kind of blessing.

'You need to understand where you're going,' he said. 'It's no ordinary place. The people in the street . . . they buy bread and milk, like me and you, but they breathe a different air. It carries the memory of ancestral insurrection – seventeen ninety-four, eighteen thirty, eighteen sixty-three; it carries the heat of recent destruction. Brack, Róża, the informer . . . the Shoemaker, the Friends . . . they all know the taste of history. It set them against each other in a fight to the death.

'During the Second World War, eighty-five per cent of the buildings in Warsaw were destroyed, seven hundred thousand people perished in the displacement, fighting and massacres. There were two uprisings and then the districts west of the Vistula were systematically blown apart street by

114

street. The suffering was apocalyptic, the latter stages observed by the Soviets calmly eating borscht on the eastern banks of the river.

'When the Nazis had finished, the Red Army crossed over to liberate the ashes. They never went home. Their opposition lay buried under the rubble. People like Róża crawled out of a hole and managed to stand up again. Brack and his like were waiting. They're always waiting . . .'

Anselm made a grimace, and not just at the history and warning. His friend was pale and tense, suffering from exclusion. Anselm was standing in his place. Fighting Róża's war, however hopeless the odds, had always been *John's* domain. He'd already explored the territory. Before going to Warsaw, he'd travelled widely throughout the Communist bloc. Protected by a pseudonym, he'd written of high cultures brought to ruin and dissident voices who kept the faith in hiding. A smart operator, the nearest he'd come to trouble was when he got arrested at Bucharest airport and had to explain to the Securitate that *The Secret Agent* was a novel by Conrad and not an instruction manual produced by MI6. By the time he'd met Róża he was already an ally, committed to the struggle. And now, when she faced her most important battle, he was . . . indisposed.

'I'm sorry it's me who's catching a plane and not you,' said Anselm. 'I know how you must feel.'

John snapped a match between his teeth. 'Thanks.'

'But there's a bright side, at least for me,' confessed Anselm. 'I wanted to help years ago, do you remember, when you came to stay at Larkwood after the accident? I'd planned to dish out some of the stuff I'd read in books or heard in the Chapter Room . . . anything that might help you deal with your blindness. Things didn't quite work out that way. Which is good, in retrospect, because I had nothing of my own to offer.'

'The time wasn't right, Anselm.'

'I know.'

'But it is now.'

The plane nosed into the mist. Down below, buildings climbed in a kind of rush towards the sky, proud and victorious, as if defying the memory of so much devastation. Glass, chrome and steel glinted amongst the flanks of brick and concrete. Leaning on the window, however, Anselm let his mind scurry back to a sort of forbidden universe.

While throwing stones by the lake and sipping coffee at the airport bar, his thoughts – at intervals – had run wild, and he'd been obliged to haul them into line, ashamed of their force and direction. Despite the Prior's warnings – and like a man drawn to the thrill of a street fight – Anselm was intrigued by Otto Brack and his dangerous world. He appeared to be a man beyond redemption. Anselm wanted to know how he'd got there and why. What could have happened in his life that had taught him to use good for evil? What was his story, once the words had been peeled back? The questions seemed indecent, unseemly, given the depravity of his actions. But Anselm still wanted to know. He reproved himself, closing an eye to the absence of any real conviction.

On leaving Warsaw's airport, a garrulous taxi driver – singing more than talking, and not requiring any reciprocal commitment – took Anselm to the Warsaw Hilton, a towering edifice devoted to contemporary extravagance and the acute embarrassment of mendicant travellers compelled by circumstance to stay there. The appointment of his room was lavish: burgundy covers, cream sheets and heavy wood furnishings. Vaguely disorientated, he unpacked his bag and placed two battered books on a large desk near a floor-to-ceiling window.

As to the purpose of his stay, John had organised everything. A faxed application to view the *Polana* file had been processed by return and an appointment made for Anselm to consult its contents. He was expected at ten the following morning at the IPN building, another modern tower whose external lights clung to the walls like limpet mines, ready to explode if anyone's secret history bumped against them. Anselm could see them now, a mere stone's throw away, resolute against a waning skyline. With a sigh, he sat down, reaching for one of the books: his Psalter, given to him by Sylvester on his first day at the monastery. Recalling the Prior's injunction to keep step with Larkwood's rhythms, he mouthed the words for Compline . . . but found himself whispering questions – of all people – to John's absent mother. Where did you go? She, too, had a story to tell, beginning with her name. On closing the cover and formally entering his Great Silence, Anselm was instantly sidetracked. Instead of turning off the light and choosing which of the five pillows would be his solace and comfort, he opted for the second volume on the table.

'It's out of date,' John had said, at the Departure Gate, another match between his teeth, 'but the important stuff never changes.'

Anselm flicked through the guidebook as if it might contain a clue to the mystery of Otto Brack's character. All at once he stopped, warmed by a sudden melancholy: he'd landed on a passage underlined in pencil . . . it was a schoolboy code linking numbers to the alphabet, the means by which Anselm and John had noted timings for a raid on the top floor dormitory. Underlined words had been thrown in to distract imagined enemies; it was only the selected letters that had mattered. Anselm smiled. It was as though John, boy and man, had come with him to Warsaw. He studied the paragraph closely looking for more high mischief. EEHGF. 55876.

None the wiser, Anselm gazed over a twinkling, sleepless Warsaw. Numberless white and yellow stars seemed to have fallen from the sky, jostling for space on the ground, colliding and blending in the darkness. The IPN building stood tall, still and curiously alone, like a gatecrasher at a cocktail party, someone who'd spoiled the fun with talk of *Crime and Punishment*. Somewhere inside its walls lay the file on the Shoemaker. Apparently it contained a copy of Róża's interrogations, carried out during the Stalinist Terror.

Anselm wondered what they'd done to her.

PART III
MOKOTÓW PRISON

CHAPTER 12

A guard kicked away the low stool. Róża collapsed to one side, but the guard caught her by the hair. Swung to her feet, she was thrown from the interrogation room into the corridor of low, yellow light. Another guard appeared walking lazily, his dull boots sagging like half fallen socks. Róża backed against the wall, facing the open door. Major Strenk was troubled, examining a fish hook under the glare of a desk lamp. Looking up, as if he'd just remembered something, he nodded at Lieutenant Brack who'd been sitting in the corner.

'I warned you, Róża,' said Brack, after carefully shutting the door. 'You should have listened to me in the sewers.'

He gave a nod, just like Major Strenk's, and the guards dragged Róża, feet trailing, to an iron staircase at the end of the corridor. Three floors down they came to a wet, freezing cellar, the air misting with the rush of their gasps and panting. Ahead, to the left, was a grey iron door.

'I warned you Róża,' he said, flicking keys on a big ring. He turned his soured face on to hers.

His hair was shaved all around, leaving a high crown of copper metallic bristles. 'You should have listened.'

He yanked open the door and the guards, slipping and grunting, dragged Róża into a low, dripping room. A single bulb flickered like a fading life. Thick pipes ran the length of the ceiling, water drizzling from bandaged cracks and joints. Heavy globules dripped from a rusty central spout. Beneath it was an open cage. The guards kicked and shoved and then locked her in.

'I warned you in the sewers, Róża,' said Brack, as if all this were her fault.

The room became silent, except for the patter of splashing. Suddenly, the twitching light went out. Róża stared at the afterglow, the fast-fading sallow bulb on the wall of her mind. She found a word, but it came as a whisper: 'Help . . .'

And then the pipes shuddered and the water exploded above her head.

Róża did not know whether it was night or day when the interrogation began again. She hadn't been conscious when they took her from the cage. She'd opened her eyes to find herself strapped to a chair by a belt. On seeing her move, the watching guard had stubbed out his cigarette and brought Róża back to Major Strenk and the footstool. Otto was sitting in the corner.

'Name?'

'Róża Mojeska . . . you know already, I'm—'

'Age?'

'Twenty-two.'

She breathed out the answers, and Major Strenk wrote them down with a pencil. It had been the same with every interrogation since her arrest six weeks previously. Always beginning again as if nothing had gone before. The same wearing questions with a few afterthoughts. Only this last time they'd led to the cage, a first departure from the routine.

'You say you're an orphan?' Major Strenk spoke as if he'd lifted the lid of a dustbin.

'Yes.'

'From birth?' This was an afterthought.

'Yes.'

'Misfortune or abandonment?'

'I don't know.'

'Do you know *anything* about your parents?' His tone of disgust suggested she might not, in fact, have any.

'No. I like to think that—'

Major Strenk seemed to lower the lid. He'd smelled enough. Dutifully, he went back to work, wanting – again – the names of teachers, staff and all the other children at Saint Justyn's Orphanage for Girls. He listened, yawning, checking the replies against his existing list. Not entirely satisfied, he moved on to slowly cover the German Occupation seeking, as ever, names along the way. For names gave associations. Associations gave suspects. And suspects were suspect. At no point throughout this quest for other degenerates did Róża so much as glance at Otto, who was watching intently from the corner. She simply left him out of the reckoning, though he too had been at Saint Justyn's, in hiding during the war. He'd turned up in 1943. They'd met in the attic by a window. Róża just kept her eyes firmly, perhaps too firmly, upon Major Strenk, recounting her early life as if Otto had never been there. It was a kind of inverted Russian roulette: Otto was taunting her, daring her to pull the trigger and mention his name; and she refused each time, not to save him, but to save herself, for she'd settled on a way to survive this measured annihilation of her humanity.

'You recall no one else?' Major Strenk sharpened his pencil, frowning at the shavings and lead powder accumulating on his desk.

'No.'

'Quite sure?'

'Yes.'

With the flat of one hand the Major wiped the debris into a cupped palm and then brushed his fingers clean over a wastebasket. Still frowning, he rummaged for a handkerchief. Between questions, his eyes on Róża, he made a short, dainty blow.

'You knew there would be an uprising?'

'Yes.'

'How?'

'Soviet radio.'

'You went to the Old Town?'

'Yes.'

126

'Your function?'

'I was a messenger, ammunition carrier, a nurse. I did—'

'—yes, yes, yes: whatever you could.' Major Strenk finished off the sentence, disliking the answer, mocking the implied nobility as if Róża were trying to clean up her background. He looked inside the handkerchief to make sure he'd got what he was after and then turned a page on to the reasons for her escape.

'I was told it was over, that we had to get out. I went into the sewer system and took a tunnel north to Żoliborz. When I lifted the cover they were waiting for me.'

'They? The power-seeking criminals who wanted to use the Uprising for their own ends? The land-owners and capitalists?' He was looking inside his handkerchief again. 'The enemies of progress and reform?'

'No. Two Germans.'

Major Strenk paused, glancing down at his sheaf of names. 'You escaped on your own?'

'Yes. Others followed . . . others had gone before, but I went alone.'

From that moment Róża let her gaze fall. She'd left Otto behind; he'd been with her and waded out of her life through another tunnel; she didn't need to protect him any more. And Major Strenk's jaded expression had become unbearable.

'Do go on,' he said, as if he was no longer that interested.

Following her arrest Róża had been taken to a transit camp in Pruszków. Three weeks later she was one of fifty packed into an open coal wagon. The train went south to Wolbrom, near Kraków, where she was allocated a shared room in a flat above a fire station. Curiously, Róża yet again kept to herself what mattered most. She said nothing of the singer and the song.

The journey had lasted almost three days. There was only standing room, the November sun high and bare, the intimacy of massed flesh intense. A single slop bucket in the corner filled within hours. At intervals the waste was tipped over the side planking on to the tracks. Occasionally apples and chunks of bread landed in the wagon, thrown by locals when the train slowed or stopped. Róża thought she might die. But then, on the morning of the second day, a child's voice climbed higher than the rattling of the train and the stench of the bucket. A little girl had begun to sing.

'Return our Homeland to us, Lord . . .'

The hymn had been sung for over two hundred years. But here, in this wagon, no one had the belief or the strength to join in. It was left to the child. Following the girl's rising voice, Róża seemed to touch the clouds with the fingers of her soul. She'd escaped once through filth, but this was a kind of rescue; a moment of salvation. The journey ended that night. After climbing out of the wagon Róża hobbled between buckled over men and women, crying out for the girl, but no reply came back. It was as though God had come and gone.

For an instant, Róża almost forgot that she was being questioned by Major Strenk: her mind was juddering from the realisation that Otto Brack and that unknown child shared the same protected space in her memory.

'When did you leave Wolbrom?'

Róża made a start. 'After the war . . . nine months later.'

'Why?'

'To help rebuild—'

'Yes, yes, yes, you tried to save Warsaw, and now you were going to help with the rebuilding. What was your function?'

Róża had worked alongside an architect retrieving and labelling fragments of ornate stonework in the Old Town. The whole area was to be restored to its original splendour using, whenever possible, original materials. Pavel Mojeska had been engaged in identical work with another specialist. She'd met him during a meeting when the experts had pored over close-up photographs of a painting by Canaletto. It had showed the buildings as they were once were. This was the complete picture and it showed them where the bits might go.

'Mojeska's date of birth?'

'Nineteen twenty-one.'

It was another pointless question. Pavel had been arrested three hours before Róża. He was in the same building, in another cell. They must already know. But they trawled *everywhere* so as to compare accounts, looking for *any* inconsistency. He was poring over his own pictures.

'As to his parents?'

'They were killed in Ochota.'

'Any siblings?'

'Yes.'

'Names.'

Róża's voice cracked. 'They're dead. Two girls and a boy, all dead. They were in Ochota . . . *Ochota*. Do you really need *me* to tell *you* what happened?'

'On reflection, no.'

As the Nazis poured troops in to crush the Uprising, special units were deployed to flush out any survivors. In the districts of Ochota and Wola thousands of civilians were executed, heaped and burned, regardless of age or gender. The Major sighed.

'Where was the criminal Mojeska?'

'Fighting in the—'

'—yes, yes, stop.' Though he'd asked the question he couldn't endure any more heroics. He started scouring their relationship, leaning forward like one of the architects over those photos.

'You were married in what year?'

'Nineteen forty-eight.'

'Your age?'

'Nineteen.'

'His age?'

'Twenty-seven.'

She gave the bare facts. She wasn't going to tell Major Strenk how they'd rebuilt each other: how Róża, who belonged to no one, had given herself to Pavel who'd lost everyone; how each had complementary wounds with a complementary power to heal. She wasn't going to tell Major Strenk how it was possible to remain injured at heart and yet laugh as if for the first time. No, the major got what he could understand: facts; dates, places and times. For two days he dutifully wrote the answers down with his pencil. On the third day he changed subject and tone.

'You are aware the criminal Pavel Mojeska is a provocateur?'

'A *what*? I'm sorry, I don't—'

'That he is planning to restore the rule of land-owners and capitalists?'

'No.'

And she had no idea that he was implicated in the publication of subversive material against the people. Major Strenk paused. He became eerily still, like a man watching a lake for the skip of life below the surface.

'Who is the Shoemaker?' he said, unblinking.

'I don't know.'

'Who are the Friends of the Shoemaker?'

'I don't know.'

'Where is the printing press?'

'I don't know.'

The one reply, uttered with every difference of inflection imaginable, all of them variations

131

of begging. Major Strenk pulled open a drawer and took out a small vice and a metal tray. Róża watched him in complete horror. First he took a fish hook from a compartment of the tray; next, he locked it between the clamps of the vice, leaving the shank free; and then, finally, he looked up, his eyes remote and dull.

'Think again. Who is the Shoemaker?'

Róża couldn't speak.

'Who are the Friends of the Shoemaker?'

This minute, transferred attention to the making of a fly, was exactly what had happened three days earlier, before she was kicked off the stool and taken to the pit. The threat was heavy between them, his unblinking, timeless gaze upon her. She opened her mouth but no sound came from her throat. Major Strenk peered into the metal tray and selected a bobbin of bright green thread. He tied a knot on the hook and reached for some tweezers.

'Where is the printing press?'

Róża began to shiver. She heard the dripping in her mind. Her voice was quiet and beseeching, 'I've told you, Comrade, I don't know.'

Major Strenk put the tweezers between his teeth and picked up his pencil. While writing down the answer, he nodded vaguely towards Brack. The guard behind Róża kicked the footstool away.

Róża woke up soaking wet and freezing. She'd been strapped to a chair with a belt. She did not know if it was night or day. The guard stamped on the butt of his cigarette and brought her back to the interrogation room.

'Name?'

'Róża Mojeska.' Her voice was so faint she hardly heard her own reply.

'Age?'

'Twenty-two.'

Major Strenk picked up a magnifying glass and examined the tied fly. He didn't seem especially pleased. Something had gone wrong. He suppressed a belch and said, 'Date of birth?'

On the third day, while testing the mechanism of a fishing reel, he asked about the Shoemaker. It whirred efficiently, like a drill, eventually slowing to a series of dry clicks. Róża watched and listened unable to speak. The major opened a drawer and nodded at Brack. Without resisting, without remembering the hauling down the corridor of waxen light, Róża fell into the darkness and the deluge. A last conscious thought, like fingernails hooked on the ledge of sanity, was about life: the irresistible, inexorable power of life. It was as though her mind was lit for a moment by a spark of divinity. She knew she was pregnant. She carried a life that Major Strenk would never catch.

CHAPTER 13

After the third visit to the cage Róża was dragged back to her cell. There were nine other women sitting on the floor. A tenth with straggling ashen hair walked around aimlessly, moaning to herself. She wagged a dirty finger at Róża, admonishing the air long after Róża had slumped in a corner. The walls were damp and gouged with hatch-patterned desperation: the days crossed out in blocks of seven becoming weeks, months and years. All the prisoners were a strange grey-green, melding them to the plaster. One of them with cropped blonde hair watched Róża guardedly over knees held tight against her chest. Róża pressed her face into the wall. She was the bearer of life. She had to survive so that this child might one day sing. Her mind turned to Otto Brack who, given time, without a war and without conflicting ideologies, just might have been the father.

A boy turned up in February 1943. He was first seen with Mr Lasky, the caretaker, helping to shave a door that had never jammed. He had to be about

134

fifteen. A few questions to one of the more indiscreet nuns produced the unlikely disclosure that Mr Lasky wasn't getting any younger and the building was only getting older, so his nephew had come to help out with the chores. Everyone knew it was another secret: he was being hidden from the Nazis, like Magda, the girl in Róża's dormitory. They had the same tragic look that comes with enforced separation.

Róża met the boy by accident one Sunday afternoon.

The top floor of the orphanage was reached by a set of warped stairs by a broom cupboard, understood by tradition to be haunted by seven orphans who'd fallen off the roof and a nun who'd killed herself with a candlestick, though no one knew how. Few used the stairs, either from fear, or because the attic held nothing of interest save bedsteads, worn mattresses and broken furniture. But Róża discovered something else: a window, the highest in the building. It looked out over Warsaw, and this was where she came on Sunday afternoons to escape the institutional existence she led down below – it couldn't be any other way, but she was tired of the discipline and the very public life of a locker without a key. She would daydream, gazing over the rooftops, imagining an existence with some colour: brothers and sisters round a table, a mother in the kitchen, and a father playing the banjo. One Sunday Róża climbed the stairs and found the door ajar. On entering she saw the boy by the window. It was wide open and he was smoking.

'Do you want one?'

'Yes.'

He'd made them out of old newspaper that had lined a drawer and threads from a doormat. His hair was rust brown, his eyes a deeper brown, flecked with green. His skin was naturally dark, as if he'd just come back from a holiday in the sun. Like Róża, he was thin, lacking muscle on his arms and legs. His shoes and jacket were too big. The boots had come from Mr Lasky.

'This is my room,' said Róża, curtly, taking the cigarette.

The boy ignored her and lit the rolled matting, his lips held tight when he exhaled. While Róża coughed and spluttered, he stared enquiringly over the bombed, sunlit capital.

'What are you doing?' asked Róża, after she'd picked some fibres off her tongue.

The boy breathed in the black fumes and said, 'I'm thinking of my father and my mother.'

Róża met the boy in that room frequently thereafter. They made no arrangement, but over the next few weeks Sunday afternoons became the time they smoked by the window. He never again revealed anything about himself or what he cared about, what he'd lost and what he hoped for. He told her his name, and no more. He was Otto. That single flash of sincerity and vulnerability was replaced by a mature frown and long simmering silences. With

136

his top teeth he'd scrape his bottom lip and Róża wondered if he might open up the skin. Once, for something to say, Róża told him her daydream: of a red dress and red shoes, and a deep green jacket, and a father who played the banjo. He listened, drinking in her hope for something better.

These two moments of brief sharing – of his loss and her dreams – created a bond between Róża and Otto. Something that could turn into love was slowly catching fire, like the dried matting wrapped in yesterday's news. By choice or chance they'd both been walked on and thrown aside; but they'd found each other among so much bric-a-brac; they'd opened a window on to something different. Which was why Róża instinctively risked her life for him the following April when the German secret police arrived with their whistles and dogs.

The community and all the children were ordered into the rear yard, but Róża and Otto made for the top floor.

'I wouldn't go up there if I were you,' said Róża to the squat interpreter, shaking uncontrollably.

'Why not?'

She was barring his way at the foot of the stairs, arms outstretched. Behind him stood two men in long leather coats. Otto was in the cupboard, two feet away.

'There's a dead nun waiting with a candlestick.'

They laughed and one of them tousled her hair – not affectionately, but as if she were a dog that had learned a trick. It took them half an hour to search the attic, during which time Otto hid in a room that had already been ransacked. When they'd gone, Róża learned that the Prioress and Mr Lasky had been taken away at gunpoint and that Magda had been found in the infirmary: she'd had no papers and no temperature.

Róża was completely distraught. At night she lay awake, staring at Magda's empty bed. During the day she kept looking out for Mr Lasky, expecting to find him mending a perfectly serviceable sash window. A couple of weeks later the explosions started. The rumour was that those in the Ghetto were fighting back. Standing beside Otto in the attic she watched part of the Warsaw horizon gradually collapse in clouds of smoke and dust. When the noise came to an end there was a ringing in her ears that wouldn't go away – not from the bombs but the lost voices.

Otto heard the same sounds. The arrest of Mr Lasky had a deep effect upon him. He was adrift for the second time in the space of two months – first from his parents and now the man who'd played a part in his rescue. Róża sensed him leaning upon her more heavily, though he never deliberately touched her. It was in his eyes and the glance that followed a brush of shoulders.

'Where've they taken him?' he asked, sucking in the smoke.

'Pawiak Prison,' replied Róża, quoting the indiscreet nun.

'He's dead.' Otto's voice was angry and correcting. 'But we aren't.'

Róża's reply didn't so much show up the base instinct of survival as reveal the peculiar duty that settles upon survivors, upon those who have been saved: to live and make the living worthwhile. 'We have to make it count,' she said, pulling at Otto's sleeve as if they might go somewhere. 'For their sake.'

A year and a bit later, they did. Soviet Radio had called for an Uprising. The Red Army was approaching from the east. The Nazis were finished. All that was needed was a quick shove.

'I'm going to the Old Town.' He lit two cigarettes, wincing, and passed one to Róża. 'Are you coming?'

'To do what?'

'Fight.'

His eyes were unable to rest for long upon her but, having strayed, they kept coming back, hungrily; and Róża saw once more the sudden flare of vulnerability, the not wanting to be left alone again to face another crisis without the support of those he . . . relied upon? Loved? It was a mortified admission of affection, made immense by where she stood in Otto's life. Róża hadn't dared believe that she might be so important. They left that night, scurrying like rats along walls until they linked up with a Home Army unit on Podwale Street.

The quick shove was soon ended by a deafening assault from tanks and planes and hammering rifle fire. The buildings seemed to spit out their broken teeth. Their bones were cracked and splintered. Róża had never seen so much death: on street corners, by heaps of rubble – the bodies sometimes splayed in the most awful shapes, so strange they seemed not to be human. She felt utterly abandoned. Where was the Red Army? Why had the Soviets urged them to rise up if they were not going to come?

In the scorching heat of this beating, Róża crouched by Otto in a makeshift hospital by the Old Town walls. There was no ammunition left to carry so they were ripping bandages from the clothes of the dead. Suddenly, Róża gripped Otto's hand. They were going to die and she didn't want to go without giving the best of herself to someone. With shocking violence she pressed into his palm all the love she had left.

And he began to talk.

As if a door had been blown off its hinges, he began to speak about what he'd seen through the window in the attic, tears pouring down his face.

'My father used to make me toys out of wood and bits of plumbing, pipes and joints, fantastic things, a musket, a revolver, a sword . . . they looked real, honestly, people used to stop and stare. He'd take me fishing, bird watching, camping, hiking and when I lost a tooth he'd put a coin under my pillow in an envelope with a funny drawing of a mouse waving at me, my name written all over the page. For years I thought the mouse came for my tooth. My mother used to cook fish in lemonade, really, I'm not joking, *lemonade*, and it made the trout all sweet, a special kind of sweet. She was always *there*, always—'

He stopped abruptly as if he'd run out of things to say. The wall behind soaked up a bang and seemed to bend inwards.

'Where are they?'

'Don't know . . . deported.'

'Why were you hiding?'

'My father was a communist.' He spoke with a savage, loud pride. 'He believed in a better world for everyone, for you, for me, for them—' He ducked the crack of an explosion. Chunks of plaster bounced on the floor; an eerie white dust floated down.

'Where are you from?' The conversation was in pieces. They were getting it all in before the ceiling came down.

'Polana.'

'Where's that?'

'Near the Ukraine.'

The ground made a judder as if the world had just been smashed off its axis. Then Róża thought of the sewers. They'd been used for gun running and messages. Pulling Otto she stumbled into the open, head low, making a scream to batter down her terror. Two hundred yards later they lifted a cover and scrambled into the hole. Thirtyfour rungs down, Róża and Otto slid waist deep into the water and filth.

High, high above, the din continued. Otto struck a match. The cavern appeared.

Corpses floated silently by like sleeping watchmen. Róża and Otto began wading east, the black bricks shuddering overhead. The match died. Otto lit another. The smell of gas, spent grenades and dirt made them wretch. On they went, pushing aside the dead. The match slowly faded. Róża whispered to the darkness, not expecting a reply:

'The Red Army. Why didn't they help us?'

The question echoed down the reeking corridor. When it died there was a silence and lapping and then Otto made a murmur.

'I thought they'd come, but now I understand.' Otto was near. She felt his breath on her neck. 'Sometimes watching is waiting.'

Róża blanked from exhaustion. Then she gradually understood, unable to accept that he meant it, wanting to believe that she'd misheard the tone of approval.

'You mean they're watching while we die?'

There was no more murmuring.

'You mean they'll only come when we've been wiped out? When there's no more resistance?' She found some energy and it made her voice jagged and loud. 'You mean they'll come when they can take over?'

Otto struck a match. His face lit up, covered in grime, his cheeks muddied from his dried tears.

'I mean the future lies with Moscow. A new future, without chains. Sacrifices have to be made.'

142

'*A future without chains*? Where did you get that from?'

This wasn't Otto. Not the boy who had been hurt and hidden. It was the ghost of a man . . . his father; it had to be his father. Otto was repeating speeches heard while they'd hiked and camped. He sloshed forward, reaching for Róża's hand, the hand he'd held up there where the bombs were falling. He raised the flame to illuminate her face.

'We're going to get out of here.'

Róża glared at his mask of disarranged dirt.

'Choose the right side,' he whispered.

'What?'

'There's going to be another struggle.' His cracked lips barked out the memory. '*Choose the right side.*'

Róża yanked her hand free and swung around. She could just make out a T-junction ahead: the tunnel joined another route heading north-south.

'I've made a choice already.' Even though she was worn out and could hardly think straight, she could grasp a basic truth. Mr Lasky used to say that what you believed was everything. It changed who you walked with and where you went. He was right. It had roused a visceral loyalty to those disfigured bodies among the rubble. 'I'm going north, Otto,' she gasped. 'You go south.'

Róża pushed her way through the water, holding on to the mental image of the junction. A small

143

flame burst behind her and Róża felt a flash of grief. Not so much for losing her friendship with Otto or for having given him her love. No, she was devastated because she'd told him about the red dress, the green jacket and the shoes. She'd given him her dreams.

Six years later those two tunnels came to another junction in the Mariensztat District when Otto and four men in long coats broke down her front door.

Róża lifted her face off the cell floor. The prisoner with the grey hair was sniggering into her hand, pointing at some fragment of her imagination. The others were like crouched gargoyles on a forsaken church. When Róża had first entered this hell she'd understood, on a primitive level, that to survive she would have to keep soft some part of her heart. Which was why she'd said nothing about her previous friendship with Otto. The revelation could put him in a cell of his own. Association was suspicion. So it was at this juncture of her fidelity to him and his abandonment of her that Róża chose to keep alive her humanity. Whatever power Major Strenk might have over her, she would remain above him, through Otto.

It was only when Róza was in the cage with water thundering upon her, when she was in this, the lowest gutter of human existence, that Róża realised what had really been happening throughout her interrogations: Otto had already told Major

Strenk about their shared past. And it was precisely because Róża never referred to it that the major knew Róża could break down and still keep important information to herself; that she might well know how to find the Shoemaker. Otto had been the man behind the questions. From that moment, Otto ceased to exist for Róża. He became Brack.

CHAPTER 14

Two weeks later Róża was brought back to the interrogation room. There, behind the desk with the small lamp, sat Brack, opening and shutting a drawer. He started asking questions even before Róża crouched on the footstool.

'Ink. Ink stains. You must have seen stains. Tell me about stains.'

He was on to something. It was how Róża discovered that Pavel was involved. She'd seen that incredibly black crescent under a thumbnail. She'd found out later that part of Pavel's role within the Shoemaker organisation was the obtaining of vital supplies. Without wearing gloves, he'd handled a leaking tin.

'People disappear, Róża,' he'd said, gripping her hands. 'They vanish. Accept my silence. It protects you.'

His dark eyes had been wide with feeling, his fair hair ruffled. He'd shoved her gently on the bed.

'Stains,' repeated Brack.

'I never saw any.'

Brack opened and shut the drawer, tension gouging out his eye sockets. He had to find a way of breaking her. But there was nothing in the desk. It had to be something worse than the cage. He changed subject.

'When did you first hear of the Shoemaker?'

'When I was child.'

'I want the name.'

'Mr Lasky. He read us stories every—'

'Don't play with me . . . Comrade.' The words left his mouth like fibres spat from one of his cigarettes. 'I have the power of life and death.'

Róża dared to laugh. He had nothing of the sort. He was wearing Major Strenk's shoes, that's all.

'The Shoemaker,' he repeated. 'When did you first learn that your husband was an associate?'

Pavel had told her after she'd swung her legs off the bed. She'd insisted on knowing about the ink. His risk was her risk. He'd thought for a long while first, getting dressed distractedly, confusing the buttons and holes. When he was done he'd put on his coat and thrown Róża's across the room.

'I'm going to introduce you to someone. I call him the Threshold.'

It was night. They went to a church that backed on to a railway line. Most of the surrounding buildings were incomplete, the reconstruction slowed by cost and a lack of materials. Heaps of rubble had still not been cleared away. Frameless windows cut black squares out of the sky. Pavel knocked on a door. After a moment he tried to light a cigarette, giving up after three strikes of a match. After several minutes a bolt slammed back and a man in a cassock pulled them inside, swearing under his breath. He was in his mid thirties. His hair, short and black, gave prominence to a large forehead. He'd shaved roughly, leaving small red cuts on his chin and neck.

'What the hell are you doing here?' he snapped.

Pavel drew the priest down the low lit corridor, whispering urgently. After listening for a few seconds the priest's mouth slowly fell open and he swore again. Róża caught their talk.

'You're *married*?'

'Yes.'

'Why didn't you tell me? If I'd—'

'I couldn't. You know the rules.'

'Rules? You break them all the time.'

'Look, stick to the point. What do you think?'

The priest drew a hand across his jaw, checking the cuts. Glancing at Róża, he shook his head in disbelief and condemnation.

'I had to find someone from outside the Friends,' argued Pavel, frustrated. 'You agreed. You said we need a sleeper. Someone who can wake the dead and shatter the illusions of many. Someone who can take up where we left off, if I'm caught. Someone who can restructure a new group of Friends. These are your words. *You agreed.*'

'Damn it, I thought you meant a man. But a young woman, your wife?'

'They'll arrest her anyway. If they pick *me* up, they'll pick *her* up.'

'Which is why you shouldn't have got married.'

'But I did. Look, they wouldn't expect her to know anything. Like you, they wouldn't think I'd tell her.'

'Have you *any* idea what these people can do?' The priest pointed towards Róża as if she was a joint at the butchers. 'They don't hand out questionnaires. They—'

'They'll do all that anyway.'

'Oh, fine. That's all right then. So let's just—'

'Excuse me.' Róża's soft voice took them by surprise. They'd forgotten she was there. 'This is my choice. I accept the risk.' She walked down the corridor to join the conspirators. 'Think about it: if they believe I'm your sleeper they won't kill me. I'd be the only one who could lead them to what they want. They'll keep me alive.'

The priest clawed at his neck, seeming to weigh her femininity and her resistance. She knew too much already. At length he murmured, 'I hope you're right.'

They moved quietly to the door and the priest drew back the bolt.

'Will the Shoemaker agree?' asked Pavel. He wanted to know that the matter was settled.

'It's not for him to decide.' The priest reached for the switch. 'And he wouldn't want to know. If he did, he might never write another word. It's our responsibility. We decide and we live with the consequences. He writes.'

149

The priest flicked the light dead. Slowly he opened the door, keeping it ajar by an inch. Leaning towards the crack, head bowed, he listened, not seeming to breathe. Finally, without a word, he pushed them both outside and the bolt slipped home.

That night, Pavel explained how the organisation was structured and what she was to do in the event of his arrest. She listened until morning, clocking the detail. Throughout she watched herself with a kind of third eye, the eye of the secret sleeper. She watched Róża Mojeska fall helplessly in love again, only this time far more deeply than before. It frightened her. She found herself bottoming out, reaching the soft sea bed; a place reserved for the elderly and those who know that their time together has been cut short.

'When did you first learn that your husband was an associate?'

Róża was being interrogated again. Once more Brack was in the major's shoes, one arm dangling, his hollowed eyes levelled upon her. The pond green jacket of the secret police didn't sit well on his shoulders. He was still thin, seemingly undernourished.

'I first heard words to that effect one hundred and fifty-four days ago.' She'd scratched them on the wall with the nail of her thumb. Brack frowned. It sounded like an admission, that he might be getting somewhere, but he knew something was

150

wrong. Róża explained. 'You told me on the night of my arrest.'

The drawer slammed shut.

Pavel had said none of the Friends knew each other. The only link between them all was Pavel. Only Pavel had a link to the priest, and only the priest knew how to get to the Shoemaker. By the same token, the Shoemaker only knew of the priest. All the other Friends were unknown to him. Róża, then, was a figure completely outside the organisation, a kind of wild card in the brutal game against the secret police: unknown to everyone, she'd been entrusted with the key to any future operation. Pavel and the priest had fixed the one flaw in the security system: they'd prepared for betrayal. In that event the Shoemaker could still speak and Róża would spread his words, fronting a new organisation of Friends.

They'd moved just in time. Two months after Róża's initiation, Pavel had lingered at the door. Unusually preoccupied, he'd given Róża his wedding ring. 'Father Nicodem's idea,' he'd said. It had been a first slip of the tongue: he'd used a name. Three hours later the front door had splintered under a sledge hammer and Otto had stepped over the debris followed by four men in coats the colour of mud.

The drawer opened, snapping her reverie.

'Tell me what you know, Róża.' It was the first time that Brack had used her name. 'We're not going to let you out until you tell us.' He was staring at her swollen stomach and the hidden life. A hint of the attic came across his face. 'You don't understand, Róża. You don't know what harm the Shoemaker has done.'

'Harm?'

'Harm.' The bark had gone; he still seemed trapped. He was still in a tunnel of filth trying to find his way out. Róża pitied him. Major Strenk had trusted him to break the girl while he dealt with the men.

'There's nothing you can do to me,' she declared, obliquely.

Brack twitched and slid the drawer shut.

Thirty-two days later the cell door opened.

Two guards helped Róża to her feet and brought her slowly down the stairs to the cellar. Ahead, to the left, was the entrance to the room with the cage. The grey iron door was open. But Róża was pushed on to a chair standing incongruously by the corridor wall. Moments later came the sounds of scuffling and dragged feet. A man whom Róża had never seen before was pulled down the stairs. He was disfigured and cut, his chest gurgling like a blocked pipe. His feet were bare, bouncing along the concrete as if he were a marionette without strings. The guards hoisted him into the room with the cage. Moments later a heavy shot crashed into the corridor. The echo was still ringing in Róża's ears when she heard more noise from the staircase, more groaning and dragging.

Another man was hauled along the passageway. This time the guards stopped at the grey door. The prisoner lifted his battered face towards Róża. She hadn't recognised him because of the quantity of blood . . . but it was Pavel. His body was limp in the arms of the green thugs, his shoulders horribly high, as if he were meat hanging on two hooks. He gaped at Róża, and sobbed, seeing for the first time the great swelling of life in her stomach. He tried to raise a crushed hand but all his energy went into a shake at the neck. As they dragged him into the room he coughed a sort of 'No'.

Brack stepped out, a revolver in his hand. He stood, hangdog and determined, grimacing at Róża, waiting for her to make another choice. She pressed her thumb against the two rings on her finger and made a confused shake of the head. Her ears were ringing. A black hole was quietly expanding, rising from her depths. Brack's mouth sagged open and he stepped slowly into the room.

The silence seeped into Róża's mind.

She waited for the sound, her knees shaking uncontrollably. Then, a compressed bang seemed to tear open her side.

They took Róża back to her cell as if nothing had happened. As the lock turned, she sank to her knees and the mental thread between her mind and her mouth snapped. She started gibbering. Her words became jumbled, losing shape and sense. Sounds poured out from her stomach like vomit. An arm came around her shoulder. The woman with cropped blonde hair was stroking her brow, saying 'Shush'. Lights flickered and popped behind her eyes. The agony of childbirth was under way, and she could feel nothing. Standing over her was the grey, distressed woman, wagging her finger, screeching nonsense.

CHAPTER 15

Róża was transferred to the prison infirmary, a ward of evenly spaced iron beds, just like the dormitory at Saint Justyn's. There, in a state of delirium, she moaned, looking up at some figment of Major Strenk. Cradled in his arms was a big fish, gasping for air, its tail flapping as if it were a kind of wild applause. A door slammed in a draught.

The following weeks were lost to Róża. She couldn't scratch them on a wall to mark their passing. Exhaustion gradually shut down the hallucinations. A dark cloud settled on her consciousness, its density drawn from the pain it absorbed. She recovered the basic functions of living without quite being alive. When she could hear and respond to simple questions, they took her to a nursery on the same corridor.

'It's yours,' said a nurse with a square jaw.

'Mine?' Róża cried, wanting wonder, feeling only a terrifying weight.

'Have you thought of a name?'

Róża sank to a chair, tears streaming down her face. She couldn't look down. She'd already glimpsed the vast ocean-blue eyes, the gangling limbs. She could hear a soft sucking sound. She'd seen the lips, the little tongue working, the nails on small fingers hooked on to the blanket.

'Name. Have you got one?' The jaw was pushed forward as if she were holding a pin between her teeth. She tapped a pencil on a pad. 'There are forms to be filled in.'

In abject misery, Róża turned her head aside, away from the bulky nurse with the muscular fingers, away from her pad, the notes, and the endless requests for names and dates of birth. Opening her eyes, Róża saw a window. The frame was large, with bars fixed on the inside. Beyond lay the sky, puffs of cloud and, most agonising of all, a tree. Róża could see the pink cherry blossoms. A light breeze came in short gusts, plucking them free. They floated away by the handful, like scared butterflies.

'I have a form.' The pencil tapped impatience.

Róża looked at the large pad of blue paper with its columns and boxes, the gaps and dotted lines. 'There will be no name.'

'Just a surname?'

'Nothing.' Róża couldn't do it. She couldn't reduce this mystery of life to just another fact in prison. 'No name at all.'

'I'll leave it blank, then.'

Róża had a consuming dread that her milk would dry up from grief and the devastating guilt that

156

came from bringing life into a prison. But as she fed the murmuring infant she looked out of the window and received something that made her strong and able to cope with the shock of hearing that first murder and the sound of Pavel's execution, all set against the grotesque monotony of prison existence. She'd seen pink blossoms. She'd seen the wind that strips the trees.

'One day we will win,' said Róża, crouched on the footstool, when next summoned for an interrogation.

She'd never said 'we' before; she'd never spoken of a struggle for victory. But now she was more than herself. She spoke for someone who didn't yet have a voice; and she joined herself to all those beyond the prison walls who couldn't speak, either from ignorance, complacency or fear, and she spoke for them. She pledged herself to a victory that they would all claim as their own, one day, with or without merit, a victory that she knew was utterly certain, a day of freedom that could only be delayed and never denied.

'I can wait,' she said. 'Today, tomorrow, either in here or out there, it makes no real difference. It's all about patience and waiting, and I can do both. Do you know why?'

Like the prisoners, Brack was barely distinguishable from the greenish walls. Even his brown hair seemed to have changed. The green in his eyes had grown stronger. He said nothing. Róża felt herself grow beyond her surroundings: even as she crouched, she filled the room.

'Do you know why?' she repeated, looking up, arms folded on her knees. 'Because you can't stop the Shoemaker. You can't lock up his words. You can't kill his ideas. They're beyond reach. They have a life of their own. They're for ever on the wind. And whether you like it or not, they *are* the future, yours and mine, because, fundamentally, your ideas and your words aren't as compelling as ours. They aren't as *good*. They require force . . . bloodshed . . . suffering; whereas ours . . . ours *demand* nothing. First they *persuade* . . . only then do they *ask* for commitment and sacrifice.'

Brack's top teeth scraped his bottom lip. He'd darkened at the assault on his beliefs, but then mastered himself, strangely unsettled – it seemed – by Róża's assurance and indifference to his authority.

'Today is your day,' admitted Róża. 'This is your winter. But we'll have the spring. Tomorrow is coming and when it dawns –' she nodded severity at him, and confidence – 'there'll be new laws, fairly framed; there'll be honest, dedicated lawyers. There'll be judges who don't pass sentence in a damp cellar with a pistol. You'll be spared what was done to me, but rest assured, you will be prosecuted for what you have done. I will give evidence against you. I will tell them about the cage and the merciless killing of two innocent men . . . whose only crime was to think differently from you and the barren system you serve.'

Once more Róża expected Brack to ignite at her attack but again he said nothing. There was no outburst about choosing sides and warnings in the sewers. He looked at Róża over his desk and the heap of Major Strenk's papers, his teeth gouging at the lip. And then Róża understood why he'd been silent throughout her credo. Like all lackeys he was scared of what might happen if the teacher went away: where he would be if, when tomorrow came, Róża was right and he was wrong. The recognition made Róża fire a shot at the present.

'You can't keep me here for ever,' she said. 'And anyway, I'm already outside. I've seen the wind in a cherry tree.'

CHAPTER 16

Róża was allowed to see her child for two hours a day. Then she had to leave the metal cot watched over by the nurse with thick fingers. Back in her cell she thought endlessly of the pink little mouth and the branches against the sky. For the first time since her imprisonment, she opened her eyes to those who were around her. She made friends with the woman with cropped blonde hair; the imprisoned nurse who'd held her hand during the birth.

Aniela Kolba was twenty-six, the mother of a five-year-old boy called Bernard who she hadn't seen for eighteen months. She'd been arrested because her brother had been an officer in the Home Army, at first a hero of the Uprising, a patriot, but then a deemed enemy of the new order. Aniela's offence was association by blood. There was no one else to go for. Her parents were dead, shot and burned like Pavel's family in the Ochota massacres.

'My boy hates fish,' she said, a hand pulling at knotted strands, her face fulsome, her arms chubby. Eyebrows, dark and fine, were twisted with pain. 'He once threw the keys to the house in the river.'

Róża told Aniela of Saint Justyn's and day trips with Mr Lasky to Chopin's birthplace or the grave of Prus, while Aniela recounted holidays in the Carpathians to see the timber churches of the Lemks and Boyks. They took turns unfolding the story of *Quo Vadis*. Neither of them was called for interrogation, though Brack's sunken face occasionally appeared at the Judas Window in the cell door. He'd watch, brooding for a moment and then vanish.

One morning the guards came for Aniela. She returned at midday, dressed in clothes from home – a light green dress with small orange flowers, a deep red cardigan with dark blue buttons. The colours were blinding, harsh against the scratched walls. Her hair was neat and tidy, shining like brushed silk. She wore new brown shoes.

'They're letting me go,' she admitted. Her loyalty bound her to Róża and the prison.

'Why?'

'They didn't say. I suppose I'm no longer a threat to the Party. Maybe they've found my brother . . . I don't know.'

It was like her arrest: there'd been no reason to lock her up; there was no reason to let her go. She smoothed her dress, ashamed to be wearing glad rags. Her eyebrows twisted. 'They've let me say goodbye.'

Róża thrust her face into Aniela's neck and the

wonderful smell of soap burned her nostrils. She pressed herself deep into those soft, open arms, from affection and to stifle the sound of gibbering from the other women – the frenzied requests to get a message out to their men and children.

'When it's your turn, come to me,' Aniela managed, against the choking. 'I'll always have a room for you.'

Then she was gone, taking with her the aroma of clean cotton, fresh skin, and the mysterious, healing power of colours, the ointment of green, orange, red and brown. Her going was like an amputation.

Róża's turn did not arrive. The months dragged on, leaving Róża with a glimpse of the changing seasons for two hours a day. All the depth of her being was concentrated into that time with her growing child. She stopped sleeping, living only for that moment of awe, veneration and pride.

On a cold night in winter Róża heard a scraping noise in the distance. She sat up, intrigued. All the other women were sleeping, shifting uneasily on their boards, one moaning, another calling out. The sound outside was familiar . . . back and forth, back and forth; then a sort of rest; then back and forth, back and forth. But she couldn't place it. The steady rhythm was comforting, oddly warming in the memory. Back and forth, back and forth. It sent Róża into a deep restoring sleep.

On entering the nursery the following morning,

Róża looked as usual to the cot and then towards the window – only this time she saw nothing but a cloudy sky. She banged into the nurse as she ran towards the dismal light. Gripping the bars she stared, unable to believe her eyes, She slowly breathed in, speaking into her lungs: 'No, no, no, no no . . .' It was as though they'd flattened Warsaw once more. They'd cut down the cherry tree. Róża almost heard a voice: this was Brack's reply to her speech in the interrogation room. He was showing her the limits of commitment and sacrifice, freely chosen: first, he'd removed Aniela and now he'd taken the tree. Where would he stop? When she had nothing left? That afternoon she was brought to the interrogation room.

'We're not going to let you out until you tell us where to find the Shoemaker,' said Brack.

Róża was shaking slightly. With all her heart she regretted her defiance while crouched on the stool. She'd got carried away, one word following another, failing to remember that for Brack the argument was concluded the day they'd taken different directions in the sewer. He watched her, running a finger thoughtfully across his bottom lip, and said, 'You got something wrong the other day, during that lecture on winter and spring. You see, we *can* keep you here for ever.'

Róża looked vacantly at the desk, the lamp, the paper, the pencil.

'*For ever,*' he repeated, quietly.

Róża could only think of the faint breeze that

had freed the tiny petals. They'd flown away. The tree's fingers hadn't got the strength to hold on.

'Despite everything, Róża, I want to help you. Even though you won't help me, I still want to help you. If you won't speak to me about the Shoemaker, if your commitment and sacrifice demand only what you freely choose –' his voice dropped a tone – 'then let the child go.'

Róża's lips shivered.

'Yes, that's what I said. Let it go. Don't keep it in this forsaken place.' He pushed back his chair and came from behind Major Strenk's desk. Kneeling beside her, he growled with naked desperation. 'Don't let another life suffer. *We've* made different choices, *we* face the consequences, and each of us must do what *we* have to do, but don't let those decisions destroy this defenceless child –' a wavering hand touched Róża's shoulder; she smelled his sweat and the violent aftershave – 'don't create another victim. We're living through a terrible time, with terrible costs, and we've taken opposing sides that set us against each other, to the death, for something that we both believe is better, but there is something we can agree upon. We can do something unquestionably . . . *good*; we can salvage something *innocent* from the bitterness and hatred, the confusion and the uncertainty. Help me save your child from what we've both known: the orphanage. Let me find a father, a mother . . . a home.'

Brack strode back behind the desk. His voice

altered, his face distorted, his green-brown eyes levelled and blind.

'I said we can keep you here for ever.' A drawer opened slowly. 'You won't be called for questioning again. Ask for me if you have anything to say. Make the choice.'

Do I betray Father Nicodem and bring them within one step of the Shoemaker, or do I keep my child? The priest had weighed her strength, but what about his? Could she pass on the obligation to suffer?

Whichever way Róża looked, she only saw catastrophic loss. If she gave in and brought them to Father Nicodem, she'd keep her child but negate the meaning of Pavel's death, and the child would almost certainly grow up to condemn her decision. If she remained loyal to the Shoemaker's cause then Pavel's death might retain its significance, but she'd remain in prison, with their child eventually transferred to the care of some unfeeling institution. Would her child thank her for that noble decision? She thought not. And that left a middle way – loyalty to her beliefs at the cost of her child, a sacrifice the child would never know about; for her child would grow in ignorance of the past, loved by another mother and a living father.

We can keep you here for ever.

There was no law. *They* were the law. Could her child wait until tomorrow, until that springtime? As if a window had blown open, Róża's mind turned to the cherry tree. She saw the burst of wind and the flight of pink butterflies. She felt a deep pain at her side; a hand went to her stomach as if to hold herself together. In the morning she asked to see Lieutenant Brack.

'If I agree . . . can I keep in touch with my child? Can I write a—'

'No, I'm sorry.' Brack's fingers were knitted, his arms resting on his desk.

'Will I get any information –' Róża began to squirm, her face breaking into creases of supplication – 'a photograph, maybe . . . once in a while . . . just a little something to let me know that—'

'It's just not possible.'

Róża felt like she was sinking to the bottom of an ocean, not breathing, her eyes wide, her lungs full of water. 'Do I have a say in which family my—'

'I'm sorry.'

'Years from now, can I ask for a meeting, even for a few minutes, just a—'

'No.' Brack slowly raised his eyes. 'There's a system, Róża. These matters are dealt with by the appropriate State department. Applicants who want to adopt are assessed for their suitability. It's only good people who apply, you must know that; people who are hungry to give, who long to receive –' he seemed to check himself, not wanting emotion to contaminate his official declarations – 'people who will raise a child far from harm. He weakened, 'It's another world out there, Róża . . . another world.'

An employee of the relevant department came the following day, a short spectacled man with a tatty leather briefcase, its top flap curving out at the ends like a huge shred of dried orange peel. Food stains peppered the dull shine of his tie. A waistcoat button was missing. Plump hairy fingers gripped the pen that filled in the forms. He seemed to talk to himself under his breath, but Róża couldn't make out any words. Her attention settled on the perspiration over his top lip.

'Name,' he said, when he got to the right column. 'You'll have picked a name, of course?'

'None.'

'None?'

Róża spelled out the word. 'N-o-n-e.'

'Fine.' He thought for a moment. 'I'll just put your surname, then.'

'No, you won't.'

He mumbled about the irregularity, wanting his papers well in order.

'You'll need to sign.'

'I won't.'

'Initials? Two small letters?'

'Nothing.'

Róża slowly opened her hands. She looked down, seeing they were empty. There would be no fine thread of attachment; nothing that would ever allow anyone to uncover the birth in prison to a murdered father; nothing that would ever lead her child back to a deranged mother in a damp cell.

'You're probably right,' said the official, throwing

caution to the wind. 'Keep well out, that's what I say. Leave the mite unencumbered.'

Róża sat motionless, feeling the weight and silence of the ocean all around her. She was sinking slowly into the sand. Sediment clouded her mind. The little man ticked some boxes and then closed the folder, slid it into his briefcase and stood up.

'Well done,' he said, dabbing his mouth with a crumpled handkerchief. He seemed surprised that a social degenerate had been capable of an act of common sense. 'You made the right decision.'

At the door, he turned, nodding profound assurances, like a nurse saying the scratch will heal. A guard appeared, summoning Róża with a lazy hand. They walked side by side down the corridor, retracing the route to her cell. Passing a barred window on the floor below, Róża slowed. Beyond the prison wall she'd glimpsed the grubby bureaucrat nodding more assurances to a slender woman dressed in a long dark coat. Her face was pale and drawn; her hair short and black. Head bobbing, he handed over the child as if it were a prize in a raffle. The guard's hand closed around her elbow.

'Can't I watch to say goodbye?' she whispered.

'Back to your cell.'

Moments later the door slammed shut.

The lock turned.

All at once, Róża seemed to surface from the deep. She sucked in the air and fell on her hands and knees. Sputtering and gasping, she rolled over, digging her nails into her breasts and stomach. The other women watched, expressionless, lined around the room like tied sacks of refuse. Róża couldn't weep. She had no tears left. When all the noise had been expelled, she went to sleep.

'Mojeska.'

Six months had passed, the empty hours falling away like water from a dripping tap. Róża hadn't spoken a word to anyone. She seemed not to hear what was said to her. She'd eaten mechanically, with a voracious appetite. She'd left the wall unscratched. A deathly composure had displaced all her emotions.

'Mojeska, out,' repeated the voice, louder.

She looked up. The cell door was open. A guard was signalling her into the corridor. Without speaking, she obeyed. They went down some stairs to a room where her photograph was taken. Then, with a shove, she stumbled through a door into the main yard. The sun crashed upon her head like the blow of a mallet. She felt a cool breeze and her skin tingled. The guard was moving quickly.

They're going to shoot me.

Her heart beat out of time. Gratitude flushed through her veins. But another guard was heaving back the entrance gate. She saw the main street. Brack was on the pavement smoking. He flicked the stub on the floor and stamped it flat. A heavy shove sent her reeling towards him.

'Goodbye, Róża,' he said, nodding at the men behind.

'*What?*'

'There's always a right and a wrong choice, Róża. You made the wrong one.'

'You said you wouldn't let me out—'

'You should have told me about the Shoemaker. That was the right choice.'

Róża spun around. The prison door had been shut. There was no outside handle. She struck it with clenched fists, kicking the iron panels, begging the men on the other side to open up. She turned to Brack, hands joined, imploring. 'Shoot me? Please, Otto, shoot me. I don't want to live, I've nothing left . . . please . . .'

'Yes, you have. You've got the Shoemaker.'

Brack pulled his revolver from its belt holster. With a flick of his thumb the chamber fell open. He withdrew a single round and held it out to Róża.

'Be grateful. This was meant for you.' He tossed the bullet up and down as if it were loose change. 'I argued for your life. But if you don't want it, take this.'

Róża saw her fingers pick up the small brass jacket with the lead cap. She felt its coldness as she closed her hand around it. Unsteadily, she walked away towards a road junction while Brack's voice roared down a kind of tunnel.

'I'll find him, Róża. One day I'll find him.'

The sky was a most gorgeous blue, like Mr Lasky's tea set. It had been a wedding present. He

170

always thought of his wife when he used it. Somewhere behind, near the gate, was the stump. They'd painted the cut face black to stop any shoots growing.

CHAPTER 17

Róża's eyes fell upon every window; she lingered, trembling, at every junction, staring down the long avenues at the lined up houses and apartment blocks. Her child was behind one of those doors. Another woman with short black hair was telling her husband about those first infant steps, the reeling on tiny feet, and the soft, surprised landing. Together they were mouthing words, 'Mummy', 'Daddy'. The evocation of family contentment was worse than any torture Róża had endured in Mokotów. She looked in different directions, trying to turn away, but only saw other windows and other doors. Finally, her agonised steps came to a block of flats built on the old Jewish Ghetto. On the third floor was the home of Aniela Kolba.

The door was opened by a little boy aged five or six. His hair was chestnut brown, his cheeks scrubbed. A white fist gripped the side of baggy charcoal trousers.

'Who are you?' he asked, cowering away.

This had to be Bernard. He'd once nearly choked on a fishbone.

'I am . . .'

Róża couldn't finish her introduction. She was overcome with emotion at the sight of the boy, his blue veins visible through the soft skin of his neck. Aniela, busy and buxom, appeared behind him, her plump hands covered in flour. Dusting them wildly on her blue flowered apron, she pulled Róża inside.

'I've been waiting,' she murmured. 'And now that you have come, you will stay.'

She gripped Róża fiercely, recognising that she'd come alone: that the baby had left Mokotów through another door; that Róża had followed a hard route taken by other prison mothers. Aniela's grip told Róża that she understood everything; that coping with the loss of your husband was bad enough without suffering a constant reminder of his murdered face; that Róża had done nothing wrong; that she'd made a difficult decision for the best. All this and much more was pressed into Róża, as if she needed some kind of absolution from another mother. Róża accepted it, neither willing nor able to explain how Brack had tricked her.

'Your home is with us, now,' said a man's voice, full of the same understanding and compassion. 'Aniela won't let you go, so you might as well get used to it.'

Edward Kolba, weathered and stocky, sleeves rolled up, shook his head at any possible objection. He was standing behind his wife, one hand resting on his son's head.

'When she's made up her mind,' he said, his arched thick eyebrows riding high with affection, 'there's no compromise. I've told her a million times: join the Party. The Russians would let go by the end of the week.'

'Have you got the bed yet?' asked Aniela, over her shoulder. 'If I told you once I told you twice. Now—'

'I'll be back in half an hour,' replied Edward, reaching for his coat and hat. 'I'll sort everything out.'

Edward sorted out a great deal – far more than the army camp bed that he set up on the other side of a wardrobe that functioned as a kind of partition in the sitting room, giving Róża her own private space. Within a week he'd found her a job at the Dubiński Millinery, a hat-making factory where his sister-in-law worked as a line manager. Róża, bewildered with gratitude, accepted her place in this new ordered world. Its structure gave her strength. It roused her dreams. She went on the night shift so that she could be free during the day. Free to find the State department that dealt with adoptions.

The relevant offices were situated in a bleak concrete edifice at the end of an alley in a southern district of the city. After being shunted from one room to another, describing to various administrators along the way the man with the ragged briefcase, she ended up in the antechamber of Mr P. R. Bondel, the Temporary Fourth Assistant to the Second Deputy Director. The room was small, the walls naked of any decoration. Two wooden chairs faced a reception desk, behind which sat a woman with scraped back hair typing feverishly. Over her shoulder, Róża saw a door of frosted glass. Looking at the shadowy figure on the other side, she explained to the secretary that she wanted to find her child. There'd been a terrible mistake. The papers had been filled in a short while back and surely—

'Sorry.' The woman hit a full stop and looked up, her pointed face frank and uncompromising. 'Once the forms are signed it's just not possible . . . didn't anyone tell you?'

'Yes,' replied Róża, 'but my situation is different. I didn't sign. It's complicated. It's—'

'Name?' Simple, unfortunately, the woman's expression implied.

'Mojeska, Róża.'

'Take a seat.'

The woman barely opened the frosted door, and only managed to slip through the gap because she was so thin. After a few minutes, she eased herself back into the antechamber and said, with that same practised finality, 'Sorry, there really are no exceptions. Mr Bondel is most sympathetic, but once the forms are completed, signed or not, there's no—'

'I want to see him.'

'You can't.'

'Why?'

'He's busy.'

'I'll wait.'

'You'll be here all day.'

'I'll stay all week.'

Persuaded that Róża meant business, the woman quickly nipped inside once more. After some heated back and forth, the door swung wide open. Behind an enormous desk, like a man hiding from a Panzer, or maybe his wife, sat the spectacled official who'd come with his briefcase to Mokotów prison.

'Do take a seat, Madam,' he said, rising, one hand brushing the crumbs off his waistcoat. 'How very nice to see you again. Can't say I thought you'd see the light of day so soon, but there we are. Glad to know you've made your peace with the forces of law and order. Everyone should get a second chance, that's what I say . . .'

Róża saw the sweat on his top lip. He took out a wrinkled handkerchief and dabbed his mouth.

'It's not too late,' said Róża, firmly, taking a seat.

'For what?'

'Getting back my child.'

'Ah . . . that's *exactly* what my secretary said you'd said. I presumed she'd misunderstood your meaning. I'm afraid it's quite out of the question, quite impossible . . . altogether –' he paused, looking for another word, something official or technical – 'unfeasible. That's what it is. Totally unfeasible.'

'Why?'

With a heavy sigh, he shoved the handkerchief into his trouser pocket, settling his beetle brows into a kindly smile for the criminally obtuse. He was used to explaining things official. And not everyone appreciated the work of the Department. Unsung, it was.

'Madam . . . sorry, what was the name?'

'Mojeska, Róża.'

'Quite right, Madam Mojeska, you have to understand how these things *work*. You see, there's a *great* demand for an infant, you know, when they're *young*. Free of attachment. Wouldn't know their mother from a spring chicken. Makes life easier for everyone. The older they get, they don't hook on that easily. And that makes them hard to place. It takes time and folk don't always want to wait. They want a simple life. Sad, but true. A child's a child, that's what I say, but not everyone agrees with me. And you see Madam . . . Majewsky . . . the facts are your child would have been placed within days. Even before I got back to the office. The queue for infants reaches from here to Kraków. That's just an expression, mind you, we have a national remit, of course, but—'

'The papers were only filled in seven months ago,' objected Róża. 'I was tricked and misled. You have to help me, I beg you. Tell me who has my child. If they knew what had happened, they'd understand, I'm sure of it . . . and they can stay at the front of the queue, there are other children out there. But we have to find my child. I'm free now . . . I'm here . . .'

Mr Bondel nodded a painful recognition of the fact but then began to shake his head as if reverting to the thrust of his previous expostulations. He waited and waited, expecting Róża to rise and leave, but she only stared back, resolute, uncomprehending . . . obtuse, criminally incapable of falling into line. Mr Bondel thought for a moment and then a sort of light brightened his official regret. 'Perhaps, this once, I can do something.' Pondering, a finger flicked his lips. 'What was the name?'

'I've already told you.'

'Not yours, the child's. What was written down on the forms?'

'None. I didn't choose one.'

'All right, no grave problem –' he spoke as if it most certainly was – 'that's what we might call a hiccup. But we have the surname, of course, so we can—'

'No,' said Róża, paling. 'The space was left empty . . .'

'Ah.' His hairy fingers tapped the desk. 'Now that causes me some difficulty. Considerable, I'd say. The name's the key, without the key I can't open the lock.'

'What are you talking about?'

'Filing systems, Madam Majewsky. Formalities.' He lowered his head as if to duck the attention of his secretary. 'Frankly, I'll be honest. I'll break a rule to show my goodwill. I remember placing your child. Nice woman, expensive shoes. Handmade, I'd say. Classy all round. But I wouldn't know her from Adam . . . or Eve, for that matter. I've no idea where she came from or where she went. I never do. From our end, once everyone's happy, we send off the forms to Section Three and they put them in a red binder, but without a name, well, what's to be done? There's nothing to ask for. I can't ask them to find something if there's no label. Can't use the index. Can't look up "None". God knows where they'd put "None". Never thought of that one.'

'But that's not possible,' protested Róża. 'All it takes is a little—'

'Now don't you start blaming yourself, Madam,' said Mr Bondel, freeing the bottom button of his waistcoat. 'There's nothing we can do. None is none. I shouldn't have raised your hopes, that was my fault and I ask your pardon. But you can rest assured that all the children who pass across this desk go to the best of homes –' he tapped his fingers as if they were tiny feet – 'and the lady I met was altogether captivating. A cut above your usual—'

'But I was tricked,' whispered Róża, harshly.

'Madam Majewsky, you got out of prison,' he whispered back, kindly. 'Your child did, too. Be grateful. It doesn't always end that well, as you should know.'

'I was tricked.'

Mr Bondel's tone dropped even lower. 'Madam, allow me to give you some sound advice of a general character. Always fill in the forms. Tick the boxes. Sign the bottom. It's what makes the world go round.'

'I want my child back,' persisted Róża.

'Unfeasible.'

'You have to listen to me, forms or no forms—'

'No, *you* listen.' Mr Bondel's patience with the criminal classes abruptly snapped. Disgust and disapproval, previously suppressed, boiled to the surface, making scum of his certified courtesies. 'I shouldn't have seen you, and I did. I'm a family man, and I felt sorry for you. But *no one* can help you find nothing. Your bird has flown. You let it go, not me.' He stood up, short and ridiculously imperious, crumbs trapped in a fold of his waistcoat. 'Olga,' he bawled. 'Madam Majewsky is leaving.'

The door opened. Róża walked hesitantly away from the man who'd filled in the forms, turning round when she reached the thin, terrified woman.

'My name is Mojeska,' said Róża, quietly, to Mr Bondel. 'M-o-j-e-s-k-a.'

'Quite right. I'll make a note. Olga, jot that down, will you?'

When she'd left the antechamber and walked twenty or so yards down the corridor, Róża swivelled on her heels and strode back to the reception desk, her limbs shaking, her teeth grinding. The lean assistant recoiled and made a weak scream as Róża reached over and grabbed the typewriter. In a wild swinging movement, ablaze with rage, she hurled the machine straight through the panel of frosted glass.

Róża stepped out of the alley and began her long walk back to the Old Ghetto, choked by impotence, blinded by tears. The Temporary Fourth Assistant to the Second Deputy Director knew exactly how to find her child, but he wouldn't; and probably couldn't. He was just as much a cog in the wheel as she was. They turned in opposing directions, that's all, their teeth meshing in a kind of obedience to the vast grinding machine that shaped their lives, determining what was possible, establishing an order of right and wrong, free from appeal or question. The only difference was that Mr Bondel moved willingly. In a way he was a collaborator – the most contemptible kind because he knew he would never be blamed: all he'd ever done was go through the motions. Just then, Róża's hand found the bullet in her pocket. Pausing in the middle of the street, she took it out.

Brack said it had been meant for her.

Why, then, had he kept her alive?

Róża stumbled on, turning the thing around in her hand. He'd kept her alive not from any residue of affection or friendship, but because he hoped she'd lead him one day to the Shoemaker. His commitment to the machine was without limitation. He would never tire or waver in his purpose.

Róża was only alive so that someone else might be brought to death. At that instant, she felt watched, tabbed and tailed. She heard the clatter of a typewriter and the clang of the return carriage. Her file would never be closed.

'Why have you gone this far, Otto?' said Róża, out loud, stumbling forward aimlessly. 'Wasn't killing my husband enough?'

Shouts of warning rang out, seemingly far off.

'Is it all because I went north and you went south? Is this my punishment?'

Róża was wavering on the pavement holding up the bullet as if she were Hamlet talking to that skull. Passers-by looked on as if she were mad. Suddenly, she closed her fists and started walking, head down, wondering how she would ever face tomorrow.

Róża moved on to the day shift. Sitting between two other women at a long table she sewed ribbons on to hats for export to the Soviet Union. Each evening on the way home she found an empty pew in Saint Klement's and listened to the silence. After an hour she went home to her side of the wardrobe. Then she ate, slept and went to work again. Occasionally, like a drunken masochist, she'd rise to watch Bernard sleep, listening to his breathing, feeling the cut of a saw's teeth with each intake of air, with each long, slow exhalation. Events passed her by. Talk of riots and deaths somewhere in the north or strikes on the coast were like distant noises, not entirely real, sounds from other people's mouths. If Brack had arranged for someone to follow her, he'd wasted his time. Róża was going nowhere that would interest him. He'd played too hard and gone too far. He should have left her with some purpose in life, something to fight for, a reason to go back to the Shoemaker. Whereas she had nothing left. Her days were empty. Their meaning had gone, flown from her own hand.

PART IV

THE *POLANA* FILE

CHAPTER 18

Anselm examined the sequence of framed maps on the wall of an airy, well lit office, situated on the fourth floor of the IPN. They charted the loss of national sovereignty to the Prussians, the Austrians and the Russians, their invasions in blue, brown and red constantly rearranging the green homeland throughout a hundred and fifty years of resistance, at one point erasing it completely. I'm in an obstinate country, he thought; one that waits for spring.

The display had been brought to his attention by a red-haired woman dressed in a white trouser suit, who'd then left him to retrieve the Shoemaker material for his inspection. Presently she returned carrying an oblong cardboard box. She placed it on the desk beneath the maps and turned on a lamp. Unable to speak English or German, she pointed once again at the maps, as if seeking confirmation that Anselm had got the message. Loud and clear, he nodded. After she'd gone, clipping the door shut behind her, Anselm polished his glasses on his scapular, conscious that his task to find a secret police informer was part of that

187

greater picture of shifting boundaries; that the losses and gains were moral and spiritual and not just national; that even a single betrayal in 1982 carried the entire weight of a people's devastated expectations. John had warned him as much.

With that sense of solemn engagement, Anselm sat down and removed the lid from the box. Inside were two files, one thick and orange, the other thin and green. He took the first and untied its bow with a quick tug. Opening the cover, he paused.

The text had not been translated. Glancing down the three short paragraphs, Anselm gleaned two names: one in lower case, Róża Mojeska, the second capitalised, OLEK. Beneath this document Anselm found two prison photographs, the first of a girl with wavy hair, the second of a haggard woman, someone so absent that Anselm thought she'd just risen from an autopsy table. They were each marked 'MPB WARSZAWA' and dated 1951 and 1953 respectively. Then he realised they were one and the same individual. This was Róża Mojeska, before and after. The rest of the file held page after page of meticulous pencil-written notes – these presumably being a contemporaneous record of Róża's various interrogations. This was the neatness of that most frightening of individuals, the bureaucrat and torturer, whose violence is a kind of humdrum administrative activity. Anselm moved them to one side, grateful that he couldn't understand the questions and answers.

Reaching into the box he withdrew the file with the green cover. It was so flimsy it might have been empty. This, presumably, was the *Polana* material from the joint Stasi-SB archive.

Anselm was right. Inside were two letters in German. The first was dated 17th June 1982, reference MW/MfS/XV1/1982. It had been sent by a Stasi major in Warsaw to a general in East Berlin. A single paragraph was relevant to Anselm's purpose:

> Contrary to the protocol of December 1978, Colonel Brack declines to share key intelligence. Day to day running of *Polana* is left to his deputy, Lieutenant Frenzel who keeps matters firmly in the SB camp. We know, for example, that an agent named FELIKS has been reactivated but to date we have not been told who that might be.

The second letter was dated three weeks later. It came from Colonel Brack to the general, copied to the major, reference IO/SB/XVI/1982. Again one element spoke to Anselm:

> As you know, agent running is a delicate task resting upon the absolute trust of the informer with their handler. Their contract is with the SB, not the Stasi. To disclose their names at this stage is neither necessary nor desirable. That said, at the

189

completion of the operation I am sure some accommodation can be found.

That was it. John had assumed the file would contain everything that had been compiled to catch Róża, which would include the name of the informer. But there was nothing of the sort. The bulk of the contents had evidently been removed. Anselm pushed back his chair to seek the woman in white. He found her ticking boxes in another office some distance down the corridor. Behind her stood a man in a dark suit examining a photocopier as if it were a lethal gadget made by Q.

'Excuse me,' said Anselm, hesitating at the door. 'The file is incomplete.'

The nurse's signals suggested he might like to try again but the conversation did not improve until the man prodding the paper tray tuned in. Shaking Anselm's hand he said, in assured English, 'Nothing's missing. They've been destroyed.'

Sebastian Voight had read law at Warsaw and then pursued post-graduate studies in London and Washington. He'd specialised in criminal procedure, with an eye to war crimes and the problems of transitional justice, thinking originally of a career at the Hague. However he'd been knocked off course – or on course, depending on your perspective – by the offer of a job at the IPN. Amongst the many investigations he'd instituted into what were now called 'communist crimes', few had been as important or urgent as that of Otto Brack.

'Important because his case links crimes of the Stalinist Terror to those of the martial law years; it's the beginning and end of Communism. Róża's story symbolises the entire epoch. A trial of Otto Brack would be a trial of post-war authoritarian ideology and its murderous consequences.' Sebastian's office, it transpired, faced that allocated to Anselm. The order was in surprising contrast to a rather appealing anarchy in his clothing. He was smart, but something rebelled. The stiff shirt collar refused to stay inside the jacket. His soul was in a pair of trainers. 'And it's important regardless of any inherent symbolic qualities, because we're dealing with a double killing.'

The orange file contained not only Róża's interrogations from the early fifties but a secret report referring to the interrogation and execution of two men believed to be part of the Shoemaker organisation: Pavel Mojeska and Stefan Binkowski.

'There was no trial,' said Sebastian, leaning on the edge of his desk. 'They were simply killed. At the time Róża was in the same prison. I'm sure she knows what happened. As things stand there is no evidential link between the murders and Otto Brack.'

'How do you know there is one?'

'Intuition. I could feel it when I met Róża. She was there. I *know* she was there.'

191

Anselm glanced at the wall planner, marked with red dots for pending actions. There were no blue ones for the holidays. Along one wall was a rack of shelves packed with box files. Presiding over the lot, in a central gap, was a photograph of an elderly woman standing behind a wheelchair.

'You said urgent,' resumed Anselm, legs crossed, remembering the savage energy generated by papers organised for a trial.

'Róża is the last and only witness,' replied Sebastian. 'The known guards are dead. And if they weren't I doubt if they'd talk. It all hangs on Róża. But she's trapped by her own decency. Brack threatened to bring a plague on an informer's house if she ever opened her mouth. She's worried they'd take a running jump.'

Anselm sipped a glass of fizzy water, picked up from a machine in the corridor outside. 'Well, she was present all right.'

'Where?'

'In the prison when her husband and Stefan Binkowski were shot.'

'Shot? How do you know?'

'She flew all the way to London to tell John Fielding, a friend of mine. She asked him to walk through fire to find the informer who betrayed her in nineteen eighty-two. She'll only meet them if they're willing to talk honestly. If they won't, she'll let them go. If they will, she hopes to persuade them that Brack's worst isn't that bad after all.'

'Well, well, well,' murmured Sebastian, dragging a hand through his black hair. 'She really did change her mind.'

He spun off the desk's edge to open a front drawer.

'I'd been chasing Róża for weeks but she wouldn't talk to me.' He took out a folder and opened its flap. 'Eventually, I persuaded her to come here and see the SB files. I tricked her, and she knew it. I'd set up recording equipment, right there in front of the shelves. I'd put up some pictures showing the chaos of her life and times. I'd made it difficult to walk away.'

He'd asked her to talk about the period between 1951 and 1982, saying it was for a voice archive. Which was true, only what he really wanted was a list of all the people she'd known. The informer had to be among them.

'I knew what I was looking for. There are only two types of candidate that would explain Róża's willingness to leave Brack unaccused. First, someone intimately connected to the Shoemaker operation with a high enough profile to make public disclosure almost unthinkable. Second, someone to whom she felt indebted . . . someone to whom she owed far more than she ever stood to gain by seeing Brack banged up for life.'

'Either way,' said Anselm, commending the classification, 'someone who might choose the Vistula if exposed.'

Sebastian gave a nod. 'But Róża saw the ruse:

193

she gave no names. After she'd finished, I thought I'd never see her again.'

But a week or so later she'd come back with a revised statement, identifying every person of significance in her life.

'She, too, was transformed,' explained Sebastian. 'She'd worked out a plan of some kind, but she wouldn't elaborate. All she'd say was that she intended to wake the dead and shatter the illusions of many. And now you've turned up.'

Anselm rather liked the ring to that declaration. He took off his glasses to shine the lenses, baulking, suddenly, as Róża's expectations came into focus.

'She brought that statement to London,' said Anselm, blinking uncertainly. 'In effect, she called it a tool to help find the informer. Thing is, she never gave it to John.'

'Why not?'

'When they met, she saw he was blind.'

'And?'

'She left. Devastated. Not knowing that John would come to me, and that I would come here, in his stead, without that statement.'

The two lawyers appraised each other, both of them – Anselm was sure – reviewing the law of agency, for unless Anselm could be described as Róża's representative, the IPN couldn't disclose a copy of her statement.

'The words "authorised", "express" and "implied" spring to mind,' purred Anselm. 'I've forgotten the rest but I think we can frame an argument to the effect that I'm Róża's sub-agent, with John as the absent principal.'

'Agreed,' replied Sebastian, taking a document from the folder. 'This is the text. To sharpen the focus, I've cut out the material where no names are mentioned. I'll get it translated now. I've traced the addresses and telephone numbers of all the people mentioned. You'll find them listed at the back.'

It was an East meets West triumph: a sort of indigenous Pizza Express, only they sold dumplings. *Pierogi.* Anselm wouldn't have thought it possible, but these fast serving mono-thematic eateries were all the rage. They'd sprung up all over the city. Could a dumpling seriously vie with a pizza? Anselm was privately awed. Out loud, over a shot of *Śliwowica Paschalna* ('. . . just fermented plums. Nothing added. Not even water . . .') he wondered if Sebastian had given any thought to FELIKS.

'Oh yes. I looked him up in one of the SB agent registers. And sure enough, he's there in Róża's statement all the way from the fifties to the eighties. For the first time I got a glimpse of her predicament fleshed out. FELIKS is a friend. FELIKS is part of a family. FELIKS is surrounded by people who've no idea he's a swine who got his swill. People Róża doesn't want to harm.'

Anselm took a sip.

'The second type of informer,' he whispered, eyes watering.

'Yes. She owed him her life.'

Assuming FELIKS is our man (continued Sebastian, after draining his glass) the circumstances showed up the moral perversion of Brack's actions. Sure, he'd used her goodness against herself, but he'd also gambled on a lack of honesty among the very people she sought to protect.

'Not everyone wants to hear the truth,' he avowed with a knowing wink to the waiter at the bar. 'They wouldn't want to know that Daddy was an informer and they wouldn't thank Róża for telling them. She'd have known the score immediately: if she wanted to keep popping round for dinner and watch the telly, then she'd better keep her mouth shut.'

Anselm nodded, thinking – curiously – of John. Given the choice, he'd preferred the lie of a happy family to the truth of his mother's betrayal. He wasn't grateful for the enlightenment, even now. He hadn't wanted the pain. Neither had his father or Melanie. They'd all been playing Misery ever since, trying to get back to the good times. All of which demonstrated the complexity of Róża's position and the risks involved in persuading someone to step centre-stage.

One arm behind his back, the waiter refilled Sebastian's tiny glass, aping shock when Anselm declined a top-up.

'But, of course, FELIKS may not be our man,' said Anselm, wetting his bottom lip.

'No. I spotted that, too.'

Colonel Brack's letter to the general, copied to the major, referred to 'agents'. Plural. There were other ears at Róża's door. But only one of them really mattered.

'I've got to find the informer that led Brack to the Powązki Cemetery in nineteen eighty-two,' said Anselm. 'The rest are just bit-players.'

How to proceed, then? Anselm could hardly go through an SB agent registry like one of those telephone-based salesmen, asking if the house-holder would like to change their heating system. He needed to know for sure that he'd found Brack's main actor, so he could plan his approach, plan that 'better story' mentioned by the Prior that would persuade them to meet Róża.

Sebastian, it transpired, had already tried to narrow down the pool of candidates. Cross-referring the IO/SB/XVI/1982 reference with SB employment records, he'd identified Irina Orlosky as Brack's bilingual personal assistant. The revenue people had traced her address but, like Róża, she'd refused to talk. Unlike Róża she'd been hard and brittle; hysterical when pushed. And while neither of them had a choice but to co-operate with an IPN investigation, Sebastian recognised he couldn't hope to mount a successful prosecution without willing witnesses.

Anselm stared at his glass and then swallowed fire in one swift movement.

'Odd, really, that the *Polana* file isn't completely empty,' he said, after a long burning pause. 'The letters left behind are more like adverts. A hint of what's on offer. I was reminded of a mail order catalogue.'

'Catalogue?'

'Yes. You know, bargain sales. Basement level.'

Sebastian didn't follow so Anselm explained.

'We need the papers that are missing from the *Polana* file. The one name left on view to anyone who opens the cover is Brack's deputy, Lieutenant Frenzel. I find that an intriguing state of affairs. I think it was deliberate. I think he wouldn't be surprised if we gave him a call. I think the man is open for business.'

Sebastian leaned back slowly, viewing Anselm with reluctant admiration. Annoyance, too, that he'd missed the true meaning of the surviving correspondence. For months he'd been poring over those two letters, seeing nothing more alluring than a reference number, and then this monk had turned up, this herald expected to shatter the illusions of many, and he'd seen the implications in five minutes.

'I think I might join you after all,' said Anselm, signalling to the waiter.

Warmed by Sebastian's silent praise, he thought it right, however, to advertise his ignorance. He'd wanted to know something long before he'd dared to question the eminence of dumplings.

'So, tell me, who was FELIKS?'

CHAPTER 19

IPN/RM/13129/2010
EDITED TRANSCRIPT OF A STATEMENT
MADE BY RÓŻA MOJESKA
Timings refer to the complete recording.

0.15
The guard behind shoved me out . . . but I didn't
want to leave. I'd forgotten how to live and I
didn't know what to do out there, on an ordinary
street. For years I'd been in a cell with a tiny
window so high that I had to strain my neck to
see the clouds. I turned round and banged on
the gate . . . but they wouldn't let me back in.
Brack just watched me . . . and, when I finished
beating on the gate, his eyes followed me to a
junction a few hundred yards up the road. That's
when I thought of Aniela Kolba. We'd shared a
cell. She'd told me to come and stay when they
set me free.

0.56
Aniela and I were bound by memories of prison
while Edward, her husband, became my guide

199

and friend. He knew how to live *na lewo*, on the left . . . outside official channels; he'd learned how to *załatwić sprawy* . . . to wangle things. That first night he obtained an old British Army camp bed and set it up in the sitting room, between a wardrobe and wall. He called it my apartment. A few days later, he pulled some strings and got me a job sewing ribbons in a hat factory. I was part of the family. No rent. No payments of any kind. I sat at their table as if I'd always been there. I didn't leave it until four years later, when – thanks to Edward's back door wangling – I got a place of my own. But by then there was no leaving. I belonged.

5.37

Work at the factory gave a structure to my life. I sat between two women and we just sewed from morning till night. To my left was Barbara Nowak. Her husband had gone for a long walk and never come back. She had a pram with a doll, bought in the hope of having a child. She had a parrot in a cage that yelled 'Let me out'. She was unhappy; and that made us friends. We both sat there, lost with our own thoughts, endlessly pulling a needle and thread. Thirty years later, never having attended a strike or demonstration in her life, Barbara organised a system of distribution for *Freedom and Independence*. She used to wear a flowery apron, even in the street. The SB never gave her a second look. But that was all to come. At the time I met her, we were both in a kind of troubled sleep.

8.09
The fifties were a difficult time for everyone. And yet I didn't really notice the hardship. I remember once seeing blood on my thumb but I had no recollection of having felt the stab of the needle. That sums me up, back then. From day to day, I felt nothing. The greater part of me was still in Mokotów . . . by a large window that looked on to a cherry tree. Events passed me by – great, terrible events, which burned themselves into those around me, and I looked on, numbed, as if I'd found someone else's blood on my fingers.

It was through Barbara that I heard about the riots in 1956. She leaned towards me saying the workers from the Stalin factory in Poznań were on the streets. They had banners. 'We want Freedom', 'We want Bread', 'We are Hungry'. She said the farmers had taken on the Soviet army. Bombs were falling out of the sky. Folk were being dragged off to Siberia. I listened from afar, only stirring at a detail that turned out to be true. Children had climbed trees to get a better view of the tanks and the soldiers. When the army opened fire, aiming high to warn the rioters, they hit these little sparrows. Children fell dead from the branches.

18.23

Such was my life. Every night I'd go to Saint Klement's for an hour or so. The silence reminded me of a voice I once heard on a train. This girl sang a song that took me out of myself. In my life, which has seen so many demands for names and dates of birth, here was someone important who'd escaped being nailed down. There was no name. I don't know who it was, or what she looked like but I found her again in that quiet place.

The cleaner was called Lidia Zelk. A timid woman, we didn't speak for three years. She'd never married. Like Barbara, she eventually joined the Friends of the Shoemaker.

CHAPTER 20

While waiting for Róża's statement to be translated, Anselm sat at his desk humming Bunny Berigan's trumpet solo from 'I Can't Get Started'. His eyes drifted on to the orange file. He'd left it open. Róża's two faces peered back from the prison photographs. All that lay between each snap of the shutter release was a couple of years, during which time . . . Anselm's humming came to an abrupt halt: he'd noticed a tiny scrap of blue paper sticking out towards the bottom of the pile.

Swivelling the block round, he lowered his head to examine the fragment more closely. It was held in place by the string fastener that kept the documents together. The relevant sheet had evidently been detached from the bundle, leaving behind the corner section. Puzzled, he closed the cover. He'd only just tied the bow when Sebastian entered with the translation of Róża's statement.

'Let me know what you think,' he said. 'Our rat is in there somewhere.'

As he reached the door, Anselm heard himself say, 'Can I just ask an idle question?'

'Absolutely.'

Sebastian turned and leaned on the jamb, hands in his pockets.

'Can't understand a thing in here, of course,' said Anselm, tapping the orange file, 'but why are there two kinds of paper . . . white and blue.'

'The white was used by the interrogators, the blue by the nurses.'

'Nurses?'

'Yes. The colour coding was common to all prisons. In Róża's case, having any medical notes is laughable. I mean, what did they do? Dish out the aspirin when they'd finished with the rack? That's probably why it's blank. They didn't do anything.'

'Blank?'

'Apart from her name at the top. I don't know why it's in there at all. I imagine they lumped all her papers together, even when they hadn't been used.'

Anselm's mind made a sort of grinding noise. Sebastian was talking as if the blue paper was still in the file. He'd seen it. He knew it was blank. But it wasn't there now. Some primitive caution stopped Anselm from revealing his thoughts. Instead he asked if he could venture some more questions peripheral to their investigation.

'Is anyone else involved in this case?'

'No.'

'Anyone else read the files?'

'No. Why?'

'Just wondering if you'd got a second opinion on the *Polana* material.' That was completely untrue. Anselm had wanted to know who might have had access to the orange file. His intuition had already leapt at the answer. He quickly pressed on, seeking confirmation. 'I know this is neither here nor there, but what did Róża do when she saw the transcripts? That white and blue paper must have knocked her flat.'

'She didn't even open the cover.'

'Really?'

'The sight of the files winded her. Wanted to be alone. When the door opened her eyes were on the "Way Out" sign.'

'How did you change her mind?' The question was entirely superfluous. Anselm had found out what he wanted to know.

'I said I had a story, too,' replied Sebastian. 'She stared at my shirt and shoes and then, for some reason, she just weakened. I pushed some more and she finally gave in. The fact is, she wanted to speak. Everyone who's been brutalised has to speak, needs to speak. And Róża went as far as she was able . . . but I very nearly lost her.'

Anselm made a mischievous nod. Sebastian was no different. That reference to an untold story had come from a dropped guard. Already the lawyer was backtracking, heading into the corridor before Anselm's curiosity could tug at the admission.

'Don't ask,' he intoned. 'I'll tell you after Brack's conviction.'

Until that moment, Anselm had thought that Sebastian was simply a dedicated lawyer born of the generation that dealt with the sins of their fathers. There was clearly another facet to his energy. Anselm recalled the box files and the photograph of the elderly woman standing behind a wheelchair. Who should have been sitting there? Were they linked to Sebastian's investigation into Brack? Anselm turned as from the ghost to have a quick word with Róża.

'I said nothing to Sebastian, because you didn't,' he said, confiding and quiet. 'I'm respecting your privacy. You removed the blue paper because you didn't want anyone to know you'd been in the infirmary. Fair enough. Your choice. Don't worry, your secret's safe with me.'

He waited, but no reply came to his imagination.

'But I'm in some difficulty. You went to John for help and, for all I know, he'd just walk straight through the fire. But you've ended up with me. I'm different. I'm easily distracted. And I can only help by stumbling around on the sidelines – it's my way. Comes with monastic life, you know, head half in the clouds. So bear with me, because I now want to know why you vandalised the national archives.'

With that resolution in mind, Anselm picked up Róża's statement.

Anselm read the document three times with increasing attentiveness – a monastic practice vaguely similar to deep sea diving without the benefit of lead boots, each appraisal an attempt to break beneath the surface tension of the page. The objective: to descend into the dark and find the strange light not always visible from the side of the boat. He lingered here and there on individual phrases, letting his mind sink and swim where it willed.

His first reaction on drying himself down, so to speak, was completely irrelevant to the matter in hand. He was hurt. And confused. At first he'd found the references to John touching. They'd given bright glimpses on to the young man who'd left East Berlin for Warsaw, the gifted journalist driven to document the struggle of an oppressed people. But then, like a sudden power-cut, came that reference to John's mother. He'd told Róża what he'd never told him. Suppressing his disappointment, Anselm focused instead on Róża's staggering misfortune. She'd walked out of Mokotów into the house of an informer.

Anselm's second reaction, then, was pity. Immense pity for Róża, but also for the husband and father who'd become FELIKS. Presumably there'd been pressure or the allure of reward, but Edward Kolba had evidently come to an arrangement with Otto Brack. With or without his wife's connivance, he'd kept an eye on their guest. For sure, Róża had been welcomed with open arms. But she'd also been placed at the centre of an ongoing surveillance operation. If

207

FELIKS did betray Róża in 1982 then that would certainly explain Róża's silence afterwards: her loyalty to him, but perhaps more so to his wife, Aniela, who'd shared the unforgettable experience of Mokotów. She too got Anselm's pity.

His third reaction was more clinical.

Róża had amended and amplified the transcript, making it a carefully polished document. Each section dealt neatly with people and places and their significance in her life. Every word had its place. Which made Róża's mistake all the more illuminating.

She'd slipped up.

The tiny window in her cell was so high she had to strain her neck 'to see the clouds'. Eight minutes later she confessed that the greater part of her remained in Mokotów 'by a large window that looking on to a cherry tree'.

Where was that big window? It had to be located in the prison infirmary. Róża wouldn't have had the run of the place. There was no gym, television room or sauna. Where else could she have been if it wasn't her cell? The textual inconsistency was of no small importance. It explained Róża's startling opening remark that she wanted to remain incarcerated. Fine, she'd forgotten how to boil an egg, but think again (Anselm said to himself): she was effectively saying that she longed to remain at the scene of a double execution. Dogs do things like that, not human beings. Not wives. But this is what Róża said she wanted to do. And it was not credible. In an otherwise crafted testimonial where nothing had been given away without a specific reason, Róża had made an accidental admission. She'd kicked and screamed and beaten the prison door not because she wanted her cell back but because she longed to be near that larger window; an infirmary window. Where else if not there? It haunted her. And all because it looked on to a tree?

'Well, what do you think?'

Anselm made a start. He hadn't heard Sebastian enter. The lawyer pulled over a chair and straddled the seat, his chin lodged on his folded arms as if he were looking into that eye testing machine at the opticians. He worked too hard, that was Anselm's verdict. The whites were yellowed and bloodshot.

'Something isn't quite right,' said Anselm.

'In what way?'

'I'm not sure.' He made a sigh of self-deprecation. 'Can't read a damn thing without brooding on it for months. At Larkwood we tend to chew words slowly, swallow them even more slowly and then wait for this sudden kick of understanding, right here –' he pointed at his stomach – 'it's a bit annoying, really. I read stuff ten years ago and I've still got indigestion. The only cure's watching and waiting.'

'Well, you've got till nine-thirty tomorrow morning.' Sebastian reached into his inside jacket pocket and took out a scrap of paper. He held it up to Anselm so he could read the address scrawled across the middle. 'You have an appointment with Marek Frenzel.'

Locating the former secret policeman had been no more difficult than tracing Irina Orlosky. According to the tax people, Brack's assistant, now aged sixty-two, had left the SB to join the peace of mind industry and was now a branch manager in central Warsaw. He'd shown a flare for insurance. He was still looking after the People: house and contents; the whole caboodle.

'Does he know what we want?' asked Anselm, taking the paper.

'I told his secretary that an old policy had finally matured.'

So the stage was set. If Anselm's hunch was correct, he'd shortly buy back the missing contents of the *Polana* file. And that would confirm if Edward Kolba had gone the distance. But in truth Anselm's curiosity, lambent with expectation, lay just as much elsewhere: on the sidelines, far from the fire.

CHAPTER 21

IPN/RM/13129/2010
EDITED TRANSCRIPT OF A STATEMENT
MADE BY RÓŻA MOJESKA

33.41
If it wasn't for Bernard, I might never have gone
back to the Shoemaker. When he was a child, I
told him the story of the dragon and I like to think
that his first steps towards resistance came from
hearing that tale of intellect against brute force.
Later, without prompting, he began to ask the
'wrong' sorts of question, like, 'Why do we have
a special relationship with the Soviet Union?'.
Edward used to pull his hair out, begging him to
stick to algebra. Clean problems that could be
solved cleanly. He just wanted his boy to do well
at school.

36.22
At university Bernard started talking about all
kinds of freedom . . . freedom to read books
banned by the censor; freedom to watch any film
he wanted; to say what he liked; to meet whom

he liked; freedom from the restraint that kept everyone in line, an ideological line drawn more for Moscow's approval than theirs; freedom to pick his own leaders; freedom of information; freedom protected by the law. Freedom, pure and simple. Edward would shake his head, stabbing one finger upwards, warning Bernard that they might be bugged, while Aniela would dust the flour from her hands, round on him and shout back, 'What are you on about? You're getting a free education!'

38.54

Bernard belonged to that group of intellectuals whose strong belief in socialism – its vision of fairness and equality – had turned restive. Their problem was that, in practice, it wasn't working properly. They demanded *reform* not revolution – a reform that had been promised year on year by the Party leadership. All they wanted was for the apparatchiks to stand back so that he and his educated pals could lift the bonnet on the government's engine. With a bit of major tinkering they were sure they could fix those grinding noises that everyone was complaining about. But eventually he lost his faith. One of his professors was expelled from the Party for condemning the lack of political, social and economic development. That was when he – and many others – realised that without a revolution of ideas there was little hope for change. He wrote a letter saying so to both the rector and the Party leadership – actions for which he could have been kicked out of the university. Happily he only received a disciplinary warning. Bernard got his degree later that year and I still remember Edward when the results came out. He sat with his mouth open, tears of joy pouring on to his thick moustache. There was a scholar in the family.

41.52

They got Bernard after he'd started post-graduate studies. One domino hit another: in 1968 the censor banned *Forefather's Eve* after the audience had a field day jeering the czarist agent as if he were a latter-day soviet stooge. The students took to the streets in protest so the rector shut down a string of Departments. Thousands of young people – Bernard, among them – had their schooling cut short. They all got 'wolf tickets', blacklisting them when it came to finding a job. Edward's face set into a mask. This was one affair he couldn't resolve by wangling. He had to watch his boy scratch around for bit work.

42.58

Bernard didn't only lose his future; he lost a child-hood friend, Mateusz Robak. They'd gone in different directions, Bernard to books on philosophy and Mateusz to an electrician's manual. When the demonstration had erupted Bernard the Student had wanted Mateusz the Worker by his side. But Mateusz had laughed him down: 'I'm not risking my job so you can watch a play written two hundred years ago.' They never spoke again, not until 1982. By then Mateusz was in charge of my security.

53.21

I lost a friend, too. Magda Samovitz. We'd met in Saint Justyn's, where she'd been hidden during the war. The German secret police had taken her away with Mr Lasky in 1944 but she'd survived Treblinka and come back. Well, the government now blamed the student unrest on Zionists, and Magda lost her job simply because she was Jewish. I couldn't believe that those who'd survived and returned, like her, would one day leave again with the little they could carry in their bags. Thousands lost their jobs and left the country. Magda went to England.

54.39

Bernard became heavily involved in unofficial union activity, which was how he met his wife, Helena. A close friend of theirs was shot dead in 1970 at Gdynia, one of a crowd chanting 'We want bread! We want truth!' at the machine guns. They carried his body on planks behind a banner saying 'The Blood of Children'. Others were killed in the Radom riots of 1976 when food prices doubled. Demonstrators unfurled the white eagle and set the Party building on fire. I listened to the news, still not feeling the stab of a needle. According to the presenter, 'drunken hooligans and hysterical women led the crowds'.

1h.02
Bernard always said that Solidarity grew from that banner and those martyrs, because afterwards the students and workers came together. But I would add something else, a remark I heard on the bus last week: no Church, no Solidarity, no revolution. And it's true. Behind this coalition of minds and hands was the presence of those strong arches, arches that had refused to bend or break despite the weight of Soviet Occupation. Even if there were men of God who'd become men of Brack, that changes nothing, and it never can: the story has been told; the arches didn't sway. I, and millions like me, stood beneath them.

Anyway, the students and workers, united to this spirit of resistance, overwhelmed the Party. Our special friends had to swallow it. Solidarity became official.

What followed, however, was chaos. Strike after strike. I ended up brushing my teeth with imported Bulgarian toothpaste. Frankly, though, I was more interested in Helena's pregnancy. I watched her slowly grow large. I didn't quite notice the hunger marches or the trucks jamming the central roundabout or the rumours that the Russians were mobilising. I just saw Helena's radiant face. Aniela watched her, scared there'd be a knock on the door; that they might come back in their leather jackets and jeans.

1h.08
They came on the night martial law was declared, barging in, guns everywhere, masked men dressed like warriors from the Middle Ages, with helmets and big sticks and whatnot. And shouting, terrible shouting. Aniela screaming, Edward pulling at his son. This time they'd really got him.

That's when it happened. Moments later, sometime after midnight. Just as they dragged Bernard away, Helena fell to her knees. Aniela dropped beside her. I was frozen to the spot, overwhelmed with . . . fear . . . no, awe, I suppose. The child was born there, in the flat, before my eyes, with Aniela stroking the mother's hair.

1h.15
I went on to the street next morning. Soldiers were warming themselves by makeshift fires. Tanks rolled over the snow. By a lamppost I found a sheet of paper. There were others, lying around like litter. On it was a list of names . . . the names of people who'd been picked up the night before. The ink was running in the melt water. I think it had been made from tea or carrot skins, I don't know, but someone had printed off this bulletin before morning, even before the soldiers had gone home to bed.

That's when I decided to go back to the

Shoemaker – not because of martial law or Solidarity or because I was worried about the cost of meat or the Russians. I went back because a little boy had been born. His father had been taken to prison before the child had even got his name.

1h.19
I packed some clothes into a shopping bag, knowing I'd have to vanish, for as soon as *Freedom and Independence* appeared again, Brack would come for me. Half an hour later I knocked on the door of Father Nicodem Kaminsky. He was the Threshold to the Shoemaker. I'd last seen him with my husband in November 1951.

CHAPTER 22

The beaming secretary in the tight skirt opened the door for Anselm on to a cramped office with half-closed blinds. The furnishings were modern and shiny: wood veneers and chrome; stripped pine flooring, convincing to look at, but manufactured by the sheet, soft underfoot where the fitters had skimped on glue. Sound-proof panelling seemed to soak up the dry rasp of Anselm's breathing. He was instantly scared.

Marek Frenzel sat with his paunch pressed against his glass-top desk, squashed from behind by his red filing cabinet. A computer screen threw an unkind bluish light on to his features. Mouse grey hair, parted and creamed back, topped a surprisingly smooth forehead. Heavy, dark-framed glasses, a throwback to the seventies, momentarily distracted Anselm from the small eyes that appraised his habit with disgust. His cheeks sagged off the bone. His lips were delicate, almost feminine. He reminded Anselm of a strip club singer who'd fallen on good times. He went straight to the point, speaking so quickly that Frenzel's jolt at hearing German was overcome by the substance of the words.

'I represent someone who wants to make a claim on a policy opened in nineteen eighty-two. The papers are lost. The name is *Polana.*'

Frenzel became remarkably still, like a man on a rope finding his balance. Only he wasn't afraid of the fall; he was just weighing which way to tilt his stick. He clicked his mouse and the light dropped a shade darker.

'Can't say the name rings a bell.' He smirked, leaning back a fraction till his head touched the wall. To one side, a print of Monet's water lilies made a desperate bid for recognisable culture and homeliness. He was the man who could protect your house and garden. 'I can do a search if the payout reaches a neat grand.'

'Sorry?'

'A thousand Euros. Used notes.'

Anselm was still standing. There'd been no invitation to sit. He wavered in confusion, not knowing what to say. He'd been right about the catalogue but he'd given no thought to the prices.

'Tell you what,' said Frenzel, using his helpful voice, his face sunny with reassurance and competence. 'I'll see what I can find out. First, I'll need a copy of your passport.'

He called out and the secretary nipped in and nipped out, her legs moving quickly, her stride reduced.

'That'll be three hundred.'

'Sorry?'

'Euros. Three hundred. To do the search. There's a cash point round the corner. Where are you staying?'

Anselm told him and Frenzel's lips paled with a snigger. 'The *Hilton*.' He leaned back again. 'Well, well, Father. Give me three days in the tomb and maybe we can have lunch together.'

Anselm returned to the Hilton unnerved by Frenzel's swagger; the sneering confidence that he could still take someone's background to pieces. He was a fearless man. He knew how to protect himself. And his representatives were even now picking over Anselm's past, his associates, his movements. The activity alarmed him all the more because Anselm, seated at the large table in his bedroom, was about to do something very similar to Róża's narrative. Both he and Frenzel were aiming to flush out a private figure and strip it down. Uneasy, but holding on to the sheer difference in their motivations, Anselm turned once more to Róża's statement.

The document had been crafted to raise the dead and shatter the illusions of many.

It also had depth – that much had been demonstrated by his first three readings.

But there was another aspect that might be called a deeper depth: a second level that Róża herself had not intended to disclose – its existence evinced by that slip about the cherry tree and the strange craving to remain at the site of an execution. The text, like Róża herself, was not as simple as it appeared.

How then to expose what she would hide or had not seen?

There was a way.

At the Bar, when faced with a knotty witness statement, Anselm had often turned (furtively) to the techniques of German Biblical criticism: *Formgeschichte* and *Redaktionsgeschichte*. They were tools of deconstruction; in Anselm's hands, secret weapons during many a difficult trial. Secret because most of his colleagues would have laughed him out of court; weapons because they'd enabled Anselm to penetrate the most innocuous deposition, the results furnishing him with an unusual and frequently devastating cross-examination. Thinking of Frenzel scratching around his past, he now set to work on Róża's amended transcript.

It was a painstaking exercise. He classified the types of information presented. He examined the authorial viewpoint. He grouped similar phrases. He looked for recurrent motifs. He made some lists. He did some maths. Gradually certain features began to emerge forming another narrative behind the words, like a palimpsest: a wholly different picture, drawn by the hand of the subconscious. Between readings he went for a walk, trying to resist the suspicion that someone was following him. He looked around, finding ambiguity at every corner. Every now and then he remembered that

John had told Róża the truth about his mother and the cut opened wide again.

The job complete, he joined Sebastian for tripe and vodka. After the plates had been cleared, Sebastian produced an envelope containing the 'search fee' and the one thousand Euro 'payout', funds obtained – after some special pleading – from the IPN investigation budget. Displaying the controlled agitation of the hunter, Sebastian barely spoke. His hands shifted restlessly. There was excitement, too, because he knew that Brack was ignorant of their approach. At one p.m. on the third day the phone rang in Anselm's bedroom.

'Your guest is in the dining room,' said Krystyna, the cheery girl at reception.

CHAPTER 23

The ambience was plush; the seats an ivory white; the carpet a fractured pattern of different red and black squares. Frenzel had booked a table in a corner. Dressed in a grey pinstripe with a Burberry check tie, he'd already drunk half a glass of champagne and was busy trying to prise apart an oyster. Scowling contentment, he dragged the knife along the sealed lips, feeling his way towards a weakness.

'First class, Father,' he said, as it snapped open. 'The taste of the sea. Nothing like it. Do you get these at Larkwood? No matter, I'm sure you dine well when you're not sucking blood, and why not, hey?'

Anselm sat down and Frenzel paused, his eyes rigid and severe, as if some social sin had taken place. Anselm passed over the envelope and Frenzel's mouth started working again. He slipped the money inside his jacket pocket and began talking.

'I can't remember everything,' he said, pulling the bottle out of its cooler. 'I had other fish to fry and Brack, well, he kept things to himself. This

223

was his case. Only case he cared about. My view? I thought it was chicken shit.'

He dabbed his lips on the white towel and hung it back over the bottle.

'He wanted the Shoemaker. He'd been after him since . . . God knows when. You don't mind the theological references, do you, Father? Sure you don't. Well, he'd had an agent in place since fifty-two. A wimp named Kolba. Edward. Date of birth, third of August nineteen twenty-three. Don't write anything down –' he pointed with his oyster knife at Anselm's hand as it moved towards his pocket; his eyes were unseeing and severe again – 'that's not meant to happen in confession, is it? Maybe that's what you get up to, when you're all boxed up in the dark. I wouldn't be surprised. But not here.' He snatched an oyster off the ice bed. He locked his thumb against the shell and twisted the blade in a crack. 'He'd come on board to get his wife out of custody. Stupid idiot. They'd have let her out if he'd waited. But that's love for you. Said he'd keep an eye on Mojeska – the slut, not the hubby. Pavel. You don't want the date of birth. He'd been seen to by the . . . shall we say, the properly constituted organs of state security. Not sure he had one of you lot in his final moments. Gray's Inn, wasn't it? Roddy Kemble's Chambers? Anyway, he could've done with a lawyer and a priest. But there you go, times change. We didn't need 'em back then. Where was I?'

Anselm didn't reply. He didn't even touch the stiff white tablecloth for fear of having some kind of connection to this man. Frenzel was sucking the juice from the shell, holding it like a spoon at an English tea party. He smiled, happily distracted, 'The taste of the sea. Nothing like it.' Anselm flinched. This pantomime of life's pleasures, held in the palm of one strong hand, wasn't the only salt that Frenzel savoured. It was power. Even though the Wall had come down, he still licked his fingers, knowing he could point at anyone and have their life delivered on a plate. His mocking eyes flicked over Anselm as if he hadn't been worth a single phone call – except that it was good fare, afterwards, to show your biceps to the weak. Part of the saltiness was other people's fear. That, too, had the taste of the sea.

'FELIKS was next to useless,' he resumed, pouting at his glass. 'According to the monthly reports he cried every time he clocked in. Imagine that. A grown man. Ponce.

'Wanted out. Said Mojeska did nothing but work and pray – she was your sort, you know, diligent and reflective – that she had no dealings with anyone, blah, blah. No mention of the Shoemaker. He produced nothing in over fifteen years.

'We had to put the screws on him in sixty-eight. The son, Bernard, date of birth second of May forty-six, was running amok. Ungrateful swine. We educated that little runt. But he stood up for Kołakowski. To keep him in at his books Daddy

225

agreed to watch a childhood friend of Mojeska's, a Zionist, Samovitz, Magda, date of birth—'

Anselm closed his ears, mind and eyes. He'd met some seriously bad men in his life – calculated murderers, blackmailers, pimps and thieves – but there was something unique about this boor slurping salt water from a shell: he spoke with authority; the confidence and carelessness of someone once backed by a system. Instinctively, Anselm jolted back his chair.

'You're not off, are you? I haven't finished yet.' He sipped his champagne and, tilting his head, halted naturally, as if he'd touched the wall in his office. 'After a year or so the Jew cleared off of her own accord . . . well, to be fair, we'd kicked her out of a hospital job. Surgeon. Ears, nose, throat. Anyway, the kid went too far. Started chucking stones in the street, I suppose. I don't know. Don't care. He didn't know which side his bread was buttered. He'd hooked up with other Jews and pro-Zionists who hadn't seen the light – not your Light, Father, ours, the light put on this land after years of toil and sacrifice and dedicated service to raise something permanent out of the darkness, something *enduring* . . .' He half-smiled, mocking his own remembered passion; puzzled perhaps that he'd cared that much. Lost love, he seemed to say, raising his glass, nothing quite like it. The tide comes in, the time goes out. That taste of the sea again. Wonderful.

Frenzel had joined the Shoemaker bandwagon

in eighty-two when a special unit was set up with the Stasi to stamp out underground printing. German speakers only need apply. He'd been assigned to Brack, effectively being second in command and taking all the noise from the Germans. He didn't like Germans. Then or now. He'd only learned the language because his stepfather had beaten it into him. He didn't like the English, or, no offence, the French . . . anyway, first off, Brack told him the Shoemaker had turned up again. *Freedom and Independence* had appeared, first with lists of names, of terrorists and mob leaders, extremists . . . and then there'd been articles about tomorrow. When – listen to this – there'd be justice, rule of law, fairness. What a bloody joke. Frenzel refilled his glass and held up the bottle to check how much was left.

'Brack was obsessed with the Shoemaker. You'd have thought he *mattered*. Christ – oops, sorry – all he had was words. Nothing else. We had the sticks and stones. Who read the thing anyway? Who cared about ideas? Don't get me wrong, if I'd caught him I'd've put him and Mojeska against the wall and pulled the trigger myself, the point is, there were bigger fish in the sea. Big ones with teeth. But Brack wanted him, and he knew Mojeska was the way to his door.

'So Frenzel went to have a chat with FELIKS. He was worse than useless. More tears and handwringing. Is there anything more pitiful than a man who pities himself? The country was falling apart. They'd even dragged school kids on to the streets, and here was this selfish, spineless piece of . . . I won't say it, Father. He gave us weekly reports on his wife and the daughter-in-law but there was no meat on the bone. We had him over a barrel, of course. The bolshy son was where he should've been since the sixties – locked up. He'd just become a father himself and the granddad, well, he was beside himself.

'But we still got nothing.' He held his breath and seemed to lose colour round his loose cheeks, but seconds later he let out a low belch and sighed relief. '*Rien* – your mother was French, wasn't she? – just a last sighting before Mojeska vanished. She walked out of the door after the birth of the child. A couple of weeks later, the rag appeared.'

From a tangent, Anselm noticed that there were no other diners near them; that the waiter didn't check on his customers; that Frenzel's power reached right up to Anselm's feet. Nothing had changed in his world, just the furniture. It was plush, now. He was very much at ease. He'd never had it so good. Unable to bear the man's presence any more, Anselm found his voice. He wanted out.

'Could you just confirm that Edward Kolba was the only informer? That he brought about Róża Mojeska's arrest in November nineteen eighty-two?'

Frenzel didn't seem to have heard. There was no response. He'd turned the champagne bottle upside and down and was pretending to wring its neck, squeezing out the remaining drops. One by one, they fell into his glass.

'You know, my memory's beginning to fade,' he moaned, reading the label, head back to angle his glasses on to the tiny writing. 'Must be my age. You begin to forget the good times. Fact is, I didn't only work for Brack. I helped out against you lot.'

Anselm didn't allow a trace of interest or confusion to flicker on his face. And there was nothing wrong with Frenzel's memory. Shortly, he'd be asking for more money.

'I said you lot. Department Four. The Church. We had a file on every one of you. Got a lot of inside help, too, thank you very much. And not always unwilling. But that's another story.' His sneer moved like a wave as his tongue slid beneath his upper lip. 'But if you want my opinion on how things stood before I moved to sunnier climes, I'd have said FELIKS wasn't your man. I'm sure he'd have told us how to get Mojeska if he knew, but the bitch wasn't stupid. She kept away from everyone she knew. You've got to keep things *simple*. Don't they teach you that when you're learning about sin and the sinner? Back then, I'd have put my money on the son. The runt we educated. He hadn't even seen his child. He was locked up. If anyone could get to Mojeska, it would have been Bernard but –' he held up splayed fingers, admitting the limitations of his humble view – 'I was a busy boy with lots of things to do. And you can't always trust your memory, do you know what I mean?'

Looking over Anselm's shoulder Frenzel made a nod. Dabbing his lips with his serviette, he became confidential. 'You know, Brack was never . . . *swój człowiek*, one of us. I even wondered if he fancied Mojeska. It happens, you know. Sleeping with the enemy. Nothing like it. Forbidden Fruit. It tastes good. You should know that. And Brack's banging on about the Shoemaker just didn't add up. Sure we all believed in socialism, but come on, get a life. He was too . . . involved.'

He drew out the last word as if he were trying to remember its flavour. Shaking his head, he pointed at Anselm. The waiter had emerged and come to Anselm's side, one hand behind his back. He placed a large plate on the table.

'*Pierogi*,' said Frenzel, waving away the young man. 'Dumplings. A speciality of the chef. I was going to eat them myself but, frankly, I'm bored.' He eyed Anselm from afar, perhaps with a few of those files in mind. 'You're not good company. You don't say anything. You sit there thinking you're better than me . . .' He held himself in check, his bottom jaw moving lazily. He stood up and dropped his napkin on his plate. With big hands, he tucked his shirt back into his trousers and hitched his groin. Anselm hadn't noticed, but he was a thick-set man, with heavy, lumbering movements. 'To find out who pulled in Mojeska, you'd have to look at the file on *Polana*. I understand the payout on that baby is two and a half grand. Used notes. Worth every centime to a man like you, I'd say. Think about it and keep a pen and paper by the phone.' He nodded assurance and competence. 'Thanks for the lunch, priest.'

Anselm slowly worked his way through the *pierogi*, drinking lots of water, unable to forget the creamed hair, the imposing glasses, the delicate lips. Having signed for the bill, he went to his room and was violently sick.

CHAPTER 24

IPN/RM/13129/2010
EDITED TRANSCRIPT OF A STATEMENT
MADE BY RÓŻA MOJESKA

1h.22
Although I'd only met him once – and even then
only for a few minutes – I had enormous respect
for Father Nicodem. If I include my next few
meetings, I've only known him – to this day – for
about two hours. And yet he remains immensely
important to me. It explains something about the
nature of friendship and loyalty.

This was the man my husband had trusted
implicitly. And I did, too. He was our link to a
voice we'd only heard, someone we'd never seen
– the Shoemaker. All we had were his words.
Whoever he might have been – and I still don't
know, and don't want to know – what he said was
more important than who he was. His identity, if
revealed, would have been a distraction, for in the
great struggle for truth, personalities don't matter.
It was his words that kept hope alive, spoke
honestly at a time of lies, said what you thought

but couldn't or dare not say, reduced the big ideas to phrases you could easily understand. He educated, cajoled, amused . . . revealed. His words were free. They flew round Warsaw. They gave you a taste of freedom that was within reach . . . beginning inside yourself.

We were pebbles on the path to his door, whereas Father Nicodem . . . he was the Threshold. So he bore a terrible responsibility. It was etched into his face. On those two occasions when we met – in 1951 and 1982 – his cheeks and neck were covered in cuts from a razor. I'm sure it was from the strain, from a shaking hand. Some of them were quite large and I often wondered why he didn't give up trying to keep still and grow a beard.

1h.32

When Father Nicodem opened the door it was as though he'd seen Brack. I had a fright of my own. He'd changed . . . almost beyond recognition. His eyes were heavy, pulling his head between his shoulder blades. He was in his late sixties by then, his hair a shocking white, as if he'd seen unmentionable things. A small detail comes to mind, in contrast to his face. His nails. They were beautifully clean and filed. They gave away his delicacy and sensitivity. They told you that he'd handle your soul with care.

1h.36

I asked him if the Shoemaker was still alive. He

said, 'Yes'. I asked why he'd said nothing since 1951. Father Nicodem said, 'He'd been broken.' By what? 'The death of two Friends.' He didn't have to say any more. We understood one another. But he wasn't ready for what followed. I told him the Shoemaker had to speak again and that I would spread his words. 'Remember, I'm the sleeper. I've come back to wake the dead.' He waved his arms around as if trying to warn a train that there were children on the line, but I told him he had no choice. He *had* to go back to the Shoemaker. He was to tell him that I, the widow, demanded it. Not just for the sake of those two Friends but for a child who'd just been born and left without a name. Father Nicodem was pacing up and down the room, saying, 'No', and that's when I recognised an appalling truth about myself. I'd done what he was doing for thirty years. My life since fifty-two had been one long walk, head down, murmuring 'No'. But there comes a time when you have to say, 'Yes'. When life becomes a 'Yes', whatever the cost might be. When we have to take the word back from those who control what will and what will not happen. This was *my* choice, *my* decision. Not Pavel's. But I needed Father Nicodem's, and the Shoemaker's. We all had to stand together once more and say, 'Stop, enough.' We had to say 'Yes' to a future of our choosing, and to put words out there to wake the dead . . . to shatter the illusions that make oppression acceptable.

I told Father Nicodem that the first edition of *Freedom and Independence* would need to be ready within two weeks. He thought for a long, tortured time and then gave me the key to his back yard.

1h.44

Pavel had told me how to set up the Friends – how to keep them separate in order to keep them together. He'd told me who to contact for paper and ink. I didn't even know if these old Friends were still alive or if they were still willing or in a position to help. But that's what happens with a 'Yes'. You have to work everything out afterwards. It's only with a 'No' that all the problems have been lined up beforehand.

1h.52

As the hub of the wheel, my job was to hold the spokes, keeping them apart. I went first to Barbara and Lidia, women the SB would never notice; women who'd never thought they could fight back. I went to Mateusz, Bernard's friend, who'd had his chance but fluffed it. The system was simple. We used prams. I collected the print run wrapped in parcels from a dustbin in Father Nicodem's back yard. Over two or three days, trip after trip, I brought them to Barbara and Lidia who then trundled round Warsaw posting, dropping and giving. In time, as the circulation grew, and unknown to each other, they organised distribution teams. How they did it, I don't know – any more than I knew who printed the paper. Sometimes I'd pick up my parcels and find an envelope with a shopping list and money. With the funds I'd go back to those old Friends who still had their ways and means, not to mention their children with minds of their own. The materials – paper and ink – would be delivered to me at a playground, a hotel, a station – it varied – and I'd drop them in Father Nicodem's dustbin. It was magnificent. We were beating the tanks and armoured personnel carriers with a convoy of prams.

1h.59
Mateusz found safe-house lodgings and I moved every two weeks, borrowing clothes and shoes along the way. Glasses, too, and hats. I never looked the same; I was never in the same place long enough for Brack to catch me. I paid my way by housework and cooking. I became, for the first time since leaving Mokotów, content.

CHAPTER 25

After a long, scalding shower Anselm placed a pen and paper by the phone (as instructed) and then rang Sebastian to outline the contours of Marek Frenzel's monologue. He left out those remarks demonstrating limited affection for the Church because they were broadly conventional – he'd read far worse in the English press – but he recited the rest, summoning again the man's devouring presence. They agreed to meet that evening in the lobby bar, where, given the demand for more money, they might consider their options. With the remainder of the afternoon free, Anselm decided to make a 'site-visit' to the crime scene central to what had become a second, unofficial enquiry: the reason behind a mysterious attack on the national archives.

Outside it was sunny with a fresh breeze. The hint of a cold evening was in the air. It tugged at Anselm's hair and cleared his mind. And the first insight to crash home was that the luxurious showers of the Warsaw Hilton didn't work. There'd been lots of levers, high pressure and free, heavily scented shampoo, but their combined force had failed to shift the dirt beneath Anselm's skin. The Prior had seen this coming. He'd warned him about Brack's world. He'd said it was a dangerous place. Anselm was reminded of those *big* mistakes in life where all you can do is accept what's happened, hoping the years to come will remove the dreadful sense of failure. Anselm's meeting with Frenzel belonged in the same camp, even though he'd had no choice but to sit near him and feel the cold, lap-lapping of xenophobia, anti-Semitism, and racism, that hint of homophobia showing what else he'd discover if he stayed in the mud much longer. The man was a swamp and Anselm had only just about managed to crawl to the bank. But he'd still failed. Before leaving he should have tipped the bucket of shells over Frenzel's head.

The second insight to crash home – with the force of a motorway pile-up – was that Frenzel had confirmed an important element in Anselm's deconstruction of Róża's statement. They'd agreed about something. It was like a pact in hell. They were, in a limited sense, companions in thought. Crossing the road as if to escape the consuming fire, Anselm let his mind run over the remaining, untarnished conclusions.

The single most important characteristic in Róża's narrative – the pattern behind the words – was the primacy of children. They determined her engagement with events (nonexistent, save and except for the fall of 'sparrows' and 'The Blood of Children'). They established her viewpoint (exclusively focused on the growth of Bernard from boy to man). They coloured her phraseology ('children on the line'). They ordered her priorities and interests, sometimes to an absurd degree (Helena's pregnancy over a potential Russian invasion). They determined her moment of action (a traumatic home birth), who acted (initially the childless) as well as the manner of their acting (the use of prams). There were other instances, all springing from this fundamental authorial orientation. In terms of Róża's vocabulary 'child' or 'children' occurred 16 times, 'boy' 7 times, 'girl' twice, and 'son' once.

Children. They kept turning up like boils on Job's back. Why?

Anselm was cautious in his judgement. The text beneath the text, the deeper depth, evidently disclosed a primitive yearning; an obsession. For an instant, Anselm was transported to a smoky basement near Finsbury Park.

He'd fallen silent once again, leaving John to twiddle his thumbs. The guest singer had just finished a soul tearing rendition of a Billie Holiday number, a lament about unrestrained murder in the south. To hear it more than once, Anselm followed her from club to club. After each performance he couldn't speak. John presumed it was on account of the singer and not the song.

'You're obsessed,' he declared.

'I'm not.'

'Trust me. All obsessions stem from unfulfilled longing.'

'Do they?'

'Yep. Without treatment, you turn really boring and fat and sad.'

'Is this the voice of experience?'

'It is. And you, my friend, have turned. You've curdled.'

Anselm woke to the sounds and sights around him. The singer had gone, leaving behind the echo of 'Strange Fruit', that Marseillaise of the oppressed. Disorientated, he looked to his left. He'd reached a vast building, an improbable hybrid of the Empire State Building and the Vatican. A glance at John's guidebook told him this was the Palace of Culture and Science, a 40-million brick monument to 'the inventive spirit and social progress' donated by the one-time Soviet overlord. Statues with stern expressions gazed down from the entrance facade. Like Billie they didn't look too pleased with how things had turned out.

'Nor do you, Róża,' muttered Anselm, pressing on.

To use John's expression, she'd 'turned'. A deep sadness lay beneath her words. It had soaked into the paper of her statement, persuading Anselm that if Róża was to be *restored*, deeply and *comprehensively*, then she'd need more than a colour picture of Otto Brack in a prison cell. She'd need to deal with this underlying longing linked to children: their absence, caused by the brutal murder of her husband. Which brought Anselm face to face with his own mission, and its importance: to find the informer and persuade them to co-operate with an abused and abandoned widow. There was nothing left for Róża to hope for. Anselm instantly rehearsed the final part of his telephone conversation with Sebastian. It had not gone smoothly.

'Frenzel doesn't think FELIKS was the informer.'

'Who, then?'

'Bernard, his son.'

'If the cap fits, make him wear it.'

There'd been a note of impatience in his voice. Sebastian hadn't quite chimed with Anselm's disgust at the man who loved the taste of the sea.

'Easier said than done,' Anselm had replied. 'If Bernard handed over Róża in a bid to get out of prison, the whole truth would have to come out: that Edward had made the same move, years back, to save Bernard's education. It's not a pretty picture. I doubt if Bernard would look at it for long . . . not after he sees the blood drain from his mother's face.'

'That's not your problem.'

'Yes, it is. Because Brack made it Róża's problem.'

Sebastian's replies had been quick and mechanical, like the fall of a guillotine blade. He didn't seem to realise that Róża would have to be there for any public execution of Bernard: she'd have to stand with the baying crowd.

It was an eventuality that would almost certainly come to pass. This was the unhappy point at which Anselm and Frenzel had found an uncomfortable agreement. If Róża's statement was meant to guide John to the door of the informer – and it was – then the use of names would be an important feature. Numerically, Father Nicodem Kaminsky was top of the list with 20 references, but he could be excluded from suspicion because of his direct link to the Shoemaker. It was Bernard who clocked in next with 14. Edward staggered home with a mere five. All the signs suggested that the rebel student who'd once defended Professor Kołakowski had switched sides when the struggle turned personal. He'd kept his place in Solidarity but he'd changed irrevocably: he'd become Brack's man, for the love of a child born into a crisis.

Anselm shelved his deliberations. He'd arrived at the crime scene.

Mokotów prison had all the demoralising features that characterise any place of detention: high surrounding walls, the dull brick curiously hard on the eye; stolid buildings set back with narrow, dark windows; a heavy sense of compressed humanity; the embodiment of architectural aggression. It was all fancy, of course, but Anselm had the impression that birds didn't fly over the leaden airspace.

As site-visits go, Anselm wasn't expecting to discover much. But buildings speak. They, too, have a memory, and he wanted to listen to the echoes of Róża's time. He began by examining the species of trees that flanked the perimeter walls, all the while turning to check the rows of windows sufficiently elevated to afford a view on to any foliage. After half an hour he found himself back at the main entrance, a large blue gate almost as high as the wall of yellow bricks. There'd been no cherry trees. Not one.

Suddenly the low buzz of an electric surge came from the gate's lock mechanism. The iron clanged and scraped. Moments later a straggling group of relatives left the premises. They were mainly women, several pushing a pram or holding a boy or girl by the hand. Apart from one or two joking teenagers, their facial expressions wore shades of darkness, the tell-tale hollows of dejection. Anselm had arrived in time to catch the end of visiting time, the departure of innocents torn apart by the crimes of someone they loved.

He stepped off the pavement to make some room, but a woman lunged towards him, someone whose age and appearance fell somewhere between the laughing youngsters and the gloomier adults. Her skin was pocked and smudged with make-up. She wore tight stone-washed jeans and white, dirty trainers. The long, red tongue on a Rolling Stones T-shirt seemed to stick out beyond the open, padded jacket. She grabbed Anselm's arms, her eyes drawn to his habit. For a moment he thought he was back at Wormwood Scrubs, or any of the other prisons where he'd bumped into the people who stuck by his clients. The young woman spoke quickly, shoulders hunched, one hand jabbing at the monolith behind her, as if she hoped to punch a hole in the State's defences. She began to cry, tattooed fingers tidying her hair as if improving her appearance might sway Anselm's mind. What did she want? An advocate? Prayers? A miracle?

'I'm sorry,' murmured Anselm. 'I don't understand . . . I'm a stranger . . . I'm just passing by.'

On hearing his voice, realising that he didn't speak her language, she suddenly stopped crying. Her emotions were sucked back inwards. A numb, glazed appearance displaced the turbulence. Looking through Anselm, she pushed past him on to the street and wandered aimlessly away.

Anselm looked down and saw that his hands were shaking. Powerlessness doesn't erase a sense of responsibility, and he felt he owed something to the woman whose cries had fallen on ears attuned to desperation but not meaning. She'd given him something important, even if he didn't recognise it. In a most dramatic and disturbing way, she was, for him, Róża Mojeska. The past had returned to the present, and Anselm had been there to see her walk away from Otto Brack. He'd seen all the women walk out of all the prisons in the world.

At that very moment, Anselm received a sort of kick to the stomach. Deconstructive insights aside, he at last understood why he'd found something incongruous with Róża's statement. It was obvious, really.

CHAPTER 26

The rich crimson carpet of the lobby bar reminded Anselm of the fractured pattern in the restaurant, making him wonder if Frenzel was nearby, listening while he licked his fingers. The interior design people had plumped heavily for variants of red. Scarlet fixtures, ruby lights, cherry napkins. The choice seemed incongruous. Anselm would've picked green. Something to do with spring. Outside the evening sky was a tender, pale orange, visible through vast glass panelling.

Before turning to the question of money raised by Frenzel, Anselm decided to resume his last conversation with Sebastian. The driven lawyer had listened on the phone to Anselm's anger and disgust with the former SB officer, but there'd been too many moments of silence on the line and too few return shots of indignation. Anselm had waited, bracing himself, but the ball had simply died on the other side of the net. He wanted to know why. He sensed a rift between them.

'Strange man, Frenzel,' began Anselm, pouring

fizzy water into two glasses, making sure the distribution was fair.

'Yes.'

'Can't imagine how his mind works.'

'No.'

'I'm not sure I want to.'

'No.'

'But I'm still intrigued.'

'I'm not.'

'Really?'

'No.'

'What about the dark places? Don't you want to understand why he does what he does?'

'No.'

Dressed in tatty jeans, split trainers and an expensive pink shirt, Sebastian looked as if he owned the place and was thinking of selling. He sat, elbow on the chair rest, his hand locked in his tousled black hair. Anselm advanced a little further.

'You surprise me. Maybe it's just a monk's view on to the mental engine, but I wouldn't mind a quick look beneath the bodywork to see the state of his shock-absorbers.' Anselm watched the irritation grow on Sebastian's face. The lawyer reached for his glass as if he didn't like water.

'He handled people's lives as if they were tools in a drawer,' resumed Anselm, carelessly. 'He blunted them, one by one, and then threw them away. Even now he'd pick up some chipped and broken file if he needed it to force open a window.'

'But he got results.'

'Pardon?'

Anselm had arrived at the fault line between them. He played out the surprise, giving Sebastian room to show where he was standing and why.

'What do you mean, results?'

'He found out what he needed to know. He opened windows. He got inside without having to kick down the front door. The alarm didn't go off. The kids were left sleeping upstairs.'

'But at what cost?'

'I suppose that depends on who's paying and what they got in return.'

Anselm's bemusement was genuine. He waited for enlightenment, sipping his water.

'We, too, need to apply some leverage,' continued Sebastian, almost harshly. 'Maybe quite a lot. Maybe to the point of damaging the house . . . waking up not just the kids but the neighbours on all sides.'

'You mean *I* have to apply some leverage.'

'If it fell to me, I'd pull with both hands But Róża didn't ask for my help.'

'Doesn't that tell you something?'

'Like what?'

'That she wants things done differently. That she doesn't want us to behave like *them*.'

Sebastian put down his glass, the water untasted. He became politely firm, repressing impatience like a teacher tasked with instructing a dim fee-paying pupil whose parents he couldn't afford to upset. He raised his hands as if he were holding out the bleeding obvious.

'Look, Róża has given us . . . you . . . a document designed to lead you to the door of an informer. She thinks a quiet chat is all that it'll take . . . a few well chosen words out of everyone's earshot. She wants the informer to take responsibility for what they've done . . . and it's crazy. What she doesn't understand is this: the informer isn't going to admit *anything*, even if we ask him nicely. You know, Father, blunted tools aren't what they once were. There's no longer any point in handling them carefully.'

'I don't believe you mean that.'

'In these circumstances, with this individual, I do.'

'It isn't what Róża wants.'

'It's what Róża needs.' Sebastian appraised Anselm as if he, too, was eyeing up a tool for the job. 'For some reason, she pities them. You don't have to. She needs *you* to act differently. She needs *you* to be merciless. Look –' the teacher emerged again, smiling woodenly, trying to wipe up the spilled impatience – 'we're not trying to understand the human condition, or work out why someone ticks in the way that they do, we're trying to bring Otto Brack to court. And to do that we need the informer to play ball – this time for us. Subject to our rules and timekeeping.'

'And so we become like Frenzel, after all?'

'Yes.'

'Then we lose what sets us apart.'

'No, we don't. We become like them for the right

reason. In the end, the world we're fighting for is better than the one they kick-started in the torture chambers. It's as simple as that. And if there's a risk of getting dirty hands, well, frankly, there's no other way. This is the nasty business of law enforcement.'

As opposed to the abstract pastures of monastic contemplation. Sebastian had the grace to keep that conclusion to himself, but Anselm now fully understood the irritation he'd detected on the telephone. And he wasn't enjoying the elucidation, the substance of which was that the mumbling monk might be swayed to compassion by the calamity of human frailty; that the former barrister, softened by his prayers, would neglect to confront FELIKS, or whoever, with the degree of animosity required to secure his co-operation.

Sebastian hadn't finished.

'Whatever the pressures, these low-life agent runners and their collaborators played *God* with people's lives for a benefit,' he said, introducing an analogy that might reach Anselm. He'd seen the blank face, not sure if it was scruple or persisting incomprehension. 'The runners got *information*. The collabos? They've had their passport, their reprieve, their promotion. Now they have to pay the people they robbed. We want our information.' He sighed, still not convinced that Anselm was ready for the exam. 'Do you really think that an appeal to conscience is enough? That remorse will come so cheaply, so easily? Don't you realise, this informer, whoever it is . . . he's already watched Róża grow old? He's eaten at the same table and said *nothing*. He's waiting for her to die.' Sebastian sat back, dragging a hand through his hair. 'When she's gone, they're free. You see, Father, whoever it is, and whatever goes through their clouded mind when they drift off to sleep, they're not that different to Brack. He's waiting too.'

Anselm had taken a mental and judicious step backwards – it was his way of managing rising anger. He considered himself an old hand when it came to handling a witness. He knew when to take the gloves off and experience had taught him that the occasion rarely, if ever arose, because there's nothing quite so effective as kindness and courtesy. And Anselm had never come across a case where, in the end, the deeper human question – the how and why of the ticking – hadn't been a matter of decisive importance, all the more so when it wasn't evident on the face of the papers.

But having stepped backwards, he'd gained a sudden perspective on something he hadn't noticed, and it calmed his irritation: Sebastian's altogether *personal* engagement in the hunt for justice. All at once, Róża appeared less the victim and more the means of his way of getting to Brack. He examined the lawyer's troubled features, seeing the strain in a subtly different light.

'I'll bear all that in mind,' he said, magnanimously.

'Thanks. I hope you don't mind me being so direct.'

'Not at all.'

'Once we get the name from the file, you'll have to lean on the informer.'

'Indeed.'

'Hard.'

'Absolutely. Right from the shoulder.' He frowned, innocently mystified. 'I appreciate that material considerations aren't my *forte*, but aren't you forgetting something? Frenzel wants more money. Rather a lot, in fact.'

'I've asked for a shoebox to be lodged in the hotel safe.' Sebastian reached for his glass of water but thought better of it. 'You'll find ten grand inside. He'll keep holding back what we want, raising the price along the way, dragging out the premiums. Let him have his day. Give him what he wants. As we used to say, ours is the spring. Now, can I offer you something stronger than water? *Zubrówka.* Bison Grass. Róża drinks it every Sunday.'

Anselm didn't notice the approach of the beast, so to speak, until an hour or so later. It came from behind, its hooves in slippers, and whacked him on the back of the knees, just as he stood up to shake Sebastian's hand. Smiling inanely, he shambled to the lift, prepared to catch his head just in case it rolled off his neck. Lying in the dark of his bedroom he pondered the one part of Sebastian's argument that had roused no anger. Instead, it had disturbed him: the recognition that people who set out to clean up a mess always end up dirty. It was, indeed, bleeding obvious. There was no escape, even for the kind and courteous. John had said something similar: in the search for the truth, sometimes you had put your hand in the sewer. Maybe Sebastian and the Prior were right after all: Anselm hadn't been trained for this, either at the Bar or at Larkwood. He wasn't entering a courtroom or the confessional, he was crawling behind a skirting board . . . perhaps he'd have to learn some new tricks, even from a rat like Marek Fre—

The phone rang, jolting Anselm upright. He turned on the light, squinting and blinded.

'Do you have the funds?' came a woman's trembling voice in heavily accented German.

'Yes.'

'Then present yourself at the following hotel . . .'

Anselm swung out of bed, abruptly sober, and jotted down the details using the pen and paper ready to hand.

'Make a booking for room forty-three.'

'What's your name?'

'I will arrive at eight p.m.'

'Your name?'

'You will come alone. Sebastian Voight stays behind.'

'Who are you?'

'I have no name. I just have what you're looking for.'

The line cut dead. A sort of echo rang in Anselm's mind, carrying that alarming confession: 'I have no name'. He listened for a long time, discerning more fear than authority, inexperience rather than the familiar exercise of low trade. Who was she? Frenzel had almost certainly been there in the background, feet up, picking his teeth, unrelenting.

CHAPTER 27

IPN/RM/13129/2010
EDITED TRANSCRIPT OF A STATEMENT
MADE BY RÓŻA MOJESKA

2h.04
The Shoemaker had not lost his eloquence. He
spoke like one released from a long and imposed
confinement. An outpouring of fresh ideas filled
the pages of *Freedom and Independence*, born from
having watched events in silence and from having
reflected deeply upon them. He wrote simply,
speaking directly to the crisis of the times. It was
his gift . . . to choose words and order them in
such a way as to light a fire in winter. He wrote
about the past as if it was ours and the future as
if it had already arrived. It was the rhymes and
rhythms of independence; a meter first heard
during the Nazi Occupation. The Shoemaker was
back. And I felt proud; he'd only spoken because
I asked him to. I'd set him free to speak again.

2h.33
His words travelled further than I imagined. An

English journalist from the BBC sent a message from a café along the distribution chain. It reached Barbara, who told me. John Fielding he was called. He wanted to meet the Shoemaker. Mateusz delivered my reply: he was to wear his overcoat like a cloak and wait at the grave of Prus. I tailed him from the entrance of the cemetery . . . but he didn't go straight to where he'd been directed. He went first to another grave, lingered there a while, and then made his way to the meeting point. I lingered, too, and then joined him.

2h.39

He was writing a number of articles on the underground media entitled 'Lives Lived in Secret for the Truth' and wanted a representative for print, radio and film. To that end he hoped to interview the Shoemaker. He had to make do with me, and I spelled out his ideas. The piece, derived from several interviews, appeared under a pseudonym in the *Observer* but then got reported on all over the place . . . *Le Figaro*, *The Washington Post*, *Die Welt*. *Voice of America* even did a broadcast on his thinking, sending his words right back to Warsaw.

While dealing with my life lived in secret, we naturally dealt with his. In time he told me about his mother's death when he was a child, of his father's swift remarriage. How his family had never even mentioned her name. I refer to it now because this was his reason for coming to Warsaw. Like all of the Friends, he had a personal story that was tied up with the greater struggle.

2h.41
The 'Lives Lived in Secret' series brought him into contact with a journalist involved in visual media. An article on how film-makers steered between the truth and the censor duly appeared in the *Observer*, exciting a similarly international reaction.

2h.56
John couldn't speak of her without blushing and he'd clam up if I asked any questions. A comical ritual soon fell into place: he would ask about the Shoemaker, and I would ask about the film-maker. He shoved me, I shoved him.

3h.34
Throughout 1982, those who'd been interned were being gradually released. And as they came home, I began to wonder if *Freedom and Independence* had done its job. The debate about the future had been taken up in numerous other publications and, as Mr Lasky used to say, once you've been heard there's no point in repeating yourself. The Shoemaker's contribution had been made. Every time I saw John he'd ask to meet him and I'd say no. But I increasingly asked myself, 'Why not?' Didn't our 'Yes' involve a move from secrecy to openness? Pavel had said 'Yes' too soon, that's all.

And that act of trust was part of the meaning of his death . . . it rang out as a summons, not a warning.

3h.41

Mateusz didn't tell me where we were going. He just picked me up and drove me to the Łazienki Park. After all the usual checks he brought me to a bench. Five minutes later a man pushing a pram sat beside me. I looked at the baby and turned to the father . . . he was grey and thin and tired, his cheeks hollowed. It was Bernard. They'd let him out. The boy in the pram was Tomasz, born the day I'd gone back to Father Nicodem.

3h.51

Bernard wanted to meet the Shoemaker. He'd read back copies obtained by his father and he wanted to get involved. He, too, had ideas that he wanted to share; and he knew others whose thinking on the crisis deserved a wider audience than a crowded basement. The war on ideas could never have been more important, he said, because we were winning.

Was I angry with Mateusz for setting up a meeting without my initiative? I don't know, I just looked at the child's fingers gripping the edge of his blanket, the clipped nails. Something inside me snapped.

4h.05

Father Nicodem opened the door and swore.

Come to think of it, he swore each time I'd met him. It was a sort of surprised greeting.

I told him *Freedom and Independence* should finish with the next edition, and that the ensuing silence would serve to amplify and preserve everything that had been said beforehand. Oddly enough (he said) the Shoemaker had come to the same conclusion. Our minds had been running along similar lines. I was relieved. A moment of shared calm opened between myself and Father Nicodem. We'd travelled a very long journey, without the chance to talk along the way. I was the first to speak. I said that before going home I wanted to meet the Shoemaker. That I had an idea for the future.

You'd have thought a train had come through the garden wall. Father Nicodem was on his feet, jabbering, 'No, no, no, no, no.'

The conversation, far from calm, went something like this:

'Our time is over,' I said. 'Something new has to take our place.'

'Like what?'

'A new publication run by new people running things in a different way.'

'Different?'

'Yes, relying on trust rather than fear.'

'Trust?'

You'd have thought it was a dirty word. He was standing over me, looking down as if I was insane. But he was old school, trusting to an absolute minimum. As a system, it had worked well enough, but we had to move forward, now, and leave all that behind.

'I've learned that whoever trusts the most is the most free,' I said. 'We have to live as normally as possible: that's how we fight *them*. We live ordinary lives, giving fear the smallest room in the house.'

'That's how you get caught,' he shouted. 'Fear is your friend, Róża. Give it the double bed and sleep on the floor.'

'Not any longer.'

I told him that there was a new generation of activists ready to speak – friends whose strength came from open, shared risk. All they required was an outlet for their ideas. They were married. They had children. They didn't want to fight as if they were on their own. And they were all children of the Shoemaker. They wanted to meet him.

'He is a hugely symbolic figure,' I said.

'A hidden one.'

'I know, but before falling silent, he has one last task . . . to hand on the responsibility for tomorrow. To tell them that his day is over, and theirs begins . . . with a new publication, under a new name.'

In effect it would be the child of *Freedom and Independence* – using the Shoemaker's press and distribution system. The transition from one voice to the next would be without a pause for breath.

Father Nicodem appeared to waver between more shouting and giving up. I then said something I regret, because it was heavy with implication. I didn't mention Pavel, I just said, 'If anyone has the right to meet the Shoemaker, it's me. And I've earned a say in the future of his Friends.'

Father Nicodem slowly sat down. He pointed towards the door, signalling his defeat and consent. I told him I'd be back in a week.

4h.13

The Shoemaker had agreed, he said. I named the day, November 1st. The place: the grave of Prus. The time: six in the evening. I left him and went to the dustbin in the back yard. In it, ready for collection, was the last edition of *Freedom and Independence*. Its theme was mercy and justice.

CHAPTER 28

Anselm took the Metro Line 1, south bound. Clutching his old duffle bag he sat with his head against the window, feeling the jolt ride down his spine. His thoughts drifted to Róża's statement. John's mother had died. He'd never told him and yet he'd listened to Anselm's disclosure, glancing when he could at the drama on a cricket square. He'd come to Warsaw with a personal story which even now Anselm did not know. Anselm let the matter drop. Apprehension stirred deep in his guts: someone on the train was probably watching him.

Fifteen minutes later, after a short walk in the rain, a spectacled manager, hunched and kind, asked for Anselm's passport and credit card details.

'You're very welcome, Father,' he said in English, handing him the key to room 43. 'Turn right at Saint John.'

At the top of a gentle ramp Anselm passed a large statue proper to a cathedral. He slowed, knowing that this was Frenzel's joke. He'd picked this place on purpose, knowing the decor, knowing the manager's public devotion. His contempt seemed to echo down the corridor, all the way to the locked door.

The room had a single bed with a deep blue cover. An old television on a wall bracket had been angled like a spotlight towards two chairs and a table. White gleaming floor tiles ran from wall to wall. The lights were low and yellow. Abstract paintings hung slightly askew. There were no saints on the lookout. He put his duffle bag in the bathroom. *What on earth am I doing here? Frenzel's taken a decent man's hotel and made it into an expensive brothel for the sale of cheap information. And here am I, a punter with money in his back pocket.*

After five minutes a knock sounded.

Riding a surge of agitation, Anselm slowly turned the door handle.

Standing outside like a janitor on his day off was a podgy man in his late twenties dressed in a tracksuit. Gloved fingers gripped a shopping trolley filled with bulging refuse sacks. His face was red and flabby, still wet from the rain. Anselm couldn't imagine him doing anything more athletic than opening the fridge door. He waved him in, thinking this was the first act in some TV prank. Instantly, as if attached to the man by a thread, a hooded woman appeared, brushing past into the room. When Anselm turned, the man was squatting on the edge of the bed, his arm resting on the parked trolley. The woman, hood removed, was standing beneath the television, arms tightly folded. She was fifty or so. As if following his cue, Anselm took a chair.

'You have the money?' she said in German.

She'd seen his habit and it had unsettled her. Why hadn't Frenzel told her? To keep her on the leash in case she had misgivings?

'Yes.'

She seemed unable to ask for it. A glance begged Anselm to cut short her embarrassment. But he didn't move. So, Sebastian thought Anselm didn't have it in him? He thought a monk was too self-righteous to take lessons from Frenzel? He'd show him how fast he could learn. The first lesson was already under his belt: snatch the advantage from the weak.

'Show me the file,' he ordered.

Her hair was greying and frizzy, her facial bones fine. Wire glasses flashed as she opened her shapeless damp coat to reach the brown envelope held to her side. Anselm didn't move. Lesson Two: wait for them to come to you. After hesitating, she walked over, holding out the packet. Her jaw was incongruously strong, without undermining an essential delicacy. Her eyes were blue, the lips dry and full. She wouldn't look at him. Lesson Three: show no gratitude.

The envelope contained four sets of documents, held at the corner by tags of green string. Swinging to his side, he placed them on the small table and started reading, whipping through the pages one after the other. He had a few questions to ask. He spoke while reading.

'Is there nothing else?'

'No.'

'You're sure?'

'Yes.'

'Why?'

'I took them in the first place.'

Anselm looked up, unsmiling, clouding his face with judgment and disapproval. He'd done that in the Old Bailey with the more intractable witnesses. The jury had loved it. Not caring, Anselm noticed that this was probably Frenzel's Lesson Four.

'Tell me how the archive was structured,' said Anselm. 'Why is all the material in German?'

'That's how Colonel Brack worked,' she replied. 'It meant he could control what the Stasi knew. He decided what got translated and put into the files . . . and it wasn't much. He kept the rest to himself . . . with *Polana*, anyway. The last thing he wanted was interference from the Stasi so he kept them in the dark.'

Lesson Five: pretend you haven't heard and that you're not that interested anyway.

Lesson Six: let 'em stew when you've got 'em hanging in the air.

Anselm slowly examined the first batch of papers. It was a series of interviews carried out with known associates of Róża Mojeska (RM). Few had anything worthwhile to say. One said she worked, another said she prayed. A third, while keen to co-operate, was judged half mad. She'd taught her parrot to scream, 'I'm free'.

Anselm turned to the second bundle.

The weekly bulletins from FELIKS made pitiful reading. He'd grovelled and scraped. He'd scoured Warsaw looking for RM. He'd followed his wife. He'd finally come up with a good idea. But they'd have to let his son out first. No, he wasn't making a threat, he just thought that RM would do anything for the boy. End of the trail. There were no more reports.

Anselm glanced up. The squat man was eyeing the television, as if wondering what his mother might say if he asked to put it on. His designer shaved head was wet from the rain. He had his mother's fine nose. One foot tapped the ground. The trainers were squeaky new and white, like the floor.

'The reports from FELIKS aren't complete,' said Anselm, his voice smooth but accusing.

'That was Colonel Brack,' said the woman, wringing her hands. 'I've already told you, he ran the operation himself, he picked what went to the Stasi. He wanted to keep them in the dark. We were all in the dark. That's what he was like, especially with *Polana*, it was his baby, he—'

Anselm shut her down with a raised finger, settling his attention on the third set of papers.

Error, Frenzel seemed to say, with a hitch to his trousers. You went too far. You should have listened to what she was about to tell you. You're interested in Brack aren't you? Lesson Seven: don't enjoy yourself too much. Keep your eye on the ball. When they start blathering, let them hang themselves.

That's fun, too; they do all the work . . . Anselm had listened enough. He made a mental dash away from the tutorial; he raced over the operational detail for a planned arrest of RM on the 1st November 1982. A well-placed agent had reported that she would be making an appearance at the monument to Prus. Brack would deal with the matter personally, assisted by Lieutenant Frenzel . . . Anselm skipped to the end, looking for a name, and then, finding nothing, threw it aside. He opened the fourth and final bundle.

In his hands was the missing correspondence between the Stasi and the SB. Anselm, still running, went straight to the back page. Brack had originally refused to disclose the names of any agents, indicating that an accommodation might be found at the termination of the operation. That accommodation, it seemed, had been found.

A cough sounded. It was his own, though it seemed to come from someone else.

Staring at the letter signed by Frenzel, he'd come to a standstill. It couldn't be, he thought. His head was shaking a 'No'. He couldn't believe it was possible.

'It was him,' said the woman. She seemed to share his shock and dismay, only she'd got used to it. She seemed vaguely apologetic. 'He worked for Colonel Brack.'

Anselm was still shaking his head.

'He was well paid, thank you,' she said, growing confident; wanting to get her own back. She'd been stung by Anselm's manner. 'Signed for every instalment.'

Anselm put the papers back in the envelope and went to the bathroom. In a daze he counted out two thousand five hundred Euros and came back to the woman and her son.

'Here,' he said, holding out the notes. He was like an automaton. 'This is a one-off. You don't have to sign for anything.'

She took the money hurriedly and said, 'There's more, if you're interested.'

Anselm's eyes came into focus. She was trying to fit the envelope into an inside pocket of her coat.

'Sorry?'

'That lot,' she said, nodding towards the bed. 'That's everything he gave them . . . for over thirty years.'

'*Them?*' Anselm looked from the woman to the bin liners and back again. '*You're* one of them.'

'There are forty-two files,' she said, ignoring the jibe. 'All his reports. They're from the main SB archive. Mr Frenzel thought you might be interested. He says they're special. If you want them it's going to—'

'What?' snapped Anselm, exhausted by this wrangling in a cesspool. 'Cost the earth? The skin off my back? Or yours?' He looked at her with a sudden savage pity. She was still fumbling with the first wedge of profit, trying to get it past the pocket lining. Mouth open, the son was lost.

Languages weren't his thing. 'How much did Frenzel tell you to go for? Five? I bet it was five. Well, I'll give you three.'

Anselm didn't wait for the woman to work out what she'd say to Frenzel. He went back to the bathroom, counted out the notes and then returned, throwing them on the bedroom floor. Sinking into his chair, he paled with loathing as she brushed them together and made a pile, watched stupidly by her son with an arm around the refuse bags. Housework wasn't his thing.

'How much does Frenzel take?' asked Anselm, quietly. His anger had gone like a popped balloon. His ears were ringing. 'Half?'

She didn't reply. Her problem was trying to find a pocket big enough for the cash.

'He checks out the punters, he sends them to you, he gets his cut?' Anselm angled his neck, trying to look up into her face. 'If need be he'll break a bone or two?'

He's the pimp. And you? You're the poor woman who takes all the risks. If anyone's going to get busted, it's you. Mr Frenzel just looks after the house and its contents. Anselm kept the thought to himself.

He was calm now, with the shuddering stillness that follows an accident; when the shock of seeing mutilated bodies has lost its primal power; when one's mind turns to how anyone will live normally once the wreckage has been towed away.

'You don't know what it's like,' said the woman, tying the belt on her coat. She pointed at her son.

There wasn't much affection in her look, just indebtedness and resentment. 'You didn't grow up getting beaten up for what your mother did during the communist years. You could walk safely down the street. You had friends, you had birthday parties . . . you had good times. No one turned their back on you.'

Anselm nodded. Her eyes were clear behind her flimsy glasses. She came closer, lowering her voice, just in case a saint was listening.

'I just took a job, you know,' she said, one hand pressed against a bulging pocket. 'I knew two languages, I could type. I had a child. I needed money. That's all. I wasn't for them, I wasn't against them. I just wanted a job. All I did was type up what other people had said. I never gave an opinion; I never shopped on my neighbours. I just wanted some security . . . for him, for me.' She appealed to Anselm with open hands as if she were begging at the door to some church. 'I'll always be an outcast. And all because I spoke two . . .'

Languages, thought Anselm. *And you could type. And you were neither for nor against.* She didn't say it in her defence but she could have done: how many people did no worse than her?

The woman was at the door. The son was already outside, idly running the zip of his fleece up and down. Looking at her straight back Anselm wanted to say sorry, but his mouth wouldn't open. But he meant it: he was sorry for what had happened to her; and sorry for his behaviour. He'd forsworn the power of kindness and courtesy – and all because he wanted to tell Sebastian he could hold his own with Frenzel.

'Madam, you do have a name,' said Anselm, at last. 'He can't take that from you.'

The woman didn't even turn around. She closed the door with a trailing hand.

Anselm didn't move for a long time. He sat facing the television and the shopping trolley with the sacks. He thought of the agent whose code-name was SABINA and his long, dedicated service to the secret police. He thought of the woman who'd just left, Irina Orlosky, Brack's bilingual personal assistant, thankful that he'd resisted the temptation to use her name; glad that by so doing he'd cut back on her due quota of humiliation.

Anselm pushed the trolley to the reception desk. The manager was troubled. He ran a clean establishment. His eyes lingered on the sacks while Anselm paid for the room he wouldn't be needing after all. There were no farewell wishes, Father; no *bon voyage*. Turning to leave, Anselm noticed a crucifix above the entrance. And he knew, with a cold certainty, that Frenzel was somewhere near, perhaps in a car outside sucking a remembered shell. He stayed up late to watch the fun. The joke was far too good to be missed.

CHAPTER 29

IPN/RM/13129/2010
EDITED TRANSCRIPT OF A STATEMENT
MADE BY RÓŻA MOJESKA

4h.16
I only told Mateusz, Bernard and John about the meeting with the Shoemaker. They were a group representing more than themselves: the Worker, the Intellectual, and the Messenger.

4h.22
I chose the 1st November because it's All Souls Day. A day of memorial, a day for Pavel and that other man. I knew there'd be thousands of lit candles. I knew there'd be lots of people. I knew it would be easy to blend into a crowd if Father Nicodem had been right and I had been wrong. Of course, I was about to break Pavel's Golden Rule, to never meet a stranger. I was about to meet the Shoemaker.

4h.37
I don't know who saw who first. I hadn't seen Brack in thirty years. He'd been twenty-odd and

he was now in his fifties. But our eyes met over the hats and headscarves. Nothing essential had changed. He'd always looked hungry; he'd always scraped his lower lip with his teeth. I was about to slip away when I saw Father Nicodem.

4h.39

He was standing ten yards or so from Brack, hands in his coat pockets, as if there was nothing to be frightened of . . . and then my mind blurred. I realised that I wasn't the only one who'd been betrayed. The Shoemaker was somewhere nearby; and he was only there because of me. I had to cause a diversion so that he could get away. So I walked over to Brack and said, 'Well done, Comrade.'

4h.42

And then all hell let loose. John appeared with his camera, just as two *ubeks* grabbed my arms. More of them pushed through the crowd and seized him. I was marched straight past Father Nicodem. He looked on carelessly. I've thought often since: in the circumstances, there was nothing else he could do. He was simply being professional.

4h.50

I was brought to the same interrogation room that they'd used in the fifties. The colours had changed, that's all . . . from a sickly green to a sickly yellow. The desk looked the same and Brack was behind it. The lamp had gone. They gave me a chair rather than a footstool. The door closed and we were alone.

'I don't suppose there's any point in my asking about the Shoemaker?' he asked.

'None,' I replied.

He leaned back and opened the desk drawer. Looking inside, angling his head, he muttered, 'If you'd only answered that question all those years ago, then everything would have been so different. For both of us.'

He seemed to be blaming *me* for what *he* had done.

With his head still bent, he said, 'I wanted you, this time . . . as much as the Shoemaker. There's something I think you ought to know.'

He slid the drawer back and forth.

'Do you remember you once said there'll be laws one day to get at people like me?' He glanced up, just to make sure I'd heard him.

'Yes,' I said. 'That day will come.'

'I think it will, too,' he said, 'given how the Party has messed up everything. But that doesn't change a thing for you.'

'What do you mean?' I asked.

'You called it justice,' he said, dropping his gaze into the drawer again. 'You need to understand that you won't be getting any.'

I stared at him, waiting.

'Justice,' he said, quietly, drawing out the word. 'You won't be getting any.'

I stood up, feeling so much bigger than him, his system, his prison, and I said so, but he shut me up with a small gesture . . . a closing of the thumb and third finger, like when you extinguish a candle. I sat down, suddenly obedient.

'Have you any idea who betrayed you?' he asked, smiling.

'No,' I replied.

He took a passport out of his coat pocket and slid it across the table.

'I've always given you a choice, Róża,' he said. 'I've always been fair. I've always let you pick the consequences of your actions. So, here's another choice: if you ever want to bring me to court, then bear this in mind – I don't want to speak on my own behalf. I'll rely on my informer, and they can tell the judge what I did to defend my country from agitators and parasites. How, together, we fought and lost. I'll stand up and be counted, Róża, but not on my own.'

And then he told me the name and what they'd been doing for years on end. That was all he had to do. He knew I'd never want to see their story spread all over the papers. That's when I noticed he'd dressed for the occasion; he'd shaved, combed his hair . . . for this moment with me in Mokotów. Without waiting for a reply, he slowly shut the drawer and walked out of the room, not even bothering to close the door.

I went home, leaving the passport on the desk. That was his one act of mercy – a chance to get away from where my life had fallen apart. To start another in the West. This was his moment of complete triumph. He knew I wouldn't take it, because we both knew he'd locked me in Mokotów for ever. He'd even left me with the key. I hold it still, in my hand.

END OF TRANSCRIPTION (4h.56)

CHAPTER 30

The *Polana* file named SABINA as Father Nicodem Kaminsky. According to his 'Statement of Intent', written in 1949 and carefully filed away in the dossier bearing his chosen code-name, he'd been a dedicated communist since reading the *Manifesto* of Marx and Engels, considering its trenchant paragraphs to be a 'watershed document in the history of social, political and economic thinking'. Fair enough, thought Anselm; but he'd volunteered his services to the organs of State Security. He'd wanted to do his bit in the struggle between the age-old servants of Capital and the newly woken brotherhood of oppressed Labour. He'd counted the cost of losing; and a price was to be paid for the winning.

'He wrote it with his own hand,' observed Anselm, recalling the precise signature. 'He chose his own words. He knew what securing the win would involve.'

'And he lost,' observed Sebastian, drily. 'Now he picks up the tab.'

Sebastian was lodged at his cramped desk, slowly

turning the pages of an orange folder. Stripped of their plastic sacks, SABINA's massive output lay on the floor like columns of paving stones in a builder's yard. For an hour and a half Sebastian had been leafing through selected volumes, murmuring to himself, occasionally swearing under his breath. Legs crossed in an armchair, Anselm had reviewed Róża's statement, his gaze shifting on occasion to the night sky and the fallen stars on the streets below.

'And to think . . . he's one of *my* lot, a *Gilbertine*,' said Anselm, ruefully. 'Where are the Jesuits when you need them?'

Father Kaminsky's short manifesto revealed that the priest had left his monastery before the war and never returned. His political convictions would not sanction a 'self-interested' withdrawal from the crisis. The forging of a new future, built on the disillusionment of yesterday, required 'uncompromising engagement with the times'. He had committed himself to social action within the concrete circumstances of history.

Anselm berated himself for not having recognised Róża's guiding hint, now seen as glaring and underlined in red pen. Only once in her entire statement did she explicitly refer to the activity of informers: she'd identified those men of God who'd become men of Brack. And if that wasn't enough, Anselm's own deconstruction of Róża's text had drawn a bright yellow highlighter over the priest's name. He'd topped the poll of references, in a document crafted to lead its reader to one specific individual.

'He's the last person she'd have suspected,' said Anselm, talking to himself. 'Why? Because she and her husband had entrusted him with their lives. He's the last person she'd want to see exposed. Why? Because a bombshell would hit the arches of Saint Klement's and every other church in the country; because the Shoemaker would find out that his closest confidant had betrayed him from the outset; because Róża was worried that Kaminsky might choose to drown himself rather than face the jeering in the street.'

Sebastian turned a page. One finger moved slowly down a margin.

'I can imagine Kaminsky squaring historical materialism with his belief in God,' continued Anselm, as if delivering judgment in the Court of Appeal, 'and I can accept that he dreamed a costly dream, but the sand in the gears is capital. He got paid –' at the back of an expenses file Sebastian had found an account of monthly instalments, running, without interruption, between 1949 and 1982 – 'so what was his motive? The money or the dream? And who could dream dreams after Stalin?'

Sebastian looked up. 'Sorry?'

'Oh nothing, just the idle thoughts of the disenchanted.' Anselm dropped Róża's statement on the floor by his side and knitted his fingers on his chest. 'Tell me what you've learned about my confrere. Since I'm going to wrestle with his conscience I'll need to know what he's done, and why.'

Sebastian closed a file, pushing it away as though he'd tasted foreign food. He hadn't enjoyed himself.

'Brack became his handler in nineteen fifty,' said Sebastian, drawing a hand through his tangled hair. He swung round, crossing his feet on the edge of his desk. 'They met every month for three decades. He informed on friends, associates, priests, bishops, two cardinals and a shooting gallery of dissident thinkers. He moved around, did Kaminsky. In high places and low. And he told Brack everything he heard. I've never seen anything like it.'

The overall effect, laughed Sebastian, mordantly, was a kind of multi-volume encyclopaedia on opposition thinking. Quite apart from entries revealing the informed reflections of 'ordinary' citizens, the views of almost every major dissident intellectual in Warsaw were represented in the files. Their arguments, neatly laid out and persuasively presented, were frequently penned in Father Kaminsky's elegant script. Sometimes he'd obtained a Samizdat draft from the author's own hand, with key passages underlined in red. It's a howling irony: the SB preserved for posterity the very ideas that had been banned by the Party. They'd built up an archive of the books the censor would never have printed. Come on, you've got to laugh.

Anselm tried and failed. 'I'm troubled.'

'By?'

'Two questions. First, Kaminsky knows the Shoemaker. He was the Threshold. But he never told Brack. He kept quiet, leaving his handler to look under all the beds in Warsaw. Meanwhile Róża is being tortured. Her husband is taken out and shot. So is Stefan Binkowski. How does all that fit into the price worth paying? Why didn't Kaminsky lead Brack to the Shoemaker in nineteen fifty-one?'

Sebastian had been nodding while Anselm spoke. The point had struck him, too. He'd arrived at an answer while examining the files.

'My guess is this. When Kaminsky presented himself after the war, he was planning on a long and lucrative arrangement. Long, because he genuinely believed in Stalinist socialism; lucrative because, as he said, tongue in cheek, he'd counted the cost of losing and wanted to be paid for his trouble . . . up front, right now.' Sebastian loosened his tie, one finger pulling at the knot. 'He retained the one piece of information that his controller wanted because that kept their relationship *vital* . . . and it kept the payments coming. He gave his controller a few gems close to the target, like Róża and Pavel, but the main prize, the Shoemaker, is left out of reach, keeping Brack on the move. And along the way, rebel voices, drawn to the Shoemaker like bees to jam, are systematically betrayed.'

The snapshot appalled Anselm: Kaminsky had

280

been using Brack in a counter-subversion operation of his own invention; by leaving the Shoemaker free, he'd caught more insects. In that light, the money appeared more as a salary for having managed his handler than a top-up for his stipend. Anselm stared at the night sky behind his own reflection. 'And Brack thought he was running the show when, in fact, he was being led by the hand . . .'

'Yes, led to do the rough stuff required by an "uncompromising engagement with the times",' added Sebastian, swinging his feet off the table. He walked to the shelving units that covered the wall and pulled out a box file. Back at his desk he flipped open the cover and took out a flimsy publication.

'This is a copy of *Freedom and Independence*,' he said, bringing it to Anselm, 'the last edition before printing ceased in October nineteen fifty-one.'

Anselm held the paper in his hands with an instinctive reverence. His eyes ran across the imposing letters and words, his finger traced the soft indentations made by the stamp of the press. Not being able to understand anything, a blasphemy instantly suggested itself: why would anyone die for these impressions on paper? How on earth could they matter so much? They were just shapes; they made an arresting pattern. But then again, what was an idea if not flotsam in the mind? How could anything so insubstantial turn out to be so strong; so insignificant, and yet so important?

'The publication was silent until thirty years

later,' said Sebastian, leaning against the front of his desk, arms folded. 'He only spoke because Róża insisted. Prior to that moment he'd been silenced by Kaminsky. Even the Shoemaker was being led by the hand.'

Anselm looked up, 'How?'

'It all comes back to those executions,' replied Sebastian. 'As the Threshold, Kaminsky knew how the organisation was structured. He knew that the Shoemaker was the indispensable figure who had to stay out of reach, for the sake of *Freedom and Independence*. Others could die, but not him, never him; he was the living breath behind the living word. He had to be protected. But that was all in theory. No one had been killed. But then Pavel and Stefan were shot in Mokotów. What did Kaminsky say to the Shoemaker afterwards? I reckon he told him enough is enough. He told him the cost of his words was a touch too high. He roused the guilt that came with the privileged position of the protected. Who'd argue with that? Who'd want to write about freedom after Róża had been tortured and widowed?' Sebastian drew breath, arching his eyebrows. 'Kaminsky ran a brilliant operation: he hid the Shoemaker from the SB because he was a lure; manipulating that lure, he snagged the capitalists who were out for a fight with Marx; and, almost by default, he secured what he and Brack wanted above all, the suppression of the most powerful and respected dissident voice in the country. The real professional was Kaminsky. Brack, with his obsession for one man in hiding showed himself to be what he was . . . an amateur. The butcher used by the State to work in its secret abattoir.'

Anselm couldn't argue with the harsh lines drawn by Sebastian. The former Gilbertine was the still point in a world of whispering and death. He was, ironically, a man who'd skilfully effected a 'withdrawal from the crisis', leaving Brack to think he was leading the charge, using the likes of Edward Kolba to watch Róża the widow and Magda the Zionist. Far away in his parish, with his eye on the greater picture, and without attracting the slightest suspicion, he'd no doubt consoled the Shoemaker. Assured him that he'd done his bit. Cried with him over the untold fate of the unsung martyrs. And as soon as Róża turned up, he sucked in a few more flies and then told Brack where to catch them.

'You have a second question?'

Sebastian was looking upon Anselm with the camaraderie of shared disappointment. While it was illogical, he understood only too well that Kaminsky's standing as a religious figure affected him personally.

'How am I going to speak to such a man?' murmured Anselm, trying to envisage the encounter. The former monk was alive and well, his address listed at the back of Róża's statement, along with all the others. 'What can I appeal to in his past that might have some bearing on the present? Why would he agree to co-operate with Róża's quest for justice?'

Sebastian's humph showed he had no answers this time. As if to leave him completely empty-handed he took back *Freedom and Independence* and filed it away.

'Funny, really, that he never cleared off altogether,' said Anselm, recalling Róża's cited dictum: no church, no solidarity, no revolution. 'He stayed on as part of the institution. An institution that had helped put a nail in the coffin of his beliefs . . . his political beliefs.'

The mirroring of that word gave Anselm a fresh angle on to Father Kaminsky's complex character. 'He still *believes*,' said Anselm, obviously.

'What?'

'Roughly what I believe and what Róża believes about the silence in Saint Klement's. It's got a shape, a pattern, like those strange marks on the page, even if you can't understand them half the time . . . and to him who listens, to him who believes, it's important. It's worth a fight with a lion, knowing you're going to lose. And whatever else, Kaminsky cares enough about his church to forgive her role in the demise of his utopia.'

'You've lost me.' Sebastian had returned to his desk and was bending a paperclip to occupy his hands.

'Kaminsky has two faiths,' explained Anselm, tentatively. 'One for this world and another for the next. How they impinge on each other is anyone's guess, but a meeting point might be murder. Maybe the executions were a step too far, a price he didn't want to see paid by anyone – least of all on the back of his informing.'

A picture of Father Kaminsky radically different to that described by Sebastian began to filter into Anselm's imagination: a tormented man, perhaps, limping through the years, powerless to go back and erase his footprints, not daring to turn around and see once more where they'd been. Leaving the monthly payments aside – a feature difficult to excuse from any angle – Kaminsky could have been horrified by Brack's brutality, finding himself implicated in actions he would never have sanctioned.

'He handed over information,' reflected Anselm. 'He gave them essays, lectures, illegal books . . . the ideas he didn't like . . . it's a long way from endorsing summary justice.'

'Where are you going with this?' asked Sebastian.

'I have one chance,' said Anselm, increasingly sure of his ground. 'If Kaminsky feels any compassion for what happened to Róża, then he might be prepared to help her – especially when I tell him that the only reason she chose silence over justice was out of respect for their shared beliefs.'

Sebastian leaned back, agreeably surprised. From a height he dropped the paperclip into a wastebasket, and said, 'Looks like I was wrong. The way folk tick matters.'

'You were right, though,' replied Anselm, with reciprocal charm. 'Kaminsky did use Brack – in relation to the procurement of *information*; but

285

Brack also used Kaminsky – to suppress evidence of gutter killings, State murder beyond the law. It's all there on the last page of Róża's statement: he placed Kaminsky's name and his faith right at the heart of his scheme to silence Róża, and I don't think Kaminsky would swallow that . . . not even for the sake of a better tomorrow. He didn't sign up in forty-eight to finish his days as Brack's spattered shield. I'm hoping it's the one price he won't pay.'

CHAPTER 31

When a journey ends one looks back. Certain features that were obscure *en route* stand out with ruthless clarity. And the one that most troubled Anselm, now that he'd arrived at the guilt of SABINA, was his treatment of Irina Orlosky. He'd trampled over a weak, already defeated woman. He'd stomped around in the mud of her failings, showing off that Old Bailey footwork. It had been ugly, unnecessary and almost certainly harmful. Again he found that the Hilton's showers weren't up to the task. And this time the situation was worse than before: the inner dirt that wouldn't shift was of his own making and he couldn't blame Frenzel.

The recognition sent Anselm first to a florist and then to a rundown corner of Praga, a central district on the east bank of the river. This was where Stalin's army had watched the Nazis crush the Uprising of 1944. It was where the Tsar's troops had massacred 20,000 civilians following the Uprising of 1794. It was where Brack's personal assistant now lived, a survivor without her name.

Anselm walked into a narrow courtyard of tall cramped buildings. Paint blistered off the crooked window frames. Red and black graffiti marked the cracked walls as if they were stitching to hold the place together. Higher up, the stucco had fallen away, the remnant oval sections like flaking scabs on the facade of orange brick. It was early evening and the light was slipping away with something like relief. Having stepped gingerly through an open, communal door, Anselm mounted a creaking staircase and halted on a second floor landing. Rapid gunfire sounded from behind Flat 8. It ceased abruptly on Anselm's firm knock. A long, sliver of light appeared like a drawn blade.

'I'm sorry,' said Anselm to the dark, spectacled face. 'I was rude, superior and insulting. You were right. I have no idea what it was like. Can I have some tea? My name is Anselm.'

The door chain slid from its groove.

'Yes, of course, come in . . . I'm . . . I'm Irina.'

Taking the flowers, she smiled uneasily, one hand nervously brushing back her grey hair. Set against the dull wallpaper, the bunched yellows and greens turned bright. She held them out like an Olympic torch, beckoning Anselm to follow, but he paused by an open door just inside the entrance. Stretched out on the faded carpet lay the podgy son dressed in a Man United top and camouflage trousers, his legs splayed, his hands gripping a plastic Kalashnikov. Secure behind a cushion for a sandbag, he was shooting Afghan insurgents on a large computer screen, his kill rate mounting against the clock.

'Please, this way,' she called from the kitchen at the end of the short corridor, her voice embarrassed, already pleading for more understanding, already fearing another kind of condemnation.

The room was small and clean, the white enamel on the cooker chipped but shining. A small, polished window looked on to the courtyard and a fragment of sky. Anselm drew back a chair by a small Formica table and said, 'Irina, it's important you know something: Frenzel doesn't have your name. Certain things always remain in our possession.'

Her back was against him. She was arranging the flowers in a vase, jiggling the stems to get the arrangement right. Without turning around, she said, 'He didn't take it, Father. No one did.'

Still not facing Anselm, and without prompting, she began to speak of August 1989 as if she'd forgotten to mention it first time round and was now making up for the lapse. She'd been called into work early. Mr Frenzel had rung to say there was housework to be done. The place needed cleaning from top to bottom. For the next three months all the staff had worked like mad to tidy up the files.

'It was non-stop shredding,' she said, turning on the electric kettle. 'In every room on every floor the machines were whining and whirring. There were

289

rows and rows of garden sacks filled with all the sliced up paper. After a week others were brought in, more people, more machines, more sacks. Department and Section Heads sat at their desks, picking the files to be destroyed. It was one long office party . . . with laughter and joking and larking around. Some of the senior officers were maudlin, leafing through old folders. "Do you remember that one?" "I wonder what became of him." Others were frantic, knowing they couldn't pull all the weeds out of the garden.'

Irina broke her recollection to pour the boiled water into two cups. She sliced lemon and placed cubes of sugar on the saucers. Three harsh shots came from down the corridor, followed by the crump of grenades and the cries of the Afghan dying. The son had ambition. He was going to succeed where the Russians had failed.

'That's when Mr Frenzel selected which documents to keep,' sighed Irina, wiping some spillage with a cloth. 'He took them home every evening in his car. Told me to keep my mouth shut if I ever wanted to work again. If my son was ever to get a job.'

At last she turned round and travelled the great divide between them – just two short steps – her eyes lowered, not wanting to meet Anselm's gaze. She was wearing a McDonald's T-shirt and neat green trousers. Her expression was hard behind the frail wire glasses.

'The only person missing was Colonel Brack,' she

290

said, sitting down. 'He made his appearance on the last day, after everyone else had gone. He came late at night . . . I only found him because I'd left my keys behind.'

Anselm stirred his tea, flipping over the slice of lemon. 'He'd kept away from the party?'

'Yes.'

'Didn't he have any files for the shredder?'

'No. He wasn't like the others . . . he was a believer. He was *proud* of his work . . . *proud* of the ministry; he wanted whoever came next to see what he'd done. His junior officers saw things differently – they cleaned his cupboards to protect themselves.' She dropped a cube of sugar into her tea and began to break it down with the teaspoon. 'For him, there was nothing to celebrate. Quite the opposite. He wanted a funeral. When I opened the door to his office, he was there, sitting bolt upright holding a gun to his mouth.'

Irina had approached him stealthily, like a cat, speaking assurances in a low whisper. She'd edged round the desk and put her hand round his, slowly drawing the barrel from between his teeth. It had been the first time she'd ever touched his skin and he'd been cold; simply cold and still, no clammy surface or shaking limbs; no fear or tension. He'd watched her from afar, letting her unpick his fingers from the handgrip. Irina, trembling violently, had stepped back and dropped the gun into her coat pocket.

'I've still got it,' she laughed, bitterly. 'I didn't

dare leave the thing behind so I brought it home and shoved it in a safe place.' Her head made a tilt to some shelf out of her son's reach. 'To this day I don't know why I did that . . . why I stopped him from killing himself. He meant nothing to me. He never once so much as asked if I was all right, or if my son was doing well. He just worked, fighting "the enemy". Years later, when I realised that most doors in the free world were shut to me, I thought of him and everything he represented; I saw him at his desk, reading files by a lamp, biting his lip. And if I could have gone back into that room, I'd have taken the gun from him and pulled the trigger myself.' Irina coloured at the admission. 'I hate him . . . and as the years go by I hate him even more. Isn't that an awful thing to say?'

'Yes,' replied Anselm, simply, with the empathy of a doctor. They both knew that hate is the infection from an unhealed wound; that it's difficult to treat properly.

'I couldn't find interesting work,' she said, glancing towards the corridor and the battle of her son. 'Every conversation, every memory, every story . . . they all led back to the ministry. I was part of it. I'd drawn my pay. Like you said, I was one of *them*. People who'd never bothered to care when Brack was opening their next door neighbour's mail became former activists. They'd all been underground. They'd all taken risks. They'd all fought the good fight, whereas me . . .' Irina turned aside again, showing Anselm her profile, the fine nasal bone and the strong but delicate chin. Her tone was flat without a trace of self-pity: 'I've paid the penalty for everything he represented. I've picked up the responsibility for everything he did . . . as if I'd fought for his ideas . . . as if his ideas were mine. I carry the virus. And what about him?' For the first time she looked at Anselm directly, her eyes naked, the hate creeping quietly like a flame on the edge of some paper, invisible, but alive and black. 'He's paid nothing . . . I'm sure of it. And I saved his life. Do you know what he did afterwards? He didn't say a word. He just opened a drawer, looked inside and then walked past me as if I wasn't there.'

Anselm sipped his tea, unsettled by her calm self-disgust, that secondary infection often found in good people who can't see any road to forgiveness, especially for themselves, never mind the person who wounded them in the first place.

'Why do you let Frenzel keep his hold on you?' asked Anselm, wanting to find some way out for this cornered woman.

'He offered me some money,' she replied, not quite answering the question. 'He said that some investigators were sniffing around *Polana*, that they might embarrass Brack . . . that I could play my part and line my pocket at the same time. He's a very difficult man to turn down, Mr Frenzel –' the strain appeared in the fine lines around her mouth; she looked inward, it seemed, her eyes glazed – 'and anyway, I'd nothing to lose.'

With slow deliberation her attention shifted towards the gunfire: she hated it; she hated the computer screen; she hated the game. But it's what her son had wanted. She'd bought the lot with her cut from Frenzel (thought Anselm); she'd treated her son to an upmarket toy with adult specifications, the kind of indulgence he'd never received when he was so much younger, excluded from the other kids' birthday parties.

'He's addicted to *kompot*,' she said, abstracted. 'It's a drug made from poppy stalks . . . weaker than heroin or morphine, but harmful all the same. He steals from me . . .'

She stared at Anselm, begging him to ask no questions, to simply understand why she needed Marek Frenzel's backhanders.

'Irina,' said Anselm, nodding understanding and pity, 'I'm not here to embarrass Brack. I'm here in an attempt to bring him before a court.'

'Oh really?' She regarded him with polite but mocking disbelief. 'For what? For crushing someone's will to live?'

'No, for murder,' supplied Anselm.

Irina's glasses flashed.

'Yes, Irina. Maybe you got paid. Maybe you didn't have much of a choice. But you've helped to bring Otto Brack closer to justice. You've made a step towards finding your name.'

She smiled reluctantly, as if Anselm had produced more flowers.

'It goes right back to the beginning,' explained Anselm, 'to the building of the system and the institutions that you're now ashamed of . . . which you wish you'd never served.' He leaned over the table slightly, giving emphasis to the trust he was about to impart: the confidence one only shares with upright, decent people. 'Róża Mojeska witnessed the execution of her husband and another man in nineteen fifty-one. Otto Brack pulled the trigger. Róża, like you, has been trapped – but not by shame or regret. *Polana* wasn't all about finding the Shoemaker. Brack wanted to confront Róża . . . to tell her the name of the man who'd betrayed her from the outset; to tell her that she couldn't condemn Brack in the future without exposing someone at the centre of the Shoemaker's organisation and intimately connected with his reputation, not to mention that of the Church. Out of esteem for them both Róża kept a long, long silence. But now she's changed her mind.'

'Why?'

'The time is right. The fact is, whatever your motives, whatever your past, she'll be grateful to you.'

Irina had asked the question in a disconnected way, as if her curiosity was a yard behind her memory and understanding. In a searching, faraway voice, she said, '*Polana*, Róża . . . it all makes sense, I suppose. No other operation meant more to him; no other woman so unsettled him.' She glanced at a wall clock as if it was time for work. 'My son asked for a pizza. Will you stay for something to eat? We have a speciality here, *pierogi* . . . they're difficult to describe, but I've got some in the fridge.'

CHAPTER 32

Irina took some persuading, but Anselm insisted that pizzas all round was by the far the simplest option. He didn't want to say that the national dish now reminded him of Frenzel. The son ate in the sitting room, presumably still hiding from the mujahedeen behind that plumped up cushion. During the break in offensive operations, a homely quiet occupied the small and tidy flat. Stray, dying sunlight stole through the kitchen window. The large plastic clock ticked like a soft pulse. Irina had laid the table precisely, with gleaming cutlery and well-pressed napkins.

'You said Róża had unsettled Brack,' said Anselm, inviting more. The phrase had snagged his interest.

'I'd always thought it strange,' said Irina, elbow on the table, her face resting against her hand. She was relaxed. Anselm wondered if he was the first guest; first because he'd come uninvited. 'At one point he ran over six hundred operations aimed at specific publications in Warsaw, but the one that mattered most was *Freedom and Independence*, even though there were other papers with a far wider circulation. *Polana* is the only file that stands out in my memory . . . even though I knew nothing about what was happening on the ground. And that's because right at the beginning he called her Róża . . . just once, by accident, but it was enough to tell me this was no ordinary case; and she wasn't just another woman.'

On her first day of work in 1982 Colonel Brack had sent Irina to the main SB archive to obtain a file on one Róża Mojeska. A meeting had been planned for the afternoon with the Stasi and they'd asked to see any existing intelligence. All he brought along to the conference room were her interrogation papers from 1951. The reports of FELIKS – which ran from '52 until '69 – were left on his desk. He was only going to show them the bare minimum, with nothing up to date, and nothing that might put them on to her present whereabouts.

'The point of the meeting was to discuss how to track down the Shoemaker,' said Irina. 'Colonel Brack and Mr Frenzel represented the SB and there were two officers from the Stasi . . . I can't remember their names. Anyway, Colonel Brack explained that *Freedom and Independence* first appeared at the dawn of time and so on, but that the paper wasn't that important and hardly worth the effort of a joint operation. He said the only known link to the Shoemaker was a woman who'd vanished into thin air. There was a lot of back and forth, and then the name just came out . . . he said, "Even if we catch her, Róża won't tell us anything." There was a pause and then Mr Frenzel looked up, all innocence and light, and asked, "Would that be Mojeska, Sir?" Colonel Brack was beside himself . . . he went red in the face with embarrassment and rage. He never forgave Mr Frenzel for that.'

But Mr Frenzel had stumbled on to something. Throughout the following months, this so-called unimportant paper showed itself as Colonel Brack's obsession. It was the only operation he cared about. And Mr Frenzel, sniggering and suspicious, knowing it had to be personal, made the case his own priority. He had right of access to all the intelligence . . . and he went off and interviewed FELIKS before Colonel Brack could think of stopping him. In the end, the Colonel had no choice but to work with him.

'Even so, he found a way of side-stepping Mr Frenzel,' said Irina, serving Anselm some salad. It was crisp and fresh. 'I only found out by chance and he asked me not to say anything . . . and I never have done, until now.'

A second phone appeared on Colonel Brack's desk: one day it wasn't there; the next it was. She was never to answer it. He'd obviously installed a secure line – evidently part of some covert operation. In itself that wasn't out of the ordinary, so Irina didn't give it a second thought, not until the day she dropped an earring. Irina's office was part of Colonel Brack's, a small area separated by an arch without a door. She was on her knees behind her desk patting the carpet when she heard Colonel Brack enter his side of the room. Moments later a phone rang . . .

'He let it ring for a long time and for some reason I couldn't move,' said Irina. 'I just knew he was looking into my corner, checking if I was there . . . and then he finally picked up the receiver and said, "This is the Dentist."'

'The Dentist?' repeated Anselm, with a light cough.

'Yes,' replied Irina. 'He said, "I'll come immediately." And that's when I stood up. He swung round and looked at me as if I had a gun in my hand. I'd never seen him look so smart. Normally he wore his uniform or a limp suit, but this time he was well turned out, as if he was off to a wedding.'

'When was this, Irina?'

'Towards the end of the *Polana* operation, November nineteen eighty-two. The whole thing was wound up the same week. The phone vanished overnight.'

'How do you know he was side-stepping Frenzel?'

'Because he asked me not to tell him about the Dentist. He said it was an operation unrelated to the joint SB/Stasi mandate . . . then he was off . . . presumably to meet whoever it was that had just been on the line.'

Anselm couldn't order his thoughts properly. The caller had almost certainly been John; Brack had been John's legitimate contact, a voice on the end of a telephone line. Anselm couldn't get the measure of the surprise because Irina had returned to something they'd touched on earlier: Frenzel's intuition that Brack had met Róża in the past.

'Mr Frenzel is not a nice man,' she said, without apparent understatement, 'but he's clever. He has a nose for things. And he'd sniffed something out of Brack's past. After that slip where he'd used her first name, Mr Frenzel was always making smutty allusions, insinuating that there'd been some lost love in Brack's life before he'd joined the service. I won't repeat the kind of disgusting things he used to say.'

'You don't need to. I can well imagine.'

'Maybe that's why I stopped him shooting himself,' said Irina, as if finding a new angle on to her own behaviour. 'I suppose I felt sorry for him. Don't misunderstand me, but he was like a monk – early to work, ascetic, dedicated, diligent, one thing on his mind . . .'

Anselm didn't quite nod in recognition, but he coughed again, trying to wave on the epithets, wondering whether to let slip a few details about life at Larkwood. He opted for mute submission; the subject was just too big.

'. . . self-sacrificing, unswerving . . . but for all that he was hollow. His emotions had been poured out somewhere . . . that's why I found him such a frightening man. He was all ideas, simple ideas, without feeling . . . cold . . . hard . . . terribly, terribly *sure* about everything . . . about what he was doing and why. But as far as I could see, he felt nothing. He used to look straight through me. I was there for a purpose, not as a person. He was like that with everyone . . . they had a function rather than any value. For that reason I couldn't imagine anyone loving him. The stuff that love latches on to just wasn't there, he was like a ladder without rungs; somehow he stayed together without falling apart, but I had no idea what kept him upright.'

She paused to clear the plates and Anselm made a flap, trying to help, but there wasn't much to be done. Irina's back was towards him again. She'd switched on the kettle and was spooning out coffee.

'You know, I met his wife, once,' she said, still following the stream of her previous reflections.

'Brack was married?'

'Yes.'

'What was she like?'

'I only met her once. There'd been a final party after all the shredding and this overweight brunette on the other side of the room kept giggling at someone's jokes, shoving his shoulder and spilling her drink. All I knew was that she was married to some top brass who was a son of even higher brass. Then Mr Frenzel came over and whispered that she'd once been Mrs Brack.

'Couldn't take him any more, he'd said, laughing. Who could? She'd divorced him for . . . get a hold of this – *Kyrie Eleison* – a go-getting careerist higher

302

up the SB ladder. The best part: the new hubby's father had been stumping Brack's promotions ever since the second wedding. Does it get any better than that?

'Mr Frenzel had done his homework,' said Irina, her face soured by the reproduction of his voice and manners. She came to the table and laid the cups of coffee between them. 'But he didn't know everything and that bothered him. He hadn't found out why *Polana* was so important to Colonel Brack, or why Róża appeared to be significant. It frustrated him. He liked to know things, to have information on people, no matter how insignificant, but especially about their mistakes. He used to say that mistakes were currency for the future –' she slowed a fraction, and Anselm instantly realised that this was part of Frenzel's continued hold on her; he had something jingling, deep in his pocket: her past – 'that mistakes never go away and their value always goes up . . . and he knew that *Polana* wasn't what it seemed. That's why he cleaned the file himself. He reckoned Colonel Brack had made some big mistake.'

In August 1989 the Stasi, unhappy about the scale of shredding, had arrived with a truck to collect all the joint operations material – a concession made by some high-ups who hadn't cared where it all went anyway. Sensing an opportunity, Frenzel had let them take Róża's interrogations, which should, by rights, have been returned to the main SB archive. 'Your right hand shouldn't know what your left is doing, isn't that how it goes?' he'd said with a smile, holding up most of the contents lifted from the *Polana* file. 'Everything comes down to give and take, doesn't it, my girl?' Frenzel might not have known everything about Colonel Brack's past but he knew enough to make an investment.

'When I found Colonel Brack at his desk with that gun in his mouth,' said Irina, 'I think he'd just found out that Róża's file had gone missing. Now I understand what must have been going through his mind. He'd glimpsed the future . . . that someone, someday would uncover those executions, that they'd go to Róża with questions, that all he'd have to rely on was her willingness to protect an informer.' She looked up suddenly at Anselm, smiling broadly with amusement in her eyes. 'To think . . . I saved his life so he could stand on trial.'

The plastic clock ticked, slicing up the quiet between them. It was dark outside now. Anselm noticed that there'd been no gunfire. The Afghans had either called it a day or their nemesis was planning a surprise attack. There hadn't been a sound from the living room, and no used plate had been brought back into the kitchen. It was as though Anselm and Irina were completely alone. The sensation prompted him to push the boat out.

'Irina, did you ever read Róża's file?'
'Yes.'

'Why?'

She leaned her cheek on the back of her hand, eyes cast down. One finger drew a circle on the Formica table, going round and round. 'She was a woman, like me. I wondered why we were so different . . . what it was I lacked.'

'Did you read each and every page?'

'Yes.'

'Even the blue one?'

Irina's finger stopped dead. She slowly straightened her back, appraising Anselm with a surprising but unmistakable coldness.

'Yes,' she said, 'even the blue one.'

'But it was blank. There was nothing to read. But that didn't render it meaningless, did it?'

The clock's ticking seemed to grow louder.

'I'm not Marek Frenzel,' said Anselm. 'Information isn't my kind of money. Usually, people give me secrets for nothing. They know I won't spend them. But in this case I came across one by accident. Róża removed that piece of paper from the file – no one knows, except me and you. I've said nothing to the powers that be. But I suspect that it's important . . . only I don't know how.'

Irina chewed her bottom lip, wondering what to do. Keeping a secret was part of her dignity, the last vestige of self respect: the woman who'd sold out to work amongst the information gatherers had discovered something by herself and she'd kept schtum. To give her a gentle push,

Anselm said 'Can't you tell me about the infirmary?'

Irina's finger began another circle on the table. 'Is this why you came here?'

'No. I came to say that I was profoundly sorry. I didn't expect to ask you anything about Róża because I didn't expect to trust you, but I do, entirely.'

Watching the circle grow smaller, Irina said, 'There was more than one infirmary in Mokotów. They were at different ends of the building. The first was for the sick, the second was for mothers.' She nodded at her hand, assuming Anselm was unbelieving. 'That's right, in those days, during the Terror, some women gave birth in prison. They didn't let you go just because you turned out to be pregnant. They kept you for as long as they wanted. I don't know if Róża had a child or not. When I worked at the ministry I knew there were registers in the archive that had been brought over from Mokotów in the sixties, but I wasn't allowed to see them . . . I was just one of the administrative staff and I didn't have the clearance.' She laughed to herself, sadly. 'In a way, I didn't care if Róża was one of those secret mothers or not. For me, it was just something important that I would never reveal to Mr Frenzel; and when I looked at Róża's prison photographs, wondering why we were so different, I just thanked God that while I'd lost everything that Róża had preserved, I'd at least kept my child.

The comparison was a kind of comfort . . . it made sense of my situation in life.'

A certain transparency comes with shared confidence. One can sense things that haven't yet been said. And when Anselm rose to leave, he vaguely knew the answer to his own question. It had grown at the back of his mind during the soft lulls in conversation, when he'd pitied Irina Orlosky.

'Who owns this building?'

'Mr Frenzel.'

Always that 'Mr'; that *appellation contrôlée* of respect.

'He's my landlord,' she continued, leading Anselm into the corridor. 'The whole block has been sold to developers. Everything's going to change for the better . . . They're going to build a football stadium for the opening match of the European Cup, there'll be a metro station for the fans, and an Olympic swimming complex . . . There'll be lots of other changes and all for the better. Mr Frenzel calls it his favourite investment because he bought the place with his SB pension.'

She drew back the door chain but Anselm involuntarily paused, looking to his left. The son for whom so much had been sacrificed lay fast asleep or sedated on the floor, one arm around the cushion, his Kalashnikov by a plate of uneaten pizza crusts. He'd lost the battle. He was one of the nameless fallen, known only as Irina's child. Her voice roused him.

'Mr Frenzel didn't take my identity,' she said, evenly. 'I lost it on the day I entered the ministry building. I can't get it back . . . I tried, and it didn't work out. But if Colonel Brack stands trial . . . if I really have helped to bring about justice for Róża Mojeska then, who knows, maybe I'll have the right to walk on the same side of the street. That would be nice.'

CHAPTER 33

Disgust and melancholy tailed Anselm through the dark, empty streets of Praga. History – always alive in this city – asserted itself once more. It was precisely because the Soviet Army had been camped here during the Uprising across the river that the buildings in Praga had remained standing. This was all that was left of the old Warsaw that Róża would have known. And it was here that Marek Frenzel, the cute investor in people's mistakes, had made his fortune, bleeding profit from Stalin's shameful failure to stop the slaughter. The irony was toxic. Hands in his habit pockets, Anselm dwelled upon another history of destruction, that of Róża, and the murmur of her uprising.

Irina may have been undecided, but Anselm was certain: Róża had given birth to a child in Mokotów. He hadn't considered the possibility because he hadn't known what the blue paper might represent. But now he knew. And, thinking now of her statement, he understood at last why children lived and breathed on every page.

'Even so, I should have seen it from the

pavement,' he said, out loud. 'The writing was on the prison wall.'

He recalled the young woman in the Rolling Stones T-shirt. Her emotions had imploded, disappearing comprehensively with shocking speed. At the time he'd simply perceived the incongruity at the heart of Róża's statement: there was no hint of visceral feeling on the page despite the traumatic events she recounted. Intellectual commitment to the Shoemaker, yes; but no fire in the belly; no stabbing passion.

'I knew then that your emotional life had remained in Mokotów. And now I understand why you wanted to stay there. It was the place you last saw your child.'

There was another certainty – Anselm looked up to take his bearings, retracing his steps towards the river, noting the streets were less dirty, the buildings smarter; that the tide of investors was on the way, bringing all sorts of changes for the good, Frenzel riding the wave like a sea slug on wreckage – Róża arrived at the Kolbas alone.

'You let go,' he declared, opening his hands with dismay. 'Why? Because you looked into the eyes of someone who, one day, would have to be told about their father; someone who could be spared unnecessary pain. This is what it all comes down to, isn't it? It's always about avoiding suffering. Your child's, Kaminsky's, the Church's, anyone's, but never yours. You just accept it, for them.'

Róża had accepted adoption. She'd let her child

out of prison. She'd let another family take her place: a better, simpler, happier family where people laughed and cried for all the usual reasons, where no one spoke of torture, martyrdom and the magnitude of the Shoemaker. But Róża had still made a big mistake, because shielding other people from suffering isn't always possible. It's not always a good idea. Which is why her decision to see Brack in court had become her last obsession.

'You realised what had always been obvious,' said Anselm, compassionately, 'easily missed because you were guided by love; you saw, at last, that you had a debt to your child greater than your loyalty to the Shoemaker and the Church, greater than the claims of any political cause or institution. You faced what you'd run away from; the obligation to bring your husband's killer to justice, *in the name of your child*, even if *that child* never knew it.'

He passed a brooding, abandoned factory, its windows sealed with breeze blocks; he nipped through an arch adjacent to a substantial residence that had been halved, the outline of floors and rooms like scars on the wall, its doorways bricked up. Rotten fruit lay on the pavement and strips of white plastic banding curled up in the gutter. A cheap market had been and gone. The warm smell of decay entered Anselm's lungs. He increased his speed, trying to escape the sudden recrudescence of the Dentist.

A chess match came to mind.

Anselm had been toying with an unusual sacrifice: a queen for a pawn – something to shock and disturb his abstracted opponent.

'I had this source,' John had said, moving a bishop to QP4. 'He listened at closed doors. Told me what he'd heard. Fed me good stories.'

He'd been a voice on the other end of a telephone, a man who'd called himself the Dentist. His stories turned out to be sweeteners, because the Dentist turned out to be a high-ranking officer in the Ministry of Internal Affairs, trying to lure John on side.

On side for what?

John had said he didn't know, because he'd been kicked out of Warsaw.

Only, thanks to Irina, Anselm had learned a little bit more about this episode in John's life. Before taking that plane to Heathrow, John had been locked in a prison cell, his jaw swollen from a good kicking. He'd called Brack, and Brack had come to say goodbye . . . and all this happening in the immediate aftermath of Róża's capture.

'Which isn't surprising,' replied Anselm to his clouded mind. 'John was arrested at the same time as Róża. Brack's creeping around as the Dentist had nothing to do with *Polana*. They were separate operations. Remember? Brack's interest in teeth fell outside the joint SB/Stasi mandate. His dealings with John had nothing to do with his plan to catch Róża and the Shoemaker.'

Anselm came to a junction he didn't recognise.

He must have taken a wrong turn. Not caring he pressed on as if Frenzel's pals were on to him, wanting blood because he'd bought those flowers for a piece of the boss's property. Ahead was the bright, modern skyline west of the river; he'd easily find a bridge. Like one of the Magi from the east, he'd found an unexpected truth, and the only way home was by a different route, because truth changes where you're going and how you get there.

'The Dentist was Brack.' Anselm wouldn't let the matter go. It was as though he'd turned round to check where he'd got lost. 'Now there's a truth I didn't expect.'

John's hand had reached into the darkness of a sewer to touch Brack's outstretched fingers. The touching had troubled John (he'd said), and it troubled Anselm now, because unexpected truths, lined up, often make greater sense of each other. And Anselm had stumbled across another one in Róża's statement.

John had told her a family secret: his mother had died during his infancy. Mr Fielding, an indecisive man, had remarried swiftly. He'd ended up exiled to a Washington basement, his career in the slow lane. Róża called it a personal story tied up with the greater struggle. It had been the reason for John's coming to Warsaw . . . where, by chance (unknown to Róża) he'd shaken hands in the dark with Otto Brack.

'What's the link?'

What connection lay between the death of John's

mother and Brack's emergence as the Dentist in the life of her son? There had to be one. Proximity of two mysteries in time and place was unlikely to be a coincidence – that was Anselm's rule of thumb: it served him in theology and it had served him at the Bar (he'd never been at ease with chance as an explanation: it was harder to justify than a miracle). The connection, if there was one, remained obscure. But this much was clear: Brack had been manoeuvring John as much as he'd been manipulating Róża.

'Why didn't you tell me, John?' asked Anselm. 'Why not tell me about her death and the greater struggle? For God's sake, we drank stolen altar wine together. We played Misery. You came to Larkwood and learned how to pick fruit that was ripe.'

Darkness entered his mind like a cold, paralysing wind. All at once he came to a halt.

There ahead, on a small piazza, in the blue night shadow of trees and shrubs, were a group of musicians . . . five of them . . . all in various attitudes of performance: a violin, an accordion, a drum, a guitar and a banjo.

But there was no sound and no movement.

On approaching the band Anselm saw that they were statues . . . life-sized figures waiting for the dance to begin, for the people in all the sealed tenements to come out and stamp their feet and clap their hands. They were waiting for Róża, and Irina, and so many others . . .

The imported meaning bounced back, smashing straight through Anselm's disquiet. This gathering of folk playing in unison was like a prophecy whose fulfilment no servant of Brack or Frenzel could hinder, even if they were to come running round the corner right now and beat Anselm senseless – as another band of thugs had once beaten Róża and so many other friends of the truth. Ultimately, the executioners couldn't win. The entertainment had been booked . . . for anyone who dared to come out of their blocked up lives.

Fired up with a quite foreign energy, Anselm strode away, easily finding the bridge back to the west bank of Warsaw. He was being drawn forward, no longer leading an investigation but following the beat of a drum. He'd found the name of Róża's informer. He knew why she'd been silent and why she'd now speak for her child. Everyone's illusions would soon be shattered – Brack's, Kaminsky's and the Shoemaker's, for sure; and maybe those of Anselm and John. It didn't matter. They were all moving relentlessly towards a time of music.

PART V

KLARA'S CHILD

CHAPTER 34

A thick-set man in jeans and a leather jacket quickly opened the rear doors of the light blue Nyska van. The engine chugged, pumping sickness into the cold evening air. As John was thrown into the back, a fist crashed into the side of his head. A siren screamed. The van lurched forward and the two big lads standing over John lost their balance.

At a police station they kicked him into a holding cell. As the man in jeans ripped the film out of the camera, John spat the blood from his mouth and said, 'When you've finished dial 55876. Tell him Conrad needs a dentist.'

The door slammed shut. Footsteps sauntered back to the main desk. John rolled over on the bed, seeing Róża in the hands of those louts. He lived out the scene as if he were watching a film reel jammed on the same few seconds, the figures juddering back and forth. Two hours later a key turned in the lock and a man in a long camel overcoat sauntered into the cell. With affected delicacy he used one finger to close the door, leaving the guard in the corridor to turn the

319

handle. John sat up, staring at the man in astonishment.

'Well, well, well,' said the Dentist, shaking his head. 'You have been a silly boy.'

This was the first time they'd met. Until now, their dealings had all been verbal, over a secure telephone line using a secure number. But this was a face he'd seen before . . . in the cemetery.

'You shouldn't have given them the number,' said the Dentist, critically.

He'd opened the buttons on his overcoat and sat on a chair, hitching his trousers at the knee. He was very smart. The shoes were brand new, with that mirror-shine. The socks were pulled high.

'They wouldn't let me use the phone. They kicked me in the teeth instead.'

'I didn't think you'd go and take pictures.'

'That's what journalists do. I collect news.'

'Not when it can burn the hand that feeds you. My hand.'

'I didn't know you'd be there.'

'Maybe we should talk more often.'

The Dentist shrugged inside his camel coat. He seemed uncomfortable. The material of his grey jacket was bothering his neck. The knot in the silk tie was fat, making a sort of maroon pedestal for his face. He was well shaved, his skin shining. Short, parted hair had a faint tinge of oxidised brown.

'Well, did you get to meet the Shoemaker?' His greenish eyes flashed a passing interest.

'No. Thanks to you.'

John swallowed the complaint. The Shoemaker had been there. He'd been within reach. If only the blockhead had stayed in his office, wherever that might be. If only he'd left John alone to get on with his job.

'You've not been following me, have you?' John's leg began to bob up and down.

'What did you say?' The question had stung. It had struck at the heart of their relationship. 'Who the hell do you think I am? Do you have any idea how much I've done for you?'

'I'm sorry, it's just that I got a beating in the van, and I . . .' John stroked his swollen jaw. Confusion erupted at the thought of Róża walking calmly towards the Dentist. She *knew* him. How could Róża know the Dentist?

'I want you to let her go.'

'Who?'

'Róża Mojeska.'

The Dentist frowned. His top teeth stabbed at his lower lip. 'You're not serious.'

'I am. Let her out.' John had influence and he was going to use it. 'Otherwise the deal's off.'

'My goodness, you *are* serious.'

Unless John was completely mistaken, there was a hint of humour in his voice. The faint mockery riled him. 'Do you think I'm joking?'

'No, of course, not. It's just that, well, I've got a job, too, you know. You seem to think I can just pick and choose my fights.' He stood up,

321

shrugging his coat again, thrusting his hands deep into the wide pockets. 'I'll see what I can do.'

'No, that's not enough. She has to walk free. It's not my fault a wheel came off today. And I want to see her . . .'

'You're going too far,' said the Dentist. 'You're wading out of your depth. You're heading into my waters. They're dangerous.'

All at once the Dentist looked tired; even bored; and possibly . . . sad. He examined John from afar, nodding to himself. His eyes moved around his clothes and features, just like John's had moved over his. The mutual appraisal was like that awkward weighing up when someone new enters the family. What you think doesn't really matter; they're here to stay. You put the best foot forward and hope for the best. And, by the look of the leather, the Dentist had gone for *Churches*, the *Oxford* style. He'd put on his Sunday best.

'I want her address.' John stood up as if finding height over the Dentist might add some pressure. 'Don't you see? I have to tidy up what happened in the graveyard. I was there. You were there.'

The Dentist made a face, as if to say he hadn't thought of that. Part of his remote sadness predisposed him to being helpful. His teeth nipped his bottom lip. 'Thirty-seven Miron Buildings, Niska Street. You say nothing of me, do you understand?'

'Yes.'

'Nothing.'

'Okay.'

'Don't get tetchy.' The Dentist moved towards the door. 'You've compromised me once already.'

Turning around he studied John with a new intensity. 'You shouldn't have called, you know. It complicates things.'

John nodded. He'd made a mistake. He made lots of mistakes.

'We can't meet again, do you understand? Our relationship is over.' The Dentist looked aside, absorbed by his thoughts. 'For now, the deal's on hold.'

'Okay,' replied John, uncertainly. As far as he was concerned, nothing need change. There was still a lot of work to be done. They needed to talk more, that's all.

'See if you can get her out,' said the Dentist, standing up.

'Who?'

'Róża,' snapped the Dentist, his voice low and running. 'You're right. She's seen us together. If you can persuade her to jump, I'll get the passport.'

The Dentist knocked on the door and waited for the guards, rocking impatiently on his heels, his back to John. When they came, he stepped outside without even a glance behind.

CHAPTER 35

Anselm's street map led him to a parish church ten minutes walk to the west of the city centre. It stood on the edge of a residential complex by a railway line that climbed towards a bridge. Anselm could almost smell the presence of the river. Flanked by major thoroughfares, the neighbourhood was somewhere and nowhere, a triangular patch of land left behind when the road and rail people had done their bit for Warsaw's post-war infrastructure.

Father Kaminsky spoke English quite well. His French was good, though his German was better. To get at Dante and Cervantes he'd learned Italian and Spanish, which left him comprehensively unprepared for small talk. His Russian was faultless. He liked Czech. Latin was another option, though the vocab might not cover the nuances of life under Stalin. So said the visiting curate from the United States when taxed on the phone by Sebastian. He viewed his host with unadulterated awe.

'He's seen everything, you know,' said the curate to Anselm. 'From the Nazis to the Reds. They say he smuggled Jewish kids out of the Ghetto, made Molotovs in the Uprising, and then, after Yalta, went out into the Cold. But he won't tell me anything. Sweet whatever. He only talks about his childhood.'

They entered a parlour facing a garden running to outbuildings and a wall. On the far side lay an embankment sloping to the tracks. A train thundered by out of sight, tearing towards the bridge.

Father Kaminsky was lodged in a wheelchair, his legs painfully thin in flimsy black trousers. Bony feet in large slippers had been lodged on the footrests like pedals on a bike. A grey woollen cardigan with buttons missing hung upon his shrunken chest. Around his neck was a bright yellow scarf. The room had the feel of a passenger's waiting room. Newspapers were heaped on a table. Anselm's eye picked out *El País*, *La Repubblica*, the *Sun*.

'Ah, my youth has come to scold me,' Father Kaminsky said in English, fondly noting Anselm's habit. 'I'll come back, one day.' He pointed towards a wicker chair, his voice throaty and soft. 'You want to speak about Róża Mojeska.'

'In the first instance, no,' replied Anselm, picking up the *Sun*. 'I thought we might start with Pavel, her husband. Or Stefan. Or maybe Otto Brack. Or perhaps we could just cut to the chase and talk about retribution, human and divine.'

The old man started, gently. 'You surprise me, Father.'

'Really?' Anselm turned the pages, not seeing. 'Do you know this paper's most famous headline? It's "Gotcha!"'

The curate knocked open the door with his knee and brought in a tray laden with tea, sliced *panettone*, nougat, Lady Finger biscuits and poppyseed cakes. After pouring and stirring he loitered, hoping to join in the chat, but Father Kaminsky made a firm nod towards the door. He was frail, like Sylvester back home. His bones were clear beneath the soft skin on his face. White hair, in wisps, had managed to get tangled, making him look more of a boy than a man. It was hard to believe that collaboration could leave no identifying marks. His eyes were wide, the blue running out of colour.

'Tell me about SABINA,' said Anselm, closing the paper. 'The rest will come out in the wash.'

I'm old school, he said, taking no nonsense. I'm telling you all you need to know and not a breadcrumb more, do you understand. You'll be getting nothing about the Shoemaker, the Friends, *Freedom and Independence*. Don't ask how I met Pavel Mojeska because I won't tell you. Same for Stefan Binkowski. They were both shot because someone said something they should've kept to themselves. Trust is all well and good, but it has a boundary. It's not an open field. And don't ask about me. I won't tell you. Understood? Check the door will you?

He was Sylvester in reverse. Anselm, unsteady on his feet, had a quick look: the curate had gone. The old man was rolling on with his story even before Anselm had sat down. A premonition told Anselm that playing smart with a headline had been a spectacular mistake. And the old man was talking . . . talking fast, as if he'd been primed to explode.

'I approached them in nineteen forty-eight. We needed the money.'

'We?'

'I've already told you: don't ask for breadcrumbs. Where was I?'

'Money.'

'Ah, yes, and we needed to keep them at a distance.'

So he'd drawn them *in* to keep them *out*, and drawn a decent wage while he was at it. A group of prominent figures, well known to him and of interest to the authorities, had agreed that he should inform on them. Patriots with ideas. Nationalists who didn't accept Soviet domination. They'd met regularly to decide in advance what Father Nicodem was to say. They'd hoped to influence minds.

'Whose?'

'*Theirs.*'

It was a word that seemed to point. He'd identified the opposition, en masse. Back then, at the beginning, the ideological conflict had been acute, cleaner, and simpler. Some people's minds were for the taking. The country had been devastated. Something new had to be built, both psychologically and materially. It was a terrible, tragic fresh start. And it was important to get the thinking right for this new purpose and the new future. It was, in fact, an opportunity for everyone to start again. But it was persuasion against imposition; words against violence. The intellectuals known to Father Kaminsky had hoped to infiltrate the system itself and lure away its agents with ideas, with arguments . . . to poison the entire edifice of oppression by injecting free-flowing words into its bloodstream.

'You see, we all believed passionately that ideas *matter*,' said Father Kaminsky with an old undying fervour. 'That ideas, properly worked out, bring peace, prosperity, equality of opportunity, justice . . . that if we could only get them into the minds of the jailors, then they'd find it harder to turn the key, that eventually – maybe not in our lifetimes, but in generations hence – the words would do their work.'

'And the money?' asked Anselm, weakly.

'Paper and ink. A good education doesn't come cheap. We thought they ought at least to pay the running costs.'

The scale of Anselm's misconstruction was colossal. Father Kaminsky's innocence completely demolished his understanding of Brack's scheme and a good half of Róża's presumed motivation. All that remained was the vindication of her child.

He listened with a kind of humility, embarrassed that he'd condemned a man who'd risked so much for so long.

'In those days, my handler was a man called Strenk,' said Father Kaminsky. 'A hardliner with a mind dead to any feeling. Like so many of his kind, he'd separated thought and emotion. All torturers do that. It's how they make sense of wading in blood, doing what ordinary folk could never stomach; it's how they step back into ordinary life thinking they're heroes.'

A few years later Brack took over. Strenk and Brack were like father and son, pupil and master and Brack was being given a chance to show he could drive the car on his own, that he could work the gears.

'I was in my forties then, and Brack, well, I'd say his mid-twenties.' A white hand with knotted veins rose to his mouth, touching his pale bottom lip. 'I remember when I saw him first . . . this young man, this . . . *apprentice*. He was being schooled. They were forming him into their own kind. For a long time I just looked at him . . . at his eyes, his mouth . . . wondering what else he might have done with his life, other than *this* with *them*.' The old priest's gaping eyes burned with compassion. He spoke slowly, nodding out the words. 'He was obsessed with the Shoemaker. He wasn't trying to please. There was something personal to his drive.'

Father Kaminsky's meetings were, of course,

limited to the report of conversations with suspected persons, but Brack never failed to remind him that he was to keep his ear to the ground, that if he heard one word about the Shoemaker he was to let him know.

'He was sullen and angry,' said the old priest, abstractedly. 'My old friend Jozef Lasky used to say "Harm the boy, you harm the man" and Otto Brack was a man with deep wounds. Whoever was responsible carries a heavy burden . . . for who Brack became and for what he did.' His face became eerily still; even his eyes ceased their slow blinking. 'Have some *panettone*,' he resumed, quietly. 'It's the real thing. From Milan.'

A train rushed along the line, shaking the window in its frame. Anselm found his arms were folded tight as if he were cold. He'd been spellbound by the confused tussle between judgement and mercy.

'In fifty-one Pavel told me he'd broken a rule.' Father Kaminsky had stepped away from the first meeting with Brack. His hands became lively on his lap. 'He'd met a stranger and brought them into the running of the operation. He wouldn't tell me who it was and I didn't want to know. He was innocent, you see. Impulsive. He was too . . . *good* for the dirty kind of fight we were in. He was drawn to the brightness of an ordinary tomorrow. I remember now, he said, "A friend is someone who was once a stranger". What could I do? What could I say? I said we had to find a sleeper, and that's when I found out he'd broken another rule:

330

he'd got married. I could have wept. Marriage is trust, and trust, in our game, was a weakness. And so I met Róża. She was to be the sleeper, he said. I could have wept again.'

He told Pavel to give her his ring. It's the worst thing he'd ever said, but Father Kaminsky had an awful foreboding that something was about to go wrong. That Pavel would go out one night and she'd never see him again; that she'd be left with nothing . . . sacred. Because Pavel had opened the door to someone who hadn't been *picked*; he'd shaken the hand of someone who wanted to meet the Shoemaker; he'd made a Friend out of a Stranger.

He'd trusted, thought Anselm, with feeling. He'd wanted to walk in an open field without walls and fences; he'd longed to stroll beneath an open sky without having to look where he was going. Róża had made an identical mistake.

'The first I knew about the arrests was from Brack.' Father Kaminsky's cheeks were nicked here and there from clumsy shaving; a hand touched the healing cuts. 'He was spitting rage . . . Pavel had set up a dummy meeting so when Brack moved in, he only caught Pavel and Stefan. Pavel had tried to patch up his mistakes. He'd tested the trust of the stranger. And he paid for it.'

Willingly, as did Róża, thought Anselm. He thought of the figure in hiding for whom the sacrifice had been made; this man of vision and determination, kept safe by the dedication of his Friends. How did he bear the outcome?

331

'He didn't.' Father Kaminsky's head was shaking slowly right and left, his voice hoarse. 'He lost the ability to speak. He couldn't write a single line. *Freedom and Independence* died with those two young men.'

Father Kaminsky was broken, too. He felt responsible because he hadn't been put against the wall. This is what happens with deep friend-ship. Everything is shared. And he wanted to share death. But it wasn't his task, his duty. His job was to survive. But how could he go on? It was as though the lights had gone out in his life. Doggedly he'd carried on working with the SB. He'd 'informed', diligently passing on the ideas of a new generation of intellectuals who'd tired of the broken promises for change. This had been his duty, and the reason for being alive: whoever had read those files had received messages of hope. The money? Given to the families of those impris-oned for what they believed.

'Then, in nineteen eighty-two, Róża came back.' Father Kaminsky's wide eyes and open mouth showed the surprise had never faded. 'I hadn't seen her for thirty years, and here she was, strong and sure and . . . forgiving. She had a message for the Shoemaker from the widow of a Friend. The fight goes on, she insisted. Tell him he has no choice, she said; tell him the choice has already been made.'

Father Kaminsky looked outside, turning away from remembered emotion. He stayed like that as if waiting for his train to arrive; waiting for the guard to carry his bags and find his seat; waiting for his big trip over the bridge.

Anselm knew the rest: it was a matter of history repeating itself. Róża had made the same momentous blunder as Pavel. Eventually, they'd both tired of deceit and caution, suspicion and doubt. They'd decided to live as human beings. They'd chosen to live by trust. They'd said, 'Yes' when they should have said, 'No'.

'When Brack saw me in the cemetery, he knew I was linked to Róża,' said Father Kaminsky, with the look of a man tired of delays.

Anselm was quizzical. It was All Souls. He was a priest. Being there had an innocent explanation.

'One gesture.' Father Kaminsky smiled, the jagged cracks in his skin turning supple. 'After Róża was taken away, I turned round and looked . . . and he saw the expression on my face. He saw how much I cared. The scales in his eyes came crashing down – scales carefully laid one upon the other for decades until he was blind – and I said, "Join us, won't you? We're going to win, eventually", and he came right up close –' the old man leaned forward, aping the disbelief and confusion in Brack's face, his thin arms rigid on the arms of his wheelchair – 'and he replied, as if he were mourning, "I know you are. But don't you see? Neither of us will join the celebrations."'

Of course they wouldn't, thought Anselm. Brack

had told Frenzel to name Father Kaminsky as his agent: to link him to a betrayal he could never explain away, contaminating all the SABINA files in the SB archive. There and then, in the cemetery, he'd planned for Father Kaminsky's future condemnation. He'd seen everything with frightening clarity and staggering speed.

They drank tea, Anselm eating the *panettone*, the old man struggling with the nougat. There used to be a wonderful shop in the Jewish Quarter that made poppyseed cakes bigger than the ones on the plate. A wall had been built twenty feet high. Children were smuggled out and hidden in homes and institutions. Father Kaminsky's remembrances began to scatter. He moved back and forth in time, 'they' variously being the Nazis, the Soviets and the City Council. Brushing crumbs off his lap, he said, suddenly, 'Whoever betrayed Róża is trapped.'

Anselm looked over the rim of his teacup.

'That's how Brack works. It's how they made him.'

Anselm didn't move.

'Whoever it might be is trapped by their past.' The old man was nodding his words again. 'He did it to Róża and he did it to me. When you find them, don't be too harsh.'

The curate brought Anselm to the front door, wanting to know if everything had gone well. The exclusion was still eating away at his curiosity. He was staying with an unconfirmed legend, a man of rumour who wouldn't tell any tales.

'What did he say about his childhood?' asked Anselm, gripping the *Sun* under one arm while he'd buttoned up his coat. Apparently the sports pages were muscular and without a trace of ambiguity; as for the leader page . . .

'Not much, frankly.' The curate made a clucking noise, going over the dross. 'Just that he'd been happy.'

CHAPTER 36

John didn't like the Dentist. He'd expected an ascetic, an intellectual with tortured eyes, one of the brains in the SB, whereas he'd been . . . what? Unconsciously vulgar? He'd wanted to impress, sporting handmade shoes and a stockbroker's coat from Aquascutum. There'd been something wretched and lazy about his way of walking, as if he'd felt there wasn't much point to sorting out the mess; as if there wasn't much point to anything. The Dentist wasn't what he'd seemed.

John's shaking hand eventually got the key in the hole. The door yielded and he stepped into the flickering shadows of his flat. A projector clattered on the dining table, a roll of film unwinding from one spool to another. Images of tanks trundled across a sheet pinned to the wall. Soldiers tramped through the snow.

'You're late.' Celina was hunched in the darkness, bent over a writing pad. Her hair was crazy, clipped back. Her glasses caught the sharp light. She was a wild cat in a wild night. John could just see the pencil moving. 'What kept you? I've been worried.'

Do I love her? Or is it what she means to me? What she represents? Am I using her?

He drew back a chair and sat down, the projector whirring between them. 'I got held up with a story.'

'It's always a story.'

'Yep, my life's a story.'

She was everything he needed. A real dissident. Her father had been a mover in the Club of the Crooked Circle, a shaker in the Band of Vagabonds. He'd been a man of secret societies. An uncle on some side had rotted in a Tsarist prison. An aunt had been deported to Siberia and she'd died walking back. Celina's mother had dumped the father because he wouldn't swallow official ideology. She'd wanted the special hampers that came at Christmas for those who towed the line. She'd found a cleaner, sharper mind with access to the special shops where scarce goods could be bought at low prices. They were a family ripped apart by principle.

'Have you eaten?'

'I'm not hungry. What are you doing?'

'I've got a meeting with the censor tomorrow. I'm cutting out the best bits.'

Celina was the non-conformist renegade daughter, kicked out of school and educated underground. She dressed outside known fashion trends. Torn jeans, bright coloured socks, beads and bangles, careless scarves, huge shapeless jumpers. No makeup. Oval, dark framed glasses, windows on to a delicate uncompromising intelligence. She walked on the other side of any drawn line.

'I'm starving,' she said, twisting the knob. The riot police with their floppy long white truncheons vanished, swamped in darkness. Celina's chair creaked; she was leaning back, straining for the light switch. Snap. The white sheet appeared, pinned to the wall and hanging like a shroud.

'What happened?' She was standing up, a hand over her mouth, her dyed hair in ordinary disarray. Her tone was shocked and quiet. Moving round the table, keeping her hands on its edge, she whispered, 'What story was this? What happened?'

Do I love you? Is it those untied laces? The jumper with holes? Or is it your past? The allure of the heretic?

'Tell me what they did?' She was on her knees, holding his hands. Her nails were painted different colours. There was no pattern or sequence. One of them had minuscule blue dots. She must have used the single hair of a paint brush.

Is there any love in this? Or is it the romance of straying near the fire that burns around your feet? The fire you stoke and bank, mocking their norms and laws and incantations?

'John, speak to me.'

Am I using you to redeem the shame of my past?

Her hand was stroking his swollen jaw. Horrified, she touched the dried blood on his lip. John sank off the chair on to his knees and pushed his hands into her tangled hair. His mind and body lost all individuation. He reached out, into the flames, wanting to get inside her skin and bones, her difference, her purity.

He told her he'd been at the Powązki Cemetery when someone got arrested. He'd tried to capture the moment on film and then the brawn had burst out of nowhere. It made you think. 'They might just be everywhere, do you know what I mean?' Celina nodded. Maybe they were, she said. Maybe we can't breathe any air but theirs. They breathe it out, we breathe it in. They're in our bodies. Their atoms mingle with ours, making new gases and compounds. There's no escape. They haunt grave-yards and kitchens, breathing out their sickness. They climb into your bed and reach over to turn out the light. She spoke with immense disgust, counting up the planned cuts to her film: the removal of scenes she knew the censor wouldn't like; images of the riot police in action. The ZOMOS, Caesar's Praetorians.

They stayed up all night watching images flicker across the shroud. After breakfast Celina went to her meeting with the censor, John went to the woman who knew the Dentist.

John knocked. No reply. He knocked again. He tried the handle. The door gave way.

Róża was sitting on a dining room chair. She'd pulled it back and sat down without drawing herself towards the table. It made it look as if she were stranded, facing nowhere. She still had her coat and hat on. She wore light blue woollen gloves, the only colour of substance in the room. Her hands were on her knees. John's eyes shifted to an empty bookcase in one corner, to a drab-looking canapé that hugged a wall, to an armchair with the appeal of an unwanted visitor. There wasn't much else . . . a lamp stand holding a washed out shade, tassels dangling. John looked again, not quite sure at first: a bullet on a shelf beneath a mirror. He came to Róża's side.

'It wasn't me, Róża,' he said, sinking to a chair, daring to place his hands on her arms. 'I promise, I swear, it wasn't me. I don't know what they were doing there, I don't know how they knew, I said nothing to no one, I'd never risk doing or saying anything that might have . . .'

She wasn't listening. She stared ahead in a kind of trance, as if she were watching Celina's film. Deep shadows like heavy paint lay around her eyes. John had never been this close before. He couldn't help notice the fine hairs on her skin. She appeared at once innocent and fragile despite what she'd seen, despite what had been done to her, despite what she was looking at now.

'Róża, I have friends . . . on both sides of the fence.' John squeezed her arm, trying to get a reaction. It was like holding a bone from the butchers. 'I can try and find out what went wrong. It's my job, you know. I'll dig around and find out who—'

'John.' She spoke his name like it was a kind of

slap to the mouth. Her voice crackled, strangely detached, unwired from the muscles round the lips. Harrowed and still in a stupor, she turned to John as if she'd fallen overboard, water framing her oval face, the hat, jaw and chin; her eyes wide with knowledge . . . knowledge of a life lived and a coming death. The mouth slowly opened, the skin of the lips seeming to tear across the centre. Her tone was dried out and paper thin. 'John, promise me you will do and say nothing.' She seemed to wait for a reply whereas she was trying to stay afloat. 'Forget about the Shoemaker; forget about the Friends, forget about me.' Then, not even noticing his beaten face, she turned away and drowned. She'd gone. There was no point in mentioning a passport.

John tiptoed out of the flat – a sort of reverential act to the body he was leaving behind. He crept down the stairs, hugging the wall.

'How did she know the Dentist?'

The question echoed in the entrance hall. It tore at John all the way home. Had the Dentist said anything to Róża? Had he told her about CONRAD? Did Róża know what John had been doing? Of his place in the Big Game, his central place? The answers circled lazily like buzzards above carrion, black and distant, wings large and still.

John couldn't get the key in the lock. Metal rattled against metal with his shaking. He knocked. Celina opened the door. Without looking, she walked back inside, dark against the light.

'They won't allow the film,' she said, slumping on a chair by the dining table. Her eyes were bright and wet, her cheeks horribly black from the run of thick eyeliner. She'd given face paint a go. She'd gone out looking like Nefertiti. Now, she was . . . something from the Hammer studios. The bandages had been unwound and a curse unleashed.

'I can't take it any more, John.' Her bare feet pointed inwards, her shoulders were low. A pink silk scarf had been wrapped into her hair. 'My life has been cut into long strips. I want to be whole again. I want to be –' she dropped her head into her hands – 'I don't want much, I've never wanted much. I just want to be happy and free.'

John's insides turned. He thought they might tip out on to the floor of his flat.

Do I love her? Or is it what she represents? She cleans me. She gives me tomorrow.

He looked at her narrow black jeans. Everyone else wore blue denim bell bottoms. Her toes were curled as if she were clinging on to a perch. He'd seen the nails that morning. They were coloured like a row of Smarties.

The telephone rang.

John made a start. But he couldn't take his eyes off Celina. Her tears were dripping like rain from a blocked gutter.

The ring seemed to grow louder. Impatient. Angry.

John made a snatch for the phone, sending the console crashing to the ground, the wire tangled round his wrist. He yanked up the receiver and barked out some words – he didn't know what he said, his eyes were still on Celina.

The announcement came after an offended pause. A few obvious details were confirmed first, but then the nameless functionary read out a text written by some other nameless bureaucrat. John sank to the floor, worked his wrist free and threw the phone as far as the wire would allow.

'They've kicked me out.'

Celina didn't react at first.

'I've got two days.'

She sat up, turning around, one arm hanging over the back of the chair. She looked like a painting out of the Louvre, something unseen by Ingres, David or any of them. She was classical, offending and timeless.

'My accreditation has been withdrawn.' He was leaning back against the wall, hands loose in the gap between his legs. He wanted a beer. He wanted to be happy and free. 'I'm finished. For collecting materials of an espionage character.'

He told her because it was going to come out. This was a fire he couldn't hide. Now he was going to get badly burned. The masterpiece wasn't moving. She was awfully still, terribly sad, agonisingly attentive: the watched and the watcher. He longed, desperately, to crawl over to touch every brushstroke, feel every rise and fall in the impossible contours of her face, her arm, her hands, asking himself, 'Is this real?', but he daren't move.

'I can't take it any more, John,' she repeated. The black had reached her lips. The pink silk scarf had come loose and lay along one cheek.

She suspects nothing, thought John, coldly.

'I've had enough,' she said, with a brutal, hopeless finality.

The phrase turned in John's mind like a light switch. Instantly, he saw something odd. Anselm had used the very same words only recently, just before John had come to Warsaw. For some inexplicable reason – ostensibly for a jaunt – he'd brought John to a monastery in Suffolk. They'd gone up the bell tower. He'd looked down and said, 'I've had enough.'

'What of?'

'Trying to find reasons.'

'For what?'

Anselm had just leaned on the stone ledge, four whopping bells behind his head, looking down at the dots of people on the ground – like Harry Lime in *The Third Man*, high up on the Ferris wheel in Prater Park. Only Anselm hadn't got the eyes of a man cynical about the boundaries of pity . . . he'd been melancholy, outreaching, vaguely desperate . . .

'You're not in love, are you?'

There'd be no reply.

'Who is it? That ballet dancer? Your clerk? No . . . the jazz singer with the veils? Veil after veil will lift, but there must be veil upon veil behind?'

Anselm had just kept his gaze on the dots and

344

the pink tiled roofs below. Obliquely, he'd muttered, 'It's like a stone in the shoe. Asking why it's there doesn't get rid of it. Chasing reasons is like . . .'

What had Anselm said? John couldn't remember, damn it, but the message was clear enough: there's no point in trying to find out why you love something . . . or someone . . . you've just got to get on with it, regardless of the implications.

'Come with me,' John blurted out.

Celina stared back, like Anselm had stared down.

'Bring your film to London,' mumbled John. 'I've got friends. We'll get it out in a diplomatic bag.' She didn't react. She just looked at him as if she were grieving. John made it across the floor and took the dangling hand. It was warm, the nails a dark purple, like mussel shells. He kissed each one, feeling the bangles against his forehead. 'Please come with me.' His eyes closed and he made a leap into the dark. He let himself fall, no longer resisting, knowing this moment had been coming ever since they'd first met to discuss art and resistance.

'I love you,' he said, for the first time.

John dialled 55876. Celina's passport was organised for the same day. Later in the afternoon, he tried to call back. He had to know if the Dentist had spoken to Róża about CONRAD; and he wanted to ask about the file . . . the file at the heart of their relationship. But it was too late. The line had gone dead.

CHAPTER 37

Anselm walked away from Father Kaminsky's church like Róża had once left Mokotów prison: wondering where to go when he reached the junction. The collapse of his theorising had an immediate and profound effect: a loss of confidence in his judgement and the utility of Róża's statement which finally showed itself for what it was – altogether useless. There were too many names on the quarterdeck. There was no way to allocate a stronger suspicion to one above another. Standing at the intersection a flood of irritation filled the void left by Father Kaminsky's innocence: all he could do now was accuse someone. If they were guilty, he might reach their conscience; if they were innocent, then they might be enraged enough to point the finger at someone else.

Half an hour later Anselm passed beneath an eagle on the elaborate entrance to Warsaw University. Neoclassical grandeur – rebuilt of course – was home to the one suspect likely to speak a language known to Anselm. Róża had watched him grow from boy to man; she'd never want him exposed for what he was. Having found a reception desk, Anselm passed over a name written on a scrap of paper. Moments later, the telephonist handed him the receiver. Anselm skipped any introduction and went straight to the point, opting for French, the idiom of intellectuals across nineteenth century Europe.

'I'm in Warsaw to find out who betrayed Róża Mojeska in nineteen eighty-two.'

There was a very long pause, followed by, 'You are?'

'I am. You could say I'm Róża's representative. I thought we might talk through the circumstances of your sudden release from internment.'

'You do?'

'Yes, because the word convenient springs to mind.'

Anselm placed Bernard Kolba at sixty or so. He wore loose jeans, a black roll-neck sweater and scuffed suede shoes. His hair, chestnut brown and rimed with age, was short and smart. The felt hat in his hand evoked an artist rather than an academic philosopher. Without speaking he led Anselm to a car park and a yellow Fiat with a dinted passenger door. He seemed neither insulted nor troubled. In fact, he had the air of a man ready to talk.

'I thought we'd go the Powązki Cemetery,' he said, struggling with the ignition. 'Lots of national heroes are buried in quiet out-of-the-way corners

– heroes, of course, according to your convictions. It's a good place to talk about the past.'

In that spirit of openness, he invited Anselm to say a little more of his mission. Anticipating reciprocity Anselm hid nothing of substance, recounting all that had taken place between John's coming to Larkwood and Anselm's departure from the church by the railway line, leaving out, of course, the distraction of the blue paper whose private character commanded Anselm's continued confidence. He'd just about finished when Bernard parked and yanked the handbrake. Walking in step, they passed through another ornate gate to enter the graveyard where Róża had been arrested by Otto Brack.

'I'm here to make an appeal to conscience,' said Anselm, in conclusion. 'Róża seeks an admission, freely made, without any preliminary accusation. Your thoughts on the matter would, I imagine, be instructive.'

Bernard nodded with appreciation, as if a professor in the law department had come up with a novel scheme to deal with plagiarism. He turned right, his hand guiding Anselm down a long lane flanked by carved angels, bare trees and a scattering of lit candles.

'I used to think that it was my teachers who'd shaped my mind,' he said, as if taking up the proposal raised by his learned colleague. 'But it was Róża. As a child she told me the story of the Shoemaker and how he'd destroyed the red dragon with a homemade bomb. Later she told me that words were more powerful than any explosion and that set me reading.'

The fairytale had led him to academic philosophy, non-violent resistance, factory work, Union activism and, finally, a return to the formal pursuit of wisdom. After the collapse of communism in 1989 he'd gone back to university and finished the studies which the government of another day had suppressed. Six years later he'd begun his career as a junior lecturer.

'By and large my doctoral thesis set out the ideas I'd have published already, if Róża hadn't been arrested by the SB. They'd have appeared in *Freedom and Independence*. That's why I wanted to meet the Shoemaker. To talk things out and get his guidance. In those days ideas weren't kept in the academy, they were running wild on the street. He was the giant on the block and I was the pygmy wanting to climb on his back and see that little bit further.'

Anselm had a rather depressing sense of déjà-vu. The tenor of these winsome disclosures carried no hint of an impending declaration of guilt. Bernard's conscience was evidently clear; but he was talking and moving with purpose.

'I've always wondered why Róża just threw her hand in,' he said, turning left. 'She's never spoken of that day to me or, as far as I'm aware, to anyone else. We've all been wondering why. We've all been trying to figure out who tipped off the SB. Obviously, it had to be someone close to her, someone she wouldn't suspect.' His hand directed Anselm to the right. 'Someone like me, you might think.'

Shortly, Bernard came to a halt. He looked around, gathering in a memory. 'This is where it happened; this is where Róża was betrayed . . . at the grave of Prus.'

Bernard pointed to a large distinctive monument. A small girl, carved in relief, was reaching up against the stone. Her arms were spread out and her head was thrown back. At her feet were yellow and red flowers. A candle burned in a green glass jar. The surrounding trees seemed to reach out to the atmosphere of sadness.

'Róża chose this place for a specific reason,' said Bernard. His hands were in his pockets as if he were extemporising in a lecture hall. 'She picked it because of the girl. She saw herself in those shoes.'

Like Prus, Róża had been a child soldier. They'd both joined an uprising; they'd both been imprisoned and never quite recovered. Prus . . . he'd fought in eighteen sixty-three against imperial Russia. The succeeding experience of prison gave him lifelong problems with panic attacks and agoraphobia. He'd turned to writing, but couldn't decide if resistance was best through ideas or guns.

'Róża was scarred by Mokotów,' said Bernard. 'But she was always sure of the ground where the fight would eventually be won; in the mind and heart. Which is all the more significant now that I know of her husband's execution.'

He began walking away with that steady purpose, so Anselm followed, his intuition tingling with anticipation, undecided as to whether it was agreeable or not.

'We'd all seen the two rings, we'd all wondered what they meant,' said Bernard. 'We'd all been stunned when she turned out to be linked to the Shoemaker. We'd all been baffled when she went silent in eighty-two – realising, with retrospect, that she'd done the same thing in fifty-three . . . and that the wedding rings were part of her silence.' He slowed down and took a narrow pebbled lane to the left. 'Róża is the most mysterious person I've ever known. Without speaking she was always crying out for help and I couldn't do anything . . . I didn't know how to reach her. So I'm glad you called. I'm glad, at last, for the chance to do something *significant*. I've waited thirty years for this.'

Bernard took off his brown felt hat and scratched the back of his head. He turned his face sideways to find Anselm.

'You've heard of Mateusz Robak?'

'Yes.'

'He got close to Róża, too. He's another man with a doubtful profile.'

There was a sliver of irony or sarcasm in those strong, hazel eyes, but the surrounding light carried a heavier regret.

351

'We fell out, once, over a play by Mickiewicz,' resumed Bernard. 'And we nearly fell out again over Róża's arrest. But he was a very careful man. And he had to be careful for Róża. So he followed her sometimes, even when she thought she was alone, just in case of trouble. So when I accused him of collaboration, like you accused me – though I failed to choose my words as finely as you did – he had a reply. He brought me here.'

Once more Bernard pointed towards a grave. The headstone was a fraction too tall, making Anselm think the incumbent had been given a straitjacket for eternity. He stepped closer to read the inscription. There was only a name and some dates: the barest elements of identification. No loving words had come to the husband's mind. It read:

Klara Fielding
8th March 1925 – 1st July 1953

Anselm read the inscription several times as if more information might suddenly appear on the stone. This was John's secret. He'd only told Róża. It was why he'd come to Warsaw.

'A BBC journalist wanted to interview the Shoemaker,' said Bernard. 'Róża told Mateusz to arrange a meeting. When the guy arrived, Róża tailed him . . . and Mateusz tailed Róża. In turn, they came here, before convening at the agreed location as if nothing had happened. Mateusz thought nothing of it until much later, when Róża walked into a trap.'

Bernard had tracked down Klara's family. Not the English one, by marriage – they'd left the country – but the Communist Party members who'd come to Warsaw from Poznań after the war: her parents.

'They were still fiercely proud of her memory,' said Bernard, stepping to one side, moving his shadow off the grave. 'Even though they knew nothing of her work for the state, they clung on to the fact that it was significant. That's what the man in the dark suit had said at the funeral. He'd come round a week later with her medals, recognition from Warsaw and Moscow of her service to the people . . . difficult service.'

Anselm did the maths. 'She was only twenty-eight.'

'Yes.'

'What happened? She had a husband; she was a young mother.'

John, the child, had only just been born.

'Suicide.'

Anselm breathed back the word.

'She hung herself. But not in the garage or her bedroom. She chose an unguarded section of railings around the Ministry of Internal Affairs. Her parents didn't know that, of course – it would have shattered the myth. And myths, even false ones, can heal if you believe in them.'

Mateusz had also tracked down her friends.

She'd been carefree and funny. Talented, too, a musician who'd won prizes at home and abroad. She'd been naive, thinking she could marry an English diplomat without attracting the attention of the security service.

'Not one of these old friends knew she'd been recruited,' said Bernard, buffing the felt with the back of his hand. 'All they noticed was that she'd lost her sense of fun. They'd thought it was because of the Englishman, you know, that stiff upper lip and the stiff embassy parties. But then she made a confession of what she'd done, to these people that mattered. She planned to tell her husband, too. A couple of days later she vanished.'

One of those shattered friends, a former love – kindly rejected – hadn't accepted the police explanation of a road accident. So he'd gone to the undertaker's with a bottle of vodka and a Molotov cocktail and given him a choice. They'd got smashed making vows of secrecy about the tell-tale bruising to Klara's neck and the laugh of the *ubek* who'd unhooked the body from outside his place of work.

'But how does all this relate to John?' asked Anselm, moved and sad, his mind drained of curiosity. 'Did Mateusz ask himself that question? Did you?'

'Yes, we did.' Bernard scratched the back of his head again, not especially enjoying the moment he'd waited for since 1982. 'Your friend told Róża that he'd come to Warsaw to make up for a mistake . . .

that's what Róża told Mateusz. She'd been overwhelmed by his honesty; she'd wanted to help him; she'd brought him into the struggle. But things looked very different once Róża was back in Mokotów and Mateusz had unearthed the nature of Klara's mistake. There were only four people who'd known about that planned meeting with the Shoemaker: Father Kaminsky, Mateusz, me and . . .'

Bernard left a sort of gap for Anselm to fill but, not wanting to name his friend, he made a kind of last-ditch loyal defence. He thought of his father sighting the Indians at Little Big Horn. He sensed an impending death and grief.

'But John has no motive. He'd mapped the failings of communism from East Berlin to Bucharest and everywhere in between. He told me once of a betrayal – he meant her abandonment of him. He'd never forgiven her . . .'

Bernard listened, nodding with agreement, following the steps in Anselm's thinking, not accepting – with immense regret – where they were leading. He stepped back, as if to get some distance from Klara, not wanting her to hear what he was going to say.

'I'd imagine that for a child, the suicide of a parent could be a sort of betrayal. They weren't important enough. Something was bigger. But that doesn't mean they cease to love them, deeply, and all they stood for.'

Anselm didn't respond because he knew it was true.

'You know, a child can grow to spend their life trying to find what they've lost. To reach the person taken away. They can seek out the streets on which that vanished parent walked . . . to see what they saw, to smell the air they breathed, to feel the same breeze on their skin. And they can do something even more desperate, a gruesome act of necrophilia: they can dig deep into the grave to salvage what their mother or father cared about. To bring those ideas and feelings back to life. To live them out, in the flesh, in mystical union with the person who turned their back upon them. Everything's forgiven. They're together again. It's another kind of suicide. This time the child is dead. Everything they might have thought and felt has been buried in an unmarked grave. They've made the ultimate sacrifice, dying so that someone else might live.'

Again Anselm couldn't speak. He was looking at Klara's inscription, her life reduced to two dates. No wonder Mr Fielding had been lost for words.

'We think he came clean to Róża because it gave him the best kind of cover,' continued Bernard, in a changed voice; less compassionate, more logical. 'The remorse of a child salvaging the mistake of his mother – it's a good story and credible. The mapped failings of communism from East Berlin to Bucharest? Part of a long and detailed preparation. I think it's called a legend. When your friend came to Warsaw, it was a homecoming. He'd arrived to finish off what his mother had started.'

Sebastian didn't argue as much as Anselm had expected. Perhaps it was Anselm's crisp retorts, the impatient authority of a judge in control of his court. Holding the phone some distance from his ear and mouth, he spoke to the Warsaw skyline. No, it wasn't Father Kaminsky who'd led Brack to Róża and it wasn't Bernard Kolba. Their innocence had sparkled. Anselm cut short the remonstrations, asking him to check the SB archive for material on Klara Fielding and her son, John. Perhaps they might discuss the outcome the following evening. It had been a long day, he'd said, and tomorrow he fancied a spot of aimless sight-seeing.

CHAPTER 38

Cooking when you're blind isn't as difficult as one might think, but it takes years of practice – at least when it comes to the more demanding recipes, and those heartbreakers, like Yorkshire pudding, which rise, or don't rise according to a caprice of their own. John had been down the roast dinner road many times and, after almost thirty years, it held no terrors for him. Except for that pudding. It wouldn't fall into line.

John's hands were shaking, too, and that didn't help. The risk of accident hovered in his darkness. Róża had said she'd come round. *You're a fool*, thought John. *You should have left well alone.* Only, all was not well.

John felt his way across the kitchen, tapping the edge of the worktop. His hands wandered towards the knife stand and he picked out the second from the left. Mechanically, he chopped some garlic, moving fast towards his thumb and finger.

Róża wanted justice.

He'd nearly fallen over when he'd answered the phone and heard that voice. He'd gripped the door frame, leaning his head against the wall. He'd

358

listened, trying to hear the traces of accusation in her rushed explanation – the blind are good at that; they can hear things above the frequency of ordinary sighted folk; but Róża was too good; she was too smart; she was wasn't giving anything away. She just stayed within the conventional waveband, leaving him to pick up the signal. She wanted to know who'd betrayed her. She'd said whoever betrayed her in eighty-two could help her bring Otto Brack to court by facing their past. All they had to do was agree to meet her.

Dear God, what had the Dentist said to her? How much did she know?

John had listened with his eyes squeezed shut, trying to locate the slightest crackle of accusation. He couldn't hear it. She just sounded resolved, her need for help almost tearing at his clothes. It was as though Róża were on her knees, forehead touching his shoes, her hands knotted into the hem of his trousers. It had been awful.

And – out of genuine affection, but a colossal lack of prudence, in the face of everything the Dentist had ever taught him – he'd said, 'Róża, come round, will you? I'll give you the taste of an English heaven.'

When he'd finished off the clove, he trussed up the meat with string.

For the first time since the bandages were taken off his eyes, John wished, with a suppressed screaming desperation, that he could see. Róża was there, four steps in front of him, seated at the end of the dining table. She smelled of 4711 cologne. Her hand had been cool and soft, the wrinkles like the striations in some living stone. Her cheek had been warm, those fine hairs touching his skin when he kissed her.

'Do you remember the grave of Prus?' she said, her knife clinking. She'd put it down. Which meant she was watching.

'How could I forget?' John kept his hand against the table to control the shake. For the moment, he'd have to leave the wine. He didn't want any spilling. 'I never asked, why did you pick that spot?'

'The caretaker at Saint Justyn's once brought us . . . he was a wonderful man, always dressed in patched overalls. Mr Lasky. His eyebrows were huge, like woollen hats for his eyes. He played the banjo.'

He'd told them stories when she was a child. His job was fixing doors and windows and pipes but he found an excuse whenever he could to drop his tools and be with the children. He'd loved children. That's why he'd taken the job in the first place. They'd shot him in the ruins of the Ghetto while the stones were still hot.

'Hot?' John's breathing scraped out the word; his chest was tightening.

'There was an Uprising before ours. After they'd crushed the remaining Jewish community, they blew the Ghetto to pieces. I'm told the Shoemaker was in there.'

Her knife clinked. She'd picked it up . . . but

she wasn't eating . . . she was looking away. John snatched at his glass and gulped some wine.

'The grave of Prus,' he said, playing dangerous, going back to the place of Róża's arrest. 'I loved the carving of that child.'

'Me, too.' Her knife clinked; so did the fork. 'Do you remember that article you did on me for that series on lives lived in secret for the truth?'

'I do-o-o-o.' John drew out the last word as if he'd just been brought to something fondly packed away in the attic.

'The title embarrassed me *hugely*.'

'Really?'

'Oh yes. It made me sound like a hero.' Her gruff voice showed smiling and affection. 'That was the beginning, wasn't it?'

'Of what?'

'Our friendship.'

'God, of course, sorry, yes.'

'Don't worry.'

'No really, I'm half out of it. Getting the old Yorkshire to rise did me in.'

'It meant a lot, what you told me, John . . . about your mother.'

'It was just . . . natural.'

'I could tell.' She picked up her cutlery. 'I followed you, you know.'

'What?' John coughed and dabbed his mouth. 'Sorry, it's the string on the beef, ha. Don't know why we do that. The thing's dead. Why tie it up?'

'I said I followed you.'

'That's right. Sorry again. Where to? The ends of the BBC?'

'No.' Her tone was smiling and warm again. 'To her grave. If you hadn't gone there, you know, I might never have met you. I might have changed my mind at the last minute.'

'Really.'

'Oh yes, agreeing to see you was the breaking of a golden rule.'

'Rule?'

'Mmmmm. Never meet a stranger. But having seen her stone, I thought you had roots. Deep roots in my soil.'

'I'm glad, because I have; because . . .' John coughed again. 'Blasted stuff. It's part of an Englishman's understanding of paradise. You can't get in without a ball of string and penknife. Dear God –' he banged his chest, thinking what to say – 'roots. You never leave them behind.'

'No, you don't.'

They ate in silence, John composing himself, trying to classify the signals from the other end of the table. There was no doubting the use of code – the lives lived in secret, that tilt towards the Shoemaker, and the tailing to a grave and the beginning of it all – the problem was cracking it; being *sure*. What had the Dentist said to her? If only John knew, he could play out this meal and make it to the shore. And with that thought, he hated himself: deeply and angrily. Róża wanted justice. She'd waited the length of the Cold War and more. The

362

Big Game was over, and John was still ducking and weaving over a Yorkshire pudding. It was ignoble.

'Do you remember the film-maker?' asked Róża.

'Blimey, I haven't thought of her in thirty years.'

'You would ask about the Shoemaker so I would ask about her. It was the only way to shut you up.'

'Ha, yes, that's right. Dear oh dear, I was pushy in those days.'

'I think you'd have given your back teeth for that interview. I'm sorry it wasn't possible.'

'No matter. I got you instead.'

'Yes, John, you did.'

Back teeth? Was that a reference to the Dentist? Was she slowly eating him up? Was she getting ready to spit out the gristle of what she knew? John made a kind of dash for the door.

'She came to London, too, you know?'

'Really?'

'Yes.'

'Brought a film with her. She'd lined up a string of clips . . . the forces of order at work, from fifty-six to eighty-one. Not that subtle, I have to say, but hard-hitting. It was shown on BBC2. Unfortunately –' one finger strayed near his dark glasses – 'I never got to see it.'

She was drinking some wine. There was no soft thud: the glass didn't return to the table . . . she was watching again, cautiously. She was thinking, appraising, making a decision. Oh God, what was she going to say now? Or was that last, pointed

363

reference to his blindness going to save him? Had he silenced her with a bid for pity?

'What happened?' she asked, very quietly.

'I went off the rails . . . well, off the road actually. Hit a tree.'

'I'm sorry.'

'Don't be. As a kid I always tried to see in the dark. That's why I'd eaten the carrots.'

The smell of bread and butter pudding was almost loud, the promised tang of raisins taking the top note.

'I'd better be going.'

John didn't argue. He'd won match point with a blow below the belt. Or had he? He just didn't know. But he wasn't going to stay in the ring to find out. He said how pleased he'd been to hear her voice and natter about the old days. And she was silent, feeding her arms into her coat, settling her hat, working her fingers into the gloves. At the door a cold blast of air swept off Hampstead Heath, bringing back the recollection of snow in Warsaw, and tanks and soldiers. Suddenly her hands grabbed his arms and squeezed them hard. Her fingers were on him, as his had once been upon her in that dreary flat, when he'd seen the bullet beneath the mirror; when he realised how close to suicide she'd sailed. He could feel the desolation breathing mist in the darkness.

'Goodbye, John,' she said, 'and thank you.'

★　★　★

364

Thank you? What for? Throughout a seemingly endless night John gnawed at his thumb bone to keep his teeth from tearing off his nails. He curled up, writing with anxiety. *What for? A Yorkshire pudding that rose to the occasion? Or that punch to the kidneys?* The wind moved listlessly across the common. A car crawled to a halt and then pulled away rapidly . . . it had to be a taxi. Feet stumbled on the pavement. Another gust of wind, stronger this time, rattled the bay window downstairs. At times, he didn't like the wind. It carried too many sounds, too many signals. It made him feel confused.

When morning came John made a pot of strong coffee, chilled by a certainty that had grown as the heath fell silent. She hadn't taken back her request for help. Surprised by his blindness, Róża hadn't mumbled, 'Forget what I said on the phone.' She still wanted justice. She was still looking to him with that bullet in the background, despair misting her eyes.

After four large cups of Fair Trade Arabica from Peru, John picked up the phone and dialled one of the few numbers he knew by heart. All his life he couldn't commit them to memory. Finally, the Old Duffer put him through.

'Anselm?'

'Yep.' The goat had managed it. 'What's up?'

'I need a lawyer.'

CHAPTER 39

A special kind of quiet reigned over the empty corridors of the IPN. Most of the staff had gone home. The outcome of Sebastian's research lay on a long mahogany table in a large conference room. There were two sections of material, but each had their own piles with individual sheets laid out for ease of reference. The matching chairs on one side had been pulled back to the wall, allowing Sebastian and Anselm to move freely, as if they were choosing what to eat at a self-service counter. Heavy gold curtains had been drawn. Ornate wall lights cast a pleasant, soft light. Sebastian had made coffee and the woman in white had found some Austrian biscuits. There was an unmistakable atmosphere of finality, embarrassment and secrecy, which was odd because the substance of everything on the table would soon be on the TV and plastered over the front pages of the national press.

'I'll start with Klara,' said Sebastian, moving to the far end of the table. He'd taken off his jacket and thrown it on the back of a chair. 'Her file is missing. Maybe it went into one of the shredders.

Its absence is unfortunate but not fatal to our purpose. There are lots of clues left behind and they give us a fairly clear picture of her value as an agent and the kind of work she carried out.'

He pointed at an open ledger, very much like a school attendance register. His finger tapped 'Klara Fielding' in a left-hand column. Alongside, to the right, was the agent name: JULITA.

'While we have confirmation of her recruitment,' he said, loosening his tie, 'we don't know whether she was a volunteer or whether she agreed to co-operate following an approach. The timing is significant. She goes into the book within a month of her marriage. That suggests a friendly tap on the shoulder after the exchange of rings.'

Confirmed by her friends, thought Anselm. They'd found her changed by close proximity to English phlegm. She'd lost her sense of fun.

'Obviously, as the wife of a British diplomat, she was a well-placed and potentially high-value source.' Sebastian stepped from left to right, drawing Anselm along. He picked up a sheaf of photocopied correspondence. 'She didn't disappoint. This letter is typical and shows what kind of material she was feeding to her handlers. When Churchill went to Washington in January fifty-two to show the world that the Brits and the Americans were ever the best of friends, JULITA had reported that there were, in fact, strong differences over policy to the Middle and Far East, defence strategy and the supply of US steel. I suppose Klara just listened to table talk and repeated what she'd heard.' Sebastian tapped an annotation at the bottom of the page. 'But it was important: this missive was copied to Vyshinsky in the Foreign Affairs Department in Moscow. Klara was listening for Stalin. She'd become his ears in the British Embassy.'

Sebastian shuffled further to the right.

'Now these are as frustrating as they are enticing.'

Three books lay open in a line, like new acquisitions in a public library, the pages chosen to seize the curiosity of anyone who happened to pass by.

'It seems Klara's value was domestic as well as foreign. These are entry and exit registers. They show that Klara attended various locations, presumably to report back to her handler or other interested parties. The addresses are revealing, as are the names of the persons she met. Klara was talking to members of the Public Security Commission.' Sebastian spoke with heavy significance, but it was lost on Anselm, so he spelled out the implication. 'The Commission coordinated the Terror. Presumably Klara had information on friends and contacts of the UK government. Or the Commission was asking her to keep an ear to the ground about certain people. Without her file, we'll never know.'

He moved a step to the left, stopping in front of the third volume. Slowly he ran his finger across the bottom of the page as if to underline an entry.

'JULITA came to Mokotów in nineteen

fifty-two,' he said, drily. 'She'd an appointment with Major Strenk. I'd love to know what they talked about.'

'Me, too,' said Anselm, managing to make a contribution at last.

They both read the sepia script several times. Anselm wanted to lift each word off the page and squeeze out the meaning, as if they were so many sponges soaked in blood.

'She was in the building at the same time as Róża,' said Anselm.

'Yes.'

'Pure chance, but it makes my skin crawl.'

'Mine, too.'

'Is there anything in there –' Anselm gestured towards the neat piles thinking of bodies in a morgue – 'which links Klara to Brack?'

'No. But they could easily have met; Brack was Strenk's immediate subordinate.'

He sure was. Father Kaminsky had called them pupil and master, father and son. 'Anything that links Klara to Róża?'

'Nothing.' Sebastian sighed. 'Being under the one roof is just a coincidence. The Commission were talking to Róża. Klara was talking to the Commission. All it shows is two women on different sides of the fence. They'd made contrary choices. They each paid a price . . . the cost, in the end, being roughly similar.'

From that perspective, the last document on the conference table was a kind of receipt. In August

1953 a functionary in the Ministry of Public Security had circulated a letter to Departments I, IV, V, VII and section heads at Bureaus A and B informing them (in terms) that JULITA's stream of intelligence had dried up, a nice enough phrase, sufficiently wide to encompass death.

Sebastian moved along two paces, stopping at the beginning of the second group of records. Again they lay in a row like today's specials in the canteen.

'Now we come to John,' said Sebastian, almost brightly.

Who didn't know that JULITA had been found hanging from a set of railings. He knew nothing of her self-accusation. Maybe John had tracked down his proud maternal grandparents and seen the two medals that had been slipped under the door by Strenk or whoever. She'd done important work for the future, they'd have said. She'd made a difference.

'There is a file on John,' began Sebastian, opening the green cover and closing it again as if it wasn't worth a glance. 'Like every other journalist he was watched but nothing of interest was picked up. His profile and conduct are just like any other correspondent. He doesn't stand out. He doesn't attract any attention. The only record of relevance is his expulsion from Warsaw for activities consistent with espionage.'

'Any mention of Brack?'

'None.'

'Thought not.'

A second phone had appeared on Brack's desk. He'd told Irina not to breathe a word of the Dentist to Frenzel. He'd been up to something that couldn't make a bleep on anyone's radar, neither the SB's nor the Stasi's.

'At this point, I thought I'd come to a dead end,' said Sebastian, hands deep in his pockets. The black stubble showed he hadn't shaved. He'd been working hard. 'Just to be sure, I sent off a string of emails to other archive holders throughout the former communist bloc. Nothing came back until this afternoon –' he began that relentless drift again from left to right – 'when these arrived from Bucharest. This time Brack does make an appearance.'

Though not immediately, explained Sebastian, holding up a report dated 8th August 1979. John Fielding had been arrested by the Securitate at the airport as he was preparing to board a plane for Prague. They'd previously tailed him to a mountain village where he'd met a professor considered to have fallen foul of the social order.

'I'll spare you the boring bits,' said Sebastian, turning the page to a paragraph marked with a yellow Post-it. 'They already knew the family history from previous correspondence with Warsaw. Maybe that's why they let him go . . . but not before writing up a quite interesting character description. A wide-ranging interview had shown him to be broadly disenchanted with western politics. A Hollywood actor had finally made it to the Oval Office. He was "embittered" –' Sebastian's fingers opened and closed the inverted commas – 'following the election victory of Margaret Thatcher the previous May. She was, he said, "no friend of the labour movement". The Securitate analyst deemed John a potential "co-worker". Someone who might turn if approached in the right way.' Sebastian dropped the report back on the table and picked up the next papers in line. '. . . a prospect that was brought to Brack's attention two years later.'

In early 1982 he'd carried out a routine check on a journalist newly arrived in Warsaw and had been delighted to receive a copy of the report and the recommendation. Brack – terse and obscure – gave no hint of his intentions.

'Did he take it up?' asked Anselm, as if he needed to know.

'Well, this is where it all gets very interesting,' said Sebastian, reaching the end of the table and the last selection of documents. 'You'd have thought that Brack would have put this stuff from the Securitate in John's file, but he didn't. He didn't put it anywhere – remember, I had to get it from Bucharest – instead he seems to have binned the lot or shredded it later, leaving behind one tantalising clue . . .'

Sebastian opened the cover of a large brown ring binder.

'Now, on its own, this is not a helpful resource,' he said, sliding his thumb on to another yellow

Post-it. He lifted the top pages and lay the binder flat. 'This is simply an inventory of names comprising agents, potential agents and targets.'

'Perpetrators and victims?'

'Yeah.'

'All mixed up?'

'Exactly and, as I say, not much use if you've got nothing else to go on.'

'Unlike ourselves.'

Sebastian nodded, his lips firm and unsmiling. His finger pointed at John's name, as he'd pointed at Klara's. In a parallel column was the chosen title: CONRAD.

'Of course, it's not unequivocal evidence,' said Sebastian, moving across the room towards the coffee pot. 'But it doesn't get much stronger.'

'Oh yes, it does,' said Anselm, taking the little jug of milk. He made a splash in two polystyrene cups. 'Do you have details on special telephone lines set up during SB covert operations in nineteen eighty-two?'

Sebastian turned slowly, appraising Anselm with guarded respect, interested to know what the monk easily distracted by the meaning of life had been up to when he wasn't talking to Father Kaminsky and Bernard Kolba. 'Yes, we do.'

'John can't even remember his own birth date. He left a phone number in a Warsaw guidebook. 55876. Check it out. I think you'll find it rang on Brack's desk.'

★   ★   ★

Anselm's investigation had run its term. In a way, he'd come full circle, beginning with John and ending with John. For the moment – lying in bed, hands behind his neck – he simply couldn't grasp the distance between the person he thought he knew and the person whose secret life he'd uncovered. He was stunned and couldn't reflect with the necessary detachment. Quite apart from any personal considerations, he couldn't imagine how John might occupy the central plank in Brack's scheme – and how that scheme could silence Róża for so long. But he did and it had. The Dentist's private operation had been a ringing success. For some reason, Róża would never contemplate John's exposure . . .

But she'd changed her mind. She'd come to London. She'd come to John's door. She'd come with a statement to help him walk through fire: an account of her life that only showed her *understanding* of his circumstances; that held out no *blame* for what he'd done to her in return. And John had stood there, blind, playing the dumb waiter. She'd left him, devastated, as when he'd last seen her; when he'd gone to her Warsaw flat protesting his innocence, offering to find the informer. She'd left him to his blindness. She'd thrown her statement in a bin. Once again, she'd taken pity on someone who deserved to suffer.

But why on earth should Róża want to protect John? As the Prior said, she'd only known him a matter of months.

The following morning – Anselm's last in Warsaw – he took a listless breakfast. Even the personal hurt seemed far off, shrinking from his nerves. In a daze he packed his bag; he tidied the room; and, coat on, he rang Bernard Kolba to apologise for his crass accusation the day before. The lurch to make reparation yielded an unexpected dividend: the conversation rolled on to the next steps and the mystery of Róża's present location. She's still in London, said Bernard. Staying with Magda Samovitz in Stockwell Green. Róża had taken her first holiday in living memory. Was there any better diversion, thought Anselm, entering the lift, than to shatter everyone's illusions, including your own?

Sebastian was waiting for Anselm in the hotel foyer. He took his bag and drove him to the airport with the solicitude of an undertaker holding up the traffic, his mood similar to that of the quiet monk at his side. He'd come dark-suited with a mumbling apology of his own, for how things had turned out. He'd have preferred it if Róża's informer had been someone at arm's length.

'But, then, the point of informers is that they get close. It's a pity you got burned, too.'

Yes, that was the right word – Anselm woke as the aircraft tilted into dense cloud over England – it was a pity all round.

A pity for Róża. A pity for Klara and for Irina,

blunted tools thrown aside. A pity for the fat young man with the plastic Kalashnikov. A pity for Edward, who knew more than he could ever say. A pity for Bernard and Aniela who knew nothing. A pity for George Fielding whose love turned sour and Melanie who came on as substitute to play Misery. And John, too. There was pity for John somewhere.

The scale of these dark reflections obscured all thought of Anselm's one remaining task: the confrontation of his old school friend, the person who'd sent him to Warsaw to find out why Róża had come to London. Instead his mind went elsewhere, seeking a diversion of its own. And it went somewhere altogether interesting.

Mooching round his cell before Compline, warmed to the point of injury by that first sound of bells, he recalled that Róża Mojeska and Father Kaminsky had something in common. Unknown to the other, they'd each shared a friend: Mr Lasky, the caretaker at Saint Justyn's Orphanage for Girls. The name had cropped up in Róża's statement as it had fallen from the mouth of Father Kaminsky. In one of those flashes of certainty-without-good-cause – sudden perceptions that Anselm no longer presumed to question – he was sure that the relationship between the three people – an orphan, a caretaker and a priest – lay at the centre of the greater picture, the canvas upon which John had made a late and troubled entry.

'Maybe Mr Lasky is part of the pity of it all,' said Anselm, heading down to Compline. 'A man whom Róża had known as a child, long before she faced the terrors of the night.'

PART VI

THE MIND OF OTTO BRACK

CHAPTER 40

The woodshed at Larkwood remained standing by some mystery of physics not yet known to modern science. Two of three central beams were cracked. Most of the dark rafters seemed to be unattached at either end. All the main uprights, already bent, were gravely aslant. The caramel wattle and daub was crazed with deep fissures. Chunks were missing, leaving ancient silver twigs peeping out like the stems of dried flowers, their heads long gone.

'You were right,' said Anselm to the Prior.

'In what way?'

'Brack's world. It's a dangerous place. I wish I'd never been there. I wish I'd never tried to understand these people, the Bracks and Frenzels. You can't get close without losing something essential to yourself. They're leeches on your soul, they suck and suck and then excrete your best intentions in some dark corner.'

He was sitting on an old piano stool. The Prior faced him, the sleeves of his habit rolled up, the scapular tucked into his belt. But for the accent, distilled from the Clyde and the Lark, he'd have stepped straight out of a Turgenev short story. In his hands was a large axe.

'You were right,' repeated Anselm. His tone had changed from lament to accusation. 'I grubbed around buying information from a man who chewed up people's lives over a bottle of Bollinger. Why did you let me go?'

'I thought you wanted to help John,' replied the Prior, reasonably. 'Perhaps John more than Róża.'

'I did. I went to Warsaw for him. *He* asked *me* for *help*.'

'With good reason, it seems.'

'Really?'

'Yes.' The Prior seemed to test the weight of the axe, letting it swing like a pendulum. 'I get the impression you wanted to give one kind of help and you're discomfited to find you've been asked for another. But that's what happens when you grasp someone's outstretched hand: you don't know what will happen once you start to pull.'

Relatively speaking, the Prior had been unmoved by the revelation of John's betrayal. There'd been a lifting of an eyebrow; a slight tilt of the head as if to acknowledge that a Lebanon cedar had just crashed through the main Dorter window. But he wasn't overly troubled by the glass on the floor and the fault in the exposed grain. These were his woods, he seemed to say. He knew all about trees and why they fell. And how to cut them down, too. He tapped the axe on the ground.

'When someone asks for assistance, Anselm, you

count the dangers, you eye up the risks, and you take precautions. And then you help. You don't count and appraise so as to take the preventative measure of leaving. You stay. You reach out, perhaps with fear in your heart, knowing that you, too, might fall.'

'Why did he ask me to go?' mumbled Anselm, not quite hearing the Prior's rebuke. 'He knew I'd find out about his mother. He knew I'd find out that he'd worked with Brack. He even gave me Brack's old number as if he wanted me to give him a call to talk over the life and times of agent CONRAD. Why not tell me himself, outright?'

'Because there's more to John's story than a betrayal. His life is more than a list of facts. Perhaps there is too much to tell, too much to reveal, too much to explain; because he's lost to simple declarations. In those circumstances, the lost man doesn't want to talk, he wants to be found. He wants his friend to find him. He wants him to learn everything along the way so that when they finally meet a discussion can take place, one that is deep and honest and true.'

I want you to coax them out of the dark, John had said. *Failing that, bring them kicking and screaming into the light. Rough or smooth, give them a helping hand.*

Anselm studied the Prior's contracted features, the squared shoulders, the rolled up sleeves.

'Just how much do you know?' he asked, quietly, knowing the Prior wouldn't answer, seeing him

383

once more at his friend's side, long ago, listening intently to mumbled confidences.

'Enough to be sure that John needs a helping hand. As, in fact, do I.'

He nodded towards a pile of mature, dry wood stacked high against one wall. It reached the split central beams which ran to the other side of the shed where they met another pile of timber – the green stuff, fresh cut and still heavy with sap. Anselm gingerly pulled free a log and stood it upright on the block, mindful that this partnership between the old and new almost certainly held up the roof. Large flakes of snow drifted through the open door. There was a faint, freezing breeze.

'It was immense,' said Anselm, standing back, hands in his habit pockets.

'What was?' To aim, the Prior tapped the centre of the log three times with the blade of the axe.

'His deception. Look at his public life, his entire social existence. He wrote a dissertation applauding political values he doesn't hold, ideas that he doesn't accept. He *teaches* them now. He basks in the reflected glory of every thinker whose mind he managed to pick. He's held in awe in the senior common room because he tramped over the intellectual killing fields and came back with his mind intact.'

The Prior brought the axe down and the wood huffed and gave way.

I defended your reputation in the High Court, thought Anselm, looking at the two halves. *Did you think me a fool? I stood by you and fought your corner, despite the destruction of a journal, the reluctance of a witness and a total absence of coherent instructions.*

'I'm sorry, I think you're wrong,' Anselm said, dragging aside the split wood and pulling free another log. He held it between his arms, leaning back against the pile, challenging the Prior's belief in John's willingness to be exposed; his need to be helped along the way. 'He didn't want to be found by his friend. He hoped I'd go to Warsaw and find nothing. And, in fact, there was nothing to be found; the file was empty. I could easily have given up and come back empty-handed. And he'd have been reassured that there was nothing over there waiting to blow up in his face. That's what he really wanted to know. Remember, Róża had told him about the files. She'd said it was only a matter of time before the informer was flushed out by some lawyer or journalist interested in the Shoemaker. He needed to know what was inside the *Polana* file to see if he was safe.'

The Prior was listening but he didn't reply. Gilbertines were like that. He had nothing else to say, so he said nothing. Anyway, he was keen to get on, nodding strained gratitude when Anselm finally placed the wood on the block.

'And I wasn't the only one he used,' murmured Anselm. 'There were others.'

The Prior tapped the log three times.

That reluctant witness: John had urged her to

come to London. Why? Because he loved her? Or because he knew that sooner or later the press might look a little closer at the circumstances of his expulsion from Warsaw; that he might be accused; that he might have need of a respectable dissident to preserve his standing. She refused when he tried to use her. And the day he was vindicated, she walked out of his life.

The axe fell and the wood splintered.

'He gave me hints for years,' continued Anselm. Without his former caution he yanked out the next victim for the block. 'He smoked Russian cigarettes. He wore East German trainers.'

The Prior humphed and the log cracked and fell, divided.

'Worst of all, he played games with Róża.' Anselm was talking to the pile of dry wood. He spent a long time choosing the next branch. He paused while pulling it free. 'She was begging him to make a confession, to come on side, and help her bring Brack to court. To vindicate himself by himself. What did he do? He called up the naive lawyer who'd done the magic last time around. Someone with his head in the clouds. Someone who wouldn't know the meaning of a Zeha trainer if it vanished up his backside. I just don't understand. I can't—'

'Here.'

'What?'

'Take this.'

Anselm seemed to wake. The Prior was holding out the axe. His round glasses, repaired at both ends with a paperclip, caught the wintry afternoon light. Snow was creeping timidly into the shed. The Prior's breath fogged in the cold air.

'Let the head do all the work.'

'Wot?'

'You do nothing. Just guide the weight of the axe and let it fall.'

Anselm wasn't entirely grateful for the technical advice. He considered himself something of a woodsman.

'We all want to *understand*,' said the Prior, impatiently, drying his brow with a clean, white handkerchief. 'But sometimes we can't, and when that happens we just have to get on with our life.' He paused, folding up the cloth neatly. 'There are other, special situations when it's not our *job* to understand. When our task is a kind of obedience to the circumstances in which we find ourselves. Róża came to John. John came to you. No one demands that you *understand* anything. For the moment, you simply have to put one foot in front of the other. You have to do as you were asked. It's *their* job to understand and explain. Now, speaking of the circumstances in which we find ourselves, do some work. It solves all manner of problems.'

Anselm capitulated, though not in deference to that last, doubtful maxim. He'd simply worn himself out thinking. Jaw thrust forward, he squared up to the wood and began to swing the axe, thinking of Charles Ingalls in *Little House on the Prairie* – something far from the unpleasantness of the grown up world. *Suddenly he slowed and stopped.*

'What happens now?' he asked. 'What do I do?'

'I've just told you.'

'Sorry, I must have missed that one.'

'Let the head do the work. Just guide the weight and let it fall.'

'Forgive me. South of Hadrian's Wall we stick to the matter in hand, it's why we won at Culloden—'

'John needs to explain how he came to be CONRAD,' groaned the Prior, 'and Róża needs to explain why CONRAD is so important.'

'And I do nothing?'

'Bring them together, Anselm,' rasped the Prior. 'Bring them far away from all that is secure and familiar. Bring them here. And build them a fire.'

Anselm planned two phone calls but ended up making three. Sitting in the calefactory he started with John. After a few pleasantries, he told him the full cost of his trip to Warsaw – leaving out hefty disbursements paid by the IPN.

'Wow,' he said. 'It's to be expected, I suppose. Can't say I'd carried out the full calculation.'

'No, you didn't.'

'Sorry?'

'Calculations, John.' Anselm felt himself slipping away, drawing back behind his words, into the gloom of his mind. From far inside, he said, 'I was going to explain about champagne and oysters, and a room in another hotel that I didn't use, but let's put first things first. I think you need to explain to Róża everything that happened to CONRAD . . . you know, Klara's boy.'

There was a long blistering pause on the line.

'John?'

'Yes, I heard.'

'I'm sorry to mention her name. I know, now, something of her life. I've learned a little of what she did. I've an idea of how that might have affected you.'

In the corridor outside, Father Jerome hollered after Brother Benedict. It sounded like the opening shots of an argument about the work rota. Intellect and feeling were about to lose their footing.

'And that was in a file?' asked John, coldly, his voice far off as if he'd turned from the mouthpiece.

'No. There is no file on Klara. It's been destroyed. In a way, that's also true of the *Polana* file. Nothing between the covers points unequivocally to you, the Dentist made sure of that.' Anselm waited, listening hard. He raised a hand to the air, reaching out. 'John, I'm not saying you betrayed Róża. You've nothing to fear from me, or anyone else. In the world of ducking and diving, you're safe. You're home and dry. This is what I have to say: the huge issue here is not your relationship with Otto Brack and how to keep it secret. It's Otto Brack's with Róża Mojeska and how to make it public. The big question is not whether you'll ride out your days without being named, it's whether Róża will end hers with the justice she's been denied. She's put the power to decide in your hands. You can choose yes, or no. She came to see you, John, not to accuse you, but because she feared that you were going to be exposed anyway, sooner or later. But she was wrong. The file is empty. All she has left is your willingness to speak for yourself . . . because she won't name you. I don't know why.'

'Me neither.'

Anselm only just caught the reply because John seemed further off.

'Come to Larkwood. It's a good place to get things off your chest. Róża already knows what you're hiding. She just wants you to tell her yourself. It's what friends do.'

The scorching silence was back. Outside, snowflakes fell like shreds of wet paper. They were banking high on the window sills. Anselm pressed the phone hard against his ear, trying to catch some indication of John's presence. It came hard and suddenly, the words squeezed through the tiny holes of the mouthpiece.

'Fine. I'll explain. You might as well call Celina. She'll need to listen, too. You'll get her number from the BBC. There's no point in me calling. She wouldn't pick up the phone.'

Then he was gone. No goodbye. Just a light click.

Anselm's heart was beating erratically. It thumped

hard against his chest. The open blisters on his hands began to burn from the sweat. On a kind of élan of misery, he rang the BBC and two extensions later he spoke to Celina Hetman who was about to do a live broadcast for the World Service. He'd pushed, saying it was personal and urgent and that he was a monk – that last being a key to many a closed door. The conversation was brief because the engineer was raising his voice. The light had gone green. Maybe that's why she caved in.

Then, drained of emotion, he rang Sebastian to suggest that he might like to catch a flight and give Róża Mojeska a pleasant surprise. The end was near. Praise came down the line, but Anselm just held the receiver away from his ear. He felt desperately sad. The cost of his trip to Warsaw had been immense.

'I don't know how Róża will react,' he said, cutting short the tribute, 'but afterwards you'll be free to prosecute Otto Brack.'

CHAPTER 41

The Old Mill had stood by the Lark for four hundred years. The original grinding mechanism, fragile and jammed, remained visible in the large room where Anselm had made the fire. The floor was flagged and uneven, worn down by the feet of peasant farmers who'd brought their threshed wheat to be ground into flour. In the centre stood a waxed round table, brought in by Anselm as a learned allusion to the ground-breaking Round Table talks of 1989 between Solidarity, the Communists and the Church; the negotiations that had launched a new order in social relations. There were four mock Chippendale chairs – a nod towards English fair play – occupied by the delegates invited by Anselm. A standing crowd of Suffolk ghosts seemed to watch expectantly, cloth caps in hand.

'This isn't going to be easy,' said John, nudging his dark glasses. 'I don't want to make a speech. I can't see you . . . it would help if you'd ask questions, reply, anything, only don't leave me floating in the darkness.'

Róża had come by train with Sebastian who was

now in the guesthouse eating his nails. She sat upright, her back away from the chair. A face of shadows, thought Anselm. Shadows that were deep with the movements of dusk. She wore a silver brooch clipped to her white blouse. Her eyes seemed to speak a forgiving but frightened tenderness.

'Why don't you start with Klara?' suggested Anselm, his voice dry and spare. 'The road to this table begins with her, doesn't it?'

Beside Róża sat Celina Hetman. She'd been held up by the snow drifts. Anselm had thought she might not come after all. He'd remembered a vibrant intellect and a kitsch, plastic belt. They'd only met two or three times. He'd once tried to imagine her in the Royal Courts of Justice speaking on John's behalf, the judge intrigued, if not distracted, by the decorated headband. He needn't have worried. She'd fled from John's life. When the car had finally pulled up at Larkwood, Anselm hadn't recognised her. On the understanding that the outlandish don't always wear that well, he'd expected a middle-aged multicoloured prune but he'd met a timeless woman whose refinement made him stammer. She was dressed in black – cashmere wools and matt leather shoes – in contrast to the coral pink of her lips. On her little finger was a large ring: a daisy; a spot of yellow enamel with long white petals. Her hair was jet black and very short, like a distressed belle's in a Chaplin film: boyish curls by the ears and incredibly feminine. Skilled with her courtesy, she'd been delighted to meet Róża and pleased to see John once more, but Anselm – a man familiar with troubled voices – sensed anxiety and old wounds. She looked at John as he ran a finger behind his roll neck collar, but then Róża suddenly spoke, a voice soft and musical, small and knowing: 'Perhaps you should start with Otto Brack.'

The call came after John had been in Warsaw a couple of months.

He said, 'Call me the Dentist.' He said he needed help. He said he wanted out. That's how it all began: with a plea for help. He urged John to trust him, to understand how dangerous it was for him to speak to a British journalist. He didn't trust his own organisation and he didn't trust any in the West: 'I need to find someone outside the system. Do you understand?'

Anselm shifted in his seat: this wasn't the kind of call he'd expected Brack to make. Why would *he* want *out*? The point – Anselm had imagined – was to get *John in*.

'The Dentist wanted me to vouch for him with a government minister, whom he'd later name, right over the head of MI6,' John's hand, flat on the table made a polishing motion. 'He was flattering me; building up my self-importance. I was easy meat.'

John had two questions – and he asked them with all the aplomb of an experienced handler:

394

first, what did the Dentist have to offer? Second, why come to John? Warsaw was packed with foreign journalists.

'He said he'd bring the entire SB battle order. He had lists of informers within Solidarity and the Church. Copies of correspondence between Moscow and Warsaw. He knew the colour of Brezhnev's underpants . . . you name it, the Dentist had pulled it from some top drawer marked "Secret", and it was mine to hand over. Part of the dowry that would secure my place in the annals of Cold War history – unread by all, save the major players on either side of the Wall.'

Anselm was cut loose. A dowry? How could a mock defection by Brack lead to John betraying Róża? Once more – and this time with complete finality – Anselm abandoned a convincing interpretation of the evidence. John might have been CONRAD but CONRAD was no willing spy . . . and Róża's eyes were resting upon him; she hadn't strayed once; she held on to his voice as if it were a handle. *I've got everything wrong, except for this meeting; and even now, I don't know why it's right.*

'He was typical of many people I knew back then,' said John – he'd become swift and fluid; his memory set in motion by the relief of letting go – 'he was convinced that but for martial law the Russians would have invaded. They'd marched into Budapest in fifty-six, Prague in sixty-eight and Kabul in eighty. He thought they still might come to Warsaw, which was why he wanted out now, and fast.'

'But why you?' Celina's tone was frail, like tearing paper. 'Why did he pick you?'

Anselm involuntarily abridged Bogart's gin-joint line – of all the food queues in Warsaw, why did you have to walk into mine? And he understood that she grieved, even now, at ever having met him.

'Because I was a stranger,' replied John, hearing – Anselm was sure – the same tone of regret. 'Because he'd done some research. He knew a great deal about my family. Far more than me; he'd guessed why I'd come to Warsaw.'

He knew John was the son of a diplomat; the son of a woman who'd committed suicide; the son of a tragedy. He'd read his mother's file. He'd calculated that John's embarrassment went deep into his identity; that he carried a kind of trans-ferred guilt.

'Suicide?' repeated Celina, softly.

The subject was too large for the moment – like Anselm with Irina on the unswerving ardour of monks – but Celina was simply reaching out to him from a new understanding. She knew there was more to be said . . . that might once have been said, if things had been simpler between them.

'Yes,' replied John. 'I've come to see it very differ-ently over the years. Once it was a betrayal. Now? I think she wanted to eternalise her regret. To say sorry for ever – to me, to my father. Brack smelled that, too.'

He'd been deeply sympathetic. The pressures of the time had been awful (Brack said) – 'I was there, I know what it was like; I felt the heat' – with friend pitted against friend to demonstrate their innocence. He'd only raised the matter because he felt that John, of all people, would understand why the Dentist wanted out; that John, of all people, might want to rectify the past – by helping him; by purging the mistake of his mother.

'He didn't use those words, but that's what he meant.' John's hand had stopped moving. 'And that was the trick. Within minutes of listening to him, the table had slowly turned. *He* was offering to help *me*. And you might find this difficult to believe, but I was grateful. Really grateful. Without the assistance of an insider, I'd never know what my mother had actually done. I thought a great chance had come my way.'

The Dentist asked John to think about it because there were dangers on both sides. A week later the phone rang again. To prove his bona fides, he offered John copies of telegrams sent to the KGB dealing with Solidarity's—

'I didn't want them. I told him I was prepared to take the risk.'

But the Dentist said that's not how things worked. That trust was a kind of deal, a bargain, an exchange of services. And, if he was to help the Dentist, there were rules.

'First, we were never to meet. I could only call him on a secure number, five-five-eight-seven-six. Second, names were dangerous, that's why he was the Dentist, so I had to pick one. I went for Conrad. It was a joke. *The Secret Agent . . . Heart of Darkness.* But he didn't get it. Third, I was to keep a journal recording all the leads he'd send my way, each of which would focus on the fight for freedom of speech, accountability, democratic blah, blah –' John smoothed the table once more, moving quickly – 'Fourth, I was to take this journal with me to the minister he'd later name as evidence of the Dentist's values and commitment to political reform. This was the deal: if I prepared his passage to the West, he'd help me understand my mother's story. He'd bring her file.'

John couldn't see any problem: he wasn't giving anything to the Dentist. All the traffic would be coming the other way. His only role was to be a messenger operating outside the system, his task to bring a request to someone at the heart of government.

The Dentist was true to his word. He gave John all manner of information, placing him one step ahead of every other Western journalist in Warsaw. He placed John's ear at the door of the Junta. Only, John didn't notice that all the 'stuff sent his way' would have made it into the public domain eventually; that he only received advanced notice; that he was only given two scoops of substance. The first was on underground printing.

'He told me the publication most feared by the government was *Freedom and Independence*.' He looked towards Róża, as if their eyes might meet. 'It's run by someone called the Shoemaker, he said; only turns up when times get really bad, and he's turned up now. This is the voice you should hear. It had last been heard during the Terror. Get his words into the *Times*, the *Guardian*, the *Telegraph* –' he threw imagined copies on the table – 'get his message out of Warsaw.'

The only known point of contact was a woman called Róża Mojeska, and he was trying to find her.

'I got there first, Róża,' he said, heavily. He faltered, like a man stepping suddenly off the pavement. 'In all that we spoke of, Róża, I never once lied. I just didn't tell the truth of how I came to find you.'

Róża nodded but didn't speak. Her eyes were boring into him out of those mauve shadows. John seemed to fall, knowing there was no hand that could reach him. 'He called again, said he'd loved the "Lives Lived in Secret" piece, it was wonderful, marvellous, this was our win, our first strike back, he was halfway to London, and now he had someone else. A documentary film-maker. She'd spent her life winding up the authorities. She was a wild cat. Wouldn't stop and wouldn't go. They'd been offering her a passport for years and she wouldn't take it. They put people like her in prison and threw away the key. Not six months, ten years, so get on to her, she's another life lived in secret.'

'And you put all this down in your journal?' asked Celina, her voice transparent like India paper. Anselm couldn't quite see through it; something was on the other side; he wasn't sure she'd even asked a question. Her lips moved slowly, beautifully.

'I kept the rules,' said John. 'My journal was the contemporaneous account of his bona fides. It was the means to get him out. It was the way to open my mother's file . . . I wanted to see with my own eyes what she'd done to my father.' He turned to Róża, reaching out again with blind eyes. 'I didn't tell him about the plan to meet the Shoemaker. I turned up and saw you walk to a man that I'd never seen before. Then I got my head kicked in. I didn't know the Dentist was the guy in the graveyard until he walked into the cell. I was thrown out of Warsaw before the end of the week. He'd used me to find you, Róża. He'd used my pride and self-importance. He'd used my mother's mistake. He'd used my longing to change what she'd done.'

Róża showed no emotion. A hand moved to the brooch, a silver triangle, a complex of tiny sculpted flowers. The dusk round her eyes had grown dark. A kind of night settled on her face. Silence pounded from her closed mouth. The fire snapped, a log rolled into flame.

'I didn't tell you about her because I didn't know what to say.' John had turned to Anselm. 'There's nothing worse, you know. Shame without knowing why. My father never spoke about her when I was a child. At ten I'd seen her name on my birth certificate. But he wouldn't tell me anything about her life, except that she'd ended it. He'd razed her life to the ground. He'd built a golf course on top and a club house with bourbon on tap. I only learned about her past when they picked me up in Bucharest. They made a call to the SB in Warsaw and the next thing I know a sort of Eton Old Boy walks in, the real thing, genteel English with the vaguest Russian accent. "A cigarette? A cup of Earl Grey? No scones, I'm afraid." What did I think of Reagan? And what about Thatcher? Then I was free, a favour to the memory of my mother, he said. Because of the price she'd paid for socialist values. That's why I took the job with the BBC. I wanted to learn about her values. Her country, her history, her roots. My country, my history, my roots. I wanted to find her. And then the Dentist called. If only I'd known of his place in your life, Róża; if only I'd known that he'd picked me with you in mind.'

John threw his head back. He was almost done. Coming forward, he planted his face in his hands, slipping his fingers behind his glasses. He appeared at once the tragic buffoon: hands covering his eyes, with spectacles on top; hiding behind lenses that wouldn't let him see even if someone pulled his arms away.

'I didn't use you, Celina.' His voice was muffled into his palms. 'I loved you. I was completely *devastated* by who you were. Your crazy shoes and rings and torn trousers. Your hair always in a mess. Your beads and bangles. But I couldn't see straight. I didn't know if I wanted you for who you were, or because you were everything my mother should have been, a rebel, someone who'd fought back. I didn't know if I loved you because you cleaned up the weird guilt shovelled on to me by my father, by not talking, by not explaining –' his breath ran out in a sigh of fatigue and surrender – 'God, in those days I thought too much. It was all so much simpler than I realised.' He came to an exhausted halt and dropped his hands. In an act of total surrender he took off his glasses. Anselm had never seen him without them – not since he'd agreed with John (post op) that he had a faraway look . . . no, not Martian, just far off. The glasses had become a heat shield easing his entry into a new, dark world. And he'd taken it down. Tiny scars ran over his lids, above and below. The eyes were the palest brown, with tiny clouds and frail red streamers flying over the whites, the pupils awfully still, not reacting to the firelight. 'I thought too much. I did love you, simply, and innocently. I knew that after you'd gone.'

Notwithstanding John's immolation before Celina, Anselm's mind – naturally withdrawing from any display of strong emotion – lay with Róża's unmoving face: the haunted lilac shadows and the coming of night. She barely moved and she didn't take her eyes off John. It had turned into a conversation between two broken friends, with Róża watching and waiting. She was like a silent guide, always one step ahead, always observant, always waiting. A deep comprehension flickered and died in Anselm's mind. He'd barely noticed its outline before it was gone.

Stirring, suddenly, he remembered a little trick from his days at the Bar. Not so much a trick as a technique that reflected the depths of the human person; the workings of the conscience. Put the question to the person who has already framed the enquiry: ask them what they asked of someone else. The answer was often surprising. He coughed, lightly.

'Celina, of all the film-makers in all the studios in Warsaw, why did Brack pick you?'

CHAPTER 42

Celina asked for some water. Anselm went to get some, wondering if they'd ever get on to the wine. He thought of Belloc; *All, all must face their Passion at the last.* The fetching didn't break the tension. There was no escape, now. It just grew tighter. Anselm roused the fire in a vast hearth with wood that was hard and dry. There was little smoke, the perfume faint but deep. Róża still said nothing. She watched. Her eyes wouldn't shift from John.

'I'm not what you think, John,' said Celina, looking into the glass as if it were a goldfish bowl. 'I never was. Though it's what I wanted . . . wanted with every ounce of longing that dragged me down. You can't weigh longing, of course. It's a just a wisp of air. Smoke from a fire. The scales don't change. You remain what you are.'

It was true; Celina had been kicked out of four schools. But there were no aunts and uncles chalked up dead by the Tsar's secret police. Her mother had dumped her father, but not because of any high-minded principles. She hadn't got any; and he'd been no dissident. There'd been no contributions to the Club of the Crooked Circle; he'd been no Vagabond, at least, not of the noble kind. The nearest he'd got to a secret society was the SB.

'He didn't tell me outright, but you find out, eventually.' Celina sniffed quietly, finding a tissue from inside a sleeve. It was inconspicuous, petite, wholly unfit for purpose. 'It's their way of talking, the habitual evasions, the sense that they're import-ant and nobody knows it, that no one appreciates them, that they understand things that no one would ever . . .' Her delicate voice trailed off. She wiped her eyes. Folding it neatly, square upon tiny square, she made the tissue into a pellet, something insignificant to hang on to. 'My mother walked out when I was nine.'

She'd been a go-alonger, the sort of woman who didn't mind what she ate, where she went or what they did. To this day, Celina ground her teeth if someone said, 'I don't mind'. Her mother had sat in the corner doing puzzles, her shiny dyed hair in curlers. All she'd wanted to know was six down or whatever. And no matter what you said, it clashed with four across. Celina had no other memory of her. She wondered now if doing crosswords had been inevitable: she'd avoided every big question, leaving all the big answers to her husband. What more could she do? She'd gone off with another SB officer. Someone with a higher rank – someone who knew more answers to more questions. And what of the daughter she'd left behind? Well, perhaps she didn't mind.

'Despite her failings, she mattered. A mother always matters. I hit back at school until they kicked me out.'

Anselm frowned as if he'd just heard gunfire echoing down a corridor in Praga. Irina's son was sorting out the Afghans. In the kitchen, Irina was explaining . . .

'My father showed no emotion,' said Celina, as if cutting Anselm short. 'He just focused on me. I was all that counted. But, you see, these people whose importance isn't widely known, all they've got is what they think of themselves. Nothing else matters. So he tried to make me into another version of him.'

When Celina began to mock one or two teachers, he'd stood over the desk in her bedroom, legs apart, hands behind his back. He'd dished out all the official lines he'd ever learned. He'd ranted in the kitchen about duty and responsibility and choices and sacrifice and ashes. After her third expulsion he'd said she was becoming an embarrassment – the understatement had shocked her; he wasn't a man for delicate wordplay. Following the fourth, what was left of their relationship broke down. She didn't wait to be thrown out, she just walked on to the street. Homeless, she'd eventually found herself among like minds, people who gave her a floor, people who thought like she did, whose flats were sometimes turned over by the boys in jeans and leather jackets. She went to a kind of university with lectures in boiler rooms and attics, staffed by professors who worked in factories or washed the windows.

'I next saw him after I'd been arrested in sixty-eight,' said Celina. She sipped water, her lips needing moisture. 'He got me out. There were no charges brought and I was furious and sick with shame. Other people's kids were finished off, but not his. I told him to keep far, far away from my life. But he stayed there, I understand that now. Why else did they leave me alone? How else did I get a job in film? How else did I get my work past the censors?'

Celina laid one hand upon the other. Carelessly, showing the depth of her distress, she played with her ring, the big daisy. Her voice came again like the tearing of flimsy paper. 'I wanted those relatives, John. More than anything, I wanted parents in prison and ancestors scattered round Siberia. But that's not what I got. I got a mother who didn't have a clue and a father who was Otto Brack.'

At least Anselm had seen it coming, so he had an excuse for not reacting. John made a start as if the Dentist had forgotten to use anaesthetic. But Róża simply stared ahead, mute, remote, frightening Anselm with her silence. She seemed all-knowing, expectant, resigned. Her thumb strayed to the finger with two wedding rings. Celina played with the daisy. John put on his glasses as if to avoid a coming explosion of light. The fire collapsed. Shadows fled across the vaulted roof. A sort of fuse spontaneously ignited in Anselm's mind.

'I thought I'd never see him again,' said Celina. 'He completely vanished from my life. I made something of myself. Good things happened to me. We met in May, do you remember, John? I moved in towards the end of the August. It was a sunny time, wasn't it? We were free and easy and the army was out there bothering other people. But then, in the October, I came home and found my father in the sitting room, legs crossed. In his hands was a journal. He didn't say a thing, he just sat there, turning the pages.'

Celina's evocation of that encounter was so vivid – not by her words but the expression on her face, the shock lived again – that Anselm found himself in that Warsaw flat, a frightened intruder watching a mystery unfold, a mystery half understood because that journal was Brack's creation. Anselm couldn't move. The fuse was sputtering. He looked out of his own darkness at the father and his terrified daughter . . .

'He's been very stupid,' he said closing the journal. 'And that annoys me.'

'What the hell are you doing here? What are—'

'Keep your voice down. I'm here to help. Again. Tidying up after you. Sweeping up your endless mistakes.'

He hadn't shouted, but he sounded loud and piercing. Celina stayed with her back to the front door, the keys jingling in one hand. He was dressed in one of those shapeless suits without apparent colour, the cloth blending into any and all surroundings. His drab overcoat was slung over the back of a chair.

'I've been trying to help him,' he said, tossing the book on to a coffee table. 'But he's broken the rules and now he's in trouble. Serious trouble. Like you, he should have listened. Like you, he thinks he knows best.'

'What do you mean, help him?'

Her father pointed towards a chair. Out of some remembered fear, Celina obeyed. His eyes tracked her with the old, hungry disapproval. He'd greyed but the hardness was still there around the mouth. She'd always thought his face looked scarred, only there were no old cuts on the beaten skin. 'I've been giving his career a push. Looking after him like I've looked after you.'

Nausea turned Celina's insides. He was at it again. He wouldn't let go of her; and now his contamination had reached John. All she could manage was, 'He's in trouble?'

'Of course he is.' Her father nodded towards the journal. 'He's written down where he got it all from – I'm not worried, I'm a careful man. We've never met. He doesn't know my face or name – but what he's written down is proof, proof of serious crimes.'

'Take it . . . burn it.'

'I can't.'

'Why not?'

'It's been seen by eyes other than mine. I've sent them away for now, but I'll have to act on it. Eventually.'

'I'll tell them what you've said and what you've done for me, over the years.'

He looked at her with a father's contempt. 'No one but me would believe you.'

'Crimes?' She was lurching with anxiety and guilt: this was her fault. He was her father, and now he'd compromised John, as he'd always compromised her. 'What crimes?'

'The sort that land you in prison for ten years. Espionage doesn't attract a short sentence, not when it upsets Moscow. Which is why he's upset me. I was only giving his career a shove in the right direction.'

Why won't you leave me alone? The question rose from Celina's depths but she couldn't give it voice. She couldn't bear to have any exchange with this . . . there wasn't a single word to describe him, or what he meant to her. The remembered fear was eating at her guts. Why had he sent off his subordinates? Why was he still here?

'He's named you and someone else,' he said, as if in reply. 'You're all in danger now. He really should have stuck to the rules. Write nothing down was number one.'

'You'll help him?'

'Are you asking?' Again the father's contempt.

'Yes.'

'All right. But there isn't much time. He mentions a woman called Róża Mojeska. I'll need to see her, which isn't prudent for a man in my position. But it's the only way I can organise a passport. I'll have to get one for you, too. I can get you all out before it's too late. I'll make it so that your boyfriend's asked quietly to leave – among journalists, that's a kind of medal for bravery. Shows he got close to the nerves of power. Best career boost in the bag. Is that good enough for you?'

'Yes.'

'I think that's the first time I've ever seen gratitude put light on your face.'

'I'm not grateful,' snapped Celina. 'It's your meddling around with my life that's caused all this . . . all you've ever done is bring me—'

'Privileges,' supplied her father. 'Well, take this one with both hands. It won't be happening again.' He stood up to go. 'Obviously, you can't tell your boyfriend what I'm doing or that we've met.'

'Why not?'

'He can't be trusted. He breaks rules.' An ironic smile warped his face. 'And I'm not sure he'd want to marry into the family, you know what I mean? Your connection to me might put him off. Christmas with the in-law? I don't think so. That's why I'm going to keep well out of the picture. Frankly it's better for him and for you if he leaves Warsaw thinking he's some kind of hero.' Shaking

411

his head in dismay, he looked down at the journal. 'Put that thing back with his socks, will you? He really should have listened.'

Celina wondered what would happen next. She was fearful and loath to be dependent on him. 'Will you find her . . . this woman?'

'Me?' He walked to the chair and shrugged on his overcoat. 'No, you will.'

'What?'

'Who else?'

'But what can I do?' Celina was crouched on her chair, looking up.

'Save him from himself, like I saved you. Do what you don't want to do, for his good. Forget yourself. Co-operate with me.'

'But I can't follow him.'

'No. And you can't ask him either.'

'What then?'

Celina's father made an impatient sigh, as if to say he'd done enough already. 'Why not see if your boyfriend writes something interesting in his journal? For once the damned thing might serve some good purpose . . . it'll keep all three of you out of prison. Find some other way, if you like. It's up to you. I'll help, but this time you've got to pull your weight. You can reach me on five-five-eight-seven-six.'

The fire crackled and spat.

'Do you see what he was doing? What he did?' Celina's voice rose slightly. 'He'd already been to

412

you. He'd already sent you towards Róża. You'd already found her, and so he came to me. I didn't know, I suspected nothing.'

Róża made the slightest moan, so low and so unobtrusive that in other circumstances it wouldn't have been noticed. But here, in this vast yet cramped room, it was as though a flagstone had cracked. Something immense was disintegrating within Róża. But there was no collapse. Her eyes were on John, bleeding with emotion.

'I read your journal.' Celina's admission came like a tearing at the mouth. 'I knew where you'd been and where you were going.'

She'd read it every day, worried that time was ebbing away; that her father would come back to arrest them both. She finally learned of a planned meeting by the grave of Prus. Celina was whispering now. She'd dialled Brack's number as if she were lodging a complaint at the passport office. It had been a quick, cold call.

They were silent.

The truth, at last, was out. The informer used by Brack had been his own daughter . . . but Anselm was running now, following the fizz of the burning fuse, head down, not seeing where he was going. Brack had told Róża the name of the informer and what they'd been doing for years. And that had silenced her . . . but why? She'd never met Celina. Brack's delinquent child couldn't be that significant.

'You came home beaten by them,' said Celina,

413

carefully unfolding the tissue. 'The next day I didn't go to the censor. I rang my father. We met in the cemetery.'

Celina had sent him back to Prus, to where he'd betrayed her. She'd hit him hard across the face. His head had flown back with the force of the blow, but, on righting himself, he'd hardly seemed present. One calm hand had gone into his drab overcoat and he'd taken out a passport.

'I threw it on the floor.' Celina dabbed the corners of her eyes. 'I wanted my freedom but not thanks to him. Then, when I came home, the phone rang. They'd given you two days. You asked me to come. You made a call for a passport.' She clutched the tissue as if it were a shred of hope. 'Was it the embassy?'

'No.'

'Five-five-eight-seven-six?'

'Yes.'

Everything was ready, thought Anselm, awed. Everyone had been put into position. Everyone had been moved. *Polana* was a game of wit and patience for three or more players. Waddington's couldn't have dreamed up the goal, the rules or the cost. Brack had won. But only because Celina's importance was . . .

'I couldn't speak at the trial, John, because it was me who'd got you thrown out of Warsaw.' Celina was looking at her daisy again. 'I left because I knew I couldn't remain and keep the lie going, year on year. I'm sorry.'

We'd both lost out, she seemed to say. Something simple and beautiful had died, without even withering. Celina turned to Róża, her face anguished. Her hands came together. 'I'm sorry I brought him to you. To this day I don't know what my father was doing, or why.'

Anselm wasn't entirely sure that Róża was breathing. Her thumb had stopped moving. Her face remained drawn and shadowed; her eyes were open; the stare fixed. John seemed to look back, yet neither was really looking at the other. Why was Róża looking at John?

'He was saving himself,' replied Róża from her inner refuge.

'But from what?' asked Celina. 'Why use me to get to John, and John to get to you?'

'He was frightened.'

'What of?'

'The claims of the law. My claims, those of my husband . . . and those of . . .'

My child. The fuse went *phut* just as the word burst inside Anselm's mouth.

He sat, lips apart, as if watching torn clods fall in slow motion to the ground: he recalled what Róża had said in the bright light of what she had not said. There and then an elemental fusion took place in Anselm's mind between the deeper depth of Róża's statement and its surface meaning: Róża's child lay beneath the page on blank blue paper, its name the one name she'd refused to disclose on the surface of the page.

'I've understood, Róża,' he said. 'I know what happened in nineteen fifty-three.'

Disclosing certain tragedies can't be done slowly. There can be no cushioning. But Anselm was going to try. He reached over and took one of Róża's hands in his. Watching the tears spill free, he said, deliberately and slowly, 'Celina, Otto Brack is not your father.'

Anselm could feel the impact of his words. They'd crashed into Celina and a stunned hush had bounced back. As if he needed any confirmation, Anselm felt the slightest pressure from Róża's fingers.

'He's not your father,' repeated Anselm, even more slowly. 'And your mother never sat in the corner lost in a puzzle, not minding what the day might bring. She minded more than she'll ever be able to say.'

Anselm couldn't speak any more. The fire snapped and murmured, sending sparks upwards in a spray of light.

CHAPTER 43

There were many images and sounds, all seared into Anselm's memory, which kept him awake that night. His mind became a screen showing nothing but the moments any censor of discretion would have cut and hid away – the parts where the actors broke down while the camera was running; the elements of tragedy best left to inference, for fear they unsettle any respectful observer. Sophocles knew his stuff: Oedipus tore his eyes out off stage; all the audience got was a man with blood streaming down his face. There are certain things you're just not meant to see.

What was the more harrowing: the moment when Róża, trembling with fear, timidity and courage, took Celina's hand from his? Or was it the slow, seeping words when Róża – her eyes closed, her head bent in an attitude of veneration and penitence – said, over and over again, 'I'm sorry, I'm sorry, I'm sorry'? 'For what?' mumbled Celina, confused and overcome. 'For having failed you, for having let you go, for not being there as you grew and changed, changed so much.' Anselm had been rigid, choking. Róża had nothing but a frayed string

417

of lost years, and now this, this moment of regret and misery and jubilation with her daughter. So much to explain; so much to understand – with so much more time behind than was left in front. She'd looked so terribly alone, like a passenger who'd been left behind on the platform.

Or was it immediately afterwards when Celina, disorientated, asked about her father – when Róża had to explain in simple, direct words that he was dead, that he'd been shot? By the man who'd taken his place in her life.

'I tried to find you,' said Róża. 'But I'd let you go without a name, to set you free. I didn't know where you were until Brack told me what he'd done. But in telling me, he knew I couldn't come to you. I couldn't bring you the truth, because I knew it would be shattering. It's taken me all these years to understand that it was your right to know, even if it destroyed who you'd become. You had a right to know who you really are. To know what had been done to you, to me and to your father.'

Or was it the sound of Celina's breathing, catching like a broken zip, the unsteady movement jamming when she tried to reply? She'd taken Róża's other hand, tears jolting from her eyes. They'd stood like that, motionless, speechless, their arms a kind of low swing bridge between them. Somehow, they had to cross the immeasurable distance, finding their own balance, all the while terrified of a fall, of some weak plank breaking underfoot.

If Anselm was forced to choose it would have been a quiet moment late next morning, seen by accident from the kitchen window. It was the sight of Celina leading Róża through the crisp snow to her car parked beneath Larkwood's plum trees. They moved cautiously, fearing a sudden slip on hidden ice. Celina had one arm around Róża's shoulder, the other holding her elbow, their heads leaning close together. Anselm had lingered, thinking that Róża had suddenly and dramatically aged. It wasn't necessarily a dark thought, but he knew she was ready to die.

After Celina's car had turned out of the gate, its occupants beginning the longest journey of their lives, Anselm, John and Sebastian – boots and coats borrowed where necessary – went for a long walk in the woods. They were white, silent and deep, every branch collared and tied with icicles and snow. Feet crunched along hidden paths known only to Anselm; voices rose, gathering in the facts, an occasional outburst of anger echoing through the forest.

They spoke of the criminal Otto Brack.

In 1951, protected by the State, he'd shot two men. Threatened by a widow with future justice, he'd tricked her into letting go of her child as if it were an act of sacrifice. But he'd secretly taken the new life as his own, knowing that in the years to come the widow could never touch him without harming her own child: for who could tell their child that the man they hold as their father is, in fact, his killer?

Then, in 1982, when the possibility of overthrow first reared its head, Brack had organised Operation *Polana*, its goal to catch the Shoemaker; its secondary purpose to find Róża and tell her what he'd done: to warn her of the cost of justice. To give her a passport. To push her beyond arm's length.

They spoke of Celina, the child abandoned by the woman who wasn't her mother.

By using her Brack had secured her eventual silence, in the event that she ever learned of her past. A snide remark from the likes of Frenzel, if he'd ever uncovered the adoption, might have sent her on a quest. At its term she'd have learned that the woman in John's journal was her mother: a woman she had betrayed. Brack had silenced mother and daughter with reciprocal shame. Even Sophocles, the specialist in unusual parent-child issues, hadn't thought of that one.

And they spoke of the victim Róża Mojeska.

For thirty years she'd believed that Celina was proximate, if not close, to Brack. That she believed him to be her father. How had she grown? Who had she become? Róża had been paralysed by two conflicting imperatives, each with a moral character: to speak or not to speak; the claims of the truth as against the benefits of ignorance. Ultimately she'd recognised Celina's rights.

But there was more to it than that.

Brack's scheme exploited the natural bond

420

between a mother and her child. He knew that Róża would choose silence rather than damage her daughter with information she need not know. She'd been trapped by love. But Sebastian had urged her to do the last thing Brack would expect: to give her another reason for living. The challenge had led Róża to realise that shielding her daughter from the truth was many things – pity, compassion, mercy, self-sacrifice – but it wasn't love. So she'd set her hand to the unthinkable task of wounding her own child. But it had to be done with enormous care. As a preliminary, she needed the smallest indication from her daughter that she was prepared to talk about her past and the shadow of her presumed father. For that, Róża needed the gentle touch of an intermediary. Which brought them on to her statement – that implement crafted to help her representative.

Frankly, as an identification tool, it hadn't worked. But as an example of moral technology it had the qualities often ascribed to Audi engineering. It ran smoothly to its destination; and so quietly you might not know it had arrived. *Vorsprung durch Technik*. Róża had placed Celina's collaboration in its complete context: against the backdrop of the Shoemaker operation, fully described, showing, in effect, that she had done nothing to compromise its aims. Crucially, she had not used her name. She'd asked about the film-maker as often as John had asked about the Shoemaker. This had been the one, decisive clue.

They came back to Larkwood chattering with cold, enchanted by the magic of the woods. John and Sebastian left for Cambridge railway station like old friends, a certain complicity between them as Sebastian explained the next steps to be taken upon his return to Warsaw: the obtaining of a witness statement from Róża to be followed by the arrest, charge and prosecution of Otto Brack.

'You'll keep me informed?' asked John.

'As matters develop.'

It was as though John worked at the IPN. The only question was who had the senior position.

As Anselm drove slowly back from the station to Larkwood, minding snow drifts, distracted now and then by the magnificence of blank fields at evening, his thoughts turned to something that hadn't been explored during that walk in the woods: the mind of Otto Brack.

On the plane out to Warsaw, Anselm had thought about the mystery of the man's character: how he'd ever come to use good for evil ends. He'd been curious as a man might leaf through a textbook, seeking a simple explanation for why the moral cells broke down. But that was then, on the plane. He now knew what lay in Brack's dangerous world. He couldn't contain his meditation or understand its direction. He sought out the Prior, ostensibly to report back on the outcome of the Round Table talks, finding him once more in the woodshed. This time there was no work. Anselm sat on the piano stool, the Prior on the chopping block. He spoke the inimitable phrase:

'Go to the end of your concerns.'

As ever the Prior was inscrutable, not reacting when told of John's innocence, nor seeking any tribute for being right about John's intentions in coming to Anselm (he knew about Lebanon Cedars, why they fell and the direction of their grain). His only response was a sharp contraction of the eyebrows when Anselm explained the mechanism and consequences of Brack's plan. As if they were both seated in its shadow, Anselm moved directly on to the matter that troubled him. It was a kind of fear.

'I think I've been naive.'

'Never accuse yourself on that score.'

'No. I've been naive about evil, as if it wasn't there. I've always tried to excuse it away, you know, defeat it by pretending it's not what it is. When I was at the Bar, I told myself the only reason one man brutalised another without any regret is because deep down he hadn't made a free choice . . . he'd been beaten and starved as a child, he'd gone to the wrong school, made the wrong friends, and in the end, there'd been a screw loose in his free will. Or maybe he believed – sincerely but wrongly – that unrestrained violence was just one of the more unusual ways of doing something good. I still want to hold on to these . . . difficult routes to mercy.'

'And?'

423

'Well, a part of me wants to find the path to Brack's actions, precisely because what he has done is unconscionable. What happened to him, that he could do such things? Was he abused and deprived or does he just think wrongly? Alternatively, is he that which scares me most, and which I've dared not consider – a simply evil man, with all the screws intact, none too loose, none too tight, a man who can't blame his circumstances.' Anselm hesitated, ashamed. 'He killed men as if they were animals. He treated women as if they were rags to clean the mess off the floor. And now he turns the pages of a stamp album lamenting the gaps in his collection. And yet I still want to know if there remains in the darkness a narrow route to mercy.'

The Prior reached down and picked up some wood shavings and splinters. He began sifting them through his fingers as if he were looking for something. Finally, he let them drop and dusted dry his hands.

'I'm no Father Zossima, Anselm,' he said. 'I'm no wiser than you, no more foolish, but I'm sure of this: evil, simply present? You'll never understand it and neither will I. Ultimately, that's what evil is . . . it's something bad without an explanation. Which is why it's terrifying. And as for mercy in the dark – well, what is salvation if not a light greater than all the shadows, something good which cannot be explained? It, too, can be terrifying. I doubt if men like Otto Brack would dare to look in its direction.'

The Prior's words stayed with Anselm for the remainder of the day. He saw the wood chips falling from his hand, back on to the floor. And he saw Róża in a completely different light. For the naming of Brack as Brack, without any understanding or indulgence, revealed who she'd been up against, and the scale of her accomplishment in stepping through and beyond the suffering he'd prepared for her. She'd trusted again, in the full knowledge that things can end badly. She brought the truth to light knowing that Celina would be harmed and that she might reject her. She'd trusted in something stronger than his hate. She was simply a good woman.

Over the following months, Anselm waited apprehensively to learn of outcomes. As ever, he was encouraged to learn that evil, named and exposed, always loses some of its power.

The disclosure to Celina of her background had obviously been a shattering experience. She was being helped to cope with the implications by a skilled counsellor called Myriam, said John – he didn't know the surname and Anselm wondered if counsellors even had them – and one of her remarks ('you are always more than your past') had worked its way into Anselm's mouth as if it was a gem from his life of silence. When the time was right he planned to let it drop, lightly.

But there was, if anything, a sharp irony to the failure of Brack's plan. Coping with the knowledge that one's parent had been murdered was dramatically offset by the relief of learning that the ideologue who'd ranted at you from infancy was not your father; that the woman who'd chosen puzzles over the enigma of life was not, in fact, your mother; that Celina's relatives were, in truth, the dissident activists of her imagination. She had the whole package, from torture to martyrdom. She was exactly who John had thought her to be. There was a hint, too, that she had found a deep bond with him – something more prized than any collection of reinstated memories: in very different ways and for very different reasons, they'd both been abandoned; they each had to grapple with the consequences of failure – their own and other people's; Anselm sensed the unique and warming softness of people who no longer judge that easily.

CHAPTER 44

Brack's arrest caused a sensation in Warsaw and beyond. Sebastian had been right in saying the case had a unique quality. The revelation of crimes by the secret police during the Terror linked to secret police operations under martial law evoked the entire period of communist rule, presenting it as a seamless garment, dirtier in some places than others, but one thing. A strait-jacket stitched and darned by the dedicated service of certain individuals. Memory and moment came together in the media. Róża's vindication, for so long a personal concern, had become a matter of national remembrance.

Anselm followed events at a distance, thanks to faxes or calls from Sebastian and John (Larkwood had yet to obtain a computer. The idea of explaining an email to Sylvester had left the Prior speechless). He'd seen copies of press coverage, and mused over the smudged photograph of the accused, barely able to discern his features. Flinching, he'd read a transcript of Róża's evidence. But, curiously, nothing came from Brack himself. There'd been no transcripts of interviews conducted in the presence of his legal representative. And then one morning in April, the Watchman beckoned Anselm as he floated through reception on his way to the hives. The old fellow was cross.

'It never works.'

'What doesn't?'

'That.' He hit the console with his stick. 'Why can't we just have one phone? Why the wires like springs? Why the buttons and lights, blasted thing? You know, other calls come in while you're trying to—'

'Who rang?'

'A chap from a place with memories or something. Flags, too, I think. He was nice enough, I suppose. Said he'd been here once.'

Anselm immediately rang Sebastian from an extension near the cloister.

'I'm worried about this trial,' came the voice without preamble. It was as though Anselm was in the room on the other side of his desk. He pictured Sebastian, feet up, clothing acceptably disarrayed, his bloodshot eyes on the wall of box files surrounding the photograph of an old woman standing behind the wheelchair.

'He refuses to answer a single question. Won't say "Yes", won't say "No". Affirms nothing, denies nothing. But he's not playing the system. He's pleased. He *wants* the trial.'

'Wants?'

'He *wants* Róża to take the stand and say out loud what he did. He's impatient for the

428

prosecutor's opening speech. Doesn't even want a lawyer. Says someone can be appointed for any legal stuff. It's as though this were his day and not hers. He wants Róża to say whatever she likes. He is supremely unconcerned.'

Slowly, Anselm sank to a stone seat built into an arch. What had Brack done? What further step had Brack prepared? This was not a man who entered a brawl. He was a cold planner. A man who worked out his preferences. And he was obviously confident. What was the final trick? Róża wouldn't find out until she stood up in public . . . and then it would be too late. Anselm's mind careered into a manner of darkness: who else was left for Brack to use? Had he trapped someone else vital to Róża's life and story?

'I've lost the first round already,' said Sebastian. He was rapidly clicking and unclicking a biro.

'What do you mean?'

'The murderer of Stefan Binkowski won't be on the indictment.'

'Why?'

'Róża insists. Have you any idea who he might be?'

'None.'

Which was untrue. Because Anselm had thought of the empty wheelchair. And he'd recalled that Sebastian, too, had a personal story linked to the struggle. He'd promised to tell Anselm after Brack's conviction.

'He's the brother of Aniela Kolba.'

Anselm, caught by surprise, thought for a moment. His mind whirred back to the grovelling reports of FELIKS.

'Think about it,' said Sebastian. 'It sheds a different light on Edward.'

It certainly did. It took time for the picture to develop in Anselm's mind, but when the print was done, he stared at it with a mixture of revulsion and pity. Stefan had been one of the Friends. They'd arrested his sister, presumably, to exert pressure on him. Maybe, unknown to Róża, Aniela had been a Friend, too. It didn't matter. The point is they had her brother and they'd been beating him for months. Getting nowhere. Same with Pavel and Róża. To break Róża's will – and possibly Aniela's – they'd shot Pavel and Stefan. But it hadn't worked. That left the two women in the cell, either of whom could still lead them to the Shoemaker.

'I don't think Edward went to them,' said Sebastian. 'I reckon they came to him.'

'Saying if you don't watch your wife and Róża, we shoot them both.' Anselm felt the strange sick feeling that comes with recognising something deep and wicked. 'So Edward agreed – hell, what's so bad about watching someone? Just give Brack some peanuts every once in a while.'

'Exactly,' replied Sebastian. 'They let Aniela go first, but not before she'd urged Róża to come and stay. The invite must have been Edward's. Róża took the bait: she moved in.'

And Edward, who'd saved the lives of two women, who'd banked on feeding the monkeys, found himself in the cage. He'd told them what he'd seen and heard. In time, he'd secured his son's education with information on Magda the troublesome Jew. He'd become the real thing – a Comrade who played the system for what it was worth.

'Does Róża know that Edward informed on her?' asked Anselm.

'I didn't want to tell her, but once we started talking about Stefan and Aniela he became the elephant in the room.'

'How did she react?'

'Silence. But not your kind of silence. Or mine. It was something dark and awesome. She's meant to fall down with shock – that's what ordinary people do – but she didn't even waver. She just took the blow. You know, going over the case, it's always silence, every time anything leaks out of her past. A sort of agonised soaking up. She even looked heavier afterwards.' A reflective pause came down the line. 'She's ageing before my eyes, Anselm. She's not the woman I chased round Warsaw.'

'So it's a variation on the same old story' said Anselm, peremptorily. 'If the trial goes ahead for the murder of Aniela's brother, then Brack will reveal Edward's history of collaboration.'

'He hasn't made the threat, it's just built into the facts. He doesn't have to say anything. He's planned his way forward. And there's an added feature.'

'Which is?'

'Aniela doesn't know her brother is dead. Or that they had him in Mokotów at the same time as herself. For her, he's missing. For ever missing. So, getting back to Róża, she can only move forward on Stefan by telling Aniela that her brother was shot and that her husband was an informer. To say nothing of Bernard, his wife, their son . . .'

Such were the implications of disturbing the past. Was it *really* a good idea? Wasn't there a lot to be said for drawing a thick long line and living as best as possible on the other side? Even if people like Brack were the winners? Isn't it part of their crime that the suffering they've caused others, collectively, outweighs the impact of any punishment? He blurted out his thoughts, surprised to hear his own quarrel with conventional justice.

'That's why Róża's trial is so important,' replied Sebastian, clicking his pen. 'It's not just hers. She represents all the people who never got a chance to tell their story, all the cases that can never be brought. She's the epoch: its victim: its accuser.'

At the conclusion of that phrase, Anselm seemed to glimpse some of the scrawl upon Brack's mind, for he, too, was the epoch, though his role was so utterly different. And he would defend it.

'I know how he intends to stop Róża,' said Anselm, in a hushed voice. The door to the cloister had been left open. He looked at the Garth, just visible between two pillars – a rich, moist and violent green, bathed in spring sunshine. 'Everything returns to the same principle of destruction. He uses families. He sets father against son, mother against daughter.'

Sebastian followed Anselm's lead. 'He's got something on Aniela. I never thought of her. She cracked in fifty-one, she . . .'

Anselm didn't listen. He was thinking the matter through.

'. . . so if Róża pursues Brack –' concluded Sebastian – 'there'll be no more warnings. This time it's mutual, public destruction. If he goes down, Aniela—'

'It's not her,' said Anselm evenly, cold and certain. 'Brack saved his best trick till last.'

Spring is a special interlude for a beekeeper. New colonies begin and the old ones come back to life. There's a lot to do. And Anselm normally found himself oddly fulfilled pottering about the hives with his list of jobs. But not this time. He was still haunted by the reunion of Róża with Celina, haunted by Brack's intentions, haunted by the long shadow of Klara's handlers. The Terror wasn't over.

By late September the harvest was over and then, as if there was some kind of connection between the bitter and the sweet, a letter came, written in a wavering hand he did not recognise. It was from Róża. A trial date had been fixed for the spring.

Father Nicodem was too old and, frankly, not altogether well. Would Anselm take his place, even if he understood nothing? The Prior didn't hesitate to grant his permission. He, like Anselm, understood only too clearly that Róża's suffering was by no means over; that it was about to reach its conclusion.

PART VII

THE WIND THAT STRIPS THE TREES

CHAPTER 45

On a cold morning at the beginning of March, the Warsaw District Court was ready to hear the case against Otto Brack, a former colonel in the communist *Służba Bezpieczeństwa*. The sun had risen to poke holes in a grey blanket of cloud. Faint rain spat upon the streets and the crowd of onlookers and restive journalists. On the other side of the road stood an elderly couple, a man and woman. They seemed to be making a separate, private protest. Between them they held a banner made from a torn bed sheet.

'*Czekamy na sprwiedliwośća*,' murmured Róża, reading the black lettering, as the limousine swung to a halt at the main entrance. She turned to Anselm with a quiet translation: 'We are waiting for justice.'

Guided by hulking policemen in baseball caps and black body armour, Anselm followed Róża, John and Celina out of the car towards the court, mouthing the phrase as if it were sacred, ducking past the nest of microphones, the flash of cameras and the volley of questions.

'We are waiting for justice,' he mumbled, in reply.

Róża's expectation that Anselm would understand nothing had been defeated by the simple expedient of simultaneous translation delivered through a discreet earpiece. Upon arrival he was brought by a court usher to a tiny room with a window and an elevated view on to the court. The cabin was sufficiently high that no one would notice it unless they raised their heads to examine the plaster mouldings or the flamboyant capitals crowning the sequence of pillars that stood like guards around the auditorium. Anselm had a bird's eye view, with the implied detachment that comes with distance. Once he was seated at a narrow table, the translator's voice sounded in his ear, greeting him with flawless English.

'Let me introduce the lawyers down below.'

The courtroom was wood-panelled from floor to ceiling. Three robed judges sat beneath the emblem of a white eagle. Documents lay in bundles between the computer screens. The IPN prosecutors were crouched to one side, their black gowns trimmed with red: Sebastian a kind of map-reader to the driver, Madam Czerny, a woman with bleached straggling hair and a pair of gold bifocals held permanently in one hand. Fastened just below their left shoulders was a plume of crimson cloth the size of a handkerchief. Anselm couldn't help but think of blood. Facing them sat Mr Fischer, counsel appointed for Brack, the sober green border to his gown completely displaced by the pink and blue striped cuffs of his shirt. One could almost pass over the client at his side. He'd been upstaged by the few centimetres of peeping colour.

Anselm examined Brack. First with a lawyer's eye: aged eighty-four, he faced what the indictment called Communist crimes – a misnomer because murder and torture had a prevalence and character without boundary of any kind – and then, briefly, with a monk's: *Do you realise what you're doing?*

He wore a light brown jacket and a dark brown shirt. His tie was another brown. Against those combinations, even his skin seemed brown. Dark pigmentations like the spots on a Dalmatian covered his head. Large glasses with brownish lenses hid his face. He was thin, like a wooden clothes stand. All the emotion centred on the mouth. It worked as if he were chewing a piece of old leather, the top teeth occasionally pulling at the bottom lip. He ignored every whispered remark from his counsel. In front of him was a smart-looking black leather document case.

Is this truly your choice?

The witness stand was directly in front of the judicial bench. It resembled a lectern, inherently serious. Róża would stand there and tell her story. Then Brack would do the same thing. A year earlier, at the other end of the phone, Sebastian had listened to Anselm, clicking his biro open and shut.

'He'll tell the court how Pavel Mojeska betrayed his wife, his friends and his country. If he wants, he can make it up as he goes along, because no one else was there. He's going to spring a defence out of the files. He'll produce evidence that Pavel collaborated with the Nazis – a crime the IPN would prosecute now, if he was living. He'll make those executions into rough justice – unpleasant, brutal, and lacking ceremony . . . but legitimate actions of the State nonetheless. Brack's not going down, Sebastian, he doesn't play to lose; he never has done.'

Sebastian's pen had clattered against a wall.

'What have I done?' he'd said, faintly. 'I've brought her to this.'

'What have we all done?' Anselm had replied.

Drawing that thick long line between 'then' and 'now' had never seemed more prudent. Shortly after that telephone conversation Sebastian had carefully explained to Róża what was likely to happen when Brack opened his mouth, and she'd listened with that disconcerting quietness that absorbed any and all disappointment. When he'd finished, she'd simply said, 'At least I didn't remain quiet.'

She was now sitting with John and Celina in a room set aside for prosecution witnesses. She was wearing a sober dress from *Jaeger* with a silvery Paisley design. The lime cardigan – an old friend, worn at the elbows – appeared, by association, both refined and expensive. Sebastian was right, though: she'd aged. She'd taken in too much. Her movements were slow and heavy, her spine rounded. But she had a most haunting allure, a curious effect of soft skin and eyes that Anselm couldn't meet for long without turning away. Inexplicably, they'd remained vulnerable.

Looking down through the window, Anselm scanned the court as if there might be any familiar faces, not expecting to find any. But he did. He found one. And it wasn't Bernard Kolba's. They'd already met in the corridor (he was there representing the family; his parents couldn't face the strain). Anselm's eyes had alighted upon a fine bone structure, frizzy, greying hair and round glasses. Irina Orlosky was in the public gallery, her dark, shapeless coat held tight by folded arms. Her eyes were on Brack, the man whose life she'd saved.

Once the jury were installed Madam Czerny came to her feet. Her voice had alarming, deep cadences, the translation in Anselm's ear skilfully matching tone with content, keeping a sort of distance from the primary speaker. Somehow, the prosecutor was addressing Anselm without intermediary. Throughout, her right hand held the bifocals, elegantly, as if it were a glass of Muscat.

'This case concerns the Terror,' she said, deadly gentle. 'The time of denunciation and disappearing, of imprisonment upon a whim, of routine violence, pathological suspicion, false accusations and forced recantations. The epoch of complicity. The age of exile and executions, co-ordinated to secure the imposition of Soviet socialist realism.'

Madam Czerny's gaze moved around, indomitable. 'Róża Mojeska is one ordinary woman who, despite the overwhelming presence of fear and the crushing pressure to conform, said, "No". As a consequence she was brutally tortured. Pavel Mojeska, her husband, also said, "No". He was brutally murdered. They'd said the one word that millions dared not speak. They'd brought a free word to Warsaw.' She seemed to have finished but then, confiding and soft spoken, she made a reluctant declaration. 'The accused, Otto Brack, said, "Yes". He got up every morning, looked in the mirror and said "Yes". No one twisted his arm. He made his own free choice. And it is this profound affirmation of terror – its implementation and consequences – that now falls to be judged.'

To that end the prosecution would call evidence from experts to present the context within which the alleged crimes took place. An historian would describe the architecture of Stalinism in general and the Terror in particular; another would explain the organisation, powers and objectives of the secret police; yet another would outline the crucial importance of underground printing as a means of preserving an independent culture. The line of attack was clear: Madam Czerny would lead the court down to the foundations of a forgotten time, that it might better understand Brack's place in the cellar.

Then it would be Róża's turn.

'She will be on her own, as she was, once, long

ago,' said Madam Czerny. 'There is no other living witness to what took place in that prison. She will tell you what she saw.'

After lunch on the second day of evidence, Anselm sent a message to the translator: owing to a previous engagement, he wouldn't be attending the hearing that afternoon – apologies for having forgotten to mention it sooner. In fact it was a spontaneous decision. He'd been listening, hour after hour, tormented by the sight of Brack's leather document case; he'd fidgeted constantly, watching Brack make rushed notes while a professor from Kraków mocked, with scholarly detachment, the acclamation of Stalin as a 'Philologist of Genius' and the 'Greatest Man of All Times' (two of 300 unctuous tributes that had appeared in the national press in 1949 to mark his seventieth birthday); he'd been troubled by the growing certainty that even the prosecutor's evidence formed part of Brack's final scheme to escape the power of a rightly constituted court.

Outside, away from the growing tension, Anselm went to a fishmonger's and bought a fresh oyster.

CHAPTER 46

'Well . . . Hail, Mary,' said Frenzel, with a wave, full of surprise. 'Or should that be Our Father?'

Anselm shut the door and came to the edge of the desk. Frenzel's eyes were alight with pleasure at the swiftness of his jokes.

'If I'd known you wanted all the stuff to have a swipe at Brack, well, you could've paid by monthly instalments. I felt sorry for him, mind, when I saw him on the telly. Made me think of those show trials in the fifties. You know, the hype and the conceit. Hypocrites, the lot of you. What was it? Whited sepulchres or something? When I saw that bitchy prosecutor—'

His gaze settled hard on the oyster. Anselm had placed it carefully in the middle of his desk.

'Sorry, I can't. Last time round I ate a dodgy one. Sick as a dog I was and I vowed never to—'

'I want Brack's personnel file. Not just the first page and not just the last. I'd like the lot.'

Frenzel's pink lips made a curve analogous to a smile. He didn't speak at first, preferring to nod a kind of dawning avuncular support for the workings of Anselm's mind. He approved.

'It makes sense, I suppose,' he murmured, scratching his paunch. 'You lot always want the pearl of great price.'

He picked up the phone, dialled and waited. After a second's thought he seemed to spew into the receiver from a height, keeping it well away from his mouth as though it were dirty. He was talking to Irina's son, presumably. He left a message from his mother. It took an effort of will for Anselm not to lean over and thump that sagging jaw. Frenzel wouldn't expect that from someone who was meant to turn the other cheek. He clenched his fists, feeling the guilt of a bystander watching back-street violence – the frenzied kicking of the racist and homophobe.

'You played that one well,' Frenzel said with a wink, cleaning his hands on a wet-wipe pulled from a shiny plastic packet. 'If you'd started off asking for the earth, you'd have paid through the nose. But you've shown some good footwork. Made yourself look stupid when you weren't. Now you've got Brack on his knees, you want his file. Smart move. Well, you can have it for nothing. I'd like to contribute to his execution. I'll have it sent over. Where are you staying? Don't tell me! Same place?' He nestled deeper into his chair. 'Thought so. You're all the same. Nothing ever changes.' He paused to lick his lips. 'You'll be getting a brown box . . . Don't go just yet, I thought we might talk about old times, you know, the days of wine and roses. What did you make of the *pierogi*? If you want my view, when all's said and done, you can't do much with a dumpling.'

On reaching the door, Anselm turned around – not to say anything but just to have one last look at the man who'd never be brought to court. By the time the European Cup kicked off in Praga, he'd be a very rich man. There'd be a wine bar called Frenzel's or a boutique selling silk ties and brightly coloured cotton socks. He flicked open a pocket knife and began prising open the oyster.

'I'm having this one,' he said, smirking. 'Even if it kills me.'

The phone in Anselm's room rang at 8.39 p.m. Krystyna said his visitor had arrived. She was waiting in the foyer.

'I'm on my way down.'

It was a stab in the dark, but while listening to the evidence Anselm had tuned into the voices of other witnesses, other experts on the Terror. Irina had said Frenzel used people's mistakes; Father Nicodem had said Brack trapped people with their past. And Anselm had wondered if there might just be some handle on to Róża's persecutor, some mistake, some element of his past that might be used to avert what he was planning.

'Here it is,' said Irina, holding out the brown

cardboard box as if it were Christmas. 'I don't know what's inside. Mr Frenzel told me it was for your eyes only.'

The jokes didn't end. He even played at spies.

'Thank you.'

She was standing marooned on the red carpet, a short distance from the entrance, exposed, it seemed, by the bright lights. She wasn't comfortable with the opulence. She didn't belong with decent, well dressed people. Her shapeless coat was wet again with rain. The hood was up, as at their first meeting. She'd come from work in her green McDonald's trousers and black sensible shoes. She spoke in a rushed, sore voice.

'Is this for the trial? Is this going to bring him down? Am I part of it again?'

'I hope so, Irina. Do you want a hot drink? A cold one?'

'Nothing. Will it help?' She pointed at the box in Anselm's hands.

'I don't know. I want to understand him, that's all. If we understand someone, we can reach them . . . far into them, even if it's something they don't want; often without them knowing.'

'Why do you want to reach him? No one can reach him. I should know.'

'Because I'm concerned he might try to escape the grip of the court.'

'How? No. It's not possible.'

'I'm just being cautious.' He smiled an assurance into her darkness and glimpsed the hygienic hair net. 'You've helped me again, Irina. You reminded me of a truth beloved by Mr Frenzel. A man's mistakes, his past? They can work like a key to his future. I want to make sure Róża can turn the lock.'

She sniffed and reached into her sleeve for a handkerchief. A sneeze followed. 'This is my trial, too, you know. I'm there, watching every day. Working nights. I don't need the sleep.' Woodenly, she held out a cold hand. 'I've got to go.'

Abruptly she turned and hurried away, out of the light and off the carpet, heading back to the queues of people wanting a Big Mac. Anselm almost ran outside after her. But he didn't because he had nothing to offer; he wanted to give her something – so much more than a hot or cold drink – but all he had was thanks for the tip about mistakes, and he'd furnished that already.

Back at his desk overlooking the glittering skyline, he rang Sebastian. Of course, there might be nothing of interest in the brown box. But if there was . . . well, time was on the short side. Róża was due to give evidence at 10.30 a.m. the next morning.

CHAPTER 47

Anselm and Sebastian reached Róża's flat shortly before 11 p.m. The room shocked Anselm by its simplicity: a table, some chairs, scraps of furniture, a mirror, a standing lamp with a yellow shade. He looked again . . . a bullet on a shelf beneath a mirror. She made tea, not speaking, her soft footfalls pattering around the kitchen. The place was tidy and clean: the surroundings of an ordered mind; the ambience of someone who'd tamed restlessness.

'We have to do to him what he has done to others,' said Sebastian. 'We have to use his past against him.'

'Have to?' The question displayed a certain moral revulsion in Róża which unsettled Anselm. He'd had no such sensibility.

'It's the only way,' said Sebastian. 'Otherwise I'm sure he's going to take something out of Pavel's file – something made up, something planted before you left Mokotów. We have to think like that now; we have to act like it, too, just for tomorrow. Afterwards—'

'No other tomorrow will ever be the same again,' said Róża.

She sat at her dining table, her black pullover drawing her into the shadows. The light from the lamp was weak. Her face caught a faint glamour.

It was, of course, incongruous to rely on any file as a guide to the truth. Despite appearances, Father Nicodem's was dramatically incomplete and utterly misleading. Even when the papers gave a full picture, like that of Edward, the image was distorted. But the rub was this: truths were in there. They might need stripping down and cleaning up, but the files contained information. And information, as Brack knew, was power.

'Róża, we have to get to him first,' continued Sebastian. He was still wearing his suit. The tie was loose, the top button open. 'You should meet him. Before you give evidence. I'm convinced that—'

'Tell me what's in the file,' said Róża, in a voice of strained patience. 'Then we'll talk about tomorrow.'

Sebastian had ploughed through every document generated by the secret police machinery between 1948 and 1989. He'd read Brack's application form, a memo from Moscow, appraisals by Major Strenk and a string of increasingly critical internal reports from 1965 onwards. It seemed that the further Brack got away from the Stalinist culture of his early manhood, the more out of step

450

he became with the system he served. Promotions ground to a halt. By 1982 they weren't allowed to beat Politicals any more. He'd been out of his depth, no doubt. But that was all by-the-by. Sebastian had distilled the facts into two broad areas. The first was small and important, if only to explain Brack's obsessions. It was all set out in his application form.

'He was born in Polana,' said Sebastian. 'He mentions the place several times. It's as though, looking back, Polana was the safe place, as if the family should have stayed there and everything would have been different. But Leon, his father, brought them all to Warsaw. He left behind the safe and conventional because he was a man with a mission greater than any individual's pursuit of happiness. Leon's life had been given to the oppressed workers. By the late thirties he was a leading light in the Communist Party. A man with ideas and ambition. The Party was dissolved in thirty-eight by the Comintern but Leon appears to have reinvented himself, surviving the purges of the time – purges his son appears to have known nothing about. Leon, above all, was a man who—'

'—made toys out of old bits of wood and plumbing.' Róża spoke quietly.

'Sorry?' Sebastian glanced at Anselm.

'Toys. He once made a musket out of a wooden spindle and . . . I forget.'

'Who did?'

'Leon.'

Sebastian nodded sympathetically. Anselm watched Róża, sensing, like a hesitant mariner, the approach of something immense beneath the surface of rising waves. It wasn't dangerous, but it had power. Whatever it was slipped away and Sebastian was talking again.

'The Germans invaded in—'

'September nineteen thirty-nine,' supplied Róża, archly.

'Sorry, absolutely. You know better than me.' Sebastian took the rebuke but he didn't slow down. 'And they immediately began tracking down their ideological enemies, prominent amongst whom, of course, stood Leon Brack.'

Leon and his family went into hiding. What happened next was not entirely clear. Brack's application form was silent on the matter, but at some point he was hidden in an orphanage where he remained for the duration of the war. Róża's orphanage. He never saw his parents again. Shortly after Brack had been spirited away, they'd been denounced and deported.

'She cooked fish in lemonade,' added Róża, and again Anselm sensed that swell of power deep beneath the water. 'It makes the fish sweet.'

'Yes,' agreed Sebastian, uncertainly, 'I'll give that a try.'

'How does all this affect the trial?'

Sebastian joined his hands into a sort of wedge, pointing forwards. 'Directly, it doesn't . . . but it

452

gives the background to your only chance to silence him.'

'Tell me how this affects the trial,' repeated Róża, her voice lowered ever so slightly.

'Brack joined the secret police believing that his parents had died in Mauthausen. He served the cause year on year, motivated, I am sure, by genuine socialist convictions. For some reason the focus of his drive and grief came to centre upon the Shoemaker, almost certainly because his ideas were the complete antithesis of his own. The Shoemaker was exactly what he set himself up to be: the challenger to Communist ideology. And Brack was looking for him in nineteen forty-eight and he didn't stop until nineteen eighty-nine. Between times he—'

'Shot my husband and Stefan Binkowski. How is all this related to tomorrow morning?'

'Everything he did – his entire life – rests upon a tragic misunderstanding and a profound deceit.' Sebastian was leaning forward over his wedged hands. 'If you tell him the truth, the naked truth laid out in his file, I think he'll lose heart. I don't think he'll want to go on. I think it will break him.'

Róża stood up and walked aimlessly into the middle of the room, lost in thought. She turned her eyes on to the mirror . . . or the bullet. Curiously, the earlier impression of old age and round shouldered weariness – evident only a matter of moments ago – had suddenly vanished, as if dropped on the carpet, sloughed off when no

453

one was looking. She returned to the table focused and erect.

'Do you have the file?'

'Yes.' Sebastian tapped the shoulder bag, heaped at his feet.

'Let me see it.'

For the next hour or so Róża sat absorbed in her reading, slowly turning the pages, while Sebastian made quiet remarks, like a librarian, pointing up key passages and documents of special interest. She pored over the early appraisals written by Major Strenk. She stared, expressionless, at the NKVD memo from Moscow, the blunt tool (said Sebastian) that would, if used, stun Brack like an animal in an abattoir.

'Yes, I'm sure it would,' she replied, pushing the closed file towards Sebastian.

'I'll organise a meeting for tomorrow?'

'Yes.'

'Good.'

'But not with Brack,' clarified Róża, with a quick wag from her finger. 'There will be no meeting with Brack. It won't be necessary.'

'Who, then?'

'My Friends. Everyone who's come this far with me, but leave out Madam Czerny. I don't think she'd appreciate what I'm planning to do, even though it's a kind of justice.'

Stray filtered light patterned the walls of Anselm's hotel bedroom. Shards with soft edges, like the design in the carpet downstairs. They came like echoes from the city on the other side of the windows. What was Róża going to do? Why had she changed so dramatically? These were the main questions but, ever ill-disciplined, Anselm's curiosity strayed along a couple of byways. He was trying to work out if they led back to the main road.

First, Róża had evidently known Brack long before she'd been interrogated in Mokotów. They'd known each other during the war, at Saint Justyn's. Would it be stretching probability to infer that they'd been more than friends? Anselm thought not. Frenzel had sniffed something personal in Brack's obsession with catching Róża. A lost or failed love, that's the fruit he'd detected, drawn in through those flaring nostrils. The connoisseur of old mistakes had smelled a hidden blunder. Was Brack simply Brack – at least in part – because, through some wrong turning, he'd lost his hold on Róża? A hold which he'd tried to reinstate through murder and a perverted scheme that left him as the father of her child – even as he convinced himself that he'd pulled the trigger for the sake of a better set of ideas?

The second byway intrigued Anselm even more, because it represented a short step back in time: Brack must have met Mr Lasky. He was there in the orphanage, guiding Róża with his homespun maxims. Brack had told Strenk about Róża, but there'd been no mention of the caretaker. Why?

Because – Anselm concluded – he'd been grateful. In the epoch where naming names was a means to salvation, he'd shown a hidden, redundant loyalty – even to a dead man, executed by the Nazis. But why grateful? Presumably for saving his life. This byway, extremely narrow and now overgrown, led to the person whom Róża had met as a girl . . . Otto, a youth separated from his family because of his father's political convictions, someone capable of gratitude and love. And who, tomorrow, would meet Róża's kind of justice.

What was she planning? How did the all the roads come together? How would she take account of who he was, set against who he'd become and what he'd done?

CHAPTER 48

The first Anselm knew of the hullabaloo was when he saw armed police running past the room where he was waiting for the meeting with Róża. Celina, John and Sebastian followed him out into the corridor. Shouts came echoing from round a corner, court officials walked into view with strained urgency. Sebastian intercepted one of them with a pull to the elbow. He listened and his mouth fell open.

'Róża's been arrested,' he gasped, swinging around. 'She's come with a bullet in her handbag. A live round, for God's sake.'

After further frantic enquiries it transpired she'd been taken to a holding cell two floors down. Strenuous representations from Sebastian, Celina and John, with a brisk appearance from Madam Czerny, eventually secured her release after forty-five minutes. Yes, criminal charges might be pressed. No, you can't have it back when you leave the building. Yes, the court will be informed of Róża's conduct.

'Why did you bring it?' exclaimed Sebastian when they were settled in the conference room. 'What was going through your mind?'

'I just wanted to return it,' she said, completely unflustered. 'I never managed to find a use for it.'

'Return it? Who to?'

Róża didn't answer. She looked different . . . younger than the night before. Just as striking was her appearance: the *Jaeger* dress had been left in a wardrobe, along with the accessories. She'd put on rough and ready clothes, as if she were off to the market: black woollen trousers that had lost their front pleats; a loose grey woollen jumper, darned at the elbows; a white blouse. On the floor by her feet was a plastic bag bulging with old newspapers. One of the more enthusiastic policemen had raised the possibility of poisoned ink. She was lucky they'd returned it without insisting on forensic examination.

'I was only thinking the other day – when that professor from Kraków was describing the old days – I was saying to myself, this isn't really working.'

'What isn't?' asked Sebastian.

'The trial. It's just not what I'd expected and hoped for. It's narrow, somehow. I can't find myself in what's happening in the courtroom. It's as though something's missing. You see, unless you were there, you can't imagine what it was like. It was so much worse than any list of wrongs. It was a climate. And I don't want justice simply for what happened to Pavel. It has to reach wider than his or my experience.'

458

The walls were white, the lighting harsh. They were seated at a round conference table, Róża somehow at its head, though she sat to one side as if she'd just dropped in and might well leave at any moment. She was leading the meeting, but in a way foreign to any professional lawyer.

'Róża,' began Sebastian, like a fisherman, net in hand, watching the big one glinting within reach, 'don't do this, listen to me—'

'No, Sebastian, you listen. I know what I'm doing. I know how to get the right kind of justice.'

'So the trial goes on?' Sebastian's relief was only marginally in advance of his confusion.

'Yes, but not according to the usual rules. I'm going to run a trial within a trial, only don't tell Madam Czerny. If she didn't understand the bullet, we're not going to see eye to eye on my kind of gun.'

Róża's relaxed appearance, coupled with her confidence, was at stark variance with the tension in the room. Even Celina did not know her mother's intentions. John was frowning behind his glasses. No one dared speak. Róża was in control of a parallel legal universe that only she could understand. She began to explain, slowly.

'I intend to silence Otto Brack, but not by using his file,' she said, coming closer, leaning both elbows on the table. 'A family's tragic past? Strenk's reports? His ignorance? That's *their* way. I have another.'

Róża became precise in her movements: the

slight angle of the head as if she were aiming, the narrowed eye, one raised finger . . .

'You must understand that for Brack this is not a *trial*,' she said, dispassionately. 'It is an *interrogation*, and he knows all about those. They were his bread and butter. He's at home. Only this time it's his turn to answer the questions. And he wants to. He's waiting for Madam Czerny to try and trip him up, to start wearing him down with her clout, with the same, sudden shift in moods that he'd learned from Strenk – from surprise to boredom, from loathing to indignation.' Róża slowly shook her head. 'There may have been a time when he feared the court, but not any more. His scheme has done its work. The other side didn't catch him. He's lived a free life. What's at stake now is what he *believes*.' She turned to Sebastian at her side. 'Which is why I don't think he'll pull some trick out of his bag to smear Pavel's memory. He intends to state his case. He wants Pavel to be who he was, so he can say he was someone different.'

Still no one dared to make a contribution.

'If I give evidence,' she said, deliberately, her eyes roving round the table, 'he gets a right of reply. If I speak about the execution of Pavel, so will he. If I speak of those bad days, so will he. He'll be able to match me, word for word. And I don't want to hear what he has to say. I've heard it all before. He hopes to redeem what I would condemn and of course, he can't: the court won't

460

legalise his murdering, but what matters to him is that he *spoke*. He got the chance to claim the light before he was cast into the darkness. Make no mistake about it, he wants the condemnation. He wants to sink to his knees, like Pavel, and die a martyr to his cause. And I'm not going to let him.'

'What are you planning, Róża?' asked Sebastian, for everyone in the room.

'For Pavel, to pull a different kind of trigger; for me, to turn a different kind of key.'

'How?'

'By giving evidence to which there is no reply.'

Anselm glanced at Sebastian and Celina. Their eyes darted back. John nudged his glasses.

'I'm going to name his crime within the greater crime of an era. To those who weren't there, it will seem trivial and that I'm a silly old woman who's lost her mind. But he will hear and understand; and he won't be able to say anything in return.'

Róża reached for her plastic bag and stood up. Anselm watched her move to the door as if she was off to the market to pick up a few bargains. On the way she'd throw all those papers in the recycling bin. Turning abruptly, as if she'd forgotten to say the obvious, she said, 'At the same time, there is, of course, this other trial, the one being led by Madam Czerny. That goes on as if nothing was happening. And it will conclude with the one thing he didn't give me, which he doesn't want,

461

and which he'll have to accept: a kind of mercy. He'll walk away a free man – apparently and actually reprieved. But within himself, he'll be imprisoned for the rest of his life, listening to the echo of his own dead voice.' She made a humph and turned the door handle. 'It shouldn't take too long.'

'Róża,' called Sebastian. 'Wait a moment, don't go. Why any sort of mercy?'

He was robed, ready for court. Unless Anselm was mistaken, he was wearing a new suit. This was his day, too.

'Because of Strenk's reports, his family's past and his ignorance,' replied Róża. 'I'm glad you brought them to me. I think they should be taken into account.'

'But there'll be no conviction.'

'Sebastian, listen to me. He's angling with you as he angled with me. Don't get caught by what he's flashing in front of your eyes. Look deeper, look further. You'll see, my way is best.'

With that confident declaration, Róża opened the door and stepped into the bustle of the court corridor, leaving everyone behind as if they had nothing to do with the proceedings. One by one, Sebastian, Celina and John left the conference room. Anselm smiled to himself, quietly admiring, reminded of Róża's original statement. She had a certain style and it had just repeated itself. Róża had planned a deeper trial within a trial; a quest for a deeper justice. The two would coincide, nicely. Justice and Mercy would meet. And when they did, maybe those five musicians in Praga would spring to life: the time of music was almost upon them.

CHAPTER 49

Anselm adjusted his earpiece and settled forward, the window over the court reminding him of that terrifying painting by Breughel where Mad Meg leads an army of women to pillage the bowels of hell. Apparently messages had been sent to Barbara Novak and Lidia Zelk, old Friends of the Shoemaker: they were down there somewhere, waiting for Róża to arrive and lead them on. So was Aniela Kolba, who'd changed her mind about keeping away. So was Irina Orlosky, crouched on the edge of her seat. Madam Czerny, bi-focals on the end of her nose, was leafing through a statement, presumably Meg's, rehearsing a strategy of questions.

Brack was motionless. He sat with horrible stillness, like a careless lord surrounded by frantic peasants, his hands resting on his leather bag. Mr Fischer twirled a pen between his fingers, tugging occasionally at his yellow and green cuffs. He wasn't worried either. This was a case he could only lose. Then Anselm made a start: slouching by the far wall like a bored demon sat Marek Frenzel, turned out by Burberry. He was in trouble, though. Something was stuck between his back teeth.

The court became quiet. The judges were seated on their hi-tech bench, the computer screens flickering. The jury were ready to listen. The usher's voice called the last witness for the prosecution.

'Róża Mojeska.'

Almost immediately the ordinary procedure was upturned. When Róża reached the lectern she was offered a chair. She refused and asked, instead, for a table. The request was granted with a kind of puzzled tolerance, an attitude that prevailed while Róża laid out her tatty newspapers as if she were a street vendor near a railway station. And yet, this protracted activity, undertaken slowly, lent a curious authority to this Mad Meg. She was setting up her own stand. There were two courts in the room, one facing the other. When Róża had finished her preparations, Madam Czerny, blanched hair astray, rose slowly, gently swinging her bifocals in one hand.

'Your name, please.'

'Róża Mojeska.'

'Date of birth?'

'Major Strenk asked that.'

'Sorry?'

'Major Strenk. Always names, always dates of birth.'

'I'm afraid we keep records.'

'Does it really matter?'

The prosecutor had a ready, indulgent smile. She was used to difficult witnesses. From long experience she knew how to handle them. 'Yes. For the court. We note what you say.'

'So did Major Strenk.'

'Thank you.'

'You're nothing like him, of course, and I'm sorry for any comparison. The eighth of March, nineteen twenty-nine.'

The concession was entirely formal. Róża had demonstrated – right at the outset – that she was curiously *adjacent* to the system; that she would respectfully co-operate with its mechanisms; but that she intended to introduce some changes.

'You were brought up in Saint Justyn's Orphanage for Girls?'

'Yes.'

'You fought in the Uprising of nineteen forty-four?'

'I did.'

'Your function?'

'Ammunition carrier.'

Even the judges laughed. It took time for the quiet to return and find its depth.

'You were deported to the transit camp at Pruszków?'

'I was.'

'From there you heard the explosions as Warsaw was razed to the ground?'

'I have never forgotten the sound.'

'You returned to rebuild it?'

'With my own hands.'

Anselm found Madam Czerny totally intimidating, even when she was being nice. The bleached hair evoked a scouring personality; someone who got the stains off a burnt pan that anyone else would throw in the bin. But Róża was wholly undisturbed. She seemed to be giving the court only what she wanted, even though she had no control over the questions. And so the two women, prosecutor and witness, came by careful, mutually agreed steps to the Shoemaker Operation. In a series of brisk exchanges Róża confirmed her recruitment in 1951, her arrest following that of her husband, and her incarceration in Mokotów prison.

'Before dealing with the grave events which are the subject of the indictment against this defendant,' said Madam Czerny, addressing more the jury than Róża, 'I think it may be of assistance to the court if you would explain, in simple terms, what the Shoemaker meant to you. You had never met him. You had only read his words. I ask because your answer will explain not only why you were prepared to face imprisonment but – and of great importance for the purpose of this trial – it will illuminate the motives of Otto Brack, the defendant; for the crimes alleged against him spring more from his quarrel with the Shoemaker than your role as his publisher.'

This was the moment Róża had been waiting for. She appeared to pounce, though she merely gripped the lectern, fingers widely spaced in the manner of an embrace. Anselm had the strongest intimation that the trial within a trial was about to begin, that Róża's unconventional procedure was now underway. She'd said it wouldn't take that long.

'It was a matter of hope,' she said, simply. 'The Shoemaker wrote about hope. You can all come and see me afterwards, if you like, and I'll show you what he said –' she pointed towards the covered table – 'you can read him for yourself. He named hope so much better than I could. The word occurs on every page of every edition. I'll give you some examples.'

Róża leaned over her stand to find selected copies of *Freedom and Independence* while Madam Czerny, reduced to a spectator, shifted on her feet: this kind of thing was outside her experience. She was about to intervene when a knowing look from the presiding judge forestalled her. Let the old woman have some latitude, he implied, smoothing a heavy moustache. We can wait. She'll be easier to lead once she's had her say.

'These quotations are all taken from nineteen fifty-one, before I was arrested,' said Róża, opening three different editions on the lectern. 'Remember, this was during the Terror. People with a mind of their own didn't dare to whisper what they were thinking. This is what the Shoemaker said to them: "Hope is among you."' She paused. '"During a time of Occupation hope

468

is our national sovereignty."' Another pause. 'And finally, my favourite: "Hope is a tree in an open field. All the birds of the air settle in its branches."'

Madam Czerny's deep voice sounded loud enough to scare them off. 'And now, mindful of those helpful observations, we can turn to the matters set forth in the indictment.'

'That won't be necessary.'

'I beg your pardon?'

'I'm afraid the more I've listened, the more I've come to the conclusion that it's just not wide enough.'

The bleached prosecutor settled her glasses on her long nose. Sebastian, hunched at her side, lowered his head. Brack looked towards Róża, implacable but inquiring. The entire room was spellbound by the hiatus. Just as the presiding judge leaned forward to speak, Róża snatched the initiative from his open mouth, underlining the culmination of her evidence.

'A man can shoot the birds from the trees . . . and I've seen them fall to the ground.' Her tone had changed colour and pitch; it was dark and low, now. 'He can even rob the nests that are left behind. But this defendant went one step further.' She turned towards Brack and raised her arm, pointing at him with an open hand. 'This is the greater crime he must answer for. It includes all the others. He cut into the sap. He cut down the tree itself.'

Brack stared ahead. He didn't seem to react,

though Róża's accusation had echoed round the room. 'She was right,' murmured Anselm to himself. 'He's just waiting for his chance to reply.' So this must be the moment: she's turning a kind of key, pulling a kind of trigger.

'Let us take things a little more slowly, and in detail,' came Madam Czerny's reassuring, papering-over-the-cracks voice. But there was a shake to the timbre. The deep cadences had gone. She'd picked up Róża's statement prepared for the trial and Anselm knew what the prosecutor – reeling behind the bluff of calm – was thinking: she had to pull the witness into line, damn quick, and forcefully if necessary; but he also knew that Róża wouldn't be moving an inch. She wasn't singing from Madam Czerny's hymn sheet; Róża had another one. And Anselm knew she hadn't finished, either, despite what she then said.

'I have nothing further to say.'

Mr Fischer looked up as if the lights had come on at two in the morning. Momentarily, he was caught in the glare of unimaginable good luck: a win was careering straight towards him, a win he'd never thought possible. Blinking, recovered, coughing and suave, he came to his feet, oblivious that his client had suddenly begun to move, writhing in his suit.

'Moved as we all are by the words of the witness, I'm obliged to remark, however, that the crime she identifies – grave though it be – is not known to the law.' He reminded Anselm of the kind of

470

opponent he'd most disliked: denigrating in the robing room and then fussy in their courtesy after a case abruptly turned their way. He tugged a cuff into place, gloating. 'I'd be grateful if those representing the interests of prosecution would clarify – for the avoidance of all doubt – that this lady has indeed completed her evidence. The court will anticipate that in those curious—'

'I said I had finished,' replied Róża, speaking for herself. 'There is nothing more to be said.'

'In that case,' began Mr Fischer, tugging the other cuff, 'I would have thought that the proper way forward – in the interests of justice – is for Madam Czerny to reconsider her position and that of those whom she represents. I'm reluctant to state the obvious to someone as distinguished as my learned colleague, but it would seem there is no lawful basis upon which the continued prosecution of my client can proceed. It is difficult to know precisely . . .'

Mr Fischer lost his thread because Róża had reached down to her table and picked up another edition of *Freedom and Independence*. Again, the presiding judge raised a calming hand, his expression as sympathetic as it was sad: he'd recognised what the whole court must know; Róża Mojeska, the survivor of the Terror, had suffered profound, enduring wounds to the mind. She'd lost her grip; she was throwing away her only chance of vindication. He sighed, audibly, surrendering the collapse of the trial to the one person responsible. Let her have the last word, he seemed to say.

471

'Let me read you the concluding reflections of the Shoemaker,' said Róża, turning to the inside back page. 'This is what he said, in late nineteen eighty-two. He hasn't spoken since. "One day, we will win. It is inevitable. But then we must turn to the question of justice. We will have to look back, never forgetting how difficult it was to steer a morally straight course when, in the day to day, we were obliged to live a double life, one in private and the other in public. We will need to recognise that we all, to a greater or lesser extent, bolstered up the system we now accuse. We will have to recall that there was a chasm between thinking and speaking, believing and doing and that not many of us managed to cross the divide without a fall. Each of these painful truths, when recollected, should make passing judgement a delicate exercise. Remember: collaboration had a grading. Let our reprimand be proportionate. Name wrongs and move on."' Róża turned the page, coming to the final paragraph. '"But what happens when we are obliged to judge someone and, try as we might, we cannot find the shades of grey known to us all? When there is no name to describe the wrong? When we linger in mourning? What are we to do? I have this one final thought: our justice can never be like theirs. It can never be a process without hope. There must always remain the possibility, however slender, that in certain strange circumstances even great crimes can be met with an even stranger mercy."'

472

Róża folded up the paper and laid it with the others on the table. All eyes in the court were upon her. She was the only person standing, now. Madam Czerny and Mr Fischer had resumed their seats, superfluous to the drama in which they'd played a part. Brack glared from the dock, paralysed and unnaturally dark – from rage or confusion or from the choking realisation that the trial was coming to an end. Róża addressed her final words to him.

'I was going to return your bullet, Otto,' she explained, conversationally. 'But I'm glad the court took it from me. I'd be worried that when you left here a free man you might use it, and I'd only blame myself.'

Without any further acknowledgement to the court, or even the dismantling of her own – she left the table covered with editions of *Freedom and Independence*, for anyone who might want a copy – Róża began walking from the hushed room, plastic bag in hand, as if she could, at last, get to the market and catch those two-for-one bargains that weren't really bargains.

'I had hopes, too,' shouted a strangled voice. Brack was upright and wavering; a fist punching at the air. But Róża wasn't listening; she just kept strolling towards the courtroom entrance, frowning to herself as if she'd forgotten to bring a shopping list. Brack stumbled forward, pushing Mr Fischer aside. 'I have a story, too, about birds shot from a tree. Yes, tell that to the Shoemaker . . . come back . . . I have a right to be heard . . . I demand it. Come back . . .'

But Róża had gone: the door had swung shut behind her with a soft thud. The trial was over. Or rather, the two trials had ended. Only Róża had spoken. She'd achieved the inconceivable: she'd condemned a man with mercy.

There was no doubting Róża's victory – at least in the minds of those who understood her – but no celebration took place; and not because Brack's technical acquittal was a matter of regret in several quarters. There was no party because Róża did, in fact, go to the market – the biggest in Eastern Europe, on the Praga side of the river. It was just another day, it seemed. Sebastian, subdued and defeated, went back to work, leaving Anselm, John and Celina in a crowded bar near the court sipping *Zubrówka*.

'Who was that bizarre woman?' asked Celina. 'The one that wouldn't leave?'

'Some crackpot,' offered John, who'd only heard the rumpus.

'Eventually, the ushers called the police . . . it took three of them . . .'

Anselm had watched uneasily from on high. As the court had emptied Irina had simply stood there, like someone in the cheap seats who hadn't understood the play. The allusions had gone over her head. People had to push past her while she stared at the empty stage and the vacant chair that

474

Brack had occupied; from which he'd walked a free man. She'd been forcibly escorted from the building.

'She was a victim,' said Anselm with a snap.

The memory of Irina's ejection haunted him: she was the only person left behind in Breughel's hell. She'd fallen outside of Mad Meg's raid on the underworld. Anselm had tried to talk to her in the street, but her disappointment had imploded; she'd drifted away, unseeing, just like that young woman outside Mokotów. He was still thinking of her, dishevelled and disorientated, when the phone rang in his bedroom later that evening. He'd been wondering whether to call round, unannounced, bringing more flowers and a pizza, with something fizzy and sweet for the son.

'Father, there's someone here,' began Krystyna, tentatively. For once she wasn't cheery. 'They want to know if you'll hear their confession.'

CHAPTER 50

There were no appropriate quiet corners. There were no small rooms available. Every conference facility was booked, even the Warsaw Hall, a 15,000-square-foot auditorium large enough for two thousand delegates. But the place wasn't occupied for the moment. The management had authorised its use, for an hour or so, with apologies for the lack of intimacy. Amused and perplexed at the same time, Anselm followed a suited porter to the lift, up to the second floor of the hotel and through a half open door.

On stepping inside, Anselm froze.

Light fittings like coronets cast a phosphorous glow upon a red carpet patterned on loops like rows of tabletops without their legs. Rank upon rank of seats faced a small wooden podium with a microphone. Just beyond, to one side, sat Otto Brack, waiting to address the plenum. Unmoved and unmoving he watched Anselm's slow approach to the front row.

'You were responsible for that fiasco, weren't you?' His German was low and hoarse as if he'd been shouting. The glasses, dark in reaction to the

476

light, made his eyes look like deep brown holes in his head. 'I'm told there's been a meddling priest who wanted to understand why I shot men and tortured women.'

He pointed to a facing seat and Anselm sat down. They were six feet apart, sitting on either side of a circle in the carpet.

'I never had Frenzel's loathing for you lot,' continued Brack. A thin arm moved woodenly in the loose brown suit, shoving aside his colleague's aversions. 'I just thought you were too concerned about the next life and interfered too much with this one. There was work to be done. Great work.'

'What do you want?' asked Anselm. To his own surprise, he wasn't afraid. People who link their fate to greatness always appear small.

'The truth.'

'You've had it.'

'No, I haven't; and neither has Róża. She thinks I had some scheme to escape laws written by the victors. There was no scheme.' He appraised Anselm through those strange openings in his head. 'You and I hold two parts of one story. Together they make the truth that the court didn't hear. Because of your interfering, they didn't come together. This is what I propose: I'll explain the crime, if you explain the mercy. The result will be the trial I never had. Is it a deal?'

Anselm didn't have the opportunity to walk away from the negotiating table, because Brack opened up – his pitch low and grating, the phrases cold and prepared – implementing his side of the bargain. Frenzel had evidently said nothing of the file. He'd given his boss a tip-off, a taster, knowing it would send him to the priest; knowing it would flush out an old mistake.

'Have you ever seen a city reduced to a heap of stones? Have you seen the dead bodies of children floating in a sewer? Have you seen the world you know stamped on and beaten flat?' Brack rasped his authority. He knew about desolation. He'd seen things that set him apart. When he saw that Damascus wasn't there any more, he'd heard an unearthly voice. 'Of course you haven't. Few have. But I did. I've seen it and I've felt the ash in my hands afterwards.' The indignation and self-aggrandisement poured out like the complaint of a servant who'd never been properly thanked. 'That's what I faced in forty-five,' he said, stabbing his leg with a bony finger. 'I looked around and all I could see was a bare horizon.'

Brack came to his feet, head held high, as if waiting for the absent applause to stop. When he heard the hushed silence, he moved instinctively to the podium, as if drawn by a magnet. On arriving, he listened surprised but attentive as his breathing grated through the loudspeakers . . . by some awful act of forgetfulness the microphone had been left on.

'What's private property?' His voice, amplified, soared over the empty seats of the auditorium. He

478

was getting back to basics. 'I'll tell you what my father told me. It's a fence that someone's put round a field and everyone else is simple enough to think that the grass on the other side was never theirs. What's history? It's the misery of the majority brought in afterwards to do the ploughing for a pittance. Well my father didn't live to see the day, but all the fences had gone. It was time to think again, from scratch. The reconstruction? It wasn't about where the fences used to be; it was about how we shared the fields. Those of us who survived the war . . . we had a chance to build something new. Something different. Something noble and good. Except, good things are never that simple.'

He scanned the room as if Anselm wasn't there, drinking in the absent nods and shared indignation. The crowd knew where the speaker was going.

'Because those old landowners, the old *szlachta*, would never accept change. They just want to turn up with their maps and title deeds and start rebuilding their interests, putting up the old boundaries –' Brack leaned forward, urgent and raucous, stabbing the air, now – 'well someone has to stop them.'

He leaned back, listening to the echo of his real-politik, nodding significantly.

'Someone has to have the courage to do difficult things.'

He paused again, his voice resounding.

'Someone must step forward to meet the demands of the moment.'

479

Brack turned towards Anselm as if appraising a snake in the grass. He seemed to be wondering if a man concerned about the next world had the slightest idea about how to handle this one, especially when it was in the throes of regeneration. Tentative and guttural, he tried to explain.

'There's a time in a child's life when it's most vulnerable. Those responsible for its growth must protect it at all costs. They act according to high instinct. Moralities are written afterwards.' A shaking hand briefly tugged at a lapel, implying a kind of modesty. 'It is no different with the renewal of society. There is a moment in its growth, just after its birth, when it is weak and defenceless. When those vested interests can creep into the nursery and suffocate the child, the child that will grow to overthrow their kingdom.'

Anselm tried to peer inside the two brown discs that seemed to hover over Brack's face. His repugnance at the imagery of child protection was slightly overtaken by an almost technical observation: he'd heard two voices, that of Brack's father talking to a boy about the field and fences; and someone else's, making a speech about men born for the moment. Anselm thought it was Strenk's.

'There are men called to act in defence of tomorrow. They must forget themselves.' Brack's teeth chafed his bottom lip. 'They must do what others dare not do, for their sake. They must shoulder the burden. And they do it by terror. A brief wave of terror, to frighten off the agitators and hooligans.' He looked aside, as if he'd heard a noise off stage – some whispering from the wings. Replying, huskily, he became petulant, his voice barely sounding in the loudspeakers: 'Do you think I *wanted* to shoot Pavel Mojeska? Do you think I *wanted* to harm his wife? Do you think I *congratulate* myself for having accepted those responsibilities?' Turning back to Anselm and the microphone, he growled his complaint, sneering at the shallow minds of his carping detractors. 'I say, "No, no, no." But was it *necessary*? I say, "Yes, and again yes, and once more, yes." I did what had to be done.' He struggled in his loose brown suit, raising his head to give his shouting some leverage. 'Because I believed and still believe that what we were trying to bring into the world was better than what was here before. I tried to save the child before they could wring it by the neck. *They* were the murderers. Yes, *they* were the criminals. They killed an idea that would have transformed the future . . . and for what great and noble purpose?' He dropped his voice, nodding at Anselm as if he were simple like the majority, as if even he, a monk, might yet understand that the grass of the here and now was just as important as the heavens above; that it belonged to him. 'For what end? To fence off the fields again. To raise another dung heap out of the ashes.'

Anselm wished the table had legs: that the red circle in the deep pile would rise up and put something of substance between him and Otto Brack. He was glad he'd never worked at the Hague, instructed to defend the executioners – the ordinary people who'd let something slip in their consciences, who now baffled the courts with the consequences of whatever it was they'd dropped. How do we comprehend? How then do we judge? Anselm had wanted to understand Brack, the roots of his relationship with evil, and now he was appalled. He'd expected a complex, twisted political philosophy, something that just might begin to explain the killing and the torture. But all Brack had rattled off was a bedtime story: a fable about a garden and a quibble about fences, a handy catechesis cribbed from Voltaire, to hold on to while he pulled the trigger, simple propositions of faith that answered all the questions if you thought about it long enough, only there wasn't time, because an urgent moment in history had called upon men to be great first and think afterwards. He had none of Frenzel's wily intelligence, who'd learned his doctrine without caring whether it was true or not. Not Brack. He'd believed and cared. He'd never buy a slum in Prada. He'd disapprove. It would disgust him. He had a morality. And this was the man who'd argued with Pavel Mojeska. No wonder he'd said nothing. No wonder Róża had sat beneath a torrent of water. There was nothing anyone could say to challenge Brack's credo. According to Father Nicodem, this was the man made by Strenk. This is what the Major had constructed with the ruins of a boy who'd lost his family, someone ordinary, the apprentice who'd once felt love and gratitude. How to judge him?

'You spoke about a new-born child,' said Anselm, thinking it was time to put some uncomfortable questions.

'Yes, an innocent life.'

'That needed protecting?'

'Yes.'

Anselm would have leaned on the table if he could, so instead, he stared at the carpet. 'You've told me why people had to be shot, I was wondering if you might like to explain why Celina had to be—'

'Don't be clever with me.'

'I'm not,' replied Anselm, mildly. 'It's just that I follow the steps you took to assuming heavy responsibilities of historic dimensions, but I don't grasp the scheme to keep Róża quiet afterwards.'

The timbre of the negotiations shifted dramatically.

Brack didn't change, as such. But it was as though he lifted the tracing paper over a colour print. There was a certain tinting to his voice: it became warmer. The lines around his argument became clearer. The picture, however, remained something out of Breughel's unearthly imagination.

'There was no scheme,' he said, turning again towards the wings. 'I thought I could make something of her. Here was a new life, unspoiled –' a foreign wistfulness came over him; the coarse sentimentality of those without the normal palette of feeling – 'I thought I could raise her to understand what her parents had tried to destroy, to bring something worthwhile out of the father's death and the mother's refusal to co-operate . . . her obstinate . . .' The face that swung back to Anselm was a mask of worn out linoleum, the voice hard and dry. 'But I failed. Celina wouldn't listen. She turned everything upside down. At school, she wouldn't even colour in between the lines. She was a lost cause.'

There were too many shades of night in Otto Brack. Anselm couldn't fully distinguish one atrocity from another. The executioner didn't see the perversion of the adoption. He'd turned it into a salvific act: he'd brought something out of Pavel and Róża's tragedy; he'd brought the child out of Egypt into the promise of another land. He was resentful, even now, for the monstrous ingratitude of the child taken from the nursery – only the attack on Celina itself didn't sound entirely convincing. It was too brisk and short; trite, like a snap rejoinder planned for an unfinished argument.

'I did everything I could,' he murmured, gruffly. 'I tried my best.'

Anselm had tried his best, too, and he'd heard enough. Otto Brack had no comprehension whatsoever of the scale and nature of his wrongdoing. He stood on his own dung heap claiming a kind of purity. He'd killed because someone had to do it; and, it being done, like any decent man, he'd pulled out the stops to make up for the consequences. Thank God Róża had managed to silence him. Anselm was about to rise and go when Brack himself stepped back from the microphone. He walked away, diffidently, one hand rubbing an aching hip; but when he reached the chair he came to a halt, as though recognising that he hadn't quite finished. Trapped between the chair and the rostrum he started limping to and fro, his head bent. Anselm slowly sank back down, listening to the lowered, murmuring voice.

'They almost met.'

'Who?' asked Anselm, this time strangely afraid.

'Celina . . . and her mother.' Brack, thin and angular, seemed lost. All he'd said till now had been for the court, prepared and crafted, but now he was wandering. He didn't know what he was saying, or how to say it.

'What did you do?' Anselm was almost whispering.

'I found a journalist . . . first, I linked him up with Róża . . . then I linked him up with Celina –' he'd paused, standing still, his wavering hands moving objects slowly in the air from one place to another – 'through him, they would have come together. I'd got them passports . . . all I had to do was throw them out . . . but Róża wouldn't go . . . she thought I was trying to escape the law . . . that I'd adopted Celina to protect myself . . . there

485

was no *scheme* . . . she couldn't see that it was better if Celina never knew what had happened.'

'Why did you get them passports?' said Anselm very quietly; but the question broke the spell.

The two dark brown holes in Brack's head were levelled against him once more, as when he'd first entered the hall. He returned to his seat, croaking and angry. 'Because they were both lost causes.'

But Anselm didn't entirely believe him. He screwed up his eyes: behind the manifest wrong-doing that *Polana* represented he'd discerned a contradictory image . . . or at least he thought he had: there were lines drawn in Brack's behaviour that he didn't appear to know about. The decision to expel Róża and Celina had another inner logic: a kind of unconscious rebellion against himself and the voices in his head.

Recalling Celina's feverish account of meeting Brack in John's apartment, Anselm heard again Brack's first avowed explanation of his conduct: that he'd been helping John as he'd once helped Celina. From one perspective, that remained true. It also remained true that Brack's plan to find Róża through a journal entry (written by John, read by Celina and reported to Brack) had, as its chief purpose, the need to warn Róża that she could never seek justice without harming her daughter – which is what he'd told her in Mokotów. And it remained true that Brack still hoped to capture the Shoemaker. But there was more to be seen.

Brack had tried to bring Róża and Celina *together*.

He'd got them passports. He'd planned to expel them, not just because they were 'lost causes', but because he knew that if they didn't get to the West pretty damn fast, long prison sentences would await them both, for they'd never stop resisting the system to which he'd given his life.

He'd planned to expel them *together*.

And not because eyes other than his own had seen John's journal – evidence of the offences that would place John and Róża in prison. That had been a lie. Brack had come to John's flat alone, in his capacity as the Dentist, an identity unknown to Frenzel and the other SB footmen. He'd lied to twist Celina's arm . . . to make her betray John . . . so that he could bring Róża and Celina back to one another, an outcome that now revealed itself as the inner logic of *Polana*. Irina Orlosky had said it was the only case that Brack had cared about. He'd even dressed up to make the culminating arrest that would trigger Róża's departure from Warsaw. Only – for all that – Brack didn't seem to know what he'd been doing. He hadn't seen the parallel mechanics of his own stratagem. Anselm was now convinced of what he'd discerned behind Brack's argument and actions: he'd tried to return a stolen daughter to her mother. There'd been a remnant of humanity in Otto Brack: he hadn't quite managed to stamp out the fire. He'd made a confused bid for reparation.

'Lost causes, I say,' snapped Brack, coiled in his chair, arms folded tight. 'The pair of them.'

He seemed to be retracing his steps, wanting to clear up any confusion. He looked worried, vulnerable, knowing he could only repeat himself; that away from the microphone he'd said strange things off the record. He couldn't retract them; he'd let slip things he didn't fully grasp himself.

'Well?' challenged Brack.

Anselm didn't reply. He let Brack squirm in the made-to-measure suit of a killer, sensing the cloth had always chafed his skin. Anselm stared across the divide, intrigued at that lingering scrap of decency.

It was Celina who'd fanned a heap of dust into flame, bringing sensation back to his life. With her colour and craziness and cheek. After she'd walked out on him, he'd tracked her troubled steps, protecting her from the many dangers of the brave new world, torn between the two, though not acknowledging the tear into his own universe. He'd almost been rescued from moral extinction . . . by garish nail varnish worn by a girl who wouldn't stay between the lines. The chance of salvation had risen out of his crimes, but he hadn't seen it. Then, and now, he had to keep face. He'd once been the man of a moment, the responsibility handed to him by his father. He couldn't surrender that, not even for the sake of Celina.

'Well? Speak. Now it's your turn,' he barked, ill-tempered and defensive, no longer quite so convincing. 'I've told you about the crimes, now tell me about the mercy.'

CHAPTER 51

Anselm had made no deal. But he couldn't walk away from the table. There'd been a partial exchange of information. Anselm had listened. It was his duty to complete the picture: to complete the trial. However, he had a few preliminary matters that required a brisk adjudication.

'What happened to JULITA's file?'

'It was destroyed.'

'By whom?'

'I don't know.'

That was a lie, concluded Anselm, but it didn't matter, for now; at least the point had been dealt with.

'Did you let it be known to interested parties that John Fielding had been involved in intelligence gathering – an allegation which, by the way, could only damage his reputation?'

'No.'

'Who did?'

'Frenzel. I found out shortly afterwards.'

And that was true. Anselm nodded, intrigued again by the hint of another double image. For if

489

Brack had known – he'd implied – he'd have stopped his subordinate from having fun. But why? John was an enemy.

'I'm not making an exchange,' said Anselm, moving on to the trial proper. 'I'll explain why Róża chose mercy, if you insist, but this is your chance to escape. You can walk out of this hall, just like Róża and Celina could have left Warsaw, sheltered by ignorance. Or, like them, you can try and shape how you understand your life by taking account of things you never knew about. Things that were kept from you. As you kept them from Celina. It's a big choice. Think about it. The protection you offered them is still available to you. I'm offering you a passport.'

Anselm found it almost impossible to make contact with Brack now. Behind his glasses Brack was almost absent, in a chosen darkness. Anselm was talking into an abyss. Brack said, 'In eighty-nine I tried to find my file. It had gone. I wanted to see what others made of me. You see, I'm not scared of what others think. I'm more troubled by what they do. I don't understand Róża's mercy and I don't want Róża's mercy. But if I have to live with it, I need to know why.'

Anselm wondered if irony would ever leave this man alone. The one thing he needed to fear was that file. And chance had taken it from him. But he wanted it back.

'Your parents were deported to Mauthausen,' said Anselm. He'd decided to lay out the facts, simply and without padding, as he'd done with Celina in the Old Mill. 'Your mother died there but, against what you have always believed, your father did not.'

Brack made all the physical motions preparatory to speech – that sudden, light rising with the body – but then said nothing. The cracks in the linoleum round his mouth became hard again. Anselm continued.

'After the liberation of the camp he was hospitalised in a part of Austria that fell under Soviet post-war administration. Agents of Stalin's security service found him. They found him because they had a list of names, names of Communist Party members of the wrong kind. The kind Stalin no longer trusted because he was mad with suspicion and fear and dread.'

Brack's mouth moved. A lip twitched.

'I've guessed that your father never told you,' said Anselm, 'but he'd lost faith in Stalin as early as nineteen thirty-eight, when the Party was dissolved by the Comintern, before the Terror got underway. I imagine he didn't want to disillusion you with grown-up talk about in-politics, divisions and back-stabbing. Maybe he just wanted to keep the story about the field nice and simple, because it was worth believing in; because he, himself, believed in it so much that he didn't want the grass, for you, to be polluted with stories of blood spilled over . . . what? How not to build a fence? Your father saw further than Stalin, Mr Brack. He understood that the death of innocent people kills off a good idea.'

Brack's top teeth nipped his lip.

'The Terror reached your father,' said Anselm. 'He was deported to a work camp in the Arctic Circle.'

'When?'

'Nineteen forty-six.'

'Where?'

'Vorkuta.'

The interrogator's voice came and went like air from a slow puncture. Brack's face became eerily mobile, the lines appearing at once as contortions rather than marks on a damaged floor. The loose collar somehow constricted his windpipe.

'He was still alive in nineteen forty-eight when you applied to join the secret police in Warsaw.' Anselm's flesh began to prickle, his back aggravated by sweat. He didn't like this bargain, this bringing together of crime with mercy. But he was a part of unfolding circumstances. The Prior had said that you have to go along with them, sometimes, as an act of obedience; you had to let the head of the axe do all the work. 'Your prospective employers were concerned about your background. They'd received a memo from the NKVD disclosing your father's whereabouts and his resistance to current Party ideology. Major Strenk, however, spoke up in your favour.'

'How?'

Anselm swallowed hard. 'He thought you were

ideologically uncomplicated, hungry to subordinate yourself to an institution and, if offered the paternity of the service, were likely to offer back the devotion of a son. His demand that you abandon Róża was a test of loyalty . . . proof to his superiors that he'd been right to support your application.'

There was a long pause. Both Anselm and Brack seemed to hear Strenk's speech about men chosen by history for the difficult tasks of the moment: the voice that had replaced that of his father. Strenk had spoken for the institution that was dedicated to the nitty-gritty of protecting what his father had believed in. This had been the moment in Brack's life when, in discarding Róża and everything she meant to him, he'd sacrificed his own inner life: for he'd loved her, hadn't he? Isn't that why he'd taken Celina? Something had stirred when he saw the child and he'd tried to grasp what he'd thrown away, for the sake of tomorrow. Wasn't that the other image behind the failed indoctrination of the girl who wouldn't listen?

'Tymon Strenk knew that my father was in Vorkuta?'

'Yes.'

'Even as I sat in the interview room?'

'Yes.'

Anselm drew a line in his mind. He wasn't going to say any more about Strenk's relationship with Brack. Sebastian was right: the file contained copious evidence that Strenk effectively adopted

493

Brack, moulding him and directing him in the ways of the service, its ideals and its goals. That didn't need saying: Brack already knew; his mind was probably burning at the recollection. Brack was grimacing again, though he'd said nothing, the discs on his eyes moving with each brief spasm. Suddenly he spoke, his voice, like a soft gust of air.

'What happened to my father?'

Anselm sighed. He wanted to ease out the disclosure, but Brack didn't want forgiveness or compassion or understanding. He wanted the reason for Róża's mercy. Anselm said, 'He escaped from Vorkuta. According to the NKVD he'd walked a thousand miles before they found him. He'd said he was coming home to Warsaw. He wanted to see his son.'

'What did they do?'

'They shot him.'

Brack's mouth went into a slight paroxysm; his legs started shaking like thin sticks in his trousers.

'What year?'

'Nineteen fifty-one.'

The hands began to tremble, too. His head fell back slightly and the change in angle allowed Anselm a glimpse into the abyss . . . at the eyes behind their glass walls . . . they were closed and horribly creased. Brack was staring at the truth of his past: in the very year that he tortured Róża and shot her husband, his renegade father – the

494

inspiration of his life – was executed by agents of the wider security system he'd served; the system that had knowingly taken him under its wing while dragging his father to the Gulag.

He'd locked the cage and pulled the trigger for a system his father didn't believe in.

They'd given him the key and the gun.

With confounding speed, the tremors to Brack's limbs and face ceased. It was as though the plug to his nerves had been kicked out of its socket. A hand came up and settled the glasses more firmly on the nose. Once more his skin settled into a cracked, hard surface, the stains like weights on his head.

'I must leave this place,' he said, stumbling away, his voice hoarse and dry. 'I have to get out, I can't . . . think. I'm . . .'

Brack couldn't articulate his despair and confusion because it was too deep. There was too much to think about, too many events to reconsider, decisions to review. A vast crack had opened at his feet and he was falling into the darkness. The new world worth killing for had come to an end: it wasn't just a failed dream beaten flat by the old vested interests; it had never existed. But the look on Brack's face seemed to admit that this was something he'd *always* known . . . ever since Celina walked out of the door. She'd taken all the colour with her, leaving behind the grey.

'Mr Brack,' called Anselm, instinctively, rising. 'Stop, just a moment.'

The murderer and torturer who'd escaped punishment was staggering down a long aisle, row upon row of empty seats on either side. The delegates were on their feet laughing at the idiot who'd done the dirty work; the fool who'd thought shooting people in a cellar was an act of significance; the clown who'd abandoned those he'd loved. He reached the Hall doors and pushed his way out, escaping the silent applause.

Anselm hadn't moved. He'd been rooted to the spot like one of the audience, only he hadn't been clapping. As if the conference was over, he left his seat and chased after the principal speaker, but he'd gone.

One of the lifts was descending, the numbers counting down. He ran towards the stairs, hoping to catch Brack before he left the building. He'd thought of something to say, even if he wasn't sure it was true. Rounding a corner, he saw him limping ahead. He caught up and tugged his sleeve, but Brack was the one who spoke.

'I knew someone, once, and he used to say to everyone, "Harm the boy, you harm the man", but to me, he said, "Save the boy, you save the man". He meant you saved him to do something decent, worthwhile and good.' He swayed as if he might fall, and moved on, as if to catch his balance. 'You know, I was the one with the matches. I knew where I was going.'

Brack reeled away, quickly. One shoulder had fallen lower than the other, the sleeve of his brown jacket almost covering the hand. He began to drag one foot. Anselm followed, half stammering, not able to call out, wanting to reach the person who'd once loved Róża and been grateful to Mr Lasky.

'Mr Brack,' he managed, again, as if the name was all he had to say.

But Brack was in the foyer now, passing the reception desk, bright lights and glass everywhere, the well-heeled from the four corners of the earth looking idly on at an old man running away from a priest. Krystyna smiled and made a little wave. Abruptly Anselm stopped and gasped.

Standing at the entrance was Irina Orlosky. She was holding out a gun, Brack's gun, as if it were a Happy Meal. Her arms were wavering under the strain.

'No, Irina, don't . . .' called Anselm. But she made no response: her eyes were wide and levelled; and Brack was heading towards her as if to welcome his old assistant. Screams broke out and people stumbled for safety while Brack came to a slow halt, expectant and resigned, the centre of a fast-widening circle. All at once – for Anselm – the glittering foyer became a kind of dripping cellar. Brack had returned to the place where the big decisions are made and where big people must swallow hard and seize the moment.

'Don't be frightened, Irina,' he said. 'Have courage.'

Anselm tried to shout but time had seized up, and with it his reactions. His lips gradually parted, but then, suddenly, came an immense bang . . . and Brack retreated three or four juddering steps, like a buffoon at the circus after being hit on the head with a frying pan. He paused, as if to think about it, and then fell on one knee. Seconds later – with striking gentleness, and slowly – he sank to the floor, rolling on to his back.

When Anselm reached him, he instinctively removed the glasses. Clouds had gathered over green flames – they'd come to life and were burning, but they were fast turning hard, becoming cold glass, the light seeming to vanish inwards. He let Myriam's words fall out, still undecided if they were true or not: 'You're always more than your past.'

And then, all at once, Anselm noticed that he was surrounded by a hushed crowd. That Brack was dead, and that he was on his knees.

CHAPTER 52

Róża was told of Brack's death the same evening. She walked the length of her sitting room and slowly sat down, no longer quite present. Examining her face, Anselm wondered if he caught the slightest lift of that wave he'd noticed when she'd been told the contents of Brack's file. Sadness, pity or compassion, he'd never know, but it had led to mercy. And now with him dead, there was an edge to her quiet. It was almost as if she and Brack were linked by a remaining thread of understanding, that with the onslaught of terror, good and bad are swept into the one fire.

Celina seemed the most confused, battling – Anselm suspected – against the upsurge of relief which, once spent, made one feel vaguely unclean. Death did that. It demanded a moment's thought, requiring all those remotely affected to look with honesty at the empty chair and check if the life extinguished had left anything worthwhile behind: and Brack's hadn't. John was indifferent, though he drew emotions vicariously from Róża and Celina, by turns reflective and furtively jubilant.

Speaking to Sebastian on the phone, Anselm found him angry. He'd wanted a trial. He'd wanted to see the law at work, its hands reaching back in time to reclaim lost ground, making it holy again. But it remained out of reach, unsanctified. Brack had died on a deep pile red carpet. It didn't seem quite right. In truth, Sebastian hadn't understood Róża's justice: that in eschewing naked retaliation for the past she'd looked creatively forwards, where even a murderer without a defence had an open future.

Coverage by the media the next morning was spontaneously inter-connected, different commentators and presenters effectively speaking to each other in public. Brack's death, fast upon his acquittal – peculiarly condemned and pitied by Róża Mojeska at one and the same time – ignited a debate that moved from paper to screen to radio: about the relationship between retribution and compassion. The argument became heated, even in the hotel's corridors. The final words of the Shoemaker were discussed like never before. Róża, to the end, had been his loyal messenger.

Anselm's reaction? The sight of the shooting itself profoundly disturbed him: the thud and the staggering backwards kept recurring before his eyes and ears . . . followed by the slow, comic drop to the ground. Even the death of a man like Brack stirred something in the stomach. The sense of sickness wouldn't go away.

He also felt peculiarly responsible, asking himself if he should ever have entered the Warsaw Hall; if he should ever have taken that oyster to Frenzel; if he should ever have brought Irina Orlosky from Praga into the outskirts of Brack's prosecution, linking his anticipated conviction with the recovery of her self-respect.

He went to see her in Mokotów, the prison built during the days of a tsar and now a remand facility. They really ought to pull it down, he thought, as Irina was brought to the visiting room on the ground floor. It stank of disinfectant – the sort of chemical used by Madam Czerny to wash her hair. The lights were glaring, the table and chairs bolted to the concrete floor. Anselm felt the past beating all around him. Róża's shouts, Pavel's groans – the cries of agitators and anti-Socialist elements. He listened to Irina's quiet, controlled confession.

'I don't regret what I've done,' she said, drawing a circle on the table with her finger. 'Quite the opposite. I'm proud. Because now I can say that I, too, stood up to them. I hit back for all those others that were shot, and the hundreds of thousands whose lives they boxed away in a file . . . decent, reasonable people who'd never twist a woman's arm or take a man's life, even such a man as that. Like the old couple outside the court waiting for justice, holding on to that banner. Well, I gave it to them. I've done something good, something that was right.' She wiped her eyes on a green McDonald's sleeve, the tears appearing without the usual disturbance of emotion. 'They'll keep me in prison, but I don't care. I'm free now, if you can imagine that.'

No, you're not, thought Anselm, sadly. *Because in time you will come to regret this swift, personal justice. You will gouge at your eyes in self-hatred for having crossed this terrible line. Because you will gradually perceive that now you stand among the executioners; and you will long for the day when you'd simply been compromised by how you'd used a skill in languages.*

'I know about living in a cell,' replied Anselm. 'You have to face yourself like never before. Frankly, it's disagreeable . . . but persevere, Irina. The darker it gets, and no matter what you feel, just plough on: face the silent commotion. There's a peace at the end, and it's greater than the distress paid to get there.' Anselm frowned with melancholy: she, too, deserved the Shoemaker's strange mercy but it couldn't stretch that far. It had reached Brack, but it couldn't quite make those extra few inches to his typist. 'Irina, promise me something.'

'Yes.'

She'd stood up because their short time together had come to an end. The female guard had opened the door with a key attached to a heavy chain hanging from her belt. She'd given that c'mon-get-moving tilt with the head that all prison staff learn.

'When you get out, don't go back to Mr Frenzel.'

'He's given me notice.'

Already? Would a strange retribution ever fall upon that man? A slate from a roof would do. But no, it wouldn't happen. The only finger justice would ever place upon his sleeve was a parking ticket.

'Thank you,' Irina blurted out at the door, pulling back from the guard.

'What for?' He turned, seized by the throat.

'The flowers. I just loved the flowers.'

The following morning, assisted by Sebastian, two police officers formally interviewed Anselm in a central Warsaw police station. They were compiling eye witness testimony to the shooting, of course, but they wanted to know about the conversation that had taken place with Otto Brack moments before the shooting and Anselm's previous dealings with the killer, Irina Orlosky. It took a while for him to realise that the absence of smiles meant they were investigating – if only to exclude it – the possibility of conspiracy: that Anselm had some shared responsibility for Irina's actions. The matter was dealt with courteously, but not before Anselm had suggested the two gentlemen might want to raid any and all premises belonging to one Marek Frenzel. A portion of the national archives would be recovered, furnishing them with enough evidence to instigate any number of prosecutions, not to mention one against Mr Frenzel himself.

'I used to be a lawyer myself,' said Anselm, after shaking hands with the senior officer. He used a forced, jocular tone to hide his festering aggression. 'Trust me: Mr Frenzel's worth a very close look indeed. Turn all the drawers out. Take up the carpet. Full body search with gardening gloves. Same with his business dealings. Check his VAT returns and his annual accounts. Call in the forensic people and pull him apart column by column. You'll find a string of stolen pearls.' And then the anger burst out. 'Lock him up and give the key to Irina Orlosky.'

Sebastian had translated every phrase, he and Anselm drinking in the slow nods of the two investigators. Afterwards, glad to have consigned Marek Frenzel to a great deal of personal and professional inconvenience, Anselm made a discreet afternoon visit to what would for ever remain – should an inventory be made of his actions – an undisclosed location. On returning to his bedroom, still melancholy and resigned, he waited for Sebastian's call. They'd agreed to drown their mutual but different sorrows. When the phone rang Anselm picked up the receiver and said, with inscrutable calm:

'"If a lion could talk, we could not understand him".'

He was quoting Wittgenstein, hoping to establish a light hearted mood for the evening. But it wasn't Sebastian. It was Róża.

'It's not a lion that wants to talk,' she replied, as if mystical declarations were an ordinary form of discourse. 'It's the Shoemaker. He wants to meet his Friends.'

504

CHAPTER 53

The silver Fiat and the blue Citroën moved gingerly along the narrow, pot-holed track. To the left a forest tinged sea green rose gently to a cloudy cobalt sky. The empty fields to the right sloped smoothly to a winding silver stream at the base of the valley. On the far bank another wood climbed to a ragged May horizon. It was late afternoon.

After a mile or so the track turned a sharp bend. Ahead, clinging to the pitch of the land, stood a walled cluster of ancient buildings, the bell tower rising high as if to reach the kestrel hovering above the enclosure. A row of small windows faced the vast natural silence of the trees. Róża had been given the address. She was with John in the lead car that had been borrowed from Edward, Celina taking instructions at the wheel. Behind trundled Sebastian, with Anselm. These were the Friends, a symbolic group, it seemed, comprising Brack's victims, his confessor and his prosecutor. As both vehicles passed slowly through the entrance, Anselm had a fleeting premonition.

A premonition that took immediate depth when

Anselm saw the Gilbertine monk shambling from beneath an arch. The pectoral cross identified him as the Prior, though – oddly, given the Order's penchant for rule-breaking – not an especially talkative one. He led the guests in silence down a low-vaulted corridor to a cell backing on to a small garden without borders, an enthusiastic if contradictory blend of indiscriminate planting and fondness for the remnant of an uncut lawn. The room was empty save for five chairs arranged around a bed.

'He's dead, I know, and I am dying,' said Father Nicodem, propped by pillows on either side, his thin arms flat upon the crisp white sheets. 'Someone has to say something for him, if only to illuminate his responsibility . . . and my own.'

Anselm thought of the kestrel. It was out there, floating and watchful, its wings outstretched above a crazy garden. He listened to the husky voice of the monk who'd returned home to die, keeping his eyes firmly on the pallid, hollow features of the Shoemaker.

Father Nicodem went back to nineteen thirty-nine. It was the only way to situate everything that was to unfold. There were some wishful-thinkers who felt that Hitler wouldn't dare cross the border and that Stalin's interest went no further west than the Ukraine. But that was not the lesson of history. The Nazis had already taken Czechoslovakia and the West had done nothing. War was coming and that always meant a carving up of the homeland.

With his Prior's permission the young Father Nicodem, just ordained, left the monastery for Warsaw. His garrulousness, his trenchant ideas, his gift for language – increasingly irreconcilable with a life devoted to silence – were to be put to the service of an underground printing operation of Father Nicodem's invention: for, anticipating defeat, he believed ideas were the one thing that couldn't be conquered; that words were the sole means to keep alive an autonomous culture.

Single-handedly, and by stealth, he obtained all the requisite materials, the most imposing of which was a treadle-operated printing machine. It was hidden behind a false wall in the cellar of a presbytery occupied exclusively by Father Nicodem, a knowing Cardinal (and his successor) ensuring that the young man remained alone in his management of the parish. Old friends stored paper. Others spare parts. Others ink. None were aware of their confreres. One night, out for a walk, he heard by an open window a mother telling her children the story of the shoemaker who destroyed a dragon. He came home and prepared the first edition of *Freedom and Independence*. This was May 1939, just four months before the Germans and Russians invaded.

'I had contacts,' he said, testily, sensing the atmosphere of admiration and not wanting it. 'And one of them – a disaffected Communist – gave me the names of prominent thinkers and activists based in Warsaw. In those early days they were very secretive, the membership not widely known . . .

507

and I decided to print their names, to unmask them, to warn the people that these individuals had a vision and programme that was harmful to our national identity, that they'd bow to Stalin's will given half the chance. And why shouldn't I? I believed in free speech, openness, transparency, accountability. I still do. Nonetheless, I didn't know that many of the names on that list had broken with Stalin. I've often wondered if that first edition was one of the greater mistakes of my life.'

Father Nicodem didn't find out why until four years later in 1943. He was sitting in the confessional, dozing. Sinning was on a half-day week during the Occupation. A voice woke him at the grille.

'My name is Leon Brack.'

Father Kaminsky had never heard of him and, stifling a yawn, he said so – adding, with a wink in his voice, that his concern lay with actions not names.

'Good.'

'Why?'

'Because you printed mine. Now I'm a hunted man. A man with a wife and child.'

The German secret police had obtained a copy of *Freedom and Independence* and had been using it to track down their political enemies. Leon had found refuge with someone who was now part of the paper's distribution chain; they'd made enquiries and eventually directed him to Father Nicodem.

'This was the last thing I'd anticipated,' murmured the old monk. 'And yet, with hindsight, the risk had always been there. I'd seen the Nazis coming in nineteen thirty-eight. I knew what Hitler thought of the Communists.'

Speaking hastily, resolved to nip past a colossal part of his life, Father Nicodem said he'd had other contacts, folk involved in smuggling operations . . . not of guns or food, but people . . . children. His hand waved away the details – it wasn't necessary to say any more because it wasn't relevant, suffice it to say he was able to organise the hiding of Leon's son. He'd gone to the house where Leon and his family were hiding to collect the boy.

'The moment is burned into me,' said Father Nicodem. 'The promises, the tears, the whispers. Otto was distraught so he barely noticed me. That night I brought him to my old friend, Jozef Lasky –' he settled his hollow eyes upon Róża – 'which brought him to you.'

The family who'd given refuge to the Bracks was Pavel Mojeska's. For a short while they'd known each other. Looking ahead, Anselm saw the full dimensions of Strenk's test of loyalty: it hadn't ended with the abandonment of Róża, he'd required Brack to execute the son of the family who'd saved his life. But that lay in the future. Father Nicodem was still recalling the early, slightly simpler days.

'Having met me, Pavel insisted on joining the

operation,' he explained, still speaking to Róża. 'He wanted to work on *Freedom and Independence*. He wanted to meet the Shoemaker. That's when I realised that Leon had found me too easily, that the Shoemaker had to become somebody other than myself, a symbol, an emblem, a figure from a story, a writer that no one could ever find . . . for these were hard times. I told him the Shoemaker was out of reach . . . but that he could help me keep him even further away.'

Pavel became the sole link between Father Nicodem and a new group of Friends. The myth of the Shoemaker was born. Father Nicodem dropped out of the picture. But on Pavel's side of the equation, he was always breaking the rules, always trusting someone. Trust was the marrow in his bones. He trusted Stefan Binkowski. He trusted others. And one of those others betrayed him.

Not long after Pavel's execution the handling of Father Nicodem moved to Brack.

When they first met, nothing registered behind Brack's eyes. There was no hint of recognition. The distraught boy had gone: the memories of that time had been covered up, painted over. He seemed to look directly at no one; to never quite look at anything in focus. By then he'd been in Strenk's shoes for several years; he'd grown into them.

'I tried to win him back,' said Father Nicodem. 'I tried to talk to him with what I wrote, but he couldn't listen. There he was, at the heart of the fight against our ideas, and he couldn't understand them. The debate we tried to raise wasn't just with the intellectuals; it was with ordinary people, anyone who cared about the kind of society we were going to reconstruct after the war, whether they accepted Soviet Occupation or not. In a way, we faced a great opportunity. Everyone had come together to pick up the pieces, our ways of thinking included. So we were arguing with anyone who could read . . . from the vendor on a street corner to a minister in a government office . . . but Otto Brack was beneath all that . . . They'd placed him underground, out of sight, in a prison to do the kind of thing no reasonable man would ever do. That's why they put him there. Pavel wasn't handed over to a man with a mind. They gave him to someone who couldn't think.'

Isn't it always that way? thought Anselm. When extremists of any kind want to push for that apocalyptic finishing line, they always call on the people who can't understand anything more complicated than a fable. And they, in turn, protect the citadel mumbling their mantras, convinced that they've grasped something the clever ones will never understand. They're the chosen ones. And they don't seem to realise that what they do sets them against the noble ideal that gave birth to the story. Brack, proud and blind, defended authoritarian communism at the cost of democratic socialism. The man who would guard the nursery had done his best to kill off the newborn.

511

'I've called you here for another reason,' resumed Father Nicodem, after a brief silence. He was tiring. Outside, the wild garden came to light with a shift in the cloud. 'I want to thank you, Róża, for your fidelity. To *Freedom and Independence* and to me, though I don't suppose you ever thought I was the Shoemaker. Now that I'm dying we might as well name what I've never wanted to hear – because it's too painful – but now is the time. You were imprisoned for me. Pavel was shot for me. You both accepted the consequences so that I could write, so that the ideas we all believed in could be published. For sixty years I've told myself the price was too high. But I wrote for you both, thinking of you both and all the Friends that I'd never know and would never meet, and—'

'I've known you were the Shoemaker and the printer since nineteen fifty-one,' said Róża, flatly. 'Your hands were too clean. You sounded the same, out of your mouth and on paper. And I found you still grieving when I came back in nineteen eighty-two. But I came back because I believed in your words. You said what I wanted to say. You said what Pavel could no longer say. You spoke for us both and all the people who had no voice. You changed how people looked at the world—'

'I brought Otto Brack to your door, Róża,' said Father Nicodem, faintly. 'I'm part of his story. I helped make Brack into the man that you and Pavel met in Mokotów.'

'I'm afraid you didn't,' corrected Róża, as if she

512

were taking away a sticky cake, nice to look at but bad for an old man's teeth. Remorse, she implied, can be a bit too sweet. 'You're getting carried away; you always got carried away.' She leaned forward towards the bed, placing a hand upon Father Nicodem's frail arm. 'Thousands of people were executed during the Uprising . . . in Ochota, in Wola. They left children behind, Pavel among them. They didn't all go and join the secret service afterwards. For once, you must listen to me, because this time I'm the one with the words you need to hear. Otto Brack made a choice, long before he met Strenk. I was there, in a sewer, beneath Warsaw. I went in one direction, and he went in another. He knew what he was doing. No one pushed or pulled. He struck a match and walked away from his father's humanity . . . and, in the end, it's his father's humanity that returned to condemn him. Not me, not a court in Warsaw . . . but his father.'

Anselm came to his feet and tiptoed out of the cell. Once in the cool, vaulted corridor he breathed deeply and made for a rounded door that had been left ajar. It opened on to a gravel path between a hedge and a rock garden of strange, mountain flowers, flowers he'd never seen before, again randomly planted. Listening to the crunch of gravel underfoot, Anselm thought of the Shoemaker's craft and the price paid for the abstract raw materials. Words had always come cheaply at home; how could they cost so much abroad?

Anselm also felt slightly miffed. He'd been to law school and practised at the Bar for years, but he could never have conceived of a trial as fair as Róża's private prosecution of Otto Brack. She'd taken everything into account, gauging the true weight of Brack's responsibility. And the Nazis had stopped her schooling when she was twelve. How had she done it? Reaching a slight elevation he turned towards the bell tower. The circling kestrel had gone.

CHAPTER 54

Anselm and Sebastian hadn't met to drown their sorrows because Sebastian hadn't called, as agreed. The plan to meet the Shoemaker seemed to have blanked out his evening agenda. Somehow a kind of lull fell between them – of miseries not shared. They'd gone to and from the Shoemaker – three hours each way – saying little, except for those odd surges of energetic discussion that usually evince the avoidance of a particular subject. A similar mood installed itself on the way to the airport. Anselm was leaning with his head on the window, meditating on Madam Czerny's coiffure – whether she actually paid someone to do it, or whether she improvised at home with a concoction of toilet cleaner and rose water.

'Do you like opera?'

'Yes, but jazz has the edge, except for sixties Bebop . . . when something went wrong in the state of Denmark.'

'Ah.'

'Why?'

'Have you seen *Prodany a Prodaná*, *The Bartered*

and the Bought? It's Czech nationalism set to music. Melodic resistance, if you like.'

'No. Why?'

'Well, it turned out the guy who wrote the words was an informer. Did it for money, so he could write. He denied it. But no one believed him. He couldn't walk down the street for fear of being attacked. Lived in hiding. Died an outcast. He was called Sabina.'

SABINA.

Anselm flicked his wrist – a French gesture meaning lots of things, but in this case 'that was a close one'. He thought of Father Nicodem meeting Strenk. They'd have talked about this and that – the weight of history and men of moment – and when it came to choosing a code-name the mocking priest had made a reference his duped handler would never have understood. Behind every philosopher is a jester, laughing with or laughing at . . . it depends on the integrity of the person on the other side of the table: someone has to come away a fool. And Father Nicodem was effectively saying, yes, Tymon, I do appreciate the scale of the risk I'm taking , but . . .

Anselm flicked his wrist again: Father Nicodem's name remained on paper as an informer, but without any disambiguation. This wasn't a close call: this was a major accident. The SABINA joke was about to crash into the public domain.

'What are you going to do with the files?' asked Anselm.

Once they were back in the archive, Father Nicodem would be drowned in controversy. There'd be detractors and protagonists, Frenzel choking with glee on his oysters, Róża swearing by his integrity.

'What are you going to do?' repeated Anselm.

'Burn the lot. Brack's included.'

'I appreciate the sentiment, but . . . how much did the IPN spend?'

'Nothing, I did.'

'You?'

'Yep. So they're my property.' He was gripping the wheel firmly as if the car might go in a different direction. 'It's better the archive is left as we found it in eighty-nine – incomplete and dangerous. I'm not going to try and tidy it up or fill in any blanks. It stays as it is.'

'You paid for them?' repeated Anselm.

'Yeah.' He shrugged his shoulders. 'Pity to get rid of it all. It's like burning Bonhoeffer's prison papers or Havel's letters. The material Father Nicodem and his friends sent to the SB . . . it's a unique outpouring of dissident thought – all of it beautifully written. But, there you go. We can't stick a label on the front of every cover saying, "These essays were deliberately crafted for the eyes of the security apparatus and were disclosed with the consent of the various authors." How many people my age swallow that? The priest-collaborator is a far better story. Actually it would serve a useful purpose.' He'd turned mocking, now. 'The files in the archive have become a lot more than a record of informing. They're our primary documentary access to the past; and we're a nation in search of villains. We need them. You can't bring Communism crashing down without having a few executions afterwards. We have to find the traitor to make sense of the hero. Where else to look if not the files? Forget the fact that half the time they represent words twisted on to paper. With Father Nicodem, of course – and this is funny, I suppose – it's the other way around: his words were straight, trying to bend his twisted readers back into shape – but he remains, like many others, an easy, useful target. They can all take the rap . . . relying on what? The files? Half the story? I don't think so.'

Anselm tried to read Sebastian's features, distracted and surprised to learn that he'd used his own money to meet Frenzel's premiums. He offered no comment on the ethics of handling the SB's paper legacy, though he observed with gratification the parallel between Sebastian and Róża: they'd both pillaged the national archives to protect someone they cared about.

'Does the name Olek mean anything to you?' asked Sebastian, in a lighter voice, changing subject.

Anselm couldn't place it. Why use your own money? He played along. 'Composer or writer?'

'Neither.'

'What, then?'

'Informer.'

'Another one?'

'Yeah, only I knew Olek.'

He used to take Sebastian bird-watching. It was an incredibly peaceful activity . . . tiptoeing in the woods, looking and listening. Sometimes they'd just stand still, barely breathing. Olek knew a lot about birds – their colouring and habitats, what they ate, where they went, migration patterns and all that.

'He used to draw them,' said Sebastian. 'Spent ages with his pencils and crayons.'

Anselm was no longer smiling. At first he'd been taken in, but now he was thinking of the elderly woman standing behind an empty wheelchair; the hint of a couple surrounded by pending investigations.

'I didn't find out about his forgotten life until I came to the IPN,' said Sebastian. 'He'd been in a strange mood ever since I got the job. Argued with my grandmother – and they'd been a quiet couple . . . and what do you expect? They'd been together donkey's years. They'd made the allowances old people come to make.'

OLEK.

Anselm placed the name. It was capitalised in the memo attached to Róża's photographs in the orange file from 1951. He didn't immediately appreciate the significance of his recollection, because OLEK hadn't informed on Róża – she'd been arrested simply because of the link to her husband. Then Anselm took the next, obvious

519

step: OLEK had been Brack's man in his first attempt to find the Shoemaker. He was one of the strangers whom Pavel had trusted.

'He was more than an informer, actually,' said Sebastian, as if hearing Anselm's thoughts. 'He wormed his way into the *Freedom and Independence* set-up and then let Brack know when Pavel Mojeska was planning to meet the Shoemaker. So, you see, my grandfather was the one who put Róża and her husband in Mokotów. Aleksander Voight is the man who made friends with Pavel and Stefan and then sent them both to the cellar.'

And you're the man who chased Róża round Warsaw and wouldn't take 'No' for an answer, thought Anselm. You tried to make up for what Aleksander had done.

Sebastian had confronted Grandpa in private, thinking of containment, not sure what he was going to do; wanting, at least, the truth. But that was enough. That little chink of light – shone in the living room while Grandma was out – did all the damage. Sebastian's grandfather said nothing in reply. No explanation, no defence. He simply wheeled himself away as if the rare bird he'd been watching for years had finally flown off. When his wife came back, her hair nicely cut, he told her everything, stripping down their shared past as though it were an old engine that didn't work properly. At eighty-two she'd thrown him out. He'd left his wheelchair behind and died in an old folk's home three weeks later.

'Which is why I understood Róża when she didn't want to pursue Brack for the murder of Stefan Binkowski,' sighed Sebastian. 'She let Edward keep his secret. That way, Aniela kept her husband and Bernard kept his father: they didn't lose what they'd known and loved. Moving on, head down? It works, sometimes. The family stayed together.'

Whereas Sebastian's fell apart. His parents blamed him. They didn't want to look backwards. They kept their eyes straight in front. 'Can't we just draw a line?' bellowed his father, hands on hips. 'Why do people like you have to keep pushing it further and further back to find out . . . what? Bits of information. You're just another kind of informer. Damn it, we'll never know the whole picture anyway, so what's the point of having a close-up from some corner near the frame? You studied law, at home and abroad. Well, good on you. You're the man to teach us all about right and wrong. But a man willed himself to death and his wife is trying to make sense of what he did before you were born. Is that *justice*? Tell me, Sebastian, what's wrong with just turning the page? Just leaving the bad time bad?'

Because in the long run it didn't work, he'd shouted back . . . knowing full well that FELIKS had a family, too. That Edward must have burned in private while the rest of them were free, ignorant of blood stains, torture and murder, consoled, if anything, by their own engagement in the history of resistance. The difficulty for Sebastian, however, was that the Kolbas weren't the only people standing by the fire. Bad times left bad had not worked for Róża. A line could only be drawn in her case as a final step and not as a means of escape – either for Brack or the Voight family. There had to be a public reckoning, regardless of the fall out.

'I pursued Brack because he'd committed crimes that couldn't be ignored, crimes which revealed the nature of an epoch, crimes where the free choice of an individual embodied the character of a system and its institutions. But then—'

'Róża, of all people, saw things differently,' said Anselm.

'Yes.'

And you were left with a family that might as well have stayed together – that could have met the Kolbas one afternoon at a bowling alley, the adults sharing a beer while the kids knocked down the skittles. Everyone could have whooped – even if Edward and Aleksander were out of it, mooning over vodka at the bar.

'I think we all see things differently, now,' said Sebastian, with flick to the indicator.

They said goodbye at the departure gate, Anselm promising to offer his services *gratis* if, on the off-chance, Sebastian netted a case of grave international importance. Justice, he quipped, it's a slippery fish. How so? (Sebastian smiled warily, looking so much older, at ease for once in his dark suit.) You catch some, you lose some, and then there are strange people who throw them back into the river. After shaking hands, Anselm said, 'If you have any, keep the pictures.'

'Which ones?'

'The birds.'

'Why?'

'As you said, they're the result of an unusually peaceful activity, something that you shared together.'

'Often.'

'Well, have a fresh look.' Anselm shifted uneasily, reminded again of Myriam's confidence in human nature. 'Maybe they've got nothing to do with OLEK. Maybe they were drawn by the Aleksander known to you and your mother.'

CHAPTER 55

Spring had come to Larkwood, bringing colour to the fields. The orchards were pink with blossom, flimsy petals detached by the faintest breeze – making Anselm (an occasional and reluctant empiricist) wonder what was the point of blooming at all. He was struck because he found no tragedy in the swift coming and going, the sudden outburst of fragility before the fruit began to grow. There was no point, as such, he concluded. It was simply beautiful. Here today, gone tomorrow.

The observation, it transpired, had the character of a prophetic warning (though Anselm didn't quite hear the message). Six weeks after his return to Larkwood, he received a call from a man who'd thumped out Colonel Bogey while marching through the bush.

'You know, the trombone player,' said Sylvester, frustrated, holding out the phone.

It took Anselm a few seconds to enter the Watchman's lost world but then he understood. John's voice was anything but musical.

'Celina asked me to call you.'

Anselm listened, hardly speaking, overwhelmed by an incoming tide of sadness – something predictable and curiously inevitable. Róża had asked Celina if she might come to London for a short spell, explained John; they'd said goodbye only the previous week in Warsaw, but that was no matter. Both of them had wept, not wanting another leave-taking, not knowing how to handle letters or phone calls, hesitant about any more time spent apart and what with cheap flights these days and the spare room overlooking the metro line . . . She'd arrived at Heathrow thin, uncertain of herself, wanting the arm of a flight attendant even before she'd reached baggage control. She'd brought presents, cheap things from the market in Praga, desperate gestures it seemed towards the backlog of gifts never given because of their long separation. Celina had taken her home, to her flat in West Kilburn. On returning to the sitting room after a quiet evening meal – a comfortable time spent talking about an office bore, career hopes and a crack in the ceiling – Celina had found Róża apparently asleep in an armchair. For a long moment she'd stood looking down upon the peaceful face of mauve shadows, struck by a certain majesty, the frail hands open in her lap, the feet in blue woollen stockings, crossed at the ankle . . . and then she'd noticed that Róża wasn't breathing. She'd gone. It was as though she'd left her coat behind, laid neatly on the chair. Amongst her few possessions Celina

525

had found a one way ticket: Róża had come to London with that peculiar knowledge of the old.

'Celina wonders if you'd conduct the ceremony.'

'Of course.'

'She's moved on already, Anselm.'

'Yes.'

'She'd only just got her daughter back.'

The greater part of Brack's legacy was now complete.

All the world came to Róża, it seemed. A small crowd gathered at the graveside in Kensal Green: Celina, of course, with John, and their different circles – people who'd never met Róża but who now felt involved in her life and death through an attachment to her daughter; Magda Samovitz with the memory of an orphanage and its caretaker, Mr Lasky; the Kolbas from Warsaw, along with Mateusz Robak and a number of elderly women brought by Sebastian, the pillagers of hell, all mentioned by name in Róża's testimonial. The Friends formed a line, strangely together, strangely apart, like those two protesters at Brack's trial holding on to a banner about justice. Even Father Nicodem took extreme measures to be there, dying two days beforehand, setting his spirit free to join the gathering. In the late afternoon, to the rhythm of a psalm of hope, they walked in turn past the mound of moist earth, dropping a flower into the deep shadow by their feet.

As the mourners drifted away, Anselm approached Edward Kolba, a stooped figure wearing a charcoal grey trilby. This was the wangler; the one who'd learned to live 'on the left'. Anselm gripped his hand and wouldn't let go. The old man tugged but Anselm wouldn't release him. Eventually he lifted his face. Anselm had expected tortured remorse but he found a challenge, glared back with a quivering lip. 'C'mon finish it,' he seemed to say. It was FELIKS. Anselm let the soft hand drop, seeing resentment in the old man's eyes – not to him, but Róża, who'd brought the scourge of compromise into his life. 'You cannot understand,' his stare implied. 'You don't know what it's like to have a child at home and a wife in prison. Our married life had just begun. Judge me all you like . . .'

Anselm didn't, but he couldn't say so because they were trapped without a common tongue and Aniela was watching, smiling gratefully at the monk's attentiveness, assuming neither of them understood the other. It was time to go.

The rest had mourned. And Anselm, left alone by the grave with a fugitive conscience, asked himself if anyone apart from himself had dared to grieve for Otto Brack – not for who he was, but for who he might have been, knowing that there'd only been one person present in the State-run crematorium: a stranger who didn't speak the language, a troubled monk who'd seen a flicker of green light in a man's dying eyes.

Anselm returned to his monastery ill at ease. The violent storm that had begun during the Terror had finally blown itself out. And in that particular serenity that follows a cataclysm, Anselm tried to make sense of the devastation, wanting to find the meaningful ending when all those affected could finally applaud the victory of good over evil. In a sense, he'd found it – or at least he *thought* he had . . . he couldn't be certain – but the finding (if that is what it was) had made him feel dirty again, all the more so because he'd glimpsed it in a place he'd least expected to find anything worthwhile. Anselm roamed around the cloister, head down, shuffling his feet. In choir he lost his place, pulling at the wrong ribbon in the wrong book. Taking his thoughts to his bees one morning, he passed beneath the branches of the surrounding aspens to see the Prior sitting on Anselm's throne, an old pew in the circle of hives.

'Aren't you scared of getting stung?' asked the Prior as Anselm hitched his habit and sat down.

'Permanently. It comes with the territory.'

'You have other concerns? If it would help, go to the end of them.' He paused and then added. 'Why not start with John?'

Anselm couldn't help but smile. At last the invitation had come to enter the grey area between himself and the Prior. Its shadow had followed him from Larkwood to Warsaw and back again. It lay between them here, among the hives. It fell upon the wild, trampled flowers.

'I suppose I feel let down,' conceded Anselm, shifting a little on the bench. 'Pushed aside when I turned up to help; pulled back once I'd gone away. Pushed and pulled when it suited. He might have shared more earlier, willingly, rather than leave me to find out later by chance.'

The Prior thought for so long that Anselm thought he'd fallen asleep, but then he spoke, seeming to aim across the clearing, his head angled to one side.

'You're disappointed because he never told you about his mother?'

'Yes.'

'Nor about his shame and his longing to change her story and his own?'

'Yes.'

'His gamble with a man who called himself the Dentist?'

'Yes.'

This was part of the ground covered by the Prior and John all the years ago, trekking through the woods to Our Lady's Lake. The Prior wouldn't say so, of course, but leaving aside Exodus 22, previous knowledge of John's past was the one explanation for why he'd sent Anselm to Warsaw without a moment's hesitation. He'd made his mind up (in principle) thirty years earlier, when the chance to call on Anselm had seemed impossible to imagine. But then an archive had turned up in Dresden and Róża had flown to London.

'Did you ever explain to John why you came to

Larkwood?' asked the Prior from a seeming tangent. 'Did you tell him why you were leaving behind a way of life he'd shared and understood?'

'No.'

He'd tried, but his friend's mind hadn't engaged with the mesh of Anselm's words. This, too – he was sure – had been ground covered long ago in the woods. The Prior wasn't surprised, and he had something to say:

'Sometimes, Anselm – and especially with the most important parts of our lives – we cannot share who we are. We can give the facts, as information, to a stranger; but with a friend we want to give that little bit more, something that changes the facts into flesh and spirit . . . and at certain times we can't do it. Because, ultimately, we cannot give away our depths: they lie beyond our grasp. It is when we most want to do so that we realise how *immense* we are . . . more vast and mysterious than the night sky; and alone.'

Anselm nodded, thrown off balance.

'John didn't give you plain facts because you were his friend. He wanted to give you so much more and couldn't. But when the time came – and he waited patiently in the darkness – he sent you into his troubled past to find him. And now you know more than anyone else; more than you could reduce to words, if asked. This is friendship, Anselm. Knowledge beyond the reach of language. It's what bound Róża to Father Kaminsky.'

The Prior had lanced a hidden abscess, instantaneously healing Anselm of a resentment that he hadn't even wanted to acknowledge. He felt peculiarly light in his body, and clear-headed with a sharper appreciation of the matters that had lowered his head in the cloister. His head fell now and the Prior, seeming to understand, spoke with a familiar tone of command:

'Your concerns; go to the end of them.'

There was so much on Anselm's mind: not just Róża's mysterious victory over Otto Brack, but the tragedy of half-redeemed lives that peppered the surrounding landscape; Irina in Mokotów, Sebastian exiled, and Aniela smiling for no good purpose, while men like Frenzel lived as though the premiums would never stop coming in (an arrangement, admittedly, that was now under close review). But the question that most troubled Anselm was how to understand Otto Brack. What was his relationship with evil?

'Róża gave me a bit of a slap in the face when the Shoemaker was dying,' he said, scratching the back of his head. 'My entire outlook on Brack had been fixed by this inclination – and I can't get rid of it, even now – that but for certain experiences, Brack would have been just like you and me. He might even be here in Larkwood, causing bite-size trouble. So I started building up this defence, before God and Man, about a damaged childhood, a limping boy who ended up in the hands of Strenk who'd only made things worse by forcing on the wrong sized boots. You know what I mean, it's the stuff about screws, loose and tight. Damaged will, and all that. Father Nicodem was on board, too, but Róża wouldn't have it, not completely.'

'What did she say?'

'That he'd made a free choice. That damaged people can make undamaged choices, and I thought, blast it, you're right, there's a freedom in this, a total liberty, and thank God I'm not tied down to the effects of a cat jumping in my pram or someone's messing around with a flat-head screwdriver. Róża says Brack did what he did because he wanted to. He was a vengeful man who didn't want to leave his injuries behind. In Strenk he'd found himself another father who told a different kind of bedtime story, a grown-up one, and he wanted to listen so he could learn the words. Like John – like me, put in similar circumstances – he fancied his place in history.'

The Prior made a light cough, as he did when he wasn't sure about a proposed change in the work rota. He unhooked his wire glasses and began fiddling with the paperclip repair and said, 'Do you remember, once, you wondered if Brack was simply an evil man?'

'Yes.'

'Well, when you sat with him in the Warsaw Hall, what did you see?'

This was the nub of the problem for Anselm. It was why he'd been lifting up volume two in choir rather than volume three, pulling the red ribbon rather than the blue.

'He spoke to me,' began Anselm, scuffing his feet. 'It was a sort of confession. He wanted to tell the whole world about his crimes, that he was proud of them, in a way, for having grasped the nettle. And as I listened, I thought there's room here for the cat and the screwdriver, sure . . . and I still do, despite Róża's point that he'd made a lot of choices . . . but either way, the picture of the man was uniformly dim.'

The Prior waited.

'But as he was speaking I thought I saw someone else behind his words and actions . . . it was as though someone decent was trying to break out, to crack the hard surface of who he was. Whether the hardness was due to circumstance or choice didn't really matter, there was some good in him. Even as he did something wrong he was trying to do something right. And I wondered if events had layers, and people had layers, and that evil might be the obliterating painting on top, but that in time, with the right kind of chemicals – something strong but not so strong to bleach the prosecutor's hair – we might be able to get it off and find out whatever it is that still lies behind the original canvas with its unimaginable depth of colour.'

This refusal to believe that one layer saturated or transformed the other, his wondering if they could remain distinct was based not on an outbreak of pity, or a desire to reinstate the damaged childhood defence. Rather it was because as Brack had stumbled away, he'd been like a man blinded by light. The truth, revealed, had had a coruscating effect on him. Out of his confusion he'd recalled another story, told by Mr Lasky, recognising that his life should have been something noble and good.

'I tried to reach him, just before he died,' said Anselm. 'He'd made the briefest of confessions, seconds before he was shot . . . that he'd always known where he was going and I threw him a few words, not my own, but something to hang on to. I don't know if he caught hold. Something flared and then a light went out.'

'This, then, is that the end of your concerns?' asked the Prior. He bent his glasses into a workable shape and fixed them on to his enquiring face.

'No,' replied Anselm. 'I'm ashamed that I want to look past his actions. I don't know why I think it matters, but I do.' Anselm dropped his voice as if he didn't want to hear himself. 'Brack, too, had an immensity to dwarf the stars. What happened to it? Could he throw away so much? Is it even possible? Is it even right for me to try and reclaim it on his behalf when, in his shallowness, he destroyed the immensity of others?'

The Prior was squinting now. Bees were drifting round the clearing, in their own way rather busy. 'Anselm, do you remember when we were in the woodshed?'

He nodded.

'I was working and you were watching? You wanted to *understand* everything.'

Anselm considered the first remark superfluous but he agreed in order to advance matters.

'Well, I suspect you now understand far more than you want to, far more than is comfortable for any man.' The Prior examined Anselm, aiming again. 'But don't change. Don't lose heart. The hunger is part of who you are. It might enable you to help those who can't be helped. People who deserve no help.'

'What do you mean?'

The Prior stood up and settled a frown upon Anselm. He coughed lightly again, smuggling his arms into the sleeves of his habit.

'You've always wanted to understand the criminal as much as you've longed to help the victim,' he said, in a low, kindly voice. 'That's why I let you go to Warsaw. It's why I'll always let you help people who've fallen between the cracks on the pavement to justice. You look beyond crime and punishment. You're a lawyer in a habit, a man who asks different kinds of questions, who seeks different kinds of answers. And in that unusual position you'll always hear things that others could not, should not and will not hear . . . sometimes from the victim, at others from the criminal, but always from someone who'd never say them to anybody else. You'll see things, too, in the darkness.' He regarded Anselm fondly, as if he were somehow important, to him and to Larkwood. 'This gives you a special kind of opportunity which only comes to those who, understanding that little bit more – who've seen behind the screen of guilt – can't judge so easily and won't condemn. It means every once in a blue moon you just might be able to say something of importance to the person who is rightly condemned . . . who can hear it, precisely because it comes from the mouth of someone who understands better than they judge. Maybe you helped Otto Brack, Anselm, when everyone else had failed. You were certainly his last chance.' The Prior looked at his feet as if he'd drifted off a well-marked path. 'There are lots of good people out there who defend the widow and the orphan, who bring killers to the courts of justice, and still others who speak up for the Good Thief. But I think there's room for a troubled maverick who keeps an eye out for the bad one, the prodigal who never came home.'

The Prior, having finished, seemed vaguely embarrassed. He nodded a few times and made a sort of wave, and then backed off towards the aspens. He passed through the low branches, head down, his scapular flapping in the breeze.

Anselm remained still for a while, astounded by the paradox. He'd gone to Warsaw as Róża's public representative and returned as Brack's private advocate. For the first time since he'd been at Larkwood the totality of his vocation had come together. The two parts of his life, past and present, converged, without the one eclipsing the other, bringing a new kind of focus. He looked around, seeing the enclosure with sharper eyes. He listened to the hum of activity; he smelled the crushed flowers and the flattened pasture. He was whole, though he hadn't felt any previous fragmentation.

'Thank you,' he said, wondering to whom he was the more grateful: Róża for the light or Brack for the darkness. They were both curiously essential gifts to his self-understanding.

He rose, light-headed, resolved to tie up the one remaining loose end. Something from the grey region.

CHAPTER 56

A mildly eccentric benefactor had long ago made a curious bequest in Larkwood's favour: a single bottle of Echézeaux, Gran Cru 1977. Given the size of the community it could hardly be drunk; given its provenance it could hardly be sold, the upshot frustrating the express stipulation of the donor that it be 'enjoyed for a celebration of some special character'. It had remained at the back of a cupboard until Anselm informed the Prior of his intentions. Before progressing with the menu, however, he made a quick call to Krystyna, just to confirm his suspicions.

'Well, I shouldn't really tell you this,' she said, merrily, turned informer, 'I mean, he told me not to say, but since you're friends, and he paid all the bills, I suppose there's no harm. Yes, you're right, he did stay here, a few months before yourself. But that's our secret, yes?'

'As if you'd told me in the Warsaw Hall.'

In due course John came to Larkwood for a few days' recollection before the academic year got underway. It was his wont to snatch such moments.

538

Celina would have come, too, but she was inundated with work that flowed in and out of season. If she managed to finish early – this was her message – she'd join them later. John didn't say as much, but he'd evidently embarked upon a new life in recent months, tentatively making his way forward with Celina holding his arm. It was touching to observe; and consoling, knowing of the great devastation caused by Otto Brack. Autumn had dawned, tingeing the treetops with a hint of yellow. The guesthouse was empty save for the two old friends. Lunch had been prepared in Larkwood's careless kitchen. Anselm had begged for anything out of the ordinary.

'What is it?' asked John, tasting the purée.

'I honestly don't know,' replied Anselm. 'It's purple.'

'It's disgusting.'

'Try the wine. It's a deep red.'

He did, suddenly slowing his movements, his mouth warmed by a revelation. 'It's un-be-lievable. Why are we drinking holy nectar?'

'To fulfil a legacy.'

'May all your friends die with like intentions.'

John ate some purée and drank some wine, scowling and smiling by turn.

'John, do you think I'm completely stupid?' ventured Anselm.

'I wouldn't go that far. Why?'

'Well, I've been reading Wittgenstein and I've found some clever ideas.'

'Really?'

'Yes. Two, in fact.'

'Go on.'

'First, someone who knows too much finds it hard not to lie.'

John thought for a while. 'Very true.'

'And, second, a confession has to be part of your new life.'

'Agreed.'

'Get going, then . . . or would you like a little help?'

'I'm sorry?'

'John –' Anselm paused, letting the quiet grow rich and heavy, like the wine – 'you knew Celina was the informer all along, didn't you? You've known since nineteen eighty-two, shortly after you came home, I suspect, when you realised that the only other person who'd known you'd be at the grave of Prus on All Saints' was someone close enough to open your journal . . . which you then destroyed, not to get rid of the evidence against you, but because it was a silent accusation against her; just as you brought proceedings not to recover your reputation, but to absolve her from the consequences of the crisis. If you had any doubts that her arm had somehow been twisted, she effaced them when she could no longer look at you. When she left on the day you'd won, though we all knew you'd lost.'

As if to punish himself for the subterfuge, John helped himself to more purée.

'You believed that the Dentist had ruined you and you wanted retribution,' said Anselm. 'You also guessed that your dealings with him were linked with his plan to find Róża. Of course, your problem was that you didn't know the name of the Dentist. There was no way of finding out. And even if you did know, how could you bring him to a court . . . no court would recognise any wrong, against you.' He paused. 'But then the SB-Stasi archive turned up in Dresden. How did you know it had been transferred to Warsaw?'

'A report by Celina Hetman on the BBC World Service.' John dabbed his mouth with a large starched napkin. 'I went to the IPN and asked Sebastian to take me through the file on the Shoemaker. That brought me to Brack and *Polana*. And I found out, at last, why Róża wore two rings.'

'Which explains how Sebastian came across Brack's crimes in the first place,' surmised Anselm. 'There were lots of other files and he didn't just land on that one. You were the first to open the cover and then he, like you, found himself in Róża's universe, something unexpected and beyond his experience.'

John nodded, without guile, and Anselm concluded that his friend knew nothing of OLEK; that while they'd plotted a route to Brack, this had remained Sebastian's secret. When John had sat in that Warsaw office, he hadn't been able to see the pallid face of a man who'd just discovered his grandfather's role in the Terror. He'd heard the tension in Sebastian's voice, no doubt, and sensed the resolve, but had simply put them down to principle and ambition. They had a lot in common, John and Sebastian: they'd each been on the trail of family shame, driven by vicarious remorse, neither truly understanding the other. Anselm didn't pause to reflect further; he said, 'In fairness to you, revenge wasn't your sole objective. Perhaps it's not even the right word to capture the scope and breadth of your project –' he refilled John's glass – 'true, your aim was to bring down Brack for what he'd done to you, but far more important was your intention to bring justice into Róża's life, clear your name by default, and – unless my imagination deceives me – to engineer the seemingly impossible: the recovery of Celina . . . whose voice you'd tracked on the World Service.'

John's slow appreciation of the wine told Anselm he was right. Very good, John seemed to say. Lots of depth, there, with nuance and a beguiling finish. Assured, Anselm went on.

'Your primary objective – which fulfilled all your purposes – was to send Sebastian after Róża: to persuade her to give evidence in the proposed criminal trial. Because, from any perspective, the unresolved murders of Pavel and Stefan were by far the most serious matter. They stood tall in your mind, far above the risk of things turning out badly for yourself as CONRAD or Celina as an informer. Getting Róża into a courtroom was the all in all. And that is when the problems began.'

'Because Róża was trapped,' said John, slowly putting down his glass. 'Which I couldn't have anticipated. Sebastian rang me after she'd been to the IPN and we both accepted that we'd have to let Brack go. I never thought she'd turn to me. But after she left Hampstead, I thought of you, hoping that somehow, with Róża's statement, and Sebastian's help, you'd set off on the left, *na lewo*, and wangle your way to a point where the many lives lived in secret might be brought to the truth . . . mine, Róża's and Celina's. That you would speak for us all. And that with Celina's exposure, sensitively handled, Brack could be brought to court.'

Anselm had nothing else to say. At such times, Gilbertines fall silent. For some odd reason the apparent hiatus compels others to carry on talking.

'When you called me for that meeting, I thought I was finished,' said John. 'I'd hoped you'd flush out the truth without anyone having to say anything, but you forced me to speak for myself. I had to tell Róża about my relationship with Brack, which could only portray me as the informer. Which is why I asked you to invite Celina. I'd no idea what would unfold. I just realised she had to speak up, too . . . not to get me off the hook, but for herself . . . because this would be her last chance to come out of her hole in the ground . . . wherever it was she'd gone when she left me. In the end, Anselm, you said nothing; you made us all speak for ourselves.'

They finished off the purée and some braised matter that might have been lamb, chicken or pork. Fish was an outside chance. They argued about that one, unable to come to any friendly agreement. The debate threatened to turn violent, so Anselm rose to make coffee. Standing in the nearby kitchenette, he rummaged for biscuits, listening to John's voice sail through the open door. The kettle began a low grumble.

'You know, Anselm, there's something that I can't quite fathom about Brack's behaviour.'

'I'm listening.'

'This is a man who hated the Shoemaker. He was into thought control, the suppression of free speech . . . he was up to his neck in class conflict.'

'Past his teeth.'

'Well, part of his plan to trap me entailed the publication of the Shoemaker's ideas throughout the English-speaking world and beyond. They're out there now, thanks to him. Can you get more stupid than that?'

Anselm didn't reply. He was looking for the sugar.

'You'd have thought that was a price too high,' called John, wondering if Anselm was still there. 'Same thing with Celina. He got her films released. And he never even seized that last documentary . . . yet he must have known that his dog-eat-dog superiors would lay half the blame at his door, since it came from his would-be daughter.'

'You've answered your own question,' called Anselm. 'He got more stupid.'

544

More than John realised: Brack had destroyed JULITA's file, too. He'd cleaned up John's past when John would have had it exposed. Anselm flicked the switch on the kettle and the raging water gave a sigh. As he entered the dining room, a cup in each hand, John said, 'What did you make of him?'

Anselm eyed his friend – his quizzical expression, the head angled – wondering just how much to say. He'd kept quiet about Róża's blue piece of paper once, and now he didn't want to speak about the layers to Brack's skin.

'A man of hidden depths,' said Anselm, guardedly.

That seemed reasonably fair. John mused upon it, as if waiting for the finish of the wine. Satisfied, he said, as though following on, 'Tell you what, can we go up to the bell tower? It's been a long time since we leaned on that ledge and talked cross-purposes, you mumbling about the cloister and me thinking of a singer in Finsbury Park.'

There was a strong wind that couldn't be felt on the lanes below. But up here, by the arched arcade, the current was almost threatening, pulling at the hair, rousing exhilaration. Four bells, still and imposing, hung beside their giant wheels. Ahead, the woods stretched far away, rising and falling like a stilled ocean. Patchwork fields and roads knitted what remained into a sort of kingdom, lost down there, but wonderfully visible from this crow's nest high above the monastery.

'Do you remember, we talked about love? And you said chasing reasons is like . . . and I can't remember what came next.'

'Neither can I.'

'That's a shame because there are remarks that sow and remarks that reap. But yours do both, back then and since. Róża found her daughter. Celina came home.'

Words that sowed and reaped, coming from a man camped between the light and the dark: the Shoemaker would have approved.

The sound of gently churning gravel rose from far below. A car swung into the parking area. A door opened and closed. Birds fled from the nearby plum trees. Anselm picked out a slim figure dressed in black. She was elegant, even at this distance. But what caught the eye were the shoes . . . bright red shoes, like sparks from a fire.

'Let's go, John,' said Anselm. 'Tomorrow's already waiting.'

AUTHOR'S NOTE

This novel began with an interest in the three million SB files currently held by the IPN and the activity of underground printing which, during 1982 alone, compelled the security forces to confiscate (according to General Boguslaw Stachura, Deputy Minister of Internal Affairs) '730,000 leaflets, 340,000 illegal publications and 4,000 posters'. In both cases – the files and the printing – the raw material was 'words'. The SB gathered them in secret; the dissidents published them in secret. They'd been used to tell profound lies and momentous truths. They'd been used to build and to destroy. And now those involved in transitional justice had to use the same stuff to open up the future, mindful of its power to bring ruin or redemption. This, I concluded, was an appropriately vexed moral landscape for Anselm to investigate.

In order to enter this most difficult area I followed an invented character, Róża Mojeska. I placed her in Warsaw during the Martial Law years. She was, to my mind's eye, a woman who understood history, a woman who saw the present in the clear light of the past. She was fifty-something. It was only at that point, when I looked onto the city through her eyes, that I recognised what should have been obvious from the outset. Such a person would have seen – to be brief – the Nazi invasion of 1939, the reduction of the Polish people to a slave status, the corralling of the Jewish community into the Nalewki district, the deportations to the death camps from the railway siding near Dzika Street, the Ghetto Uprising of 1943, the Uprising of 1944, the razing of Warsaw, and then, when peace came with the overthrow of one tyranny, the imposition of Stalinist totalitarian communism. Róża would have witnessed all these events without even leaving her teenage years. By the time she was involved in producing the fictional paper Freedom and Independence in 1982 she'd have muttered the litany of succeeding martyrdoms: 1956, 1968, 1970, 1976, and 1981. And she, like most other Poles, would have viewed her experiences in the light of a shared cultural memory: the hundred and fifty years of partition disrupted, here and there, by other failed uprisings. In short, having put Róża on the page after the tanks rolled onto the streets in 1981, I realised that I couldn't look at the files and underground printing and transitional justice and the overarching battle of ideas without recognising that every act of resistance or collaboration had carried the weight of centuries. And with that recognition, Róża became someone so much larger than herself – a symbol of the ordinary person compelled to make far-reaching decisions in the darkness of their time without even a match to find their way. By extension Warsaw itself became more than a city that had been reconstructed after the Second World War. It was a symbol of the human refusal to be reduced to dust and cinders.

Of course, I was not writing a social history of communism. With Anselm as my guide, I intended to write a novel about one woman's choice in a sewer set against those who'd taken a different route to the surface; about the whispering that followed, set against the riot of publishing; about the moral devastation of families razed to the ground by force or compromise. About ideas and why they were important. To do this, I gave the story three landmarks: the Stalinist Terror, the Martial Law years and what I'll call the aftermath, the struggle of a society to pass judgement on what happened between 1945 and 1989. As a result, the final narrative could not reflect in any great detail the differing ideas of nation, the extent of any popular accommodation of the regime, or – most interestingly (given the themes of this book) – the viewpoint of the many party members who must have struggled to make sense of their convictions as the government responded to a succession of intellectual, political and economic crises. I hope the informed reader will understand that such questions were not germane to Róża's dedication to the Shoemaker.

As to the factual basis of this novel, there was no joint SB/Stasi unit dedicated to fighting underground printing in Warsaw (as far as I'm aware), although some 500 Stasi agents did operate in Poland under communism, beginning in 1978 after the election of Cardinal Karol Wojtyła as Pope John Paul II. The Shoemaker did not exist and there was no Shoemaker Organisation. That said, there were countless similar publishing operations (and they often used prams). The fate of the imagined character Pavel Mojeska was not out of the ordinary. A tablet on the wall of Mokotów prison commemorates the names of 283 political prisoners executed on the premises between 1945 and 1955. There were hundreds of others, though their identities are not known. For the purposes of the plot I have made a number of changes to the layout of the prison, the IPN, and the Warsaw District Court. Procedure and language in the courtroom accomodates the characteristics typical of an English criminal trial.